THE YANKEE SAMURAI

A shell whisked high overhead like a broom on rattan, splashing into the sea beyond. Fear screwed Brent's guts into an icy ball, and he felt a trembling in his jaw, his heart pumping against his ribs. But he was "The Yankee Samurai." A veteran warrior. He tightened his jaw and concentrated on his hate for the enemy. Composure began to flow back into him.

Edo answered, her 76-millimeter barking out a sharp crack like a whip. It sent a shock wave through the entire ship, stinging Brent's eardrums and filling his nose with a whiff of cordite. Glassing the target, he found disappointment. Fired on the uproll, *Edo*'s first shell had arced high and over the enemy.

"Captain!" Brent shouted, "fire on the down roll. We want her hull! Let water in her!"

"Main battery! Fire on the down roll! Down roll!" Poraz shouted into the intercom.

THE SEVENTH CARRIER SERIES
by Peter Albano

THE SEVENTH CARRIER (3612, $4.50)
The original novel of this exciting, best-selling series. Imprisoned in a cave of ice since 1941, the great carrier *Yonaga* finally breaks free in 1983, her maddened crew of samurai determined to carry out their orders to destroy Pearl Harbor.

THE SECOND VOYAGE OF
THE SEVENTH CARRIER (2104, $3.95)
The Red Chinese have launched a particle beam satellite system into space, knocking out every modern weapons system on earth. Not a jet or rocket can fly. Now the old carrier *Yonaga* is desperately needed because the Third World nations—with their armed forces made of old World War II ships and planes—have suddenly become superpowers. Terrorism runs rampant. Only the *Yonaga* can save America and the Free World.

RETURN OF THE SEVENTH CARRIER (2093, $3.95)
With the war technology of the former superpowers still crippled by Red China's orbital defense system, a terrorist beast runs rampant across the planet. Out armed and outnumbered, the target of crack saboteurs and fanatical assassins, only the *Yonaga* and its brave samurai crew stand between a Libyan madman and his fiendish goal of global domination.

QUEST OF THE SEVENTH CARRIER (2599, $3.95)
Power bases have shifted dramatically. Now a Libyan madman has the upper hand, planning to crush his western enemies with an army of millions of Arab fanatics. Only *Yonaga* and her indomitable samurai crew can save the besieged free world from the devastating iron fist of the terrorist maniac. Bravely, the behemoth leads a ragtag armada of rusty World War Two warships against impossible odds on a fiery sea of blood and death!

ATTACK OF THE SEVENTH CARRIER (2842, $3.95)
The Libyan madman has seized bases in the Marianas and Western Caroline Islands. The free world seems doomed. Desperately, *Yonaga*'s air groups fight bloody air battles over Saipan and Tinian. An old World War II submarine, *USS Blackfin,* is added to *Yonaga*'s ancient fleet and the enemy's impregnable bases are attacked with suicidal fury.

TRIAL OF THE SEVENTH CARRIER (3213, $3.95)
The enemies of freedom are on the verge of dominating the world with oil blackmail and the threat of poison gas attack. *Yonaga*'s officers lay desperate plans to strike back. Leading a ragtag fleet of revamped destroyers and a single antique WWII submarine, the great carrier must charge into a sea of blood and death in what becomes the greatest trial of the Seventh Carrier.

REVENGE OF THE SEVENTH CARRIER (3631, $3.99)
With the help of an American carrier, *Yonaga* sails vast distances to launch a desperate surprise attack on the enemy's poison gas works. But a spy is at work. The enemy seems to know too much and a bloody battle is fought. Filled with murderous rage, *Yonaga*'s officers exact a terrible revenge.

Available wherever paperbacks are sold, or order direct from the Publisher. Send cover price plus 50¢ per copy for mailing and handling to Penguin USA, P.O. Box 999, c/o Dept. 17109, Bergenfield, NJ 07621. Residents of New York and Tennessee must include sales tax. DO NOT SEND CASH.

ASSAULT OF THE SUPER CARRIER

Peter Albano

ZEBRA BOOKS
KENSINGTON PUBLISHING CORP.

ZEBRA BOOKS are published by

Kensington Publishing Corp.
850 Third Avenue
New York, NY 10022

First Printing: May, 1996
10 9 8 7 6 5 4 3 2 1

Printed in the United States of America

This book is dedicated to John Kenney Winter, Bonnie Jeanne Winter, Abbie Gene Winter, Jarret Robert Winter, Donald Charles Johnston, Patricia Johnston, David Charles Johnston, Susan A. Johnston, Donald Brandmeyer, and Elizabeth Hansen Brandmeyer who are my good neighbors and valued friends.

Acknowledgments

The author makes the following grateful acknowledgments to:

Master Mariner Donald Brandmeyer for his advice concerning nautical problems;

Major Robert L. Kingsbury, USA (Ret.) for contributing his knowledge of land warfare;

Dale O. Swanson and Alfred G. Shaheen who provided invaluable information about bombers, fighters and aerial combat;

Tomoko Levespue and Yuki Kobayashi who led this writer through the intricate maze of the Japanese language;

Umberto Piscopo, fisherman supreme, who so ably explained the details of purse seiner fishing;

Patricia Johnston, RN, and Susan A. Johnston, RN, for their assistance with medical problems;

Bebe Jean Earl for her counsel regarding character development;

Mary Annis, my wife, for her careful reading of the manuscript.

One

The China Sea, 400 kilometers southwest of Kyushu, 3 May

The day *Gobo Maru* died dawned cold and chilly. Shrouded by low-hanging clouds, the feeble sun struggled to break through but only managed a crimson glow low on the horizon. With the sunlight muted, the sluggish sea took on the cast of bruised flesh, gray with dark splotches in the troughs like old blood. Nudged by the swell, the old purse seiner rolled, chugged, and wheezed, barely keeping steerageway as she lay to next to her nets.

Standing on the starboard wing of *Gobo Maru*'s bridge, Seaman Kazuki Aoki fingered his binoculars. He was bored. *Gobo Maru*'s ancient radar had broken down 3-days out of Kagoshima and he had been instructed to, "Keep a sharp lookout." But there was little to see—nothing to report. He raised his glasses and scanned his sector again in short jerky movements. He saw nothing but the hundreds of Spanish cork-and-glass floats holding their net afloat, and the endless sea vanishing into the mists.

These were cursed waters. Many evil *kamis* dwelled here. Just 2-months earlier the big trawler, *Minokamo Maru*, had vanished without a trace in clear weather. Not even a "Mayday" on her radio. And Kazuki's old captain, Akinobu Tanimoto, told tales of the massacre of Japan's greatest battleship ever, *Yamato*, at this exact latitude and longitude. Sister to mighty carrier *Yonaga*, *Yamato* was sunk by American aircraft in April of 1945 with over 3,000 dead. Captain Tanimoto, ever bitter, had lost his brother on one of *Yamato*'s escorts, light cruiser *Yahagi*. Tanimoto hated Americans. "The curse of the 'Eight Myriads of Deities' on all their filth-eating souls," he had growled one night after downing a half-bottle of *saké*.

A soft howling sound sent an icy shiver down Kazuki's spine. Were the spirits of dead warriors crying out to him from their steel tomb a thousand fathoms below? Or was it just a gust of wind in the rigging. The men had said they were in the "Horse Latitudes." An accursed place. But the sea was calm, as flat as the doldrums, the force one wind barely stirring their red and white colors. And why would the dead beneath their keel be restless? Surely, the spirits of such heroes dwelled in the Yasakuni Shrine. Or perhaps the gods turned their backs on those defeated so ignominiously. Shuddering, he dropped his glasses, searching for more pleasant thoughts.

Suddenly, she was back. Meiko Suzuki, banishing ghosts with her heat. Meiko always broke through; when he was on watch, trying to sleep or read, even when playing *go* with his shipmates. How could anyone forget that secret place like a gift from the gods in the woods behind her father's fields. The hot, firm body, rolling and twisting in the bed of leaves. How she had clawed, screamed and dug her fingernails into his back until they broke flesh. The hot, wet depths of her. Consuming him. Draining him of life in devastating spurts. Feeling his arousal growing, he shook his head, wiped his glasses and scanned the buoys. He must tend to business. He studied the net for the hundredth time.

Laying the nylon net in a huge 130-meter semicircle, Captain Tanimoto had hoped for a rich catch of tuna. And so did the other ten members of the crew. They would all share in the success or failure of the two-month voyage. It was a group endeavour, group profit, group loss. The buoys floated serenely. No bobbing. No jerking. This was not a good sign. Even a novice knew this.

Kazuki felt boredom again and his mind wandered to his family, to the farm. Although his father, Otosan, was only a poor Shikoku rice farmer, Kazuki had been steeped in the samurai traditions of his once proud family. Otosan had never let him forget his birthright of Bushido, the doctrines of Shinto, and his loyalty to the Emperor. "Just because we are poor, does not mean we are without pride," Otosan had said many times.

And indeed they lived in the most miserable poverty, barely eking out an existence on one of Shikoku's terraced hillsides—a muddy hillside where they shared 40 acres of tired soil with 30 rice growers. He remembered pumping water by treadmill; plowing the wet soil with an ox-pulled plow; his parents, brother, two sisters, and grandfather hoeing the paddies; the topsoil piled in rows to be carried on their backs and cast by hand; the dry clods mixed with fertilizer and pulverized by the hands of the entire squatting family. It was hard, backbreaking, demoralizing work. But through it all, Kazuki attended school and excelled in mathematics.

"You will have better, my son. You are bright, will work with those new computers someday," his father had said many times.

"Yes, Otosan," Kazuki always replied. There was nothing he wanted more than education—to free himself from this enslavement to the land and help his family.

Then two things had happened to change Kazuki's life: Meiko was sent to Tokyo to school and Otosan heard a distant cousin, Akinobu Tanimoto, needed deckhands for his fishing boat. Everyone knew, if lucky, even a deckhand could earn big money.

Within a month, Kazuki had signed aboard with Captain Akinobu Tanimoto. He prayed he would earn enough money to attend Tokyo University to study computer programming. Meiko had already enrolled in the Tokyo University for Women. They could be together.

The day Kazuki set foot on *Gobo Maru*'s rough teakwood decks, he realized he knew nothing about commercial fishing. The only fishing he had ever done had been rare sport fishing trips in the Bungo Suido with his father, grandfather and brother. He had much to learn about the art of purse seining. Clumsily, he had helped when the men labored to lay the huge net by manhandling it and its floats into place by dragging it with the boat's skiff in a crude circular route. This was done when the masthead lookout, Goro Shikimoto, had called out, "Tuna off the starboard bow. Five-hundred-meters." Cursing and screaming, grizzled old Captain Tanimoto had done everything but whip his men in his frenzy to lay the net and trap the school.

Now Kazuki was watching, in fact, all hands were watching and nothing seemed to be happening. They hoped to surround the school and trap it. Then the big power winch amidships would draw the net together into a purse by hauling in the cable that ran through the rings at the bottom.

The friendly young helmsman, Shugi Tomigawa, had told him when a good catch was made, the water was whipped into froth by the trapped fish. Sometimes, they would trap as much as a hundred tons. When the catch was good the men would exhaust themselves hauling in the net with the power block boom, winch and, sometimes, bare hands. Then they would ladle out the fish with big netted scoops, dumping the squirming catch into the iced hold. But, now, there was no froth, only an occasional tuna would break the water and sound again. If they had a catch, it would be a small one. He heard Captain Tanimoto cursing under his breath and pounding the binnacle.

Abruptly, Meiko Suzuki stormed through again. She was torturing him. He cursed, called on Amaterasu-O-Mi-Kami, but he could not banish her even with the help of the supreme sun goddess. Milky white breasts, rosebud lips wide open and hungry, tongue darting like a frenzied adder, legs opening for him . . .

Tanimoto's voice banished the girl brutally. "On the horizon—on the starboard quarter!" Tanimoto shouted. "By the gods, Aoki, a ship! Why did you not report it? Are you blind? That is your sector!" Then, the old man seemed to read his mind, "Get your mind off girls and 'pillowing' and open your eyes! There is no sex out here unless you can fuck a tuna—if we ever catch one."

Bringing the glasses to his eyes so quickly and hard he hurt the sockets, Kazuki focused on the sighting. At first his landsman's eyes failed him. And then he saw it—a large dark shadow in the haze, approaching slowly. As Kazuki studied the sighting, the sun burned through the mists and the strange vessel became quite clear. It was a trawler. And a big one. Anyone could see that. Making about nine-knots, the big ship veered to starboard, steering to avoid their nets.

At least 70-meters long, the ship was one of the biggest trawlers Kazuki had ever seen. He swept it from bow to stern and back: bow winch and boom; high pilot house where men stared back from the wings through their binoculars; high foremast burdened with an astonishing array of antennas; single stack smartly raked; huge trawl winch amidships; power block boom; stacked nets; 2 motor launches on her stern; and at her gaff, Indian colors.

Captain Tanimoto moved next to Kazuki and studied the big ship. "Indian colors," he snorted. "What are they doing here? They have some of the best fishing in the world off their own coast without traveling this far."

"Is this illegal, Captain?" Kazuki dared.

"Of course not. These are international waters. There's

only a 20-kilometer limit." He waved. "And look at all that radar. What in the world . . ." He stopped in midsentence. "What are they doing?"

Goro Shikimoto screamed from the masthead, "Guns! Guns! They are uncovering guns!"

At first Kazuki did not understand, did not sense the danger. Guns? Impossible. A trawler did not mount guns. Only a whaler would. Then he saw the activity. Men working furiously on the bow, amidships and on the stern. He caught his breath in disbelief. It was true. Guns were being unmasked and cranked toward *Gobo Maru.*

Tanimoto screamed at the six men amidships manning the big winch and power boom, "Let go the rings and chop the net lines! Now! Now! Quickly!" The seaman manning the winch released the brake and the cable whipped free. At the same time other men grabbed axes and began to hack.

"All clear!" several men shouted from the waist. The net began to drift away.

"Watch the screws!" Then Tanimoto shouted into the pilot house, "Full ahead! Give me everything she has! Left full rudder!" Tomigawa pushed both throttles forward and the old diesels bellowed and backfired. At the same time, Tomigawa turned the old-fashioned big wooden wheel hard to port.

"Nets clear of the screws!" one of the men on the stern shouted. The old purse seiner wallowed ahead and began to turn.

The trawler was passing them and was off their starboard bow, turning toward the line of their course. Kazuki stared in horror as a fearsome yellow flash leaped from the bow of the trawler and a something dreadful screeched through the rigging. There was a huge splash far off their port side. Leaping into the pilot house, the captain grabbed a microphone, "Mayday! Mayday!" he screamed.

Then the cataclysm struck. Steady, pulsating yellow

flames leaped from the stranger amidships and stern. Some kind of multiple machine gun was firing. Two mounts. Kazuki could hear them, a blending of thousands of popping sounds like bundles of Chinese firecrackers ignited simultaneously. A storm of smoking projectiles stretched out toward him, approaching like a swarm of tiny lights, coming slowly at first but accelerating miraculously as they closed and then hummed past like angry insects.

Fear struck Kazuki like an icy paralysis, flowed in his veins, slithered in his guts like a great vile worm. He clutched his glasses with white knuckles, eyes wide and unblinking, jaw hanging, drops of spittle flying from his quivering lips. He was going to die. It was certain. And he was not even twenty. Had not even had time to live.

A scream as a torrent of shells ripped the crow's nest. It was Goro Shikimoto. An arm and part of a shoulder flew out of the nest and dropped in the ship's waist. More screams and it began to rain big gobs of blood. Blood was oozing from the shredded lookout's station like a colander straining boiled rice. The screaming stopped. Numbly, Kazuki wiped blood from his face with the back of a trembling hand.

A typhoon of shells blew planking from the bow, set fire to the paint locker and blasted the anchor windlass into junk. The anchor splashed into the sea, taking its chain with it. Raging aft, the explosions blew jagged holes in the deck and upper hull, destroyed the scuppers and lifelines, and blasted the bridge.

Smoke, and the burnt solvent smell of high explosives filled Kazuki's lungs. Gasping, he clung to the bridge railing fiercely as if the thin steel railing could save him. But nothing could stop the carnage.

The windows of the pilot house shattered and Shugi Tomigawa was hurled back from the wheel. Hit squarely in the face, his skull exploded, pulverized brains and bone splattering the captain, who still shouted into the microphone. But the radio had been destroyed, and then Tanimoto was hit in the chest. He, too, burst, ripped lungs, broken ribs and bloody detritus splattering Kazuki on the face and neck. Tanimoto fell on top of the decapitated helmsman.

Staring in disbelief at his slaughtered shipmates, Kazuki vomited. Then a scream of anguish welled deep in his soul and burst from his lips in a long moaning, "No! Dear Amaterasu! No!"

But Amaterasu had turned her back. Only the evil old woman of death had spread her foul loins for him. A blinding flash that sent after-images flashing from his retinas. *Gobo Maru* staggered and then leaped as a big shell hit her squarely amidships and at the waterline. The winch, boom, spare buoys and three men were hurled into the air by a geyser of flame and water. Immediately, the engines stopped and the boat took a hard starboard list while blue water rained down and spray swirled.

Self-preservation took over and Kazuki's mind was suddenly clear. The boat was sinking fast. He dropped into the water which was almost touching the tilting bridge. Swimming away he felt something slimy brush against his legs. A tuna. He was inside the net with some trapped fish. He laughed at the irony. Who was trapped?

He swam toward a small piece of a skiff's stern that was still afloat. He would hide under it. There should be an abundance of air trapped there. He looked back. *Gobo Maru* had rolled over and two men were scampering onto her keel. He could hear them screaming. Begging for mercy. Calling on the gods as the gray ship ran down on them at a slow speed. A short blast from one of the machine guns, and they were both swept from the wreck, riven like butchered game. Kazuki ducked under the piece of wreckage.

It was dark and he bumped his head on something

hard and metallic. A floatation tank. He grabbed the planking of a broken thwart. He would be safe here. Plenty of air. He would wait until the killers left and then pull himself onto the wreckage and pray for a passing ship or fishing boat. He could hear the engines of the trawler moving behind him. She would stay clear of the nets. He was certain of that. There were shots like a small automatic assault rifle. Screams. Someone must have survived. But no longer.

For nearly an hour Kazuki remained under the wreckage while the trawler cruised and small weapons fired sporadically. Once, there were hard banging sounds and the skiff jerked. Kazuki ducked, but the slugs only dug out chunks of planking or ricocheted off. Trembling with fear and cold he cried out his silent thanks and then kicked as another gray form swam up beneath him and brushed his legs.

Finally, he sobbed with relief as the engines of the big trawler began to fade. The killers were leaving. He wanted to duck under the wreckage and surface. Climb out of his prison, see the sun, and breathe fresh air. But it was too soon. They would see him.

Something tugged at his leg and he felt a sharp pain as if he had been stung. A gray shape. But this was no tuna. This was a shark. They had trapped a shark. And another one. They had smelled the blood of the slaughter and were in a frenzy. And he had been bitten, his own blood coloring the water.

Fear cut through him like a gutting knife and he screamed an incoherent cry without form or meaning. In a madness of terror, he ducked under and surfaced next to the skiff. The trawler was gone. Then another pull on his leg and pain beyond reason, comprehension. He howled in agony. Flailed at the water with his fists. Grabbed at the skiff. But a big gray shape had clamped down on his leg and was shaking him like a dog worrying a bone. Blood swirled and reddened the water and the predator was gone with his foot and most of his lower left leg. Then a big triangular fin slashed toward him. Another shark.

"No! No!" He saw a cavernous mouth open, rows of sharp teeth, and then he was struck at the waist and the jaws clamped down like a jagged vice. He actually heard his own ribs breaking as the big fish dragged him beneath the surface. Water filled his mouth, blocking his trachea, gagging him. His heart raced. He felt his neck veins bulge as if they would burst. Strange visions unreeled in his brain and Meiko was there. He tried to call her name, but he could only gurgle the last of his oxygen into the black depths.

Then the darkness. Merciful and infinite.

Two

Yokosuka, Dock B-2, 12 August

Dressed in their Number One blues, the two naval officers walked side by side on the rough, splintered planking of carrier *Yonaga's* pier. Both wore the DOP patch of the Japan's "Department of Parks" on their left shoulders, both wore a chrysanthemum badge on their peaked caps, and both wore the three gold stripes of the full commander. Curved swords in ornate scabbards hung at their sides.

The first, Commander Brent Ross, was tall, blond, in his early thirties with the broad shoulders and confident stride of the All-American fullback, which he indeed had been at Annapolis twelve years earlier. One was struck by the incongruity of the ruggedly handsome face—the face of a man who was equally at home savoring the verses of Tennyson or relentlessly tracking a target with a 50-caliber Browning. "The Yankee Samurai," the world's media called him. The sobriquet was well earned, if not appreciated.

The second officer, a Japanese, was Commander Yoshi Matsuhara, Air Group Commander of carrier *Yonaga.* Compared to the blond giant beside him, Matsuhara appeared squat, with broad shoulders crowding his tunic. He had an enigmatic old-yet-young face. And indeed, he was both. Approaching his eighth decade, he still clung to enough of his youth to man the controls of his Mitsubishi A6M2 Zero-sen. With 73 kills, he was arguably the best fighter pilot on earth, and the oldest. His hair was glossy black, face virtually unlined, stride as sure, true, and youthful as the young man's at his side. Some of the world's unfriendly tabloids had labeled him, "The Geriatric Killer." The pilot did not find this amusing.

The pair wove their way through the usual dockside clutter of fresh and dry stores, spare parts, machinery and the thousands of items—from fresh eggs to 1,000-pound bombs—that kept a great carrier alive and fighting. Most of the material had been loaded on pallets by sweating, cursing stevedores awaiting the cranes that would lift and swing them into *Yonaga's* open cargo doors.

Yonaga's sheer size defied a man's credulity. Over a thousand feet long and weighing in at 84,000 tons, the immense warship made a man feel he was standing at the foot of a vast skyscraper. Even carrier *Bennington* and battleship *New Jersey* moored astern were diminished by the leviathan. Jutting into the sky, the spire of her upper works soared above the masts of the surrounding ships like a redwood over spruce. Tiny insect-sized men could be seen high on her island, scampering over a cat's cradle of scaffolding, scraping and painting, waging the sailor's eternal war with rust. Approaching the bow, Brent Ross sighed. Never in his eleven-year duty on the gargantuan carrier had he become inured to her great size. Turning to his companion, he said, "The subchaser is moored just ahead, Yoshi-san." He pointed. "Up there, just forward of *Yonaga*."

"I know, Brent-san. But I don't see her."

"She's little." The American gestured. "There's her mast."

"That's a twig."

Brent laughed. "She's only 110 feet long with an 18-foot beam."

"A ship's boat for *Yonaga*," Matsuhara quipped.

"She's fast and packs a big wallop."

"All wood construction, too."

"Right. Mostly juniper. Shortage of steel and petrochemicals, you know."

"Your baby, Brent-san."

Brent slapped his friend's back. "I was in the delivery room, Yoshi-san."

Clearing *Yonaga's* bow, the two officers stopped and stared down at the tiny warship riding gently at her moorings. *Edo,* the ancient name for Japan's capital, was painted on her bow in English and Kanji characters.

The compact warship impressed like a flyweight with a heavyweight punch. With clean salty lines, her sharp "bull-nose" bow was high with an unbroken, graceful sweep of deck line sloping to the stern; a pilothouse with a flying bridge atop and a single mast about a third of her length abaft her bow. A long-barrelled 76-millimeter high velocity cannon was mounted on her bow, two 20-millimeter Orlikons amidships, a three-barrel Gatling on a raised deck a few feet aft of the Orlikons, two 50-caliber Brownings on the stern, and two 7.62-millimeter M60E1 GPMG machine guns on the bridge. Her decks were so cluttered with guns, ready boxes, winches, hatches, a pair of small cranes on the stern flanking the ship's wherry, and other gear, the holystoned teakwood of open spaces appeared like narrow white paths winding through an obstacle course. She would be a tough ship to sail, a tough ship to fight.

A young ensign with duty belt and pistol on his hip stood at the foot of the accommodation ladder on a tiny rectangle of deck that served as the subchaser's quarterdeck. A petty officer of the watch was at his side. The ensign was dark and Semitic, the petty officer Japanese. Both looked up, smiled and saluted. The ensign shouted in throat clearing Hebrew "sh" and "kh" sounds, "*Sholem aleichem,* Commander Ross. Coming aboard, Sir?"

"Aleichem sholem, Mister Shaftel. Not today. I have two meetings."

A signalman on watch on the flying bridge waved, saluted and shouted in the unmistakable intonations of New York's lower East Side, "Good to see you, Commander Ross. Coming on our next pleasure cruise? Plenty of girls, vintage booze and the casino will be open. Better 'n Atlantic City, Sir."

Chuckling, Brent saluted back and said, "Hope to, Becker. I need the R-and-R."

"A floating crap game?" Matsuhara asked slyly.

"You punned, Yoshi-san."

"I'm learning. Americans twist the English language in the most maddening way. You love double entendre."

"Is that right? Well, no craps, just poker," Brent said through his chuckles. "And that's not double entendre."

"No *go?*" Yoshi asked, referring to the ancient Japanese checkerboard game.

"You punned again."

The Japanese pilot laughed. "American idiom. That was an accident."

Two more men loading 20-millimeter magazines in the ship's waist, and another on the stern waved, saluted and called out friendly greetings. Brent returned the salutes and called out to each man by name.

"You're popular, Brent-san."

"Great bunch of boys."

"Israeli's and Americans? I heard more, *'Sholem Aleichems'.*"

"All three officers are Israeli and about half the crew. The rest are Americans and Japanese."

"Then, the captain is Israeli."

"Right. Lieutenant Dov Poraz. Good ship handler."

"Can he fight it?"

"The Arabs will decide that."

The pilot nodded and then stabbed a finger at each

gun mount and whistled. "He has a lot of firepower on his midget." Then he indicated the Gatling and Brent read the question in the gesture.

"That's the 20-millimeter Sea Vulcan—1200 rounds a minute, delinking feeder direct from the ship's magazine." Brent pointed to a boxy structure at the front of the mount, "It's electrically operated and those are batteries."

"Batteries can wear out—run down fast."

"They're online with the ship's electrical system, Yoshi-san. It can lose the ship's power and still operate."

"Then, why not two more instead of the single-mount Orlikons?" The Japanese pointed at the machine guns where the gunners were loading magazines.

Brent shook his head. "We're lucky we got that one. The U.S. Navy is grabbing all the Vulcans that General Electric can build. You know there is an airborne version, too—a six-barrel system."

"It looks heavy."

"That's another factor. It weighs 1100 pounds—500 kilograms. Two more would raise the center of gravity and *Edo* already has a helluva roll."

Yoshi scratched his head. "I thought you said *Edo* was a subchaser."

"I did. She's an old American WW II design."

"Where are her depth charges, hedgehogs?"

"The Israelis want her for gunboat and radar picket duty. She's so loaded with guns, ammo," Brent pointed at the clutter of antennas at her masthead, "radar and ESM, there wasn't room for sonar or ASW gear. She's ideal for inshore patrols—to intercept Arab raiding parties." His face hardened. "You know Kadafi's commandos have even been raiding bathing beaches."

"I know. Killing women and children."

"As usual, Yoshi-san."

"As usual."

The pilot eyed the ship from bow to stern and shook his head, "Can't draw much water, and she's top-heavy with all those guns. You said she had a big roll. What is her displacement? One-hundred-twenty-tons?"

"Good guess. One-hundred-forty-tons, fully loaded, and she draws about six feet at the stern and three to five feet at the bow."

"One-hundred-forty-tons! Why *Yonaga* carries more rice than that." Matsuhara swept his hand in an encompassing gesture and the warrior in him spoke, "Terrible gun platform. Worse than a Zero-sen in a force ten wind."

"True. Takes a highly trained crew." The young American rubbed his temple and smiled at his friend. "There's an old saying, 'Ships of wood, men of iron,' Yoshi-san."

"Iron sinks."

"True."

"You've been on training cruises with them?"

"Right. Took her out to the Izo Shichito for high speed trials and target practice. Her gunners are good—*very* good."

"Her sea-keeping must be terrible." Yoshi shook his head. "You actually want to go to sea on that thing?"

"Why not. You said she's my baby."

The pilot chuckled. "More like a miscarriage." A new thought swept the smile from his face. "And Admiral Fujita won't hear of it, anyway."

Brent taunted back, "We shall see, old friend, we shall see."

"Yes we will," Matsuhara agreed, grinning slyly. "We meet with Admiral Fujita at 1530."

"Right."

"Flag Plot, Brent-san?"

"That's it. Probably most of the staff." The American glanced at his watch. "It's 1205. I've got to meet with a reporter at 1230 for lunch at the *Ichi-riki*."

"A reporter. You didn't tell me?"

"Admiral Fujita didn't tell me until this morning. You know he hates reporters almost as much as he hates politicians. Somehow, I've become his PR man for this one."

"Can you blame him, Brent-san? When a reporter walks in, truth flees through the nearest exit."

"You're beginning to sound like the sage Oriental pundit, Yoshi-san." Brent ran his fingers over his square jaw thoughtfully. "Why don't you come along? It's a woman, Helen Whitaker of UAIS—the United American Information Service. Could be interesting."

"She will hear only what she wants to hear. You know that."

"Of course. That's why Admiral Fujita despises them. But the Emperor insists on good relations with the media."

"Good relations," the Japanese snorted. "Remember, I'm 'The Geriatric Killer'."

"I know. And you're talking to 'The Yankee Samurai'." Brent took his friend's elbow. "Come on, Yoshi-san. Let's feed her a lunch of unadulterated lies together and see if we can give her indigestion. Could be interesting.

"Why not. *Ichi-riki* is just outside the gate."

As the two officers turned toward the gate, Ensign Shaftel shouted, "Come back soon, Commander. We have a bunk for you."

"Keep it warm, Ensign."

"Mazel tov, Commander."

"Kol toov, to you Ensign."

"He wished you 'good luck'."

"Right, Yoshi-san. And I said 'All the best to you'."

Yoshi snickered. "Pray to your god for that 'good luck', Brent-san, because mine," he waved broadly at the small ship, "won't get involved with that little thing."

"You mean it's hopeless?"

"Hopeless."

Chuckling, the two officers walked toward the gate.

Three
Ichi-riki

Ichi-riki was a large western-style restaurant that attempted to cater to the disparate tastes of men from every corner of the earth. Finding this impossible the owner, Yohei Kono, a portly man in his mid-fifties, finally settled on a menu of American, French and Japanese cuisine. This satisfied some, but disappointed many. However, since hungry sailors did not bring gourmet palates with them, business was brisk. This pleased Yohei Kono and his bank account swelled with his waistline.

Silverware was to be found on most tables next to wooden *hashi*. However, in a far corner, several low tables surrounded by padded *zabutons* catered to those with strict Japanese tastes. Here, only *hashi* were found and the tables were lit by paper lanterns of elegant simplicity.

Because of the threat of terrorist attacks from *Rengo Sekigun*—the Japanese Red Army—Admiral Fujita imposed tight security on *Ichi-riki*. In fact, Brent and Yoshi had to identify themselves to two hulking, glowering seamen guards before they could enter. Security, in addition to Admiral Fujita's ban on the serving of liquor in the three canteens inside the Dock B-2 compound, added to the popularity of the restaurant where liquor flowed freely.

Bowing so deeply he almost tore a notch in his belt, Yohei Kono fawned, *"Konnichi-wa shinshitachi."*

Chuckling, Brent replied after a brief bow, "And good day to you, too, Mister Kono."

Leaving the beaming owner behind, the officers entered a spacious waiting alcove just inside the entrance. The walls were covered with cheap imitations of great Japanese art. Here Brent first saw Helen Whitaker. Standing next to the far wall, she was staring at a faded copy of a painting of a pine tree done by the fabled fifteenth century painter Kano Masanobu. Turning, she eyed the newcomers, smiled tensely, and stepped toward them. Tall and slender, she was a prim woman who appeared to be on the green side of forty. Her shapeless suit was gray, skirt long, white blouse buttoned at the high laced collar like a choker. The flat lines of her face and the forbidding collar gave her a Gothic look, like a Norman Rockwell vision of American womanhood.

Staring at her severely swept back hair, thick lenses on glasses that looked like they had been pried off the end of a telescope, Brent thought she might be an attractive woman if she ever dropped her glasses and unleashed her hair. Strange how women seemed to telegraph their moods with their hair: pulled up into a tight bun conveyed, "I'm all business—hands off;" loose and flowing to the shoulders, "I'm ready for passion—hands on." Brent sighed. *Well, at least some of the time,* he thought.

She seemed to know him instantly. "You're Commander Brent Ross, 'The Yankee Samurai'. I'm Helen Whitaker," she blurted in a breathless, bubbly cadence of someone half her age. She extended her hand, smile tentative and fleeting.

Taking her limp hand for a brief handshake, Brent nodded at his companion, "This is Commander Yoshi Matsuhara."

"Of course, Commander Matsuhara, 'The Ger . . .' " She blushed, trapped by her own *faux pas.*

" 'The Geriatric Killer'," Yoshi muttered, completing her thought.

"Got off to a great start," she said, self-deprecatingly. She turned her lips under and shook her head.

Both men chuckled. At least she could laugh at herself. "You're doing okay," Brent said.

The door burst open and a fortyish man in a three-piece Brooks Brothers suit entered hurriedly. He was as tall as Brent and nearly as bulky. "Gary Mardoff," Helen said. "Thought you were stuck with the ambassador."

"Got away. Couldn't miss this," the newcomer muttered, eyeing the officers.

While Helen introduced Gary Mardoff with, "My associate," Brent gazed at the lean face of a hawk, peculiar yellow-green eyes the color of dirty rice, beaked nose and jutting chin. He had heard of Mardoff, an aggressive man who fancied himself an investigative reporter like the brilliant Mike Wallace of "60 Minutes," but without the tact and polish. An insatiable lush, it was rumored he never wrote a story while sober. And his face showed it. The sagging flesh was reddish-gray, as if exposed to too much sun and a spider's web of veins striated his nose and cheeks.

Mardoff had caused an international scandal when he was sued for slander after one interview with a famous movie star. He had reported drunkenness and philandering when none apparently existed. One of the tabloids, "The International Investigator," had reportedly settled out of court. Brent was surprised he was still employed by UAIS. Looking into the man's eyes, he did not like what he saw. There was malevolence there, darkened by cunning. Yet, there was something more; a touch of wicked humor, was it? He was on guard.

"Pleased to meet you," Mardoff said, his voice mellifluous, almost greasy. He shook hands with both officers, hand as soft and slippery as his voice.

"Jochu-san!" Yoshi called out to a delicately beautiful

young woman dressed in a traditional embroidered silk kimono.

Smiling, the beauty approached them. *"Irasshai, mase,"* she said.

"What? What's that?" Helen asked.

"The waitress—ah, her name is Fumi, said 'Welcome, Sir'," Brent explained.

"Can't she speak English?"

Brent chuckled. "To a certain extent, she is conversant with a dozen languages. She knows us—talks our own language the best she can." And then to the waitress, "Table for four, Fumi-san."

"This way, please, Commander," the waitress said in heavily accented English.

She seated the party in a far corner which provided a modicum of privacy. The crowded restaurant was filled with the sounds of young men talking in high, anxious voices. Only a few diners were women. Helen and Gary placed recorders on the table. The presence of the devices made both officers uneasy.

Fumi stood very close to Brent, never taking her eyes from his face. Brent looked up into the warm dark eyes, "I had a late breakfast. I'll take *saké* and *shimaki* Fumi-san."

"Saké is rice wine," Helen said. "But what's *shimaki?"*

"Special sweet cakes usually eaten during *Tango no sekku."* Helen and Gary both looked confused. "Boy's Day—it's a festival, very big in Japan," Brent explained.

"I'll take the same," Helen said curtly. Everyone nodded and the waitress left.

"You're very 'Japanese', Commander," Mardoff noted.

Staring into the iron-hard eyes, Brent saw a mocking shadow glimmer. The words were innocent, the eyes were not. He disliked this man and wanted to annoy him—bait him. "Does this give you a problem?" Brent asked evenly.

"None at all. To each his own, Commander," was the quick response.

"They call him 'The Yankee Samurai'," Helen injected quickly, trying to thaw the ice.

"I know. I know," Mardoff said, testily.

At that moment the *saké* and *shimaki* arrived. With a rustle of *tamoto*—the long, wing-like sleeves of her kimono—Fumi poured the clear white wine. Staring down at Helen, she said, *"Sakazuki douzo okyakusan."*

"What was that?"

Brent chuckled. "She said, 'Your *sakazuki,* honored patron'." Smiling, the waitress bustled off.

"The *sakazuki* is a cup."

"Right, Helen."

Helen arched an eyebrow toward Brent, "She likes you, Commander."

"Is this part of our interview?"

Mardoff groused impatiently, "Get off it, Helen. Quit being a woman. You're a reporter. Remember?"

"You don't have to remind me."

"Then let's get to business."

Yoshi said, "Excellent idea." He raised his *sakazuki* and everyone followed. "The Emperor." Everyone drank.

"To the free people of the world," Gary Mardoff said. The cups were emptied and Fumi approached the table. Waving the waitress off, Helen refilled the *sakazukis* from a large pitcher.

Smacking his lips, Mardoff said to Brent, "You're good with Japanese."

"Not really. It's a difficult language—over 33,000 kanji characters and no alphabet."

"But you've served on *Yonaga* for a decade and . . ."

"The language of the ship is English."

Helen's eyes widened, "English!"

"Yes. We have an international force and, anyway, the language of the old Imperial Navy was English. Don't forget, the Imperial Navy was modeled after the British Navy.

Uniforms, commands and the British even built the first battleships." Both reporters nodded understanding.

Yoshi added, "Even the bricks that were used to build our naval academy at Eta Jima were brought from England. Remember, Admiral Fujita is of that era—maintains the old traditions."

"He's 'The Iron Admiral'," Helen mused.

"He certainly is." Yoshi and Brent exchanged a knowing grin.

Mardoff gulped down his drink and said to Yoshi, "I hear Colonel Moammar Kadafi has placed a million-dollar bounty on your head."

"Right. The old butcher holds me in high regard."

Mardoff moved his eyes to Brent and a sneer twisted his face into an ugly mask, "A million on you, too. It must pay to kill."

"Right again. It does. I've earned every dollar." Brent took a small drink, smiled, and said, "Just think, poison me and you can drag a million dollars out the door." The two officers laughed. Mardoff stared sullenly and drank.

Turning away from Mardoff, Brent asked Helen, "What publication do you work for?"

"None in particular. UAIS will probably syndicate this interview or sell it to a publication."

"Not a tabloid?" Brent said, refilling his cup.

The reporters exchanged a glance. "No. No chance," Helen assured him. Brent knew this was the first lie. There would be more. Helen continued, "*Yonaga* is a half-century-old."

"Older than that," Yoshi said, chewing on a *shimaki*. "She was laid down in 1937 and commissioned in 1941."

"You were on board during her entrapment in the Arctic," Mardoff said.

"For the whole 42-years."

Helen said, "Then the breakout in '83, the attack on Pearl Harbor, the battles with the Arabs, the . . ."

"All of it," the pilot said, interrupting impatiently. He thumped his cup down on the table with a hard ceramic sound. "Everyone knows this. Why do you reporters keep on harping on the same questions?"

"Sorry," Helen said. "But, *Yonaga* is the story of the century."

"Why don't you write a novel about it?" Brent offered, unable to mask his sarcasm. He gulped the last of his drink and recharged it. A warm glow began to spread.

Mardoff entered, "If it hadn't happened, no one would believe it." Then while downing *saké* like a thirsty man at a desert water hole, he asked questions about *Yonaga*'s construction. The officers answered honestly, explaining her battleship genesis as the fourth hull of the *Yamato* class. The conversion, lengthening, the division into over 1,000 watertight compartments, the armored and "boxed" flight deck, the 16 Kanpon boilers that gave her a flank speed of over 33 knots. They only balked at armaments and electronics gear. "Sorry, those departments are classified," Yoshi said curtly.

The reporters pressed on, asking about *Yonaga*'s and *Bennington*'s last massive assault on Kadafi's Marianas airfields. "You inflicted a lot of damage, according to Fujita's communiqués," Mardoff concluded. And then with a trace of bitterness, "No reporters were on board."

"Of course," Brent said. "Fujita doesn't trust the fourth estate. That's why we're meeting here."

Mardoff and Helen exchanged a hard look. "We know," Helen said, her words shaded with bitterness.

Yoshi said, "You're right about Arab losses. It will take Kadafi a few months to make good his replacements." Brent chuckled and drained his cup. Helen refilled it and added to her own.

"You took heavy losses, too, according to Kadafi's communiqués," Mardoff taunted over his *sakazuki.*

The officers became grim. "You are treading on privileged ground," Yoshi said with a warning in his voice.

"Yeah, okay," the reporter conceded, smirking. "I've heard that before." His eyes riveted on Yoshi. "This war with the Arabs started over some trivial incident back in '83."

Yoshi stared back, hard and unflinching. "I was that 'trivial incident'."

"Oh? Really?"

"Yes. A Libyan aircraft entered *Yonaga's* airspace over Tokyo Bay."

Mardoff ran a finger over the flower design on his *sakazuki.* "I know. It was an old Douglas DC-3—a helpless transport, filled with helpless people."

The line of Yoshi's jaw altered. "It was an aircraft that entered forbidden airspace."

"You fired on it."

"I turned it away with a burst into a wing. There were no casualties."

"Except to Kadafi's pride," Brent declared.

Helen said, "And the war began. Japan and Israel against Kadafi's *jihad.* Thousands have died." She raised an eyebrow at Brent, "Over Kadafi's pride? You really believe that was it?"

"You don't understand the Arab mind. The Arabs wanted it that way, not us." Brent tapped the table with massive knuckles. "Don't you see, the Arabs wanted their war—it wasn't the DC-3. It's like saying the assassination of the Archduke Franz Ferdinand at Sarajevo started the Great War." He thumped the table top hard with his fist. "Nonsense! It was the Kaiser's excuse and the DC-3 was Kadafi's Sarajevo."

"According to Kadafi, Japan and Israel have been the aggressors," Helen countered.

The officers rocked with laughter. Brent finally managed sarcastically, "Why, of course. Japan and Israel picking a fight with two hundred million Arabs." More laughter.

"This is old stuff," Mardoff said, tiring of the subject. Then he surprised Brent and Yoshi with some information that had not yet even been reported by intelligence. "This morning Kadafi tried to test fire a rocket—test the Chinese SDI system. Lost a dozen men."

"That's crazy. It couldn't work," Brent said. "And none of our intelligence services reported it."

Mardoff waved his cup, spilling some *saké.* He seemed not to notice. "I know. They miss a lot. CNN even scooped them a couple times." Brent and Yoshi squirmed uneasily. What the man said was true. CNN had outperformed the CIA, Mossad and NIC on several occasions.

Helen said to Brent, "One of the weapons platform's orbits decayed and it burned up."

"I know," Brent said. "Half the world saw that shooting star. But there are still nine left."

"It landed on Fresno."

"Fresno, California?"

Helen nodded. "That's right. Destroyed a whole city block."

"I've been there," Brent said. "No one will notice." Yoshi chuckled into his cup.

Mardoff said, "Kadafi's rocket never left the ground. Zapped by a laser within milliseconds."

Helen said, "It still looks like no jet or rocket can fly for the foreseeable future."

"Of course. The nine surviving weapons platforms adjusted automatically. They're programmed for that. Kadafi was mad to test it," Brent said.

Gary Mardoff tapped the table restlessly and turned to Yoshi, "You're an American?"

Yoshi nodded. "Dual citizenship. I was born in America, but educated in Japan. Joined the Imperial Navy when I was 15."

"You've killed men of all nationalities," Mardoff said matter-of-factly.

"Kadafi recruits renegades from all over the world." Yoshi glanced slyly at Brent, "Twenty-millimeter shells do not discriminate." The two officers snickered.

Mardoff rubbed his temples as if he could wipe out rising frustration with his fingertips. Before he could retort, Helen said to Brent, "You've killed a woman—Kathryn Suzuki. Shot her between the eyes."

"Wrong."

"But you *did* kill Kathryn Suzuki. She tried to blow up *Yonaga.*" She patted a leather embassy case. "I have it here and it's been reported . . ."

"I said 'wrong'," Brent insisted, chopping off each word with a cleaver.

"Wrong?" the reporters chorused.

"Yes," Brent said, feeling the effects of the *saké,* brazen and a little careless. "I've killed two women." He glanced at Matsuhara. The pilot nodded and smiled. He was enjoying himself.

"Two?" Helen hunched forward. "Who was the other one."

"She was a reporter who asked too many questions."

Helen gulped and then giggled nervously. "You're kidding."

"Arlene Spencer."

Mardoff downed his *saké* and spoke out, slightly slurring his words, "I never heard of her."

"So what? She worked for Nippon Press. Do you know everyone?" Brent growled.

Mardoff's face flushed scarlet and his voice became hard and brassy, "That's a small outfit, but I should've heard of the broad." He wiped *saké* from the end of his chin with the back of his hand. "That's a lot of bullshit." He recharged his cup.

Brent felt his temper flare deep like a small pile of

kindling in his guts. He felt the urge to leap to his feet and smash his fist into the arrogant face. Matsuhara's hand closed on his forearm with a tight grip, and Brent managed to speak in an even voice, "At that time—it was over two-years ago—there were security considerations surrounding the circumstances of her death. Espionage was involved. NIC (Naval Intelligence Command), CIA and Mossad (Israeli Intelligence) arranged a cover story for her death—an auto accident. It's no longer classified. I beheaded her with this," he patted the tang of the killing blade at his side, "in Suite 1410 in the Tokyo Hilton." He stared unflinchingly into Helen's eyes. "We were very close and she talked too much." He shifted his eyes to Gary Mardoff. "And she was careless about the company she kept, and that's no bullshit."

"That's hard to believe," Mardoff declared.

"I don't give a damn what you believe. You have your scoop," Brent retorted.

"Scoop! Poop! A pile of shit! That Arlene Spencer was nothing," Mardoff spat, spraying Brent with spittle.

"This interview's over!" Brent said in a loud voice that turned heads. He came to his feet. Helen stared, her face a book of anguish. Yoshi rose and stood next to Brent.

Remaining in his chair, Mardoff's face twisted into a jeering smile. He raised his cup. "We who are about to die salute you, 'John Wayne'."

Helen gasped, "For God's sake, Gary! What are you doing? You've ruined this interview."

"I'm giving this 'hero' what he deserves." The buzz of voices faded, patrons stared.

Brent felt control vanish. Growling deep in his throat, he lunged, but Yoshi caught him and pulled him away. "Easy, Brent-san. Easy. This garbage isn't worth it."

"We'll settle this sometime, Mardoff," Brent said, allowing himself to be pulled away.

"Yeah. My pleasure." Mardoff tossed off his drink and reached for the pitcher.

"Maybe you can become an instant millionaire," Brent shot back. And then added, "If you catch me with my back turned."

The two officers walked through the silent restaurant, past a crestfallen Fumi and out the door.

An anxious Yohei Kono stared after them.

Four
The "Iron Admiral"

"It is good to have you back aboard, Commander Matsuhara," Admiral Fujita said from the head of Flag Plot's long polished oak conference table. "It has been over a month." The rheumy eyes never wavered from the pilot's face.

"Yes, Sir. I've had over a hundred pilots and crewmen to train, Sir," Matsuhara answered from his seat next to Brent Ross.

"Can our foreign pilots adapt to the Zero-sen? Most have flown albatrosses, and now we ask them to mount hummingbirds."

"Some of our best candidates include five Americans, three Englishmen, two Russians, three Germans, two Frenchmen, a Chinese and an Arab."

There was a disconcerted gasp and mumbles from the ten other officers seated around the long table. The faces reflected the international character of the force: five Japanese, an Israeli, an Englishman, and a group of three Americans, which included an Amerasian.

"An Arab?" Lieutenant Akira Terada, the torpedo bomber commander, cried out incredulously.

"Yes," Matsuhara shot back. "His name is Shafeek Ghabra. He's a Druze."

"He is an Arab," Akira Terada retorted heatedly. "We

can't trust him—we cannot trust *any* of them." Silence descended on the room, broken only by the whine of *Yonaga's* blowers, the rumble of auxiliary engines, and distant pounding two decks below where watertenders labored to install new fresh water lines.

Fujita tilted his cadaverous head toward the torpedo bomber commander. Although the old sailor had passed the century mark and had been shrunken and twisted by time like a wind-whipped bonsai, his mind was still keen and alert. Running his fingers over a cheek so riven by deep lines and rifts it had become a miniature moonscape, he broke the silence.

"Shafeek Ghabra's mother, father, two sisters and brother were killed by Hezbollah because they cooperated with the Israelis. He has a few scores to settle with his Arab cousins." He thumped the table with his bent and wrinkled fingers. "And through the years, his family has fought with the Israeli Defense Force against Kadafi's jihad. There is no questioning his loyalty."

Brent watched the exchange. He was not surprised. Terada was a superb pilot, but an arrogant boor and insufferable bigot. He had never shed the aristocratic traces of his wealthy family. The imprint of the spoiled scion still broke through the military veneer. A troublemaker, he was not unlike dozens of other Japanese officers who Brent had met over the years. These were haughty men who fancied themselves samurai and wore the aegis of Bushido on their sleeves. Brent was sure the man's patrician lineage bore heavily in Fujita's decision to accept him into a key position on his staff. Perhaps pressure from Emperor Akihito had swayed Fujita. After all, the Emperor was the only power the old sailor acknowledged.

Fujita returned to Matsuhara. "You have received your new engines?"

"Yes, Sir. All of my Zero-sens are powered by the new Nakajima 2,500 horsepower Sakae 50, *Arashi,* Sir."

"The bombers?"

"New *Arashis* are arriving daily to have their engines changed."

"Good."

The dive bomber commander, Lieutenant Oliver Y.K. Dempster, spoke up. "My Aichis need heavier guns. That single rear-firing 7.7-millimeter Nambu protects our tails like throwing rice balls." He turned his hands up in a hopeless gesture, "After all, the enemy fighters are attacking us with 12.7-millimeter and 20-millimeter guns. And some of those new Focke-Wulf 190s are equipped with 40-millimeter guns."

Everyone stared at Dempster. An Amerasian, his face was a map of Korea with a U.S. overlay. His mixed antecedents had never sat well with the older Japanese, who still had strong prejudices against the Koreans. But in the last battle over the Marianas, he had proved himself a brave and resourceful leader. His dive bombers smashing three enemy airfields, destroying or damaging over 60 enemy aircraft. However, he had lost nearly half his force. His face showed new lines, and deep dark hollows like bruises underlined his almond eyes. His usual congenial demeanor had been battered by fatigue and bitterness over his losses.

Fujita gestured at his gunnery officer, Lieutenant Nobomitsu Atsumi. Atsumi said, "I have received a shipment of new American fifty-caliber Browning machine guns complete with mounts. Tomorrow I will have them trucked to your training fields at Tokyo International and Tsuchuira. You can install them immediately."

Lieutenant Akira Terada glared at Matsuhara. His squadrons, too, had suffered heavily in the attack, when they had been equipped with bombs instead of torpedoes and had attacked with Dempster's Aichis in low level dives. They had been easy targets for AA. His dislike for Matsuhara was known to everyone and he made no attempt to hide it. "It isn't just firepower," he said. "One fifty-caliber is not enough."

"Then what do you want?" Admiral Fujita asked.

Terada gestured at Yoshi Matsuhara, voice acid with sarcasm, "More fighter protection. While my boys are dying, our brave fighter pilots are charging off trying to build their scores—find their glory."

Yoshi leaped to his feet. "That's not true!"

Terada stood. "Then why don't you stay with us. You are so high, I rarely see you." He waved overhead. "At your altitude, you can play *go* with the gods!"

There was a stunned silence. A lieutenant did not talk like this to a commander. But staff meetings were open forums. Fujita would not interfere, and Matsuhara would not hide behind his stripes. This was a time to have it out—to speak one's mind. This is what Fujita wanted, expected. He remained silent while the pilots glared.

"You can't tie fighters to bombers," Yoshi Matsuhara asserted.

"Why not?"

Matsuhara's face flushed and he clenched and unclenched his fists. Still, his voice was controlled. "Fighters must fly high—hunt. That is our nature, what we are designed to do. Hermann Goering tried to bind his fighters to his bombers in attacks on Britain in 1940 and 1941. It was a terrible mistake—precisely what the English wanted. The *Luftwaffe* lost heavily in both fighters and bombers."

Fujita entered, "True. A fighter's efficiency would be compromised if forced to fly at a slow speed with the bomber formations." He looked at Dempster, and then Terada. His voice became uncharacteristically conciliatory, "I know the umbrella must appear porous to you. But the dictates of tactics force this."

The matter was closed and everyone knew it. Dempster and Terada traded an obdurate look. Both young men sank back, still unsatisfied but not daring to throw a direct challenge at the old admiral.

Fujita turned to Brent, "Commander Ross. You met with reporters today. I hope the interview was a success."

Brent felt himself blush slightly. Although Fujita hated reporters, he had been instructed by the Emperor to encourage good relations with the media. Brent had failed miserably. He said, "I'm afraid that I did not establish the best possible rapport."

The old man's face clouded. "Then it did not go well."

"I'm afraid not, Sir."

Yoshi Matsuhara intervened, "One of the reporters, Gary Mardoff, was an insufferable lout, antagonistic and belligerent and he drank too much." He gestured at Brent. "Commander Ross conducted himself with great restraint and control."

A murmur and subdued chuckle swept the room. Brent's Vesuvian temper was well known. "Restraint," someone whispered. Barely repressed laughter flowed from man to man like a wave.

The old admiral's glare halted the tittering abruptly. He turned back to the air group commander, "I did not know you attended, Commander Matsuhara."

"I requested his attendance, Admiral," Brent injected quickly.

Fujita ignored the young American and stared at Yoshi. "And you contend the reporters . . ."

"One, Sir. Gary Mardoff."

"This Gary Mardoff was malicious—hostile?"

"From the beginning, Sir. He is one to watch—could be dangerous. I feel he is pro-Arab. He obviously loathes us and was deliberately antagonistic."

The old man tugged gently on a single white hair dangling from his chin. He turned to his ancient scribe, Commander Hakuseki Katsube. Hunched over his pad like Quasimodo squinting down from Notre Dame's bell tower, the old man gripped an ancient brush expectantly. "Take a note, Commander," Fujita ordered. He described Gary Mardoff's suspicious behavior and possible pro-Arab leanings.

The old scribe cackled something incoherent, drooled, and brushed some ideograms. Brent wondered what the old man had written. Kanji characters had a multiplicity of meanings and Katsube was senile. Brent had suggested modern recorders, but Fujita had dismissed the proposal out of hand. He and Katsube had served together for nearly three-quarters of a century. Brent suspected dismissing the ancient aide would be like cutting off part of Fujita's body. "Someday, that old man will die in that chair," Yoshi had quipped one evening in the wardroom. Brent had retorted, "And no one will notice."

Fujita turned to his executive officer, Captain Mitake Arai. "You have a report on the status of our amphibious forces, Captain," the old admiral said.

Wearily, Arai stood. One of the few surviving Japanese destroyer captains of World War Two, Arai's voice was still strong and assertive. However, the strain of the Arab wars had begun to take their toll, bending him. The once-strong face now showing signs of stress, deep lines slashing downward from the corners of his mouth and eyes. He said, "As most of you know, the Americans have provided us with thirty troop transports, ten cargo ships, four LSTs and two command ships. Our own LSTs, *Muira*, *Omika*, *Satsuma*, *Motobu* and *Nemura* are ready for sea."

Every eye was on the tired face. The taking of the enemy bases on Saipan and Tinian, the very survival of Japan and the free world, depended on this *mélange* of old and new amphibious craft.

Colonel Irving Bernstein, a Mossad agent (Israeli Intelligence) on permanent liaison to *Yonaga*, raised a hand and caught Fujita's eyes. A small leathery man, he was over sixty but still appeared fit and very tough. As usual, he wore the camouflaged desert fatigues of the Israel Defense Force. After Fujita's nod, he asked, "These American ships, how modern are they?"

"Ten of the troop transports are of the Greater East Asia War vintage. The others are more modern, but all were taken out of 'moth balls'—as the Americans would say. Of course, our LSTs are modern." Arai continued, describing how the crews were making practice landings on beaches in the Inland Sea.

The lone Englishman, Commander Clive Coglan, captain of the old British destroyer *Haida*, came to his feet. Replacing the escort commander, Captain John "Slugger" Fite—who was still recuperating from wounds suffered during a dive bombing attack—Coglan commanded the growing number of escorts that totalled 21. More were expected from the United States, Greece, and Turkey. He spoke with the brisk, clipped intonations of his Staffordshire heritage, "Armor! Daresay, the LSTs can land armor, trucks, artillery—the whole bloody lot—but not with the first waves. The Americans had a bloody bad show at Omaha Beach in Normandy because Omar Bradley did not land armor straight away. It was a sodding disgrace and a lot of fine lads bought the farm. Why, Montgomery put his armor ashore immediately at Sword Gold and Juno—took light casualties compared to the bloody muck-up at Omaha." He fingered his long aristocratic nose, "Face up to it, gentlemen, we need small tank landing craft or we'll have another bloody 'Omaha' on Saipan."

There was a rumble of voices, scattered shouts of, "Hear! Hear!" and Katsube managed another damp, *"Banzai!"*

Rear Admiral Byron Whitehead, the permanent liaison officer from NIC (Naval Intelligence Command), struggled to his feet. A florid, heavyset man in his early seventies, he was obviously disconcerted by Coglan's remarks. "Omar Bradley had 79 tanks assigned to the first waves, DDs—dual drive British designed amphibious tanks. I saw the planning."

"Respectfully, Admiral," Coglan said, "the DDs assigned to the western sector landed, but the eastern sector was a disaster."

Whitehead's face turned the colors of sunset. "Your DDs wore those stupid canvas 'bloomers'. That's why they sank. Your 'bloomers' failed."

Coglan tightened his lips. He would not back down to anyone. "Sir, they were launched 5,000 yards from Omaha in a heavy sea. Of course they sank. Bradley should've landed Shermans on the sand in LCTs. You Americans mucked-up the ruddy show."

Brent squirmed in his chair, but tension still cramped his back. The bitter session with Mardoff had left him with a bad taste in his mouth. And now he was finding more warfare in Flag Plot than he had experienced in the last six months with the Arabs. Everyone was anxious. Everyone was on edge, nerves taut as violin strings and as easy to snap.

And Fujita felt the tension, read the frayed nerves. The 'iron' in him showed when he said forcefully, "Gentlemen, we are fighting the wrong war. Please stand down." Slowly Coglan and Whitehead found their chairs. The old Admiral spoke to his executive officer, "Continue, Captain Arai."

"The Americans have promised us two LSDs and 57 LCMs and we have six tank landing craft of our own." He stared at Coglan. "These craft will put our armor ashore with the first waves."

"That's not enough. We'll take casualties, need replacements," Coglan persisted. Some of the officers nodded.

Arai sighed. "I know. We are negotiating for more." He shrugged and turned his hands up. "But all of you know that Kadafi is putting pressure on the Americans at Geneva. He threatens to cut off all oil to Europe and any nation friendly to the U.S. So I do not know if the LSDs and LCMs will be available."

An angry mutter filled the room.

"Gentlemen," Fujita said. "It is obvious we cannot mount an invasion for at least four months." He turned back to Colonel Bernstein, who was thoughtfully fingering six tattooed blue numbers on his forearm. "Auschwitz, my alma mater," he would say to anyone foolish enough to ask about them.

Fujita said to Bernstein, "The Arab battle group. Has Mossad any new information?"

The thin Israeli whose skin appeared as dry as the deserts—where he had fought for most of his life—shook his head. "Carriers *Buzaymah, Al Marj* and *Magid* and cruisers *Beth-shan, Arad* and *Babur* are still based at Aden."

"Escorts?"

"Perhaps, sixteen *Gearings.*"

A funereal silence filled the room. This was a powerful force. *Buzaymah* and *Magid* were former Russian carriers of the *Kiev* class. Capable of over thirty knots, they were newly refurbished and capable of operating seventy to eighty aircraft. *Al Marj* was the former Spanish carrier *Reina de Iberico.* American designed, it was fast, modern, loaded with electronics gear and could operate over ninety aircraft. Cruisers *Beth-shan* and *Arad* were also Russian, of the *Sverdlov* class. Mounting twelve six-inch guns and displacing 16,000-tons, they were well-armored and packed a devastating punch. Cruiser *Babur* was light, but heavily armed with six new 125-millimeter rapid-fire guns.

Everyone knew Kadafi was waiting for the Japanese to make a move against his bases in the Marianas. Then his fleet would steam across the Indian Ocean to friendly Indonesia, refuel and head for the invasion forces. The last great battle, with the freedom of the free world in the balance. "The last final, decisive battle. This is what the samurai always seeks," Brent had heard Fujita say many times. He would have his wish.

"The Russians are selling everything to anyone," Terada said in a tormented voice.

"They're broke and they need cash," Whitehead said.

"Why not nuclear weapons?" Terada said.

"That has been discussed at Geneva," Whitehead explained. "And if any of the Russian republics sell nuclear devices to anyone, the United Nations will retaliate with sanctions."

"Sanctions don't kill, Admiral," Captain Mitake Arai sneered sardonically.

"They do, *if* they are at the end of a nuclear warhead, Captain Arai," Whitehead retorted. Arai shook his head as if he were a professor listening to a weak explanation from a failing student.

The men shifted uneasily. Even the mention of nuclear warfare made the Japanese sick with horror. "We have their assurances," Whitehead said, obviously piqued.

Clive Coglan could not resist the temptation to thrust another barb into Whitehead while the admiral was on the defensive and obviously disconcerted. "And as valid as the bloody word of Adolph Hitler," he offered in a taunting voice.

"I won't take that," Whitehead shot back.

Fujita intervened, "Enough gentlemen. We have Arabs to kill. Settle your differences after we sink the enemy and drive him out of the Marianas."

The old scribe Hakuseki Katsube raised his head and sprayed, "*Banzai!*" Exhausted by the effort, his head thumped down like a rock on iron.

Brent expected Coglan to remain silent. But the Englishman was not finished, quickly segueing the meeting into another channel—a dread that had plagued Captain John "Slugger" Fite over the years and worried all destroyer men. "Admiral," Coglan said. "According to the

Geneva agreements of 1984, the Russians can supply the Arabs with torpedoes, but no guidance systems."

The men looked at each other. Captain Fite had brought this topic up many times and now Commander Coglan, too, had found the same script. The escorts had already made two torpedo runs in past battles and suffered heavily from the Russian "533" torpedo. Guided "533s" would massacre them.

"Yes, that accord is still in force. Contact fuses only, for the '533' and our Mark 48, both surface and anti-submarine." And then anticipating Coglan's next question, Fujita added, "And fire control radar is still out for all combatant vessels, including *Yonaga.*" Satisfied, the Englishman nodded and fell silent.

Colonel Bernstein waved a hand and said to Whitehead, "Admiral, is there any change in the disposition of American nuclear submarines? There was one off the Dardanelles that appears to have been pulled out. We have not picked up any of her transmissions for several weeks."

No one was surprised at Bernstein's knowledge. Mossad monitored everything and, sometimes, seemed to know too much. Whitehead, poise regained, spoke down the table to the row of curious faces, "Yes, Colonel Bernstein, she was pulled out."

"But why?"

"The *Shreveport,* a SSN—a nuclear attack sub, vanished in the Arabian Sea without a trace."

The Israeli nodded. "Yes it was reported in the media—overdue and presumed lost."

"Right. That's why we pulled the sub off the Dardanelles station. She was the *San Jose.* She's taking *Shreveport's* patrol." He smiled, a tight little smile, "Or did you know that, too?"

A soft chuckle swept the room. "Negative, Admiral. We knew *San Jose* was in the Mediterranean and disappeared." Deep lines creased the weathered brow and the brown eyes narrowed. "Are you that short—so short of boats you had to abandon the watch on the Dardanelles?"

Whitehead sighed and his tone was bitter, "I'm afraid so. Our fleet's been scaled way back. We're hard put to maintain reconnaissance off Gibraltar, Norway, the Gulf of Aden, North Korea, Vladivostok and all the other sensitive areas. And don't forget, very few ports are available to our subs and they all require major overhauls after their long patrols." He waved his hand, "Why, they can't even be serviced here."

Matsuhara laughed, a sound filled with irony that turned all heads. He said, "Why, *Rengo Sekigum* would stage the riot of the century the minute a nuclear sub stood in and those cowardly women of the Diet would howl in anguish." The men nodded.

Fujita said, "Unfortunately, you are correct, Commander." Apparently tiring, he leaned forward, both hands spread flat on the table. "Are there any other matters for discussion?"

"Yes, Sir," Whitehead said. "I hate to prolong this meeting with a trivial matter." He hesitated.

"Speak up, Admiral Whitehead. Let me make that decision."

"Well, Sir, we have had reports that two fishing boats have disappeared in the East China Sea in the past five months off the Tokara Retto."

Fujita yawned. "Survivors?"

"That's it, Sir. Like the *Shreveport*, without a trace."

"Without a trace? Usually there is something."

"Yes, Sir. A few nets and floats. But they could have been left by any number of boats."

"Some of those captains are consummate fools—put to sea in floating coffins." The old man ran a hand over his bald pate where there was nothing to find but wrinkled skin. "Enemy submarines would not trouble themselves with fishing boats."

"True, Admiral. Must have been coincidence—accidents, Sir."

The old man sank back into his chair, obviously fatigued. "You must be right, Admiral Whitehead. But I am pleased you called this matter to my attention. Nothing can be overlooked when dealing with the Arab."

"Yes, Sir."

The old man's eyes wandered over his staff. "It is time to return to your duties," he said slowly. Struggling to his feet, he turned to a small shrine hanging on the side bulkhead. The tiny wooden structure was filled with Shinto icons, and a single exquisite gold Buddha. Everyone stood except the old scribe, Hakuseki Katsube, who sprawled in his chair with his head thrown back as if he had been garotted. Yoshi Matsuhara pulled him to his feet and held him up like a sagging man of straw.

Fujita clapped twice to attract the attention of the gods. All of the other officers respectfully added their claps. Fujita nodded and smiled at the response. In reverential tones, he called on the founders of Shinto, "Izanagi, the father of our islands, who produced our sun goddess Amaterasu from his left eye, our moon goddess, Tsuki-Yomi, from his right eye, and our storm god, Susano, from his nose, help us enlist the help of our god of war, Hachiman, in our struggles against our implacable foe and lead us to victory in our final great battle."

Then the expected shift to Buddhism: "May the 'Enlightened One' guide us down the Middle Path and avoid the pleasures of sense and asceticism, avoid the desire of the moth for the star, the inadequacy of the finite against the infinite. Only in this way can we find the Noble Eightfold Path that will lead us to the destruction of the forces of evil that threaten to infest our sacred islands." Fujita pounded the table. "As sure as the wheel turns, we shall annihilate our enemies!"

"Banzai! Banzai!" the Japanese and Brent Ross shouted. Whitehead and Bernstein eyed Brent and smiled.

Fujita nodded at Rear Admiral Whitehead. Whitehead would speak for the Christians, "Heavenly father watch over us and lead us to victory over the barbarians at our gates." He opened a book of psalms and read two verses from the Seventh Psalm: "My protection is my God, who saveth the upright in heart. God is a righteous judge, and a God who is indignant with the wicked." He looked long at his fellow officers and then concluded, "In the name of the Father, the Son and the Holy Ghost."

Next, Fujita gestured to Colonel Bernstein. Bernstein called on the Torah: "Arm us oh Lord against the Assyrians, Philistines, Chaldeans and Babylonians who rage at our gates. Give us the strength of Joshua who led the tribes of Judah to victory over the Canaanites—the foes of God and man. The walls of Jericho will fall again and the Canaanites will rule no more."

Fujita smiled with satisfaction. He had honored the three great religions represented in the room. In his oriental mind, his cause has been strengthened not only by an alliance of men, but, more importantly, a joining of deities. "Gentlemen, you may return to your duties," he said.

The officers began to rise. "Commander Ross," Fujita called out. "Please remain."

"Aye, aye, Sir," the American said, sinking back in his chair.

The door closed, and the old admiral sat silently, staring at the young American. Then, thumbing a document on the table, he said, "You wish to take the shakedown cruise on that new Israeli submarine chaser—the, ah . . ."

"The *Edo*, Admiral."

"Yes, *Edo*." He raised the document. "I have your written request here." Putting on a pair of thick round glasses, he scanned the single sheet. Still studying the document, he said, "Her captain, this Lieutenant Dov Poraz, plans on a run south to the East China Sea."

"Right, Sir. Cruise off the Tokara Retto."

"Where those fishing boats vanished."

The young man shrugged. "Makes it more interesting, Admiral."

The Japanese ran his fingers over his small nub of a nose like a crinkled button and removed the glasses. "You are a line officer, my JOD (Junior Officer of the Deck) at battle stations, a communications expert, one of the best NIC officers."

"You are very generous, Sir." The young man shrugged. "If I am an effective officer, it is because of my decade spent under your command."

The labyrinthine web of wrinkles rearranged themselves into the old man's version of a grin. "Now, you are becoming generous, Brent-san."

"I'm a realist, Sir."

Fujita stabbed a finger at a chart hanging on a far bulkhead, "This shakedown cruise could take nine days, perhaps two weeks. Why do you wish to make it?"

Brent hunched forward. "You know I was in on the planning, saw her built at the Tanabe Boat Works just a few slips away."

"You love small craft."

"Yes, Sir. My father had an old navy P.T. boat we converted to a pleasure craft. We'd run her out of Long Island Sound at 40 knots." He smiled expansively, "It was great."

"*Edo* is no motor torpedo boat."

"Of course, Sir. But she is small, fast. And I supervised the installation of her electronics gear. I know every man on her crew. Lieutenant Poraz is a fine skipper, and the crew is a great bunch." He hunched forward, "I want to make this cruise—if it doesn't interfere with my duties."

"No, it would not. Admiral Whitehead has a new assistant—that Italian who is such an electronics genius. Admiral Whitehead says he learns very quickly, and has become an excellent cryptographer."

"Lieutenant Giovanni Castagnini."

"Yes, Lieutenant Giovanni Castagnini. I wish he could speak better English. The Italian Navy assured me he was a language expert."

"The Italians make mistakes."

"Yes, they are very proficient in that area, Brent-san. The briefest book I ever read was a history of Italian military victories."

Brent was stunned. The old man was actually joking. Humor in the old man was very rare.

There was a knock. Brent opened the door and grinned. Lieutenant Giovanni Castagnini was standing in the passageway. It was almost as if the man had heard his name and appeared like an apparition in a cheap Hollywood schlock movie. He was holding some splintered, black-splotched wood and a small plastic bag. *"Buon giorno, commandante,"* the small, dark man said.

"Enter, but speak English," Fujita laid bluntly.

"Si, si."

"What?"

The dark skin reddened. "Ah, yes, yes, *signor* Admiral." He entered, bowed, palmed a lank of black hair back from his forehead, and stood at attention. Considered below decks, there was no saluting in Flag Country. Brent returned to his chair.

"At ease. And what is that driftwood you are carrying?"

The Italian placed some broken planking on the table and emptied some slivers of twisted metal out of the plastic bag. "A fishing *braca* found this *bosco* drifting, Sir. Near the place where the *Gobo Maru* vanished. The Maritime Self Defense Force sent it to us *immediatamente.* It just arrived a few minutes ago."

The sprinkling of Italian seemed not to trouble Fujita. Castagnini was very nervous, spoke with a guttural Sicilian accent, yet was understandable enough. Hunching forward, the old man eyed the scraps of metal suspiciously. Brent could tell every sense was attuned, concentration almost palpable. The bits of metal were bullet fragments. "The bullets?"

"Kalashnikov AK 47s, Ammiraglio Fujita."

"No doubts?"

"Senza a doubt, Sir." He held up a nearly perfect round. "We dug this *fuori di* the planking. Seven-point-six-*due*-millimeter, steel *giacca."*

"Steel jacketed, and the planking is from the boat's skiff?"

"Correcto, Ammiraglio."

Brent said, "The Russians and Chinese have flooded the world with those assault rifles. Why, street thugs in the U.S. shoot policemen with them. *Anyone* can get them."

The old man scratched his chin and turned the pencil-thin lips under, "Could be pirates."

Brent said, "True, Sir. Pirates have been preying on refugee ships for years, especially Chinese and Vietnamese."

Castagnini said, *"Con rispectto, Commandante, Ammiraglio* Whitehead said the *piratas* do not usually attack fishing *barcas."*

Brent shrugged. "Who knows? Maybe they needed rations, or they were spotted and would leave no witnesses."

Fujita nodded. "Possible. But I do not believe this is a matter for our forces. Let the Coast Guard look into this."

Brent said, "Only two of their vessels survived the Arab air raid of '89, and they keep on breaking down."

"I can't send destroyers down there for such a trivial matter," Fujita said.

"We could alert our air patrols, Admiral," Brent said. "Have them report all suspicious vessels off the Tokara Retto. After all, two fishing boats have vanished in that area, not just the *Gobo Moru."*

The Italian said, "*Ammiraglio Fujita.* The other fishing *barca* was the *Minokama Maru.*"

"Sir," Brent said. "*Edo* will cruise that area on her shakedown. If any suspicious vessels are spotted by aerial reconnaissance, we can investigate."

The old man nodded. "Good thinking, Commander, and be prudent. You could meet something quite vicious and lethal down there."

"I understand, Sir." Brent ran his fingers through his hair thoughtfully. "Admiral, I would suggest chemical and metallurgical analyses of the bullet fragments and those burned spots on the planking."

"Burned spots?" Fujita leaned forward and stared.

"Could be explosives—shell fire. Analyses could help identify the attackers, or, at least, the source of their weapons."

"Good suggestion, Commander, but *Yonaga* does not have the facilities."

"The Maritime Self Defense Force does, Sir."

"Or the Tokyo *polizia,*" Castagnini offered.

The old man turned to Castagnini, "See to it, Lieutenant. Contact the Maritime Self Defense Force first."

"*Si,* ah, I mean yes, Admiral."

"You are dismissed, Lieutenant."

Quickly, the Italian gathered the wood and fragments, bowed and walked to the door.

When the door closed, Fujita said, "It is possible, Brent-san, you may find a formidable enemy off the Tokara Retto."

"Very small chance, Sir."

"But possible."

The American's face hardened. "I would welcome a chance to engage those murderers."

"Spoken like a samurai."

Sagging back into his padded chair, Fujita patted a leather-bound copy of the *Hagakure*—the handbook of

Bushido and the samurai's Bible—and quoted from it. " 'When a samurai tests his armor, he should test only the front', Brent-san."

Brent's face was softened by a smile. "That is the only part of my armor the enemy has ever seen. Remember, Admiral, years ago you told me, 'If you die, die facing the enemy'."

"I could never expect less of any of my samurai, Brent-san."

"Thank you, Admiral." He gestured at the *Hagakure,* "And, Sir, the book tells us, 'A warrior must be unattached to both life and death. With such non-attachment, the samurai can accomplish any feat and find the Way'. I seek this, Admiral."

"Very good, Brent-san. You truly are 'The Yankee Samurai'."

"Thank you, Sir."

"You are dismissed, Brent-san."

"With your permission, I will report aboard *Edo* immediately."

"You have my permission."

The young man stood, bowed, and left.

For a long moment the black beady eyes stared after the young man. Then a withered hand reached into an inside pocket of his tunic and pulled out an old leather billfold. Opening it, he pulled out a picture, faded and brown with age. It was a photograph of a strapping young Japanese who strangely resembled the young American who had just departed.

"Kazuo, my son. Your ashes will whisper through the atomic dust of Hiroshima for eternity." He looked at the shrine imploringly, "Amaterasu-O-Mi-Kami watch over him. I cannot lose him twice."

Spreading his hands on the table, he dropped his head on his palms and clutched his forehead.

Five
The Shakedown

"Tropical cyclone" is a generic term given for a revolving storm that originates over tropical oceans and contains no distinct air-mass contrasts or fronts. Differences in atmospheric pressure give the storm its power. As with all storms in the northern hemisphere, the winds swirl around the center of the atmospheric depression in a counter-clockwise direction. If the winds exceed 75 miles per hour, these storms are known as hurricanes in the western hemisphere and typhoons in the eastern.

It is not unusual for the barometer at the center of the depression to fall below 930 millibars. The changes in pressure are very rapid, frequently twenty or thirty millibars in minutes. It is the tremendous differences in atmospheric pressure between neighboring air masses that give the typhoon its devastating destructive energy. The strength of the winds follows a rigorous pattern: velocity is proportional to the difference of pressure between the place from which it comes and the place toward which it blows.

Typhoons can be over 1,000 miles in diameter, accompanied by high seas, heavy rains and gusts of wind that can exceed 150 miles per hour. They tend to move slowly; sometimes not at all. This is especially true while the storm is in the tropics. As the typhoon moves to higher latitudes, the forward speed usually increases and may reach fifty miles an hour or more.

Their range is enormous. The great winds smash the coast of Indochina, the Philippines, China, and occasionally curve as far north as Japan. They follow regular seasons, striking from May to November but are most frequent during July, August and September. Unfortunately, subchaser *Edo* put to sea in late August, just at the moment the biggest storm of the season was brewing.

Steaming a hundred miles off Honshu's east coast, *Edo* headed south and west at fifteen knots. With the typhoon raging 700 miles to the south, a large swell was running as if a giant had hurled an immense boulder into the ocean at latitude zero, sending ripples radiating to every corner of the Pacific. From the subchaser's bridge, the swell appeared like an unending succession of blue-gray ridges, one behind the other in neatly matched ranks. The waves made the ship heave and groan as her bullnose lifted to the sky, and then plunged forward and down in drawn out, sickening swoops. With the freshening wind backing to the south and east, the tops were clawed from the swell. Spray and occasional blue water hurled completely over the flying bridge. Overhead, the sky was angry, the sun bleeding copiously across a high veil of cirrus which streaked from horizon to horizon like glowing smoke.

"Anemometer and barometer readings," Lieutenant Dov Poraz shouted into a voice tube.

"Force eight from the southeast, 1005 millibars of pressure, Captain," came back quickly from the pilot house.

Poraz turned to Brent Ross and shouted over the bark of diesels, the hiss of water sluicing past, and wind mourning through the rigging. "Not a bad barometer reading, Commander." His near perfect English had an Ivy League correctness to it.

Clinging to the foul weather rail at the top of the plywood windscreen, Brent nodded. A standard atmosphere was 1013.2 millibars. Poraz knew his meteorology. "Right, Captain," Brent acknowledged. "Not too bad. I've seen the barometer drop in the low nine-hundreds in the eye. That typhoon's in the tropics, clobbering the Western Carolines. We're just getting the tailings, and with this set of sea and wind we should take most of it bow-on."

"I've never steamed this hemisphere, but we're in the middle of the typhoon season?"

"July through August—the heart of the season."

"It should move north and west."

"Right, Captain. That should be the track of the storm—toward the Philippines, the China coast, Taiwan. Usually they climb right up the China coast and knock hell out of everything."

"Should move at ten to fifteen knots, just like a hurricane."

"Correct. That's all it is, only the hemisphere is different."

"I know that, Commander. Then the wind should back to the southwest as the storm moves across our front."

"Right, Captain—if all our suppositions are correct and we're lucky, *and* the storm does what it's supposed to do, *and* Susano does his homework."

"Susano?"

"The Shinto god of storms."

Poraz grinned, a wide friendly upward turn of his lips. "Why, of course. I almost forgot. 'The Yankee Samurai'."

"That's what they call me, Captain."

"What about the god of the sea?" the Israeli asked.

Brent chuckled. "Watatsumi-no-Mikoto? We could use his cooperation, too."

"Do you think this mythology works?"

"Theology, Captain."

"Of course."

Brent turned a single palm up and shrugged. "As good as anything man ever invented in the West."

The Israeli nodded with new seriousness. "I guess you're right, Commander. Different longitudes, different gods." Quickly, he segued away from Shinto and returned to the sea. Waving over the bow at the advancing swells which, in the distance, seemed as black and as substantial as rocks, he spoke. "*Yonaga* wouldn't even feel this."

Brent laughed. He was accustomed to *Yonaga* bulldozing her way through the seas. *Edo* was a cork. "It's all relative, Captain, isn't it?"

"Right, Commander. One-hundred-forty-tons *viz-a-viz* 84,000."

The American threw a thumb over his shoulder at the stern, where several of the crew leaned over the taffrail and heaved their breakfast into the wake. "I think they would prefer *Yonaga*," Poraz said through a chuckle. "Or the Rock of Gibraltar."

"It will pass."

"It always does, Commander." He glanced at the American, and Brent knew there was a question on his mind. It was voiced as a statement, "I think I'll reduce speed."

"Good idea, Captain. Don't want to punish her *too* much," Brent gestured at the taffrail, "and they'd appreciate it."

Poraz spoke into the tube, "Pilot house."

"Pilot house, aye," came back up the tube.

"Speed twelve."

"Speed twelve, Sir." Immediately, the slowing beat of the big diesels came up through the soles of Brent's boots, and even through his gloves on the foul weather rail.

"Speed twelve, 950 rpms, Sir."

"Very well." And then Poraz threw a switch on the intercom and spoke into a small microphone, "Engine room!"

"Engine room, aye."

"Pazanowski, report, main engines."

The voice of the eccentric Chief Engineer, Chief Machinist Mate Willis Pazanowski, echoed back. "Nine-hundred-fifty rpms, boost 46.9 inches of mercury, exhaust temp both engines, 662 degrees. Fuel pressure 62 psi both engines, oil pressure port 54 psi, starboard 55 psi, fuel consumption 18.7 gallons per engine . . ."

"Very well. Very well," Poraz interrupted impatiently. "I don't want a report on every nut and bolt. Are all readings in the green?"

"Right, Sir. Purring like a contented pussy after a romantic night in an alley."

"Very well," Poraz said in a forced professional timbre. The two officers grinned at each other.

"Pazanowski's an independent maverick," Brent said.

"Right. But he knows when to rein it in, Commander."

"Anyone who grows up in Cleveland has to be strange," Brent noted. Poraz smiled a taut little smile and tightened his grip on the rail.

"Nine-hundred-ninety millibars," came up the voice tube. It was the anxious voice of *Edo*'s third officer, Ensign Ilam Tehila.

"Very well, Ensign." Poraz looked at Brent.

"The barometer will 'pump', Captain. Not unusual at this distance from the center. If it gets too rough, we can put into the Bungo Suido and ride it out. We'd be on the lee side of Kyushu there."

"I know. But she should handle this. It's a good test for the ship and good experience for the crew. After all, this is a shakedown." He lifted a flap of his lined cap and scratched his ear. "As a last resort, we can put into Kagoshima, Commander."

"Those old sea dogs would spot us as a stranger with Kagoshima as a home port—might see through our disguise."

Poraz nodded grimly. "You're right, there, Commander. But as a last resort."

Brent stared at the vast emptiness ahead. The view was

striking, yet monotonous and simultaneously frightening. It was impossible not to recognize that this vast, heaving sea was a giant creation of nature, utterly dwarfing any creations of mankind. A single wave could bury a Gothic cathedral, a swell a thousand times longer than all of man's aqueducts, bridges and roads laid end to end. And the immensity of it; the Pacific alone was nearly 70,000,000 square miles in size—bigger than all the land area of the world combined.

But it could be beautiful; an exquisite yet treacherous mistress capable of providing a man with the most delectable delights, yet, also capable of turning on him without warning with murderous fury. Maybe this was why he loved the sea so much. It was so very feminine.

Poraz's thoughts seemed to mingle with Brent's, "Immense, isn't it?" he said, staring through his binoculars.

"It's a pretty big puddle."

Dropping his binoculars, the Israeli's mood deepened, "The indifferent immensity of the natural world. Right, Commander?"

"Yes, that's it exactly."

Poraz surprised Brent with his metaphysical side. "It doesn't care about us. It doesn't care about anything. It would gulp us as quick as a shark swallows a sardine."

"You're a philosopher, Captain."

Poraz chuckled. "A pragmatist, Commander."

"And accurate."

"Thank you, Commander."

"But it can be beautiful."

"So can a cobra."

The ship labored up a mountainous swell, hung for a moment on the crest, and then slammed down with teeth-jarring force. Her bow and forepart crashed into the reverse slop with a hollow booming sound. Spray flew, and blue-gray water shot to both sides in sheets. The mast snapped and vibrated, stays strumming. Grimly, the two officers tightened their grips on the rail and rode the heaving deck like two cowboys trying to stay with an unbroken stallion.

Brushing spray from his eyes, Poraz said, " 'God moves in a mysterious way, His wonders to perform; He plants his footsteps in the sea, And rides upon the storm'."

"That's William Cowper," Brent said.

"Right."

"Well, Captain, God would have a rough ride today."

Only two nights before, *Edo* had cast off from Dock B-4 and stood out the Uraga Straits. Then, Brent had been pleased by the weather, which had been mild and still, with only a slow oily swell and bright clear moon. They had been 200 miles at sea when the first reports of the typhoon were picked up. Since that time, the wind had increased and the sea had steadily roughened.

Bending his knees to counter the sharp, quick rolls, Brent's mind wandered back to the last meeting with Admiral Fujita. The old admiral had him bring Lieutenant Dov Poraz to his cabin. "You have heard of Q-ships, gentlemen?" the old admiral had asked from behind his desk.

"Ah, World War One. The British disguised armed merchantmen with hidden guns, even added false bows and tried to lure German subs into attacks—into surfacing," Brent had said.

"Oh, yes," Poraz had added in his precise English. "Then the British would unlimber hidden guns and sink the subs."

The old man nodded. "Very good." And then with a lean smile, "If everything went to plan and the German captain cooperated."

Poraz rubbed his chin thoughtfully. "Are you suggesting we make a 'Q-ship' of *Edo,* Admiral? Try to trap that fishing boat killer?"

"Why not? I know the chances are remote, but the only sure probability in war is that war will always be with us."

"Hiding our armament would not be easy."

Fujita leaned forward, eyes aglow with new energy. He had thought it all out. "Take the 50-calibers and Orlikons from their posts and lash them to the deck. Disguise the 76-millimeter as a boom."

"The Gatling, Sir?"

"Lock it horizontally. It can easily be given the appearance of a power boom and winch. A fishing boat would have one amidships. Then cover all of it with false nets and floats, and dress your men like pigs. You will look like a 40-meter fishing boat."

Palming back his long black hair, Poraz turned to Brent. Brent answered his unspoken question, "It's worth a try."

Fujita stared intensely at the young Israeli, "There is something else, Lieutenant. This may not be your war."

"What do you mean, Admiral?"

"Japanese fishing boats have been sunk, and we do not know the nationality of the attacker. Could be ordinary pirates. They infest those waters."

A slow smile had spilled across the Israeli's thin face like warm syrup. "Sir, *your* war is *my* war. How many thousands of your brave samurai have died saving my country? With all due respect, Sir, you speak nonsense if you feel I would not be delighted to engage this murderer."

"Spoken like a samurai!"

"Banzai!" both young men shouted. Then they laughed while Fujita sank back.

Watching the young men, the old admiral's watery eyes showed no trace of the humor the young men enjoyed. Then he dampened the spirited mood with a flat harsh voice. "Gentlemen, always remember. Only one step separates fanaticism from barbarism."

The officers stared at the admiral for a moment, and then Brent said, "Yes, Sir. They *are* close neighbors."

The old man placed both hands on his desk and leaned forward. "The Arabs have taken that step."

Brent and Dov Poraz had been silent when they left.

The conversion had been done in a covered shed and completed in only two days. Then the subchaser put to sea at night.

Now as *Edo* rolled, pitched and fought her way through the seas, Brent stood on the bridge of what looked to be a completely equipped purse seiner. Nets and buoys appeared to be stacked and lashed down both on the forecastle, amidships and even on the stern. To complete the deception, *Edo* had been painted off her bow and replaced with *Akune Maru*. On her stern, "Kagoshima" announced her home port below her name.

Not the slightest trace of her armament was visible, even to men studying her through powerful binoculars. And the false nets and buoys could be discarded easily by simply releasing pelican hooks and pushing them over the side. The cannon and the Vulcan could be brought into action in less than a minute. However, to unlash and replace the Orlikons and Brownings, then load and aim, took almost three minutes. This time could not be reduced despite repeated "dry runs."

Although *Edo* was small and reacted to even a small sea, Brent liked the way the ship handled. True, she had a severe roll; sometimes the inclinometer's needle swung more than halfway from the vertical. But she was quick to answer the helm. Her variable pitch propellers and twin rudders gave her amazing maneuverability. Her pair of Caterpillar V-16 engines were the most powerful and durable marine engines made. Turbo-charged, they generated 3000 horsepower each and could drive the tiny vessel at a flank speed of over 30 knots. This contrasted sharply with the original design, which called for either two 1200-horsepower "pancake" engines, or a pair of the

GM 268A in-line diesels. Both power plants were incapable of producing speeds over 20 knots.

The dirty weather was relentless, and the barometer had dropped to 980 millibars. Turning west to enter Colnett Strait—the 25-mile gap between Yaku Jima on the north, and Hira Se to the south, which opened on the East China Sea—the seas took the little ship on the beam. Now the roll became so severe, her gunwales sometimes rolled completely under. With the forecastle slick with spindrift of solid water, it was impossible for the men who bunked forward to relieve their watches without a thorough drenching of cold Pacific water. Boots, heavy trousers, foul-weather jackets, parkas, gloves, long-eared watch caps were worn by all men on watch on weather decks. Brent Ross wore a wool double-knit sweater under his jacket, and still felt the bite of cold wind.

To add to the crew's discomfort, the diesel-fired galley range failed. *Edo*'s men were denied even the comfort of what hot food they managed to gulp while holding onto whatever support happened to be handy. So for breakfast, lunch, and dinner there was nothing but cold bread, cold meat, and cold cheese. Luckily, the big electric urn continued to work, and the men were able to wash their cold meals down with steaming hot coffee.

It was shortly after 2100 hours on the second night of the storm, when Brent lay down on his improvised bunk in the wardroom which served as quarters for the officers. Fully clothed, he was just dozing off when he was jolted awake by a hooting shriek like a giant automobile's burglar alarm gone berserk. It was the emergency alarm which clamored the warning of an engine failure or major breakdown of any kind. Rushing topside just behind Lieutenant Poraz, the pair ran head-on into the OD, Ensign Ilam Tehila, who was sliding more than running down the port bridge ladder.

"The wherry's torn loose," the young ensign shouted.

"That's no reason to leave your watch. Return to the bridge and secure that damned alarm!"

"Aye, aye, Captain Poraz," the young Israeli said sheepishly. Then he raced up the ladder. In a moment the ear shattering hooting stopped.

"Please lend a hand, Commander," Poraz said, weaving aft over the heaving deck like a drunk. Brent followed, each step supported by a hand to a gun, lifeline, ready box; anything bolted down. Finally, they arrived on the stern, where Chief Boatswain's Mate Gorsuko Uchimura, Signalman Ronald Becker and Hospital Corpsman Ezer Weizman were trying to heave in the wherry, which was still secured to *Edo* by its painter. With the help of Brent and Poraz, they managed to pull in the boat and winch it aboard.

As the four men settled the boat in its cradle, Poraz shouted, "Double the lashings, Boatswain."

"Aye, aye, Sir. It will take a 3-inch shell to blow it loose when I finish with her, Captain."

"Very well." Brent and Poraz returned to the wardroom.

Wet and very tired, Brent sank into his bunk. But now, with the rolling and pitching increasing, sleep was almost impossible. At least the hatch did not leak. Those in the aft crews' compartment were not so lucky.

In the aft crews' compartment, which doubled as a mess hall, there was a steady drip through the presumably watertight hatch. On one particularly vicious roll, the long mess table, with hundreds of pounds of provisions secured to its underside, broke loose and jammed athwartships. The same roll flung several men from their bunks. One, Hospital Corpsman Ezer Weizman, suffered a deep bruise on his right leg and a long cut on his forehead. The mess sloshing across the deck was cleaned up by cursing men, and Weizman's cut closed with surgical tape by Brent Ross, who was routed out of his bunk again by Poraz.

"Lash yourselves to your bunks," Poraz ordered.

"That leak?" Electronics Technician Tochi Nakahara asked, waving at the hatch.

"We'll replace the gasket when the weather permits. For now, dog it down as tight as possible."

There were grumbles as Brent and the captain left. "Think they'll mutiny?" Poraz jested as they descended the ladder to the wardroom.

"Quite possible, Captain Bligh."

Poraz laughed as he sank on his bunk, "Thank you, Mister Christian."

Six
The Stranger

Three days after leaving Tokyo Bay, *Edo* completed the passage of the Colnett Strait and entered the East China Sea. Brent expected even more violence from the storm. But the typhoon had struck west, ravaged the Philippines, and crashed into the China coast. The barometer climbed above 1,000 millibars for the first time in two days. Almost miraculously, the capricious sea flattened and the sky cleared as if Susano was extending a welcome. The range was repaired, hot food served once again, a new gasket fitted to the hatch and morale soared. The taffrail was unoccupied.

Then the long tedious patrol began. Steaming fifty miles to the west of the string of tiny islands called Takara Retto, *Edo* ran a southwesterly heading. Numerous weak radar signals were detected by ESM, and a few fishing boats sighted. But the boats were very small and given a wide berth. After a 300 mile run, course was reversed and the subchaser ran the reciprocal. This patrol was run day after day, without sighting a single suspicious vessel. And nothing was reported on the radio.

The only break in the monotony came from the denizens that dwelled fathoms below. Occasionally and without warning, dozens of dolphins would bound alongside like ambassadors from a contrite Watatsumi-no-Mikoto, trying to atone for the terrible pounding he had given the ship. But then the dolphins would disappear just as quickly, as if the irascible old god had recalled them with a secret signal. Now and then a whale was spotted, spouting or leaping from the sea. The men would point and laugh.

"I wish someone would give a war that wasn't so damned boring," Brent said one day in the wardroom.

"Does give a man a chance to catch up on his reading," Ensign Yoram Sheftel said from his chair, dropping a copy of *Moby Dick* in his lap.

Brent liked young Sheftel. Despite his shaggy and haphazardly-cut dark brown hair, he had a bracingly clean face. And, strangely, a gap between his two front teeth seemed to betoken his intellectual curiosity. Very early, Brent had learned that honesty and candor were two of his great virtues, along with a total lack of malice and an even temperament.

Like Ensign Ilam Tehila, Sheftel had been born in Israel and educated in the United States. Both were highly intelligent, but inexperienced. During the storm the pair had become ill, but never missed a watch. Now, with the sea calm and their stomachs under control, they attacked their duties with renewed enthusiasm. Smiling, Brent spoke. "Think we're chasing a white whale, Ensign?"

"Who doesn't, Commander?"

Brent dampened his lips. The young officer's incisive mind was challenging. He threw out a gambit. "Maybe Captain Ahab was just trying to find his own identity."

The young ensign's eyes brightened, and he deliberately grabbed the lure. "I don't believe so, Commander. The biblical Ahab pursued false gods, and so did Melville's Captain Ahab. To me Moby Dick was simply an abstraction of evil."

"Maybe Moby Dick wasn't evil at all," Brent countered. "Maybe, the whale was simply defending himself against attack. Don't forget, Melville was a sailor, loved the sea and its creatures."

The young man shrugged, and his face was broken by an enigmatic smile that could mean a dozen things in a dozen situations: curiosity, ennui, impatience, self-control. The gap between his teeth was dark, like an exclamation mark, as he conceded. "Good point, Sir."

Brent wondered if the young intellectual was patronizing him. The American continued, "There's a strange dichotomy in American literature—in a way two journeys."

"Two, Sir?"

"Yes, discovery and escape. *Moby Dick* is essentially nothing but a story of a search—and a discovery."

Now the young man was completely caught up in the discussion, realizing he had met his intellectual equal, if not his superior. Leaning forward in his chair, he asked eagerly, "And the other journey? The escape?"

"Have you read *Huckleberry Finn?*"

"I've read all of Mark Twain, Commander."

"Huck Finn moves in an opposite direction to Captain Ahab."

"He's escaping, Commander?"

Brent chuckled. "Why, yes. We agree, Ensign. When Huck Finn decides—as Twain put it—'to light out for the prairie', he's shedding his skin and losing himself in the West."

The young man bobbed his head like a schoolboy and smiled as if he had suddenly made a connection. "In a way, we Israeli's do the same."

"Trying to define your own religion and build a civilization in a jungle of enemies."

Sheftel stared at Brent in near awe. "Why, yes, Commander. You know us very well." He fell silent for a moment, and then said soberly, "Of course, Sir. You should know us. You've fought our battles since I was a little boy. I should've remembered."

Brent chuckled. "It has been a battle well worth fighting, Ensign."

"Maybe we'll harpoon Kadafi yet."

"If he ever surfaces."

On the third day, Brent requested that he be assigned to the Watch, Station, and Quarter Bill. "Give you a fourth OD," he said to Lieutenant Poraz. "No offense meant, Captain, but Ensigns Sheftel and Tehila hardly have their sea legs."

"True, Commander," Poraz conceded. "But they are learning fast."

"Great boys, but I would like to stand watches."

"If you wish, Commander. I'll give you a section and we can stand four on and twelve off."

"Good."

"Six men to the section."

"Fine. The Gatling's the ready gun, Captain."

"Right."

"Takes two men. Leaves four men to run the ship."

"Correct, Commander. One lookout on the bridge with you, a man on the helm who can man the throttles, a man on the radio, the radar, and ESM. And an engineer."

"Fine, Captain."

"Do you think that's stretching ourselves too thin?"

"Negative, Captain. We can always hit the general alarm, be battle-ready in minutes."

Brent enjoyed standing OD watches simply because it was not quite as boring as doing nothing. His lookout was an 18-year-old seaman named Hisayo Ubo from Osaka. The son of an electronics technician, he had found his father's trade boring and enlisted in Fujita's forces to find adventure. Instead, he had found more tedium, with the added curse of gut-wrenching seasickness.

Ubo was totally in awe of "The Yankee Samurai." And he was even more inexperienced than Sheftel and Tehila. In fact, he had spent more time at the taffrail during the storm than any other member of the crew. Brent had heard the grizzled old chief boatswain's mate, Gorsuko Uchimura, raucously shout at him after a violent convulsion that produced nothing but bile. "If you taste shit, choke it back. That's your asshole."

Brent found himself teaching Ubo how to scan his sector with his binoculars. Using his own magnificent MIV/IT Carl Zeiss range-finding binoculars to demonstrate, he showed the young man how to use short jerky movements that focused on a specific area instead of the continuous sweep that could miss important sightings. Luckily, he was very efficient in English and Brent could trust him with the ship's log; if the directions were specific enough.

Fortunately, the weather held and the sea remained relatively calm. But the watches crept by slowly. The hissing sluice of the water, the rumble of engines, and the occasional mourn of a gust of wind through the rigging were all numbing. It was hard for a man to keep his concentration. The usual sailor's haunts crept in, tormented. The women. They all came back.

Pamela Ward, fifteen-years his senior, who introduced him to the ineffable delights of mature love making when he was only twenty-one. Sarah Aranson, the Israeli Mossad officer. The incandescent traitor Kathryn Suzuki, who screamed "I fucked you to death!" as she led him into an assassin's trap, only to die when Brent pumped a 7.62-millimeter slug through her skull. Mayumi Hachiya, who loved him with unabashed passion in her Tokyo apartment, yet tearfully abandoned him in an arranged marriage to a cousin she despised. Dale McIntyre, frightened when she passed "the big four-oh," who broke her own heart when she shed her young lover ruthlessly. Arlene Spencer, who consumed him with fiery passion, and then betrayed him and lost her head to his killing blade in return. Ruth Moskowitz, who loved him and then died at the hands of a sadistic rapist. And there was Devora Hacohen, another

Israeli, who was sadistically murdered like Ruth Moskowitz. That time, Brent had found his revenge, pounding Devora's murderer with the heavy brass base of a lamp until his brains sprayed across the floor of Devora's living room.

Luckily, there were breaks in the monotony. Whenever he had a spare moment, Ensign Yoram Sheftel climbed up to the bridge and helped banish the ghosts. Sharing Brent's love for literature, the astonishing young intellectual had read every word that Shakespeare had written. One day, instead of writers, Shaftel showed an unusual interest in the war and he managed to maneuver Brent into telling him of the great battles in the Sinai and Negev: the repulse of the Arab attack at *Bren-ah-Hahd* and the bloody tank battle at Zabib Pass. He was particularly interested in the Battle of Zabib Pass.

The young man listened solemnly as Brent described the great tank battle and then said, "I lost my brother at Zabib Pass. He was a tank gunner with the First Armored Division."

"I'm sorry."

The young man sighed and changed direction quickly, "Do you remember *Henry V,* Sir?"

Brent was pleased by the change in topics. "Of course. One of my favorites."

"Do you remember his words on the eve of the Battle of Agincourt?"

Brent thought for a moment. "Act IV, Scene 3."

"Right," the young man said, obviously relishing the moment.

Brent began: " 'The day is the feast of Crispian, He that, ah . . .' " he stumbled.

" 'Outlives this day . . . ' "

"Of course. And the rest, Ensign?"

Shaftel stared off at the horizon and seemed to be somewhere else in another time. He quoted: " 'Today is the feast of Crispian, He that outlives this day, and comes safe home, Will stand a tip-toe when this day is named, and rouse him at the name of Crispian'."

"Oh, yes. Now it comes back." Brent rubbed his chin thoughtfully. "The Crispian brothers were Christian martyrs, killed by the Roman Maximian Herculius."

"And I am a Jew, so why should I care?"

Brent shrugged. "You *could* put it that way."

The young man smiled and his brown eyes sparkled. "But they died for their beliefs, Commander."

"And that's *all* that matters?"

"Of course, Sir. We Jews have been taught that lesson well—very, very well."

The patrol continued day after day for two weeks. Daily, Poraz ran drills. With the soft discordant buzzing of the alert alarm, the men walked casually to what appeared to be stations at the nets, winches and booms. Then, when the cacophonous bleat of the general alarm's klaxons assaulted their eardrums, they simulated dumping the dummy nets and buoys, loading and training of weapons. Fire, abandon ship, abandon ship and provide, rescue and boarding drills were also held. Everyone grew sick of them, but all hands knew they were necessary. Their lives could depend upon these exercises.

On the sixteenth day, Brent was on watch when Electronics Technician Tochi Nakahara called him on the intercom. "Report from *'Comyonaga'*, Commander. A very large trawler is headed for this area. It flies Indian colors and is loaded with antennas. Last position 27 degrees, 10 minutes north, 126 degrees, 30 minutes east. Course almost due north."

"Inform the captain immediately."

"Aye, aye, Sir."

Brent studied a chart tacked down on a small covered table in the corner of the bridge. Quickly, he plotted the position of the sighting. Taking a pair of dividers he spread the points. "About two hundred miles to the south," he said to himself. "Worth a look."

"Yes it is," Poraz said from behind him.

Brent turned and saw the Israeli staring down over his shoulder. "A large trawler, flying Indian colors and loaded with electronics gear," the captain said, almost to himself.

Straightening, Brent said, "Could be just another trawler looking for," he waved at the sea, "some of the greatest fishing in the world."

"True. But on the other hand . . ."

"You're thinking of the old Russian AGIs, Captain?"

"Right." Both men moved to the windscreen. Poraz continued, "For years the Russians kept one off our coasts trying to gather intelligence by eavesdropping on every kind of transmission. They monitored our radio traffic, intercepted and classified radar searches, our ESM and ECM signals." He waved in irritation. "Airborne, ship-borne, land-based . . ."

"I know, Captain. The US Navy was very familiar with them. Big ships up to 5,000 tons dogged us off Charleston, Holy Loch, Cape Kennedy, Kings Bay—everywhere. Why, they tailed our battle groups. NATO couldn't hold an exercise without one of them sniffing in the wake."

"You think this could be an Arab intelligence vessel?"

Brent shrugged. "Probably not. But this would be an ideal place to gather intelligence. They could easily intercept radar and radio signals here, even monitor ship to plane and plane to plane transmissions over Tokyo Bay. And, with luck, even predict when our battle group was ready to sortie."

"The destroyed fishing boats?"

"Could be they saw too much."

The Israeli moved to the gyro repeater and sighted through the vanes of the bearing ring as if he had a target in view. "She bears about 210 true and is on a northerly heading." He turned to Brent. "Commander, what would you recommend as the best course of interception?"

Returning to the chart table, Brent cut in the trawler's course with a drafting machine. Then, using parallel rules, drew a line from *Edo's* position until it crossed the stranger's projected track. Then he worked the rules back to a compass rose. "Recommended course 220, Captain."

Poraz turned to the voice tube, and in a moment the subchaser was on a new course and making eleven knots.

"We'll keep her speed down, Commander. No one in the world would ever believe a thirty-knot purse seiner."

"Right, Captain. I'll alert ESM."

"Very well."

An hour later Signalman Ronald Becker, who was manning the electronics gear, called the bridge. "E-shack to bridge," the New Yorker's metallic voice came through the speaker.

"Bridge, aye," Brent said into the microphone. Poraz dropped his binoculars and stared at the speaker.

"Got somethin' big and mean on the ESM. Could be that trawler."

Poraz said to Brent, "Please check it out. I have the deck, Commander."

"Aye, aye, Captain."

Brent raced down the ladder and entered the electronics shack, a tiny room just back of the pilot house. He heard a step behind him and Electronics Technician Tochi Nakahara crowded into the room. Brent and Nakahara stood behind Becker, who was at the operating console of the ST Research radar detection system. A red radar sensor light was blinking on the threat receiver and Brent could hear a buzzer.

A compact version of *Yonaga's* superb Model AN/WLR-1H, *Edo's* Model 1H, Mark II radar detector was half the size and nearly as efficient. A passive system, the Mark II could automatically measure the direction of arriving signals, classify them, analyze frequency, modulation, pulse width, amplitude and scan rate. It contained a thirty-megabyte threat library, and could operate on a frequency range from five to nineteen gigahertz. The entire system was managed by its own microprocessor.

Becker threw a switch, and the buzzing stopped. Then, staring at a waterfall display, he slipped an earphone from one ear and said, "This is no fishing boat, Sir. There's a powerhouse unit out there; broke through the usual YHF and UHF garbage. He's searching and he's not in my threat library." He switched on a bulkhead mounted speaker.

At first Brent heard only static and a distant, garbled voice of a weak VHF transmission in the Tokara Retto. Then there was a fuzzy beep followed by a short silence and then the blurred signal beeped through the speaker again.

The beep repeated on a steady beat, overpowering the voice. Brent checked his watch. Three-second intervals. "S-band, surface search and he's not targeting us—not yet."

"Right, Sir. He's over the curvature of the earth and his stuff's going right over us—not generating a return signal to his transmitter, yet."

Nakahara spoke up for the first time. "We're getting the downside of his beam, Commander."

"I know. I've seen this many times. If he had us, he'd focus on us and we'd get a constant beep." Brent put a hand on Becker's shoulder, "Give me a reading—all that magic box can tell us."

The signalman turned a pair of dials, changed scales twice, cursed and then said, "Bearing about 210-true, X-band, power—oh, about nine gigahertz, maybe fifteen-kilowatts, range maybe one hundred and thirty miles. Probably that trawler. Range and bearing check out."

"Right. It's definitely a small ship," Brent said.

Becker looked over his shoulder, "Why, how did you know, Commander?"

"A big ship would have a higher antenna, be targeting us by now. No, this is a small ship with a small antenna maybe no wider than three feet." He waved at the scope, "His beam width is only about five degrees. Must be the trawler."

"You're amazing," Tochi Nakahara said.

Brent chuckled. "Thank you, Nakahara. Not all officers are stupid."

Crestfallen, Nakahara recoiled. "I didn't mean that . . ."

Regretting his blunt humor, Brent placed a hand on the young technician's broad shoulder. "Of course, Nakahara. I was kidding you." The young Japanese appeared relieved. And then Brent said to Becker, "Keep an eyeball on the radar scope. We should have him soon, but he'll have us first."

"Aye, aye, Sir."

Brent raced back up to the bridge and reported to Poraz. "That's a lot of power for a mere fishing trawler," the captain said.

"True, Captain, but not unusual."

Poraz fingered his binoculars, but did not raise them. Without looking at Brent he said, "I know officers can't command on a basis of intuition, but I don't feel right about this contact."

Brent smiled. "No good C.O. ever feels 'right' when a stranger's over the horizon. Approach with caution—great caution, Captain."

Raising his binoculars, Poraz searched for a moment and then dropped them to his waist. He said, "I wish to have no connection with any ship that does not sail fast, for I intend to go in harm's way.

"That's John Paul Jones."

"Right, Commander."

"He lost the *Bonhomme Richard.*"

"But won the battle—captured *Serapis* while his ship sank."

Brent wondered at the high level of education of these Israeli warriors. There were no fighters like them in the world. A nation of only 4,000,000, these extraordinary people had fought 200,000,000 Arabs to a standstill. He said, "Can't argue with that, Captain, but a helluva way to win a battle. King Pyrrhus did the same thing. He won his battle, but it cost him so many casualties he lost his war against the Romans."

Poraz chuckled. "Well said, Commander. Well said. History does teach us well."

"Or we repeat it."

"That's what the sage said, Commander."

A hum on the speaker caught Brent's attention. Then Becker's voice, "Bridge!"

"Bridge, aye."

"They have us, Captain."

"Range?"

"One-hundred-twenty-miles."

"Do you have them on the scope?"

"Not yet, Captain."

"Bearing?"

"Still 210."

"Very well." Poraz turned to Brent, "The bearing's constant."

"Good. We're on a collision course."

Poraz nodded silently and raised his glasses to the still-invisible sighting.

An hour later, Becker announced: "I have them on S-band, Captain. A clean, bright blip. Range 110, still bearing 210."

"Very well."

Brent said, "Our combined closing speed is about twenty knots."

"Right, Commander. Should sight them in about five hours."

Poraz was off by fifteen minutes. The sea had roughened. Sharp swells mounted in the west, where line squalls slanted curtains of gray water into the sea. Suddenly, Brent sighted the stranger. Searching between the ashen, bulky squalls with his Zeiss binoculars, he found the stranger's foretop poking over the horizon precisely where it should be. "Target bearing 030 relative, hulled down."

"Radar, range in yards?"

"Seventeen thousand, Captain."

Steadying himself against the roll, Poraz studied the stranger. "Must be friendly. If he were an enemy intelligence vessel, he would have avoided us."

"Not necessarily, Captain. Could be he's had our emissions on his ESM as long as we've had his." Brent grabbed the windscreen as a swell took the ship on the starboard beam and she rolled sharply to port.

"Then he'd suspect we aren't just a harmless fishing boat," Poraz said.

"Well, he'd be curious and very cautious."

Poraz smiled, his lips in a tight line. "Of course, cautious." Bracing himself against the windscreen, he glassed the trawler that slowly heaved over the horizon. "Flying Indian colors," he said.

"Right, Captain. And he has too damned many antennas."

"I don't like this." Poraz pushed the general alert button and the muted buzzer for "Battle Stations in Covered Mode" sounded.

"Good idea, Captain. Could be 'harm's way."

"Caution."

"Always."

Casually, six slovenly clad crewmen walked to their stations, some stretching out on the nets, others sitting indifferently on top of hatch covers, talking and smoking.

Because it would not be normal for a small purse seiner the size of *Edo* to carry a 28-man crew, thirteen of the men remained hidden below, in the crew's compartments. Poised at the foot of the ladders, they would rush to their battle stations only if the klaxons called the General Alarm.

Quickly, the bridge battle stations were filled: Ensign Yoram Sheftel reporting as the official JOD and starboard lookout; Signalman Ronald Becker to man the ship's single signaling searchlight; and young Seaman Hisayo Ubo who was the port lookout and gunner. Sheftel and Arai dropped to the deck below the windscreen. Only Becker, Poraz and Brent Ross were visible. In less than two minutes all stations reported, "Manned and ready."

The crew worked hard at being nonchalant. In fact, a four-man dice game appeared to be underway on the fantail, despite the ship's roll. It took Brent a few minutes to realize that the dice were being rolled for real money in a real game. However, despite the forced casualness, Brent could see anxious glances thrown toward the approaching vessel.

"Radar, range!"

"Seven thousand, Captain." Slowly, the trawler turned until she was steaming parallel to *Edo.*

"Why would she do that?" Poraz said almost to himself.

"Doesn't make sense, Captain," Brent said.

Poraz swung a querulous hand at the swells approaching from the west, "And it would kick up at a time like this."

"The trawler's rolling, too, Captain."

Signalman Becker said, "She sure carries a lot of nets, buoys, fishing gear."

Brent swept the stranger from bow to stern. "Too much gear, Captain," he noted. "And too many men."

The captain said down the voice tube, "Range?"

"Six thousand, Sir."

Poraz gulped so hard his Adam's apple moved like a stuck walnut. His hand moved toward the general alarm.

Then Brent saw the quick, unnatural movement on the stranger's forecastle, followed by the same hasty actions amidships and on the stern. "She's unmasking, Captain!" he shouted. "She's going to engage!"

Instantly, Poraz hit the general alarm with the palm of his hand and the klaxons hooted throughout the ship. Men boiled out of the compartments and the deck crew was galvanized into action. Pelican hooks were released, nets tumbled over the sides and the 76-millimeter and Gatling appeared and began to train toward the enemy. At the same time the pair of Orlikons and the two 50-calibers were lifted to their posts and Sheftel, Becker, and Ubo unlashed the pair of M-60E1 machine guns on the deck of the bridge, locking them onto their mounts. Already belted and ready, it took Brent only a second to pull the action back on his starboard gun and let the spring slam it forward so that the first round was driven into the firing chamber. He switched the safety to "Fire" and trained the weapon toward the enemy. But the trawler was far out of range.

Poraz reacted calmly like a man who had experienced the heat of combat many times. He had no trouble uttering the two most difficult words in a naval officer's lexicon, "Commence firing! Main battery, commence firing! Commence! Commence!" And then while the pointer and trainer cranked the cannon onto the trawler, "Engine room, all ahead flank! Give me all the revs you've got!"

Chief Pazanowski's voice: "Winding them up. Nineteen-fifty, Sir, and as long as you need it."

"Watch the shaft bearings. Port side's been a little rough. We don't want it to seize."

"Shaft temps are normal."

The great Caterpillar engines roared out their full power and the subchaser surged as her screws bit into the sea. Poraz shouted into the Intercom, "Pazanowski, keep an eye on the pyrometer. If exhaust temp pushes 1,200, inform me!"

"Aye, aye, Sir. We're making thirty-four knots," came up the voice tube.

"Jesus, thirty-four, I didn't expect that," Brent said, raising his glasses.

A flash and puff of smoke on the enemy's forecastle, and a shell whisked high overhead like a broom on rattan, splashing into the sea beyond. Brent's old adversary fear screwed his guts into an icy ball. He felt a trembling in his jaw, heart pumping against his ribs. Gripping his glasses tighter, he bit down on his lower lip so that it could not quiver. He was "The Yankee Samurai." A veteran warrior. He must show an implacable face. Defeat his old nemesis. Gulping air deeply, he tightened his jaw and concentrated on his hate for the enemy. Composure began to flow back.

Edo answered, her 76-millimeter barking out a sharp crack like a whip. It sent a shock wave through the entire ship, stinging Brent's eardrums and filling his nose with a whiff of cordite like burned linoleum. His brief moment of dread flew off with the shell. Glassing the target, he found disappointment. Fired on the up-roll, *Edo*'s first shell had arced high and over the enemy. He saw a splash at least three hundred yards beyond the trawler.

"Captain!" Brent shouted in a fully controlled voice, "fire on the down roll. Her hull! We want her hull! Let water in her!"

"Main battery! Fire on the down roll! Down roll!" Poraz shouted into the intercom.

Brent focused on the enemy cannon. "Looks like a Russian 76-millimeter sixty-caliber."

"Loading machine?"

"None. Hand loaded."

"Good, Commander. Their rate of fire is about the same as ours."

"Right, Captain, she's too small to take the weight of the automatic loader."

Luck was on the side of the enemy. A second muzzle flash—an orange disc with a white-hot core burned into Brent's eyes. He did not hear the expected whistle sliding down the scale as the shell passed over. Instead the pitch rose to a screech and there was a blast overhead, as a thirteen-pound projectile struck the radar antenna. Antennas, pieces of yardarm, fragmented recognition lights, and hoists were all blown from the mast. Shrapnel rained down.

A chunk of jagged steel the size of an ax-head struck down through Signalman Becker's left shoulder. Shattering his clavicle, it ripped through his heart, pierced his stomach, not stopping until it sliced his liver and wedged against the hard bones of the pelvis. With its right ventricle torn, his heart hemorrhaged into his chest cavity and cardiovascular functions began to shut down immediately.

The dying man's scream was short and rasping as if a noose had been jerked around his neck to cut through his larynx. Spraying blood, Becker whirled from his platform and collapsed on the deck with his back to the binnacle. His head lolled to one side and he drooled blood, eyes glassy and unblinking.

Brent stared at the dead boy, stomach gnarled into knots. Ronald Becker, a carefree kid from the Lower East Side. No more light-hearted humor. No more dry quips. Now, just the end product of war—the garbage of war. So many.

"Ron! Ron!" Hisayo Ubo screamed, leaping from his platform. Then, bending over the dead man, "Get Corpsman Weizman!" Poraz and Ensign Shaftel stared, stunned and mute.

Brent pulled the trembling Ubo away from the corpse. "There's nothing Weizman can do—anyone can do. He's dead."

"Back to your post," Poraz finally shouted hoarsely. And then regaining his composure, "All stations, casualties?"

Surprisingly, only the radio shack reported further casualties. All electronics equipment except the ESM had been put out of commission. Unlucky Becker had been the only man hit.

The tense voice of Gunner's Mate Tad Jaacobi, the gunner on the Gatling, came through the speaker. "Request permission to open fire."

"Negative. You're out of range."

Both ships fired slowly, the gunlayers obviously having trouble bringing the enemy into their sights. Then, another shell ripped low through the rigging, just as *Edo's* cannon fired off another round as she rolled down toward the enemy. This time, in the strange erratic way of ballistics, *Edo's* shell struck short, became visible at reduced speed, and flipped over and over like a bottle thrown in a barroom brawl as it soared high above the enemy's midriff. Then, a Gatling opened fire.

The blaze of the revolving barrels looked like dozens of flash bulbs all going off at once. Immediately, the sea was churned short of the subchaser by hundreds of shells as if the sky was raining rocks.

Brent's glasses brought him aboard the enemy. The Gatling was blazing into his face from amidships. "Looks like old Russian NR-30, thirty-millimeter cannons mounted in a four or six-gun pack. And they have another one on the stern."

"The fool. We're out of range," Poraz said. The Gatling ceased fire.

But the cannons did not. Each ship got off round after round. But the rough seas made terrible platforms of both vessels and the shells flew wide.

A sharp roll sent Becker's body sliding from the binnacle and rolling across the deck where it wedged against the windscreen. The teakwood decking was covered with a gelatinous layer of coagulating blood. Shaftel and Ubo both threw glances at the corpse, but remained at their stations, glasses to their eyes.

"Lash Becker to the windscreen," Poraz shouted at Ubo, his voice traced with pain despite his military demeanor. "I don't want him rolling under our feet." Quickly, Ubo leaped from his platform and looped a line around the corpse. He secured it to a stanchion at the aft end of the bridge.

"We're pulling ahead, Captain," Brent said. "We're at least fifteen knots faster."

"Good! Good! We'll stay out of range of his thirty-millimeters."

"Cut across his bow, Captain. Cross his 'T'. None of his weapons will bear except his cannon, and we can rake him with everything from bow to stern."

Now, almost a half mile ahead, Poraz shouted down the voice tube, "Right to 250."

"Right to 250, Sir."

The subchaser swung hard into her turn and began to bear down on the trawler's course line. But the enemy skipper was not to be had easily. Quickly, the trawler turned with *Edo,* anticipating Poraz's tactics.

"He'll just turn with us," Poraz said.

"But we can run circles around him. He can't win this contest. Not with our speed. And we could throw off his gunnery."

Rolling, twisting, vibrating with the pulse of her straining engines, *Edo* closed on her enemy who turned with her. But the superior speed began to tell, the trawler's rear armament slowly being masked by her bridge. Now with the range down to only 5,000 yards both the cannons were able to fire off more rounds. But, the rate of fire was slow. Brent guessed each ship had fired 25 to 30 rounds. It seemed almost impossible that with all the shellfire, only one hit had been made at such close quarters, even with a rough sea. Some were very close, columns of water raining spray on the bridge and shrapnel shaving splinters from the hull.

Poraz had just changed course to 270, when the enemy scored his second hit. Slamming into the starboard side just above the waterline, a 76-millimeter passed completely through the wooden ship before it exploded a few feet off the port side. Brent never saw it. The concussion struck his back like a small shock wave and he heard shrapnel whine and hum, crack into wood.

But not all of the shrapnel found wood. There was a high-pitched scream and Ensign Ilam Tehila who was stationed aft between the Brownings, clutched his stomach and fell to the deck, blood and gray intestines pouring from a huge rip in his abdomen. Spread by the roll, a red stain trickled into the scuppers and ran off the sides of the ship. One of the fifty-caliber gunners, an American named James Mattesson, dropped to his knees and leaned over the stricken officer.

"Ensign Tehila is almost cut in half," said the shocked voice of Seaman Zeev Shabtai, the talker on the stern.

Poraz's voice was thick, but controlled. "Mattesson is to return to his gun—on the double! Corpsman Weizman to the stern."

Immediately, the kneeling Mattesson left the disemboweled ensign and gripped the twin handles of his Browning. Weizman, carrying his bag like a shoulder pack, raced aft. But, Tehila was dead by the time Weizman reached his side.

There was a cheer from the cannon's crew. A shell had struck the trawler amidships, blowing a Gatling and her crew completely off their platform. The first blast was followed by a series of smaller explosions as ready ammunition ignited and exploded and flashed white light like grounded high tension lines. Men, steel plate, smoking wood decking and flaming debris erupted into the sky.

Black smoke roiled in the ship's wake as if she were laying down a smoke screen. Immediately, the trawler lost speed. Hoarse cheers rose from *Edo* and fists were raised. But the joy was short lived.

The shell slammed into *Edo*'s forecastle like an exploding sledgehammer. The detonation blew the 76-millimeter over onto its side, held onto its mounting plate by only two bent bolts. The four man gun crew was killed instantly. The pointer and trainer were blown over the side, the loader and his assistant shredded by shrapnel and hurled against a ready box. There, two heads, a pair of arms, parts of a leg or two and ripped torsos and intestines mingled in a grisly mix like a nightmare concocted by a Hollywood special effects man.

Chunks and splinters of plywood rained on Brent and he covered his face as slivers stung his cheeks. But something mushy also rained on him. Uncovering his face, he saw Ensign Yoram Sheftel pitch onto the deck, face up. A piece of shrapnel had struck him under the chin, blown out his eyes, and taken off the top of his head. The mushy substance that rained on Brent had been the young man's brains. "Oh, God! No! No!"

Brent thought he was crying for the brilliant brain that had been blown all over the bridge. But the voice was not his. It was Poraz, pounding the windscreen and muttering, "God. God . . ."

"She's dead in the water, Captain." It was Seaman Ubo's voice.

Brent was jolted out of his shock. The eighteen-year-old Japanese showed more composure than the captain. How strange men react and change under fire. Just a moment before, Ubo had been a trembling, terrified boy. Now he showed new spirit, even courage, as though he had found his "Red Badge."

Brent stared at the trawler, which was now bow-on and perhaps 2,000-yards off their starboard side. Another flash, and a shell warbled over with a sound like the devil screeching. Point blank. Only the wallowing, pitching deck of the enemy had saved them.

Brent measured the enemy through the calibrations on his range-finding lenses. "Open up with the secondaries, Captain. She's in range," he shouted.

Stiffly, Poraz leaned over the intercom and shouted, "Secondary batteries, commence firing. Commence! Commence!"

Immediately, the Phalanx and the starboard fifty-caliber roared and yammered into action. A torrent of tracers swept the trawler's bow and killed the gunners. A half-loaded shell exploded, wrecking the breech. Then small red fire motes blossomed all over her superstructure like a pox. The twenty-millimeter shells exploded on contact, but the fifty-caliber bullets punched through the thin steel. Brent knew terrible execution was sweeping her bridge crew.

Poraz's voice: "Engine room, speed 15."

"Speed 15, Sir," Pazanowski replied. Immediately, the pulse slackened and the ship slowed. Poraz would make a leisurely run, rake the trawler from stem to stern. Brent nodded in silent approval.

"Right to 030 and make it a slow turn," Poraz shouted into the voice tube. "I want to close the range." He turned to Brent. "We'll run her reciprocal, take her under fire from end to end."

"Good idea, Captain. But she *does* have another Gatling on the stern."

"I know. But the smoke from her fires should hinder her gunners."

Slowly, *Edo* circled around to the trawler's starboard side, approaching her bow. Not one live man was visible on the enemy's superstructure. Dead in the water, she continued to burn amidships. The Phalanx and the starboard Browning continued to sweep her like streams of fire from two murderous hoses. And now the enemy was very close, almost in range of the M-60. She seemed helpless. But her sly captain still had one more card to play.

Suddenly, surging forward, the trawler angled toward *Edo.* Flashes stabbed out from her stern and bridge. Torrents of glowing white pellets whipped toward the subchaser; most from the Gatling, but some very accurate fire from a machine gun that suddenly appeared atop what appeared to be her electronics shack. "Her aft Gatling and a machine gun in her superstructure!" Brent shouted.

"Her stern! Her stern. All guns, her stern," Poraz shouted. And then to Brent, "The gun in the superstructure is yours. Kill them Commander!"

With the ships closing on each other, the exchange was savage. It was no longer a matching of wits, tactics, deception. Both commanders were intent on killing each other. It became one of those battles of extermination where blood lust gripped every man. The only intent was to kill. A primal animal frenzy that led to the slaughter at Thermopylae, butchery at Nanking, the massacres at Gettysburg, Verdun, Tarawa and Kursk. Mutual annihilation. Kill and kill again, casualties be damned. Poraz slowed even more and closed the range.

There were shocks and blasts as shells slammed aboard *Edo.* The wherry was blown to bits, and all the men astern suddenly toppled to the deck. More explosions and screams from amidships. But the Phalanx continued to fire.

Brent squinted through his sights. Pressing the butterfly trigger, he watched his tracers slam into the steel of the superstructure and ricochet. Too low. Cursing, he pressed down on the spade grip and brought up the muzzle.

The enemy machine gunner concentrated on *Edo*'s superstructure. Firing low, bullets slammed into the pilot house and then marched upward. Striking with the sound of hammer blows, they ripped through the plywood windscreen like it was paper. Splinters flew, the gyro repeater was smashed, bearing ring flying, and holes were punched into the binnacle. Alcohol poured out of the binnacle in streams and ran with the blood on the deck. Sheftel's and Becker's bodies jumped and shuddered as bullets wasted themselves on their stiffening corpses.

Ubo shouted: "You're low, Commander. Low!"

Brent raised his sights. Bullet drop was taking his stream too low. Firing three-second bursts to keep the barrel cool, he aimed just above the two-man crew manning the machine gun. His tracers suddenly arched slightly upward and then drilled straight-on into the crew. Both flung up their arms and toppled back. Two more men rushed to take their place. But, now, Brent had the range and the two newcomers joined the corpses on the deck. Another short blast knocked the machine gun from its tripod. No more men appeared.

Brent felt a warm pulse ache deep down and low. He had killed again. It was the ultimate satisfaction, curiously reminiscent of the feeling he had known with women. Strange how killing and sex were such close companions. Was he insane? The insanity of battle? He wondered about other men. Did they react the same way? Eagerly, he searched for more men to kill. None were visible. He cursed under his breath.

Suddenly, the enemy's Gatling fell silent. Cheers from amidships led by Gunner's Mate Tad Jaacobi. "We got her! We got her!" he and his loaders shouted.

"And they got us," Poraz muttered, looking around at the carnage. "Jaacobi, fire on her waterline," he shouted into the intercom.

The Phalanx traversed along the trawler's waterline. Shells burst, bounced, and water spouted as high as her main deck. "Fire Commander! Kill her, damn it!" he yelled at Brent.

Brent waved a hand. "No targets, Captain." Not one

live man was to be seen. Only corpses scattered singly and in heaps were visible. However, water from powerful hoses manned below decks could be seen spraying up amidships and playing on the fire. And the enemy was picking up speed and had almost passed the subchaser.

Poraz pounded the windscreen. Brent continued, "Captain, her hull's probably half-inch steel plate. That's how the Russians built their AGIs. We're wasting ammunition. We'd better count our casualties."

Poraz's face was seemed longer, drawn with new downslashing lines. A dictionary of fatigue. He was drained, completely drained, like all men after the hell of combat. Brent had seen this haunted look many times. He felt bone weary himself. In a low, monotone, Poraz said, "I'm afraid you're right, Commander. We can't punch through that hull."

"Her fires are almost out, Sir," Seaman Hisayo Ubo said.

"Right, Seaman," Brent said. He waved at the trawler and said to Poraz, "You can see water spraying up from below decks. Good damage control." As he spoke, the last of the fires faded into brownish-white smoke.

Poraz pounded the windscreen. "Nothing we can do." He stabbed a finger at the shattered antennas. "We can't even call in an air strike."

Slowly, the subchaser passed the stern of her enemy. The trawler, still smoking and listing slightly, plodded to the south and began to vanish into the mists concealing the curved line of the horizon.

It was time to count casualties. *Edo's* wounds were grievous. In addition to the dead cannon crew and Ensign Tehila, Signalman Becker and Ensign Sheftel, Talker Zeev Shabtai and Gunner James Mattesson had been killed on the stern. Electronics Technician Tochi Nakahara had died in his chair when a chunk of shrapnel passed through his ESM and slashed a jugular vein. Alone, he bled to death. He was found with the shrapnel still imbedded in his throat.

Four men, including Chief Boatswain's Mate Gorsuko Uchimura, had been wounded. Exactly half the crew had been killed or wounded. It was time to stand down and return to base.

The next morning while passing through the Colnett Strait the dead were buried. Brent Ross, Dov Poraz and a suddenly mature Seaman Hisayo Ubo led the survivors in Christian, Jewish, and Buddhist rites. When young Ensign Yoram Sheftel's canvas-wrapped body slid over the side, Brent said with undisguised bitterness, "Do not rouse me for the feast of Crispian."

Poraz, head covered by a yarmulke, turned. He stared curiously for a moment, and said nothing.

Seven
The Return

"We took heavy casualties, Admiral," Brent Ross said wearily from his chair in front of Admiral Fujita's desk.

Sitting behind his desk with the poise of a granite monument, Fujita looked into Brent's eyes like one studies a priceless art work. "How heavy, Brent-san?"

Brent described the battle in detail, the firepower of both ships, the savage in-close fighting, the bravery of *Edo's* crew. "They stayed at their guns, fought until they were killed."

"Wood cannot defeat steel," Fujita observed. "It is wise that Lieutenant Poraz broke off the engagement." He asked detailed questions about the trawler. Brent told him of the huge number of antennas carried by the enemy, her slow speed, the disguise as a harmless fishing trawler.

The old man's voice came out like a hiss, "Then they were gathering intelligence."

"Without a doubt, Sir."

"This so-called electronic eavesdropping."

"Yes, Sir."

"We know their old *Whiskeys* and *Zulus* watch us, but these trawlers are much more effective."

"True, Sir. Much more effective than reconnaissance by submarine. Not only can they copy our radio traffic, read our radar and build a threat library, but they can watch for changes in air-to-air and ground-to-air traffic and . . ."

Fujita interrupted, "And predict when our battle group will sortie."

"Yes, Sir. Our strength, level of training, even the nationality of our pilots."

The old man scanned some documents. "*Edo* is back in the Tanabe Boat Works. It will take months to repair her and train replacements."

The bloody bridge came back. Vividly, Brent saw the butchered corpses of Yoram Sheftel and Ronald Becker. The gore. The bloody offal. He winced. Becker the playful, insouciant kid from the streets of New York. Sheftel's great brain. His love of literature, of beauty. At least 170 I.Q. points splattered over the bridge when that piece of steel gouged his brain out. The feeling of crushing loss weighed down on Brent's shoulders and he sagged in body and spirit. As usual, the old man seemed to leaf through his mind. "You lost some good friends, Brent-san."

"Some fine young men."

"Such is the way of our profession."

"For time eternal, Admiral."

The old man's eyes softened and he looked beyond the young American, as if he had returned to the century of his birth. "The great poet Natsume Soseki once wrote, '*Kaze ni kike, izure ga saki ni, chiru konoha*'." He stared expectantly at the young man while Brent pondered.

The admiral's words did not surprise Brent. He read anything and everything and loved to test his men. Brent narrowed his eyes, tapped his temple and said, " 'The winds that blow, Ask them which leaf on the tree, Will be next to go'."

"Very good, Brent-san."

"We have lost many bright leaves—Soseki knew."

"The first to drop, Brent-san."

"The winds of war reap a bitter harvest."

"Only what men have sown, Brent-san." The old man patted the leather-bound copy of the *Hagakure,* which was always at his right hand, and quoted one of his favorite passages. " 'As everything in the world is but a sham, Death is the only sincerity'."

Brent nodded at the book. "There is much wisdom there, Admiral."

"Our Bible, Brent-san. Has it replaced yours?"

"No, Sir. But it occupies a place next to mine."

The old man was silent for a moment, and then the mercurial mind rushed down another avenue. "Most men spend their lives building cages around themselves."

Brent caught the drift. "And hopelessly imprison themselves."

"Yes, routine becomes the metronome marking time for them."

"But not the samurai, Admiral."

"No, Brent-san, in that we are fortunate. We march to our own drummer."

"To the gates of the Yasakuni Shrine."

"If we are fortunate and die well, and leave this earth with shining karma." The old man leaned forward and pressed down on the desk with his fingertips. "Consider this, Brent-san, the dead of *Edo* dwell with the heroes."

A few years earlier Brent would have laughed at the admiral's words. But now, the promise of a hero's reward seemed no more ludicrous than some of the Christian teachings of paradise and life everlasting he had been taught in his youth by Catholic priests. He nodded respectfully, but remained silent.

Sinking back, the old man ran a hand slowly over his pointed chin. He knew the head-on collision of Shintoism and Christianity could lead men into a morass of confusion. He decided to return to military matters. "You have a thirty-day leave, Brent-San."

Brent smiled slowly, "You think I'm showing battle fatigue, Sir?"

"Battle fatigue? No. Tired? Yes." His fingertips tested the oak. "You have earned a rest."

"Thank you, Sir. But don't we have an invasion to prepare for? And aren't we short of invasion craft of all kinds?"

"The American Navy is taking attack transports and cargo ships out of those moth balls you use so liberally."

"I know, Sir. But do we have enough bottoms to move a full corps?"

"Yes. They have promised us more ships."

"And the small craft to put infantry and armor ashore?"

The old man smiled. "Just last week, we were promised forty more LCMs and fifty more LCUs. And, Nakajima has built and tested a new LCVP. It will soon be in production."

"Landing Craft Vehicle Personal?"

"Correct, Brent-san. Thirty-six men, or a small vehicle."

"But no tanks."

"No tanks, Brent-san. We need the LCMs and LCUs for our armor."

Brent tugged on an earlobe and narrowed his eyes. "At the last staff meeting you said you wanted to invade the Marianas in four months."

The old head nodded. "They are a dagger pointed at the heart of Japan."

"We won't be ready."

"I know. But we will expedite—storm those beaches as soon as possible." The welter of wrinkles softened, "So you see, Brent-san, we have ample lag time. You can take your leave."

The suggestion suddenly had great appeal for the young American. His back ached all the way from his neck down his legs. "I don't think the idea is completely without merit, Admiral."

The old man chuckled. "Your leave commences now, Commander." And then a cloud suddenly erased the smile. "Do not take a room in Tokyo, Brent-San."

"Too many terrorists?"

"Everyone knows Kadafi has put a million dollars American on your head. That amount of money could make a killer out of a monk." The fingers went back to work on the desk top. "There is a fine hotel, the *Kujaku,* less than two kilometers outside the compound that I am designating as R-and-R for officers. I have detached a squad of seamen guards from Tsuchuira and they will provide security, beginning tomorrow evening. If you wish a billet off the ship, take a room there."

"Yes, the Peacock. I know it well. But if I travel to Tokyo?"

"Two seamen guards will accompany you."

"I would like to drive to Tokyo International to see Commander Matsuhara."

"That will not be necessary."

"Not necessary?"

"The Americans have given us some new aircraft. I recalled him for a conference. He should be aboard soon—by 1900 hours." Slouching, Fujita ran a finger over his thin lips and studied the young man. "You are young, Brent-san." Brent stared expectantly. "You need the companionship of women."

"I have never taken a concubine or visited the 'soaplands', Sir."

"I know, you are too good a man for that." He tugged on the single white hair hanging from his chin. "Your Ruth Moskowitz and Devora Hacohen died at the hands of sadists."

"Respectfully, Sir, I need not be reminded."

"I know, Brent-san, but Commander Yoshi Matsuhara lost two women he loved to assassins, too."

Brent remembered too well how Kimio Urshazawa had been shot down in an outing in Ueno Park, and Tomoko Ozumori raped and murdered in her own home. For a while, Yoshi Matsuhara had been *shinigurai*—crazy to die. Perhaps, still was. Brent only acknowledged the admiral's statement with a silent nod.

"He has never recovered, Brent-san."

"I know."

"And you?"

Brent laced his fingers on top of his head as if he were trying to contain mounting pressure within his skull. He took several deep breaths. "I have told myself that I was not to blame."

"Did you convince yourself?"

"No."

"Did you say the same thing to Commander Matsuhara?"

"Yes."

"But you could not convince him—he feels evil *kamis* infest his soul, curse the women he has loved."

"That is true, Sir."

"Are you the same?"

"I don't know."

"I lost my wife and two beautiful sons at Hiroshima, Brent-san."

Brent was shocked. This was the first time Fujita had ever mentioned his family. This was a level of intimacy he never shared. "I know, Sir," Brent said simply.

Fujita surprised him, "And I blamed myself."

"You did, Sir?"

"Oh, yes. I was a rear-admiral and before I left for Sano Wan I could have easily moved them away from a high-priority naval target with the stroke of a pen." He shook his head as if he could banish the horror. "But I did not."

"So you blamed yourself."

"For some time, yes. But then I realized the Wheel of Causality turns inexorably, and if they had not died there, it would have been somewhere else. We cannot control our own destinies let alone those of others. And remember, all living things are destined ultimately to become Buddha and be merged in nirvana, the absolute." He turned his head upward, closed his eyes and said softly, " 'For whosoever hath, to him shall be given, but whosoever hath not, from him shall be taken away even that he hath'."

"Lao-tsu."

"Yes. The real man who understood the law of life. Do you, Brent-san."

"I try, Sir. Oh, Lord, I try."

"Good, Brent-san. That is all a man can do." The old man ran his fingers over his pate as if he were still searching for hair that had vanished decades ago. Fatigue showed on his face, hard down-slashing lines creasing the wrinkles. Brent had noticed this was happening far more often recently. It seemed every battle took something from the Admiral, and it was never replaced.

Coming as erect as his arthritic spine would permit, Fujita said, "You are dismissed, Brent-san."

"Aye, aye, Sir." Brent stood, bowed and left.

The second scotch and soda brought welcome warmth, and Brent felt the tension in his muscles begin to ease. Stretched out on his narrow bunk, he clasped his hands behind his head and stared at the overhead. With only a lamp on his small desk lit, the dim light cast long shadows of the inevitable maze of pipes and conduits cluttering the overhead. Even in flag country, the veins and arteries of *Yonaga* were exposed. The blower hummed softly, and he could feel more than hear auxiliary engines rumbling decks below. The heart of the ship, pumping life through her. Fortunately, the work detail on the bridge had secured so that the eternal pounding and scraping of sailors warring with rust was not to be heard. In fact, not one boot stomped the passageway, not one voice echoed. Most of the men were at evening chow. For a rare moment in her long life, *Yonaga* was almost quiet.

The mattress was very restful after his thin, hard bunk of the subchaser. His eyes slitted and new shadows coalesced like fog banks above him. He felt himself drifting off into a spectral realm of half-sleep, half-wakefulness. Thumbing through the album of the past. Finding Ruth Moskowitz and Devora Hacohen. Both beautiful, passionate. Both loving him fully. Unconditionally. Without reservations. Without demands except to be in his arms. Lovers who did not hide their love. Both raped and murdered by Kadafi's assassin Paul Andre Marcel. His revenge? Smashing Marcel's skull with the heavy brass lamp base. Scattering his brains like Sheftel's.

His personal devils welled up. This happened more often now. He had changed. Composed and serene most of the time, but capable of becoming a savage, wolfish beast with an unquenchable thirst for blood. He had smashed Marcel's skull with relish and continued to kill him long after the assassin was dead.

More faces paraded by. So many had died. The good. The bright. The witty. The promising. The happy warm smiles gone forever. His dear friend Takii Yoshiro, burned to charcoal, stood out. Takii had died years ago, but he would never forget that face. No eyes, ears, nose, every inch of flesh charred black. A ganglia of pain that should have died and would not. Bound to his bed with tubes in every orifice, he had begged Brent for a samurai's death. Lord, it tore his soul.

His grip on the leather tang of Takii's own sword. Raising it over his shoulder. The hum of the perfectly balanced killing steel as he slashed it down over his head with all his strength. The spindly neck parting to the blade like a lean willow. The head rolling. Jugulars spurting blood. The screams of the horrified patients and attendants. And all the others. Shot, sunk, drowned, stabbed, beaten, burned, one skinned alive. It had been incessant. Would the war against the evil jihad ever end? Could war ever end? Fujita had said, "It is our nature." Was this really true?

His ruminations took another drift. What had brought him to this? The war? The ship where his father, Ted "Trigger" Ross, had killed himself. The ship that had ravaged Pearl Harbor forty-two years too late. His assignment as liaison by NIC. His growing responsibilities and trust by Admiral Fujita. Then the growing confusion and conflicts between the orient and the occident. The head-on clash of philosophies and theology that led to bewildering contradictions. The near mythic mutability of the orient, that allowed a man to possess multiple viewpoints at once. Schizoid to the western man, a source of strength to the Japanese. "The more the contradictions, the stronger the man," he had heard repeatedly.

And what strange people, indeed. Another universe. Turned inward by the isolation of their islands, they were industrious, methodical, obedient to every conceivable kind of authority. Smug in their isolation, all outsiders were viewed as inferior. In a very real way, xenophobia was as Japanese as *saké.*

They held the Chinese in contempt, yet borrowed their religion, philosophy, even their ideograms. Polite to the point of obsequiousness when a guest in their home, they could crush you when stampeding to a commuter train. Their love of beauty was so strong, it took the form of a sense of communion with nature. Matter was not regarded as something inert and passive to be dominated, but as life to be understood. The divine suffused everything. Yet their cities were monuments of concrete mundanity and garish neon tubes.

Arrogance and cruelty abounded. Only in this land could the samurai have tested the sharpness of his blade on the neck of the first beggar he happened to encounter. And this haughty superiority was still to be found in the upper classes; cruel disregard for the plight of those less fortunate.

They spoke around the truth, not at it. Everything was couched in a kind of code. Nuances were everything. And their Kanji characters strengthened this, meanings changing with context and ambiguities rife.

Codes of honor were iron clad. Loyalty was unquestioned, dishonor repulsive to the point of suicide, and bravery to the grave the norm. And they admired and respected "The Yankee Samurai." He had become part of them—one of them—contradictions be damned. He could not help himself. He loved these inscrutable, bewildering people.

A knock interrupted the drowsy musings. Opening the door, Yoshi Matsuhara grasped his hand. Then the two friends pounded each other on the shoulder. "Yoshi-san," Brent greeted happily, "come in. Have a drink—Chivas Regal."

Yoshi stared into the half-open eyes. "Asleep already, Brent-san. It's only 1830 hours." He stepped in and closed the door.

"Just resting, old friend," Brent said, pouring a scotch and soda and one scotch "neat."

The two friends sat across the desk from each other. "I heard about your soiree with the trawler," the pilot opened.

Brent described the battle while Matsuhara listened solemnly and sipped his drink. When he finished, Brent moved to recharge Yoshi's glass. The pilot refused. "Got to meet with the Admiral in a half-hour, Brent-san." He swirled the amber fluid until the ice cubes clinked against the glass. "I have some LRAs out looking for that trawler." He shrugged. "Not much chance for long range aircraft, though. We weren't informed until you stood in."

"Our radios—all our electronics were shot out, except ESM."

"I know."

"The trawler's in the Marianas by now—maybe Tomonuto." Brent drank and continued, "She'll head for Surabaya, Yoshi-san."

"You're sure?"

"Yes. We damaged her severely. She even had a list. Probably flooding from her own fire-fighting equipment, but she did list and we put some pretty big holes in her. She needs a dry-dock."

"Good."

"Does the media know, Yoshi-san?"

"Not to my knowledge."

"We left some dust on the sea."

"What do you mean?"

"Some men and were blown overboard from both ships, and there was wreckage from both ships. Our wherry, for one thing, was blown over the side."

"Watatsumi-no-Mikoto is fastidious about cleansing his face—erasing our acne, Brent-san."

Brent smiled at the metaphor. "True. But that area is heavily fished." He sipped his drink and poured a small amount of whiskey into his glass. "Those reporters, Gary Mardoff and Helen Whitaker, have you seen them? Did they ever write us up after our affable interview?"

The pilot chuckled. "They came out to Tokyo International one day and I had a word or two with the woman. She asked about you and I told her the admiral had you busy cleaning bilges."

Brent laughed. "She believed you?"

The pilot shook his head. "She knew you were at sea."

"Rengo Sekigun spies, probably watching us with night glasses when we stood out the Uraga Straits."

"Right, those traitors watch everything. There were rumors of some kind of secret mission, but nothing in the media."

Brent nodded. "A lone subchaser couldn't amount to much of threat—or be a big story." Another thought pushed the reporters aside, "The admiral said we were going to receive some new American aircraft."

The pilot's eyes lit up as if they had suddenly been back-lighted. "Yes, indeed, Brent-san. Twelve Douglas AD-4 Skyraiders."

"But *Bennington* has a full complement."

"No, Brent-san. These aircraft are for *Yonaga.*"

"*Yonaga!* Great!"

"Yes, indeed," Matsuhara enthused. "We're getting the new powered up version with a 3,500 horsepower R-3350 engine."

"Same engine you have in your Zero-sen."

"Right, Brent-san. Only more powerful and more efficient. The AD-4 can carry five tons of bombs or torpedoes, and our version will have a power turret with twin fifties. They saw service in Korea and Vietnam, you know."

"I know. And they held their own in the age of jets."

"A great bomber that will give us a *sumo* punch, Brent-san." Yoshi glanced at the bulkhead mounted brass ship's clock. "Got to leave. Almost time for my meeting with the admiral." He tossed off the rest of his drink and moved toward the door.

"Oh, Yoshi," Brent said. The pilot stopped, hand on knob. "I'll be staying at the *Kujaku* Hotel."

"Good, you need the R-and-R. They have great recreational facilities and the biggest bar this side of the Ginza. When are you checking in?"

"In the morning."

"Good. I'm staying on board tonight. I'll drive you

over." His eyes narrowed and his jaw tensed. "Some of our friends are still out there to greet you."

"Rengo Sekigun?"

"Right, Brent-san, the Japanese Red Army. They can't picket the gate so they began to picket the hotel as soon as they found out a lot of our officers were staying there."

"Cowardly traitorous scum."

"But that scum has the right to demonstrate." The pilot smiled humorlessly, "Don't forget, we're a democracy now."

"Thanks to the constitution MacArthur forced on you."

The pilot pressed his glass to the desktop, leaving interlocking rings of moisture. An amusing thought relaxed his tension. "There is an added twist to the demonstrators." Brent stared quizzically.

The pilot chuckled. "Christian missionaries have joined them. They are quite enthused about saving our pagan souls and helping ease our journey into the next life."

Taking a deep breath, Brent shook his head negatively. He had learned to view Christian missionaries with disgust. There was arrogance and superiority in their self-righteousness that he had found appalling. Each sect was convinced all non-Christians were heathens and damned. Every man on earth had to accept Jesus Christ or go to hell. What confused and often amused the Japanese was the in-fighting amongst the various missionary groups. There were innumerable versions, and each, according to the missionaries, was the *true* version. All Christian sects except their own were equally as damned as the oriental heathens. It made no sense to the Japanese, and Brent had learned to share their sentiments—his own Catholic background notwithstanding. Shaking his head, he could only say resignedly, "Oh, Lord."

"That's precisely it. 'Oh Lord'—the *Christian* Lord."

Chuckling, the pilot turned and left. Brent emptied his glass and fell back onto his bunk. Sleep was almost instantaneous.

Eight
To Save a Soul

Sally Neverland was first raped by a neighbor when she was ten years old. Then, from eleven on, terrible men did terrible things to her. At age twelve she was raped by one of her mother's johns, who felt cheated when her drunken mom fell asleep in the middle of a trick. Then, pleased by her daughter's natural attraction to men, her mother pimped her out regularly. When Sally was fifteen, her mother died of an overdose of heroin. Penniless, Sally took to the streets of Hollywood. Here, on "The Walk of Fame," she picked up men and specialized in oral sex because it was so easy to do.

Sally lived with other street kids in abandoned buildings, filthy crowded apartments, under cardboard in alleys, and sometimes under freeway overpasses. Most were dope heads. Soon she was hooked on coke, crack, crystal meth, uppers, downers, and any other "shit" she could get her hands on. Between hits, she drank cheap wine. The parties were wild but quiet. Noise attracted cops and everyone had been arrested many times. She was raped by most of the boys. The girls expected it. She lost count. Sometimes two of them would be on her at once. "Sucky fucky," they'd giggle. Sometimes it hurt. She didn't care. They got off fast and gave her coke.

Some of the girls enjoyed it. She could hear them

moan, groan and sometimes shout out. This, she could never understand. It always felt like something big and hard was pounding around inside of her until the guy grunted and filled her with his awful stuff. Then she got her dope and cleaned herself up. That was it. No fun. No thrill. Just something men had to do and Sally was there to do it to.

"Piano Legs" Nell, came on rough one night when a group of the girls were in the hall cleaning themselves up with a bucket of water they kept there for douching. Nell was jealous of Sally's sleek figure, and suspected she faked it with the boys. She was stoned out of her mind and scrubbing her crotch when she slurred out to Sally, "You know something, skinny butt, you wouldn't have a friend in the world if you didn't have that pussy. Too bad it's a dead soldier." The other girls giggled. Sally remained silent as she splashed water between her thighs.

Nell's best friend, "Hot Lips" Sheila, joined in on the fun. "All the guys say Sally gives great blow jobs."

"Oh, yeah. Yeah. You've got two pussies," Piano Legs added. Everyone laughed.

"You've got three, if you count that fat ass," Sally finally retorted.

This time the laugh was on Nell. She tried to slap Sally but fell down. Sally kicked her in her fat butt and left.

One night Sally was scared straight, right off the "shit." It was the night Freddie "Pillow Ass" Schnabel pulled his "River Phoenix"—OD'd on coke, crack, uppers, downers, speedballs, Valium, booze and God knows what else. He went into convulsions. Bit his cheeks and the end of his tongue off, arms and legs jerking like he was made of springs. Some of the boys tried to hold him down. Slapped his face. Rubbed him. Poured water on him. But nothing worked. He screamed, emptied his bowels and bladder into his pants, gagged on his vomit and blood. Slowly, he turned blue and then purple, tongue sticking out, eyes bulging like they would pop right out of his head like ping pong balls.

Then he died.

Some of the kids had seen this happen before. Two of the boys pulled him out of the room, down the hall and out into the alley. They left him by a dumpster. Sally told herself this would not happen to her. Could not happen to her. She quit the shit cold turkey. But she continued to drink. She had to have wine so that she could sleep.

One cold evening she met Howard Cook. A dazzling young male prostitute, she met him while trolling for johns on the concourse in front of Mann's Chinese Theatre. They moved into a seedy room off Franklin Avenue and set up housekeeping. She faked with moans and groans when he was banging her so that he would think she was having a good time. This pleased him. Then, while Howard was visiting his dying brother in a local AIDS hospice, she was raped by his best friend. This happened three more times. Howard threw her out and his best friend moved in. Howard liked men better, anyway.

Back on the streets, Sally was picked up by Nicholas Vance, a famous set decorator. Nicholas was more than three times her age. Warm and friendly, he took her to dinner and then to his apartment. He had her dance and strip while his CD player played classical music. Then he masturbated. She moved in and he supplied her with all the wine she wanted. Sally never had it so good. This went on for almost ten months.

Finally, Nicholas began to tire of her. She was almost seventeen and was growing too old for him. He took her for a ride in his Sedan DeVille, raped her in the back seat with a beer bottle and threw her out. "I should'a broke the fuckin' bottle in your cunt, you lousy slut!" he shouted after her. An older woman pulled her out of the gutter.

Wagging a finger under Sally's nose, the old crone scolded, "A man's penis is a weapon and every act of sex is an attack on you. All men are rapists and all women victims. Always remember this." Then the old woman pulled a bottle of wine from her purse, took a deep drink and staggered to a corner where a group of men were standing.

"Anyone for a good time?" Sally heard her ask. She had no takers. Sally returned to the streets.

On her seventeenth birthday while straddling Judy Garland's star, Sally Neverland found Jesus. He was brought to her by an older man with a bushy white mane, a beard to match, and electric eyes that could penetrate steel. He looked just like Charlton Heston playing Moses. "Wanna good time?" Sally asked as he approached. She was broke and very hungry.

"Only in the arms of the Lord," he answered.

"Huh?"

"Do you wish to end this life of sin, young lady? Leave this evil that would shame Sodom and Gomorrah."

"Sodom and what?"

"Gomorrah." He raised his arms and stared up at a sign over a bar that announced, "Nudie Cuties." The light from the sign caused his face to shine with a weird orange glow. He said, "Leave, and find a new life with the Lord Jesus."

Sally looked at him dumbfounded. There were other lives, people who lived in happy families. She knew. She had seen "The Partridge Family," "Little House on the Prairie," and "The Waltons" on television, so she knew some people lived differently from her. But it was probably all phony Hollywood stuff. "You don't want to trick?"

"No."

"They say I give great head."

He took her by the arm. "We'll use your head to find the Lord." He looked down on her with those paralyzing eyes. "But you must be willing?"

"Do I get something to eat?"

"Yes."

"Do I have to fuck you?"

The man caught his breath. "No. And don't use that word again."

What a nut, she thought. But the prospect of a free meal overcame her doubts. After all, she had nothing to lose.

His name was Reverend Ezra "The Word" Freestone. He belonged to a sect called "The Voice of God in Jesus." When Ezra bellowed out the word of the Lord, he sounded like a combination of Luciano Pavarotti and Placido Domingo in full aria. Walls shook and people trembled.

He took Sally Neverland to a twelve-apartment complex in Santa Monica, which had been converted into a retreat and treatment center for reforming prostitutes. Immediately, she entered "rehab" under two therapist, both ex-addicts. She was lucky. Soon, the twelve-step program weaned her away from booze.

With the craving fading, Sally began to stand out in the classroom. Here, she improved her literary skills, studied the Bible and learned to pray. She found her personal Jesus. His arrival was strange and unexpected. One evening, while kneeling by her bed and praying, he struck her like a thunderbolt—a force that permeated her every fiber and filled her soul. She trembled, burst into tears and buried her head in the bedclothes. In that split second, her whole life seemed to turn in another direction. And from that moment on she became Freestone's most ardent student.

She uncovered her brain. She could read faster and learn more quickly than any of the other girls. Within a few weeks, she committed most of Genesis and Exodus to memory and was hard at work on the remaining 37 books of the Old Testament. She was possessed by the "Book." Read far into the night, revelling in the word and storing an astonishing amount of it in her memory. "Jesus is my high," she told herself over and over. And he was there, filling her room with love every night.

Within a year, she was ready to be sent on a mission amongst the heathen. Freestone informed her in a very special way.

"There is a terrible war raging all over the world," Ezra "The Word" Freestone bellowed one Sunday morning during a service in the compound's small chapel. He looked skyward, "And the Lord hath commandeth, 'Thou shalt not kill!' " The laser eyes found Sally in the group of young girls and cut to her soul, "And you, Sally Neverland, have been chosen to carry the word to the heathen. They must repent their pagan ways and come to the fold of Jesus Christ or be eternally damned to the fires of hell. And you alone are ready—you can save them. The Lord has chosen you." The other girls looked at her, some with envy, others with amusement.

"I can save them, Reverend," Sally shouted, leaping to her feet. The spirit welled up, filling her with its power and glory.

The great man patted her head gently, "Then you shall go forth, find the stray sheep and bring them back to the fold." He quoted Psalms, " 'The kings of earth raise themselves up, and rulers take counsel together, against the Lord, and against his anointed'."

Trembling with joy, Sally answered with her own quote, " 'Happy are all they that take refuge in Him'." The girls exchanged surprised looks.

Clasping his hands prayerfully beneath his chin, he raised his eyes as if he were speaking to the Lord himself. He called upon Mark: " 'Go ye into all the world, and preach the gospel to every creature'."

Tilting her head back as if she, too, could talk to God, Sally cited the last verse in Matthew: " 'Teaching them to observe all things whatsoever I have commanded you, and, lo, I am with you always, even unto the end of the world'."

Everyone was shocked. Such knowledge was expected of "The Word" or "Old Leather Lungs" as some of the freeloading hookers called Freestone. But not a novice, a mere neophyte like Sally.

Beaming and holding Sally fixed with those great eyes, Freestone stabbed a finger grandly to the west. "Go you with the Lord to the end of the world," he thundered.

"With the Lord to the end of the world," Sally shouted back.

"Hallelujah!" the girls yelled shrilly. Sally was sure a few of them giggled. She cared not. Just backsliding whores.

"Amen," she said.

"Amen," everyone shrieked.

A month later Sally Neverland discovered Japan was the end of the world. Parading outside the *Kujaku* Hotel, she carried a sign with the simple message, "Jesus Saves." Usually there were other missionaries there; a Mormon boy and a middle-aged Jesuit novice. But on this particular morning, she was the lone servant of God. Anyway, the Catholic and the Mormon were damned to the fires of hell along with their churches, congregations and all of their converts. This morning she would have these oriental idolaters to herself. Convert them to the one true church of Jesus. This brought her a feeling of contentment. But the rest of the demonstrators were disturbing.

She felt neat and well dressed when she looked at the dozen pickets of the frightening group called the *Rengo Sekigun.* Half were Japanese, the rest appeared to be caucasians. They were scruffy, filthy people parading in a tight pack in front of the hotel's entrance. The men were bearded with unkempt hair, the women equally as dirty. All wore filthy rags and there wasn't a comb in the crowd.

Men and women alike wore their tangled hair long. They all smelled.

They, too, carried signs. "Japan Bleeds for Wall Street's Profits;" "Free the Arabs From the Jews;" and the trite, "Yankee Go Home" were the most visible. Just an hour earlier, she had tried to save them. "Jesus is the way!" she had cried, waving her sign. " 'The truth shall make you free'." They looked on her with amusement in their eyes.

"Jesus saves, huh?" a gross fat woman chided, gesturing at Sally's sign. A biological mountain, her thighs and belly were swollen, breasts like boulders. She waved her sign under Sally's nose from side to side so that the motion caused her braless breasts to flop loosely like sacks of gelatine. "Glad the guy's thrifty. Help him in his old age, if he don't get Social Security." Bending over and slapping her knees, the woman's breasts jiggled up and down.

Undaunted, Sally stopped in front of the leader, a huge, foul man with a flat twisted nose and hair of matted swamp grass. A large tarnished earring dangled from his left ear like a brass ring. Again she waved her sign and cried out from the Bible, " 'Repent ye: for the kingdom of heaven is at hand'!"

"Get outta my way, 'Virgin Mary', before I stick that sign up your sanctimonious pussy," grass hair bellowed at her. Then the others jeered and taunted, threatened to break her sign. A short rotund Japanese woman threatened to break her neck. From then on, Sally kept her distance and prayed silently to herself. She prayed for the souls of the *Rengo Sekigun* and prayed for food for herself. She hadn't eaten since the previous morning. Money from "The Voice of God in Jesus" was slow in coming. And God was listening. She was sure of that because the picketing continued peacefully for almost an hour and no one bothered her. Then the car arrived.

It was a Mercedes with *Yonaga* in both English and Japanese ideograms on its side. Stopping in their tracks, the crowd turned toward it. Everyone stared silently. Venom was in their eyes. Sally watched curiously while the Mercedes parked across the street.

Two naval officers emerged, stared at the pickets that blocked the entrance and began to walk toward her. Both wore immaculate blue uniforms with gold trim. Swords were at their sides. One was a Japanese, an older man with a proud, haughty look about him. The other was one of the most impressive men she had ever seen.

He was a giant. Broad in the shoulders and narrow in the waist, he was very fair compared to his companion. His hair was blond, eyes cobalt blue, nose fine and straight and jaw strong. A stump of redwood was his neck. Sally had seen his picture many times. "The 'Yankee Samurai'," she said to herself. Commander Brent Ross. The myth lived. She sighed. It was like finding a combination of Arnold Schwarzenegger and Tom Cruise on your doorstep. Then she remembered her work. The man was as lost as the heathen at his side. In fact, he was one of the world's most heartless killers. She moved toward him. He was an American. Maybe, with the help of the Lord, she could reclaim his soul for Jesus, lead him to rebirth. Empathy with the American seemed automatic.

Then the *Rengo Sekigun* began to chant, " 'Yankee Samurai!" "Killer of babies!" "Capitalist assassin!" "Jew lover!" "Yankee go home!"

Although the demonstrators blocked the entrance, the two officers walked directly toward it with long, sure strides. The big man with the flat nose and swamp grass hair, stepped directly in front of Brent Ross. "Killed any babies lately, oh mighty 'Yankee Samurai'?" he taunted.

The steely blue eyes bored into the demonstrator. The voice was cold steel, "I suggest you get out of my way."

"This is a free country. Remember? Walk around." The crowd tittered.

"That sign," Brent Ross said.

"What about it."

"You might have trouble picketing with it shoved up your ass."

Rocking on his heels with laughter, the man tossed his sign to floppy tits and said, "Now, 'John Wayne', make me." More laughter.

The crowd fell silent and swarmed closer. Sally edged forward until she could smell the *Rengo Sekigun.* The Japanese officer stepped ahead, but Brent Ross halted him with a hand to the chest. "This is a one-on-one tête-à-tête," he said to his companion matter-of-factly.

"You gunna stick me with that big sword, oh mighty warrior?" flat nose jeered.

Unbuckling the sword and handing it to his companion, the commander said, "No chance. The sword's valuable, and I don't want to get the blade dirty."

Face purple-red with rage, the man lashed out with a fist. The American ducked and the huge fist knocked his cap off. The crowd cheered.

Stepping lightly to the side with the grace of a dancer, Brent Ross's fists pounded out in a dazzling flurry—one, two, three times. The first rustled the swamp grass as the big man ducked and weaved, the other two blows landed; one on the shoulder and the other in the ribs, pounding the wind out of him. Dust flew from the filthy shirt and he staggered back.

There were curses from the crowd, which was growing. Guests were streaming from the hotel accompanied by curious employees, joining the spectators who ganged around in a big circle. It was then that the tall, bulky man in the fine suit nearly knocked Sally off her feet. Right behind him was a slender, prim woman also dressed in a suit. Both carried cameras. The man bulled his way through the crowd with the woman on his heels. "Careful, asshole," someone yelled at him. He didn't even pause. Sally pressed forward. She had to see the fight and, perhaps, pray for Brent Ross.

Apparently hurt, the big man was giving ground unsteadily with the American close behind. It was a ruse. He was obviously an experienced gutter fighter. Spinning on the ball of his foot, he lashed out at Brent Ross with the other. The foot impacted the commander in the chest and knocked him backward. Cheering, the mob surged forward. Sally stifled a cry with a clenched fist.

Pressing his advantage, flat nose swung big roundhouse punches. Most landed on the weaving officer. But Sally noticed they seemed to glance off Brent Ross's arms and shoulders. However, two hit his head so hard, his hair flew and drops of sweat sprayed. He was taking terrible punishment.

Sally knew it was time to pray. Clasping her hands, she spoke to the sky, "Help him, oh Lord, as you helped David against Goliath."

Brent Ross staggered to the side and his knees seemed to give way. Shouting in triumph, the big man charged in for the kill. It was a mistake. Probably strengthened by the Lord, the commander brought a fist the size of a cement block up from the ground and caught the man in the solar plexus. Even from the back of the crowd, Sally could hear the breath whoosh from his lungs. She pushed forward.

Crying out and gasping with pain, flat nose staggered backward. The cement blocks continued to rain. A straight-on punch flattened the nose even more. Mucous and blood sprayed. Another blow to the mouth sent teeth flying. The big man fell, and Brent Ross leaped on top of him. Now, at the front of the crowd, Sally was sure she heard an animal growl.

But the big man was not finished. He rolled just as Brent landed. Then brought a big fist over and hit the American on the back of the head, driving his face into the cement. Cheers. Then it was the turn of the big man to attack. Bleeding from the mouth and nose, he rolled into the officer and the pair clasped each other like two maddened lovers in the throes of passion. Rolling over and over, they punched, screamed and fought like wild animals. Sally had seen fights in the streets of Hollywood, but nothing as savage as this. These were no longer men, but beasts. The filthy man was actually trying to bite.

They crashed into the curb. The American grabbed his enemy's head and began to pound it onto the cement edge. Flat nose screamed, a spray of bloody spittle. The other *Rengo Sekigun* pushed forward, and big tits pulled a knife from her bag. "You motherfucker! I'm gunna gut you!" she screamed.

Then the Japanese officer pulled a pistol and she shrank back. Other officers, too, crowded around and the combatant were left to finish their fight.

They rolled from the curb. Flat nose tried to gouge the commander's eyes. Ross brought up a knee and caught him in the crotch.

"He kicked him in the balls!" saggy breasts screamed. "That ain't fair!"

"Yeah," one of her companions cried out. "He don't fight fair! Chicken shit!"

Flat nose grabbed an empty bottle laying in the gutter. Smashed it. Brought the shards down hard, aiming for the American's face. Sally cried out in horror. But the American caught his wrist and forced the bottle back. Both eyed the weapon fearfully as if hypnotized by it.

"Enough!" Brent's companion shouted, stepping forward.

"No!" Brent Ross gasped back. "Stay out of this, goddamnit. This is *my* fight!"

To Sally's surprise, the Japanese officer stopped. It must be their code. Brent Ross was "The Yankee Samurai." She had heard of Bushido. It was very confusing. Is this what Bushido meant? Fight to the death? Like an animal? And the *Rengo Sekigun* showed no sign of quitting. None of his followers tried to interfere. Did they have a code, too? Apparently, everyone would let them fight to the death and, she suspected, enjoy every minute of it.

The pair continued their struggle over the bottle. Slowly, Ross turned it, and with the great muscles of his arm straining, drove it slowly toward his enemy's face. The first sharp shard touched the man's cheek. Then dug in. Penetrated. Blood spurted. More cruel slivers sliced into the skin. The man screamed shrilly, continuously. He weakened. The bottle scraped upward, peeling skin like a chisel through balsa. More blood spurted and ran. Strips of flesh curled. Sally could actually see part of his jaw bone and some yellow teeth as his cheek was torn away. His screams became the howl of a mangled animal as the weapon scraped past his temple and tore off most of his ear. She felt sick.

The American rolled on top of his enemy. There was murder in his eye, face contorted by rage and hate. The bottle plunged down again, this time driving into the man's mouth, slashing gums, knocking more teeth loose and cutting his tongue. Blood sprayed from a mouth that looked like it was filled with mashed currants.

Again, Sally heard the awful, primeval growl. It was Brent Ross. He raised the bottle again and she finally yielded to a strange force that filled her with unbelievable strength despite her hunger. She was being called.

Launching herself forward, she screamed, "Thou shalt not kill!" and grabbed the upraised hand. But the bottle caught her, cut her hand. She felt nothing, the only thing that counted was to stop this work of the devil.

She set off a reaction in the crowd. Other strong hands grabbed her and the two struggling men. Officers were trying to pull them apart. The bottle was wrested away. Snarling, Brent Ross whipped a wide open hand around with unbelievable speed and caught her on the side of the head. The massive hand struck with the force of a club. A pistol exploded in her head, flash bulbs popped and she tumbled and rolled until stopped by the curb.

Black curtains clouded her eyes, but she shook her head and fought them off. More bulbs popped. Were there cameras, or was it the force of the blow? She was so woozy the ground seemed to be moving. Then, breathing deeply she managed to sit up.

Sally never saw big tits walk up behind her with the blackjack in her hand. The blow was short and vicious. Now brilliant lights flashed, whole constellations blinked and comets raced in brilliant arcs. Then darkness, absolute and overwhelming.

Nine
The Mission

Commander Brent Ross was holding his throbbing head as he looked down at the angel. She was very young, probably not yet twenty years of age and very beautiful. Her profuse mane of fine silky hair glowed like newly-minted gold, flaring around her head in a halo, reminding him of a saint in a medieval painting. Her skin, free of cosmetics, was so white and flawless it glowed in the sun like fresh snow on Fujiyama. The delicately-chiselled nostrils, well-formed cheekbones, perfect skin, marvelous hair, and long gazelle-like neck gave her an ethereal look—a look of purity and innocence. His eyes moved to her body. A long shapeless dress and cheap denim jacket could not hide her slimness, that supple elegance of long fine limbs and slender hips. He wanted to see her eyes. But they were closed. He had knocked her out. He cursed himself.

"Goddamnit, I hit this poor girl—cold-cocked her."

"No you didn't, Brent," Yoshi said. He waved, "That fat woman . . ."

"That's right, Commander," a young American lieutenant said from the crowd milling about on the sidewalk and street. He pointed at a group of *Rengo Sekigun* clustered around their battered leader. "That broad with the big boobs poleaxed her, Sir." He turned his head and looked to the north. "Hear those sirens, Sir. Ambulances will be here soon. They'll take care of her."

"I hit her," Brent said, dropping to his knees next to the girl.

"You slapped her—didn't knock her out. She jumped on you," Yoshi assured him.

"You son-of-a-bitch," one of the *Rengo Sekigun* screamed. He waved at his fallen leader. "Come over here and see what you've done—if you have the guts."

Brent stood. "No thanks, I can't stand the smell."

There were shouts of rage and menacing gestures were hurled at the American. But quickly, at least ten officers behind Brent formed a line facing the pickets. The terrorists remained in a tight group around the injured man. Two of the women were gently washing his face and trying to tend to his wounds. Groaning, he tried to twist away from them. Obviously, he was in great pain and blood had formed in a puddle under his head.

"Half his face is gone. We'll kill you, you shit-eatin' fascist pig," big tits screamed over the wailing sirens which were now very close.

"Yeah. Kill the motherfucker!" her companions shouted. Knives and clubs were pulled from the baggy clothes and they began to advance. Two of the men clutched pistols. Brent reached for his Beretta.

At that moment three police cars, two ambulances and two truckloads of seamen guards arrived simultaneously. All seven vehicles screeched to a halt in the street, forming a barrier between the hostile groups. Six police officers jumped out brandishing pistols. At least two dozen guards, armed with new M-16 rifles leaped from the trucks. All were over six feet tall and picked for their powerful physiques and belligerent dispositions. Their leader was burly, fractious Chief Boatswain Mate Shin Kanemaru, who had a gleeful affinity for cracking *Rengo Sekigun* heads.

Four attendants rushed to the wounded man. Quickly,

they disinfected his wounds, stanched the bleeding, and gently lowered him on a stretcher. Then he was loaded into an ambulance which departed, siren howling. Two attendants squatted beside the young girl.

To Brent's surprise and relief, the beauty sat up. She rubbed the back of her head and groaned. While one attendant gently examined her head, the other bandaged her hand.

"Need stitches?" Brent asked the man bandaging the girl's hand. His name tag read "Sanzo Nosaka."

"No, Sir," Sanzo Nosaka answered in heavily-accented, but understandable, English. "Not very deep. In fact, quite superficial. She is lucky."

"Thank God." Brent watched as the second attendant parted the girl's hair and studied her scalp. He nodded to himself, seemed pleased and stepped back. He wore, "Yashihiro Konubo" on his tag.

The girl spoke for the first time. "You said, 'Thank God', Commander."

"Yes. I did."

She came erect and the big blue-green eyes bored into Brent's. "Have you accepted Jesus Christ as your personal savior, Commander?"

Brent smiled and looked at a sign laying on the sidewalk. It read, "Jesus Saves!" Now he knew who owned it.

Before Brent could answer, Yashihiro said to Sanzo, *"Dekimásu tátte iru."* It was very fast but Brent caught the meaning. "He wants to know if you can stand," Brent translated.

The attendants looked at each other in surprise. Although he could not speak English, Yashihiro, like most Japanese Brent had met, had a working understanding of English. Brent continued, "Before you start saving souls, Miss, let's see if you can stand."

"You promise to listen to me?"

Brent threw a self-conscious look at Yoshi, who smiled slyly. "Of course. And what's your name?"

"Sally Neverland."

"I'm Brent Ross, and this is Commander Yoshi Matsuhara."

"I know."

They were distracted by shouts from the crowd. Brandishing small but vicious batons, the seamen guards were herding the *Rengo Sekigun* down the street. One turned and began to shout obscenities into Chief Shin Kanemaru's face. A sharp powerful punch to the chest with the end of the baton immediately discouraged the man. He turned, and propelled by a big boot to the backside, joined his retreating comrades.

"We'll get you, 'Yankee Samurai'. And you, too, 'Virgin Mary'," another man shouted over his shoulder. A blow between the shoulder blades silenced him. However, big tits screamed out, "You're a dead man, 'Yankee Samurai'!"

"Take you best shot!" Brent shouted back. "Any time." The mob disappeared around a corner.

Steadied by Yashihiro, Sally was standing. "Your vision?" Sanzo Nosaka asked.

"Fine. But I have a world-class headache."

He turned to Yashihiro Konubo and spoke in Japanese. Brent caught, *"Osoraku shokeki,"* in the blur of words.

Brent said to the girl, "He said something about a concussion. You might have one." The attendants looked at each other and nodded affirmatively.

Sally shook her head. "I have a headache, that's all."

"You should go to the hospital for observation," Brent said.

"No!"

Yashihiro Konubo spoke again in Japanese. His comrade nodded and asked the girl, "When did you last eat?" He gestured at his companion. "Yashihiro thinks you are suffering from malnutrition."

The girl drew herself up. "I am nurtured by God."

"You still need food."

"I feast on the love of the Lord Jesus."

The attendants turned their hands up to each other in a display of hopelessness and began to gather their instruments. They had obviously heard Christian missionaries before and had their fill. Sanzo handed Brent a small container of pills.

Brent looked at the pills and said to Sanzo, "These are Tylenol and codeine."

"Correct, Commander. Should give her relief from her headache. But watch her for signs of a concussion—nausea, vomiting, impaired vision."

Brent waved the pills in vexation, "I don't even know her. I'm not in charge."

"Somebody has to watch her, Commander." The attendants walked to their ambulance and left.

Turning to the girl, Brent said, "Who are you staying with?"

"I'm by myself. I have a room in town."

"Oh, Lord."

Releasing her breath with a long, drawn out, "Oooh," the girl sagged as if her knees were suddenly water. He grabbed one arm, Yoshi the other. "Maybe, you'd better go to the hospital."

"No, please." She looked at him with wide pleading eyes. "A cup of coffee and I'll take a pain pill. I'll be all right."

"Do you promise to go to the hospital if you have dizzy spells, nausea, double vision."

"Yes. I know all that. All I have is a headache and I'm weak."

"You promise in the name of the Lord?"

She smiled for the first time—a dazzling smile that radiated warmth and a sort of shining innocence, like a kitten or beautiful child. Brent was absolutely captivated.

If anyone had a direct line to God, this girl did. And if he had ever met a virgin, Sally Neverland was it.

"You're stealing my lines, Commander," she chided.

"Of course. I've read the Bible, too. I spent most of my childhood in parochial schools." They began to turn toward the entrance.

"One moment, there," a deep authoritative voice rang out. Turning, Brent saw one of the police officers approaching.

A squat, husky man, he was breathing heavily and perspiration lined his forehead like a valance of dirty beads. "I am Lieutenant Yohei Kono of the Yokosuka Police. And you are Commander Yoshi Matsuhara and Commander Brent Ross."

"Right," Brent said. "And this is Sally Neverland."

The lieutenant opened an old wound that had been a sore point between the civilian police and *Yonaga's* crew for a decade. The officer almost spit his words out, "You cannot just make our streets a battleground for your personal feuds."

Yoshi spoke, "We were attacked and defended ourselves. We'd be dead, if we had waited for you."

Kono gestured at Brent, "He almost killed a man."

"He attacked me," Brent said. "Don't try to tell me I can't defend myself."

"I will tell you. It is our duty to protect you."

"Ha! In that case, I'd have zero life expectancy."

"You tore most of that man's ear off."

"It was too big and dirty, and I didn't like his earring." Yoshi laughed, Sally just stared expressionlessly.

The officer stepped closer to Brent, eyes clouded with anger. His voice climbed octaves and he almost shouted, "It is the duty of the Yokosuka Police to maintain order in these streets. Do you understand that?"

"You couldn't even sweep them."

Lieutenant Kono almost sprayed spittle in his exasperation. "Commander Ross, do you wish to be placed under arrest?"

"Try it."

The man's round face took on a crimson hue, like the morning sun straining through thin clouds. He turned to call more of his men and found Chief Shin Kanemaru and a dozen seamen guards behind him. The chief was thumping his baton into the palm of his hand. He was smiling, a demonic grin that bared his teeth and narrowed his eyes to black beads. "You going to arrest someone, Lieutenant?" the chief asked with ominous gentility.

The officer said to Brent, "So, you would threaten the Yokosuka Police."

"No one's threatened. Just do your job and keep that rabble under control."

"Don't tell me my job!"

"The hell I won't." Brent felt the girl slump against him. He spoke to Kono, "I can't waste anymore time with you."

"I'm not finished with you!"

"Yes, you *are.*"

Brent and Yoshi led Sally Neverland into the hotel, while fuming Lieutenant Yohei Kono was escorted to his car by Chief Kanemaru.

Ten
The Devil and Brent Ross

The dining room was surprisingly large and well-appointed, the service quick and efficient. In fact, the maitre d' took personal charge of Brent, Yoshi and the girl. Quickly, Sally downed a pain pill and almost immediately began to brighten. She sipped her coffee and stared silently at Brent over the cup.

"Please," Brent began, "you're not going to try to convert me now."

"Why not? Do you deny God?"

Pursing his lips, Brent released his breath noisily. "No, I don't deny God. But at the moment, we're not speaking."

Sally surprised Brent with her answer. He expected some kind of reprimand, but instead he received the bright, perfect smile and a concession. "That's an interesting way to put it, Commander. But, I can't believe it. God listens to everyone."

Yoshi interrupted, "Chief Shin Kanemaru and his men are remaining."

Looking at the entrance, Brent could see the chief dispatching several of his men to various stations. Two took positions in the dining room. "Must be the permanent security force Admiral Fujita has assigned to the hotel."

"Good idea," Yoshi said, dabbing at his lips with a linen napkin. "Sorry, got to leave," he said, glancing at his watch. "I'm late now. A few hundred pilots are waiting for me."

"See you soon."

"In a few days, Brent-san, I'll give you a call." He politely took his leave of the girl and left.

Brent caught Sally eyeing a large lunch being served at the next table. Her eyes seemed as wide and round as his saucer, making her cheeks appear even more sunken. He was discreet. "I think I'll have lunch. Why don't you join me. They have an international menu here." And then he lied, "I'm very hungry." Actually, his jaw hurt, ribs were sore and he knew his right eye was slightly swollen. And, he was filthy. He had no appetite whatsoever.

"I would like something. But I'm so dirty."

Brent hesitated. Something told him he was about to navigate hazardous waters. But he took the plunge anyway, out of concern, not desire. "Would you care to clean up in my place? I understand I have a suite. I haven't seen it yet, but my luggage is supposed to be there and we could have lunch served there."

A tormented look racked the girl's face, like the onslaught of a tsunami on a calm sea. Through hooded eyes she stared at Brent with an intensity that distorted the innocence, twisted the full lips downward almost grotesquely, obliterating her spirit. It was frightening as if her God had been dispossessed by some vile presence. It was like looking at a different person. He was suddenly very uncomfortable.

Gulping her coffee she said, "There must be a ladies' room—and a men's room here—off the dining room. Can't we just clean up here and then have something?"

At that moment, Brent knew Sally Neverland had had a bitter, painful experience with a man—or men. He suspected she was not the sheltered, cherubic virgin he had first seen. "Of course," he said simply. "Have you had breakfast?"

"No."

"Then I'll order for you while you're cleaning up. Okay?"

"Fine." The girl stood and walked to a dimly lighted alcove with male and female figures painted on opposite walls.

Brent ordered pancakes, eggs, bacon and toast for the girl, and soup for himself. Then he went to the men's room to clean up.

When he returned, Sally was seated and drinking her coffee. Just as Brent dropped into his chair, the food arrived.

"Oh, thank you," Sally said, mood brightening. "Just what I wanted." Her eyes scanned the big meal. "But so much, Commander."

"Call me Brent."

"Then, I'm Sally."

The bright, spritely girl was back. Brent was sure it was the sight of the food. He nodded at her breakfast. "Try. You're a big girl."

"You're only having soup, Brent?"

"Navy bean."

"What else?" she chuckled.

He traced a finger down his jaw. "That bum had a big fist."

"Your jaw's sore," she said cutting her pancakes.

"All the way to my toes."

He watched her as she devoured her breakfast. He could not believe that such a wisp of a girl could have such an enormous appetite. Finally, sighing, she sank back and dabbed at her lips with her napkin. "Thank you, Brent. I needed that."

"My pleasure." He pushed a pad and pencil across the table. "Your address and phone number. I would like to see you again, Sally—if you don't mind."

She stared into his eyes with such intensity she seemed

to be staring straight through to the back of his skull. "I won't go to bed with you."

A flash of anger boiled up through the sore ribs. "I'm not asking for that—looking for that. Is that all you have on your mind?"

"Only the work of the Lord."

"Then get your mind off sex. There isn't any up there with Him."

"Sorry," she said, dipping her spoon into her cup and stirring the black liquid furiously. And then contritely, "I didn't mean to offend you. Sometimes men misunderstand."

"Well, this man doesn't," Brent said, cooling.

"You need to see me." She scribbled on the pad and pushed it back to him.

Refilling his cup from a ceramic carafe, he stared at the beautiful face as he raised the cup. It was hard to remain angry at Sally Neverland. "Why do you say that?" he asked in a level tone.

She waved. "Out there. I watched you fight that man. The devil had you."

"Oh, no."

"He was there in you. I saw him."

"Then he's everywhere."

"That's precisely it." She tapped her cup with a long, slender finger. "Remember Peter's warning, 'Be sober, be vigilant; because your adversary the devil, as a roaring lion, walketh about, seeking whom he may devour.' "

"You saw him devour me."

"Yes. Body and soul."

"And you can save me," he said with resignation.

"Through the one, true church."

Brent let his breath escape through his lips with a hiss. He had heard this many times before from Seventh-Day Adventists, Pentecostalists, Mormons, Baptists and God knows how many more. And now this beautiful girl. But she fascinated him. He was convinced she was not completely what she appeared to be; professed to be. With as much sincerity as he could muster, he asked, "And that one true church?"

"The Voice of God in Jesus."

"Located."

"The world is our parish."

"Main church. Headquarters?" he asked impatiently.

"Hollywood."

"Hollywood," he repeated.

A hint of that frightening mask crept back onto the beautiful face. "Yes. The modern Sodom and Gomorrah."

"Then why didn't you stay there—make your mission there in Sodom and Gomorrah? A lot of you do."

"Because I was sent here by our leader, Reverend Ezra Freestone."

"Why did he select Japan?"

"He didn't."

"Then who did?"

"God."

"God?"

"Yes, Reverend Freestone talks to him every morning."

Brent choked back a laugh. Jim Bakker, Jimmy Swaggart and Oral Roberts all claimed direct pipelines to God. The first was in jail, the second an admitted whoring sinner, and the third was nearly bankrupt. Obviously, their divine dialogues were paying sour dividends. Steeling himself, he managed to ask in an innocuous tone, "And why did you pick me?"

"I told you, the devil . . ."

"Maybe it wasn't the devil."

"Then why that terrible fight?"

Brent smiled, a sardonic twist of his lips that focused the girl's attention. He was fascinated with religions, eastern and western. He was an expert. All his friends knew this. Some considered him a theologian. He called on his intimate acquaintance with the Bible. " 'Greater love hath no man than this, that a man lay down his life for his friends'."

The great blue-green eyes widened. "You would throw Christ's words at me? Words spoken on the eve of his martyrdom?"

"Why not? Is he not the son of man?"

"You've had religious training."

"Yes. Some. In Catholic schools."

"Then, why do you speak blasphemy, Brent?"

"Blasphemy? Nonsense!"

Her voice rose, "Your words shame Jesus Christ. Yes, blasphemy."

Brent's patience was wearing very thin. "Then let it be blasphemy."

Rising, she stabbed an irate finger at him, almost touching his nose. " 'And when he is come, he will reprove the world of sin, and of righteousness, and of judgment'."

"John, quoting Jesus before the crucifixion," Brent said matter-of-factly. He threw the Bible back at her, "And remember, 'Resist the devil and he will flee from you'."

His knowledge irritated her even more. She spoke in a loud voice that turned heads. "How can a heretic profane those holy words so casually?"

"Profane!" he shouted angrily. More heads turned and the room became silent. The maitre d' began to weave his way toward them. Brent continued, "Do you own them? Maybe, your Reverend Freestone has a franchise. After all, he speaks to God every morning." He dropped his spoon in his saucer with a clatter. "And who's the heretic?"

Placing both fists on the table, she leaned toward him. The voice was harsh, " 'Put up again thy sword into his place; for all they that take the sword shall perish with the sword'."

"Matthew, Chapter 26, Verse 52," he said, mocking the deep, sonorous timbre of a hellfire preacher. And then with a harshness he usually reserved for men. "Go back to Sodom and Gomorrah and save Heidi Fleiss and her girls."

Wheeling on her heel, she almost walked headlong into the distressed maitre d', and then vanished out the entrance.

Brent rose, picked up his key, and walked to the elevator.

The maitre d' watched him until the doors closed.

Eleven
The Journalist

When Brent entered his suite, he was so upset he hardly noticed the small but bright living room, large bedroom with the king-sized bed and the compact kitchen alcove. Still steaming from the fight and mind churning with anger at Sally Neverland and at his own coarse treatment of her, he rummaged through his luggage. Finally, he found a bottle of Chivas Regal and took it to the kitchen. Impatiently, he searched for the refrigerator. "Where'd they hide the goddamned thing?" he shouted at the tiny two-burner stove. "It's got to be here somewhere."

Then he found it, cleverly tucked under the counter next to a miniature compactor. Grunting with satisfaction, he dropped a few ice cubes into a glass, free-poured a generous shot, and topped off with soda. Then he stomped into the living room and plopped down onto a large, generously stuffed sofa.

He sipped and his jaw hurt. Then his sore ribs gave him a start and he shifted his weight. It seemed impossible to find a comfortable position. The fight came back and he nodded grimly. He had enjoyed beating that *Rengo Sekigun* scum. Placing his drink on a Formica covered end table, he looked at his bruised fists and smiled. "Don't mind bruising you on garbage like that," he said.

But he had lost his temper again. It had happened

before and Fujita had warned him many times, "The man who cannot control his temper, digs his own grave."

He had done some digging today. For "flat nose," not himself. There was no doubt in his mind he would have killed the man. Blinded him first. Chopped him to pieces with that bottle. Driven it into his throat. Maybe Sally Neverland was right. Maybe the devil *did* possess him. Nonsense! What devil? The Japanese could be right. An evil *kami.* Maybe they were all right. An evil *kami* could be nothing more than the devil in a different hemisphere. And, maybe, they were *all* wrong.

But certainly something had burst through, drove him with a savagery known only to predators. Maybe it had been the primal jungle creature that inhabits all men. After all, civilization was nothing more than a thin veneer of superficial mores and manners painted over the heart of a Cro-Magnon brute. Why "flat nose" had actually tried to bite him, just like a wolf, a tiger, or a man out of control. Brent took another sip and smiled, a mirthless, ruthless twist of his lips. He knew, given the chance, he would have bitten him back.

Certainly Sally Neverland and her Christianity had failed. And so had Shinto. He couldn't buy devils and evil *kamis.* That was just too easy. And Buddha didn't help. Religion always seemed to offer a simple explanation; an easy way out. "Ten 'Hail Marys' and you're forgiven," some priest would say after confession. And then he would be square with God. Nonsense! Too damned easy.

As Brent stared out the window at shredded pieces of clouds streaming across the sky, he realized a man could not define life by human terms. It could only leave him completely judgmental, so that he would hate life for what he perceived as its injustices. Instead, he must realize there were atavistic, primal powers that lurked in the dark recesses. "Instincts" was too easy. They were racial memories bred into the chromosomes, were part of every cell.

He knew these were the things he could not manage. They were beyond his control; they were as ancient as man and they responded to their own reasons, which were not his.

He tapped his glass gently against the brass base of a lamp on the end table until it rang like a tiny bell. "I'm becoming a Taoist," he said to himself. "Old Atsumi would be proud."

The memory of his close friend, Lieutenant Commander Nobomitsu Atsumi, brought back comments the gunnery officer had made many times. An avid follower of Taoism, for years he had preached the same refrain to anyone who would listen. "A man's inner conflicts present the real and incredibly powerful enemy every man must face and conquer in this life. He must recognize this clash of demons and archetypes, which are as old as the race, and drive him like the winds in the eye of a typhoon until he is wise enough to recognize they exist. Then, and only then, can he make their acquaintance on a conscious level, purge himself and grow."

"Yes. Yes, that makes sense," Brent said, as if Atsumi was seated across from him in the easy chair. "There are demons, but they are personal things."

Taking a large swallow, his mind raced on through the new insight. The racial memories, the archetypes of the collective unconscious of mankind all evolve within the human body. In a very real way, these were the demons. All men shelter these personal demons and he had his share. They cannot remain static unless dreadfully repressed. He had not been repressed. Instead, he had spent a lifetime acting it all out. By acting it out, he might be changing himself, and maybe some of these demons would be exorcised.

He shook his glass gently and the clatter of ice cubes told him the glass was empty. He had no memory of emptying it. He recharged the drink and sank back. Now his ribs didn't ache quite as much, and even his jaw felt better. But he was still distressed, confused. He believed he had changed much since coming to the orient. Certainly, the exposure to the ancient wisdom of Shinto, Buddhism, Confucianism and especially Taoism had had powerful influences on him. But, then, in many ways he had not changed at all.

Sometimes, especially after a battle or a personal one-on-one fight, he felt robotic. As if he had not changed since he was a little boy scrapping in the schoolyard. Was he one of those infantile men frozen at some early age? Was he clinging to some sort of primeval agenda and re-playing a mindless role? Could he ever rid himself of those personal demons Atsumi warned about? Change, and change dramatically? Certainly, today, rolling in the gutter with that thug had been a replay of a lifetime of "The Brent Ross Story." Was this what war did to a man? Freeze him in time so that he could never really grow? If true, this was the ultimate annihilation. The thought sickened him.

Suddenly, the racing mind found Sally Neverland again, driving the depressing thoughts away. He couldn't get that beautiful face out of his mind. She had been exquisite, with the erotic appeal of the girl-woman. The wistful, innocent face of a child, the body and sensuousness of the woman. The sexiest combination. Yet, there had been something about the girl that challenged that innocence. Something Brent had sensed—something he had felt. Despite the angry parting, he wanted to see her again. But she had that typical inflexibility and arrogance of the Christian missionary. Her church was everything—her life, her heart, her soul.

He was sure she would die for it.

And he was convinced she had been deceived and mislead. It was obvious the church of "The Voice of God in Jesus" was nothing more than some splinter group of fanatical fundamentalists. Its founder, Ezra Freestone, was probably nothing more than a con man. In all probability he had founded the whole thing to line his pockets and fill his bed with young girls. And the poor deluded kids all chanted the same verse, "Ours is the only way!", while waving their pitiful signs.

He slammed the glass down on the tabletop so hard some of the drink spilled. "Bullshit!" he shouted. He had her number, her address. But, he would never call her. Never speak to her because he knew it was impossible to deal with her missionary fanaticism. Freestone had her locked in, and the bars of the cage could never be broken. An argument would be inevitable—an argument where reason and logic were doomed to failure.

A knock interrupted his musings. When he opened the door he found a familiar woman standing in the hall. However, he could not place her immediately. And then obviously piqued by his silence and blank look in his eyes, she said, "Commander Ross, I'm Helen Whitaker. We had lunch together a month ago at the *Ichi-riki* Restaurant. I'm a reporter with the United American Information Service. Remember?"

Then the memory gears meshed and Brent recalled the woman and her obnoxious friend Gary Mardoff. But she had changed, looked years younger. No glasses, hair down and coiffed smartly, a tight-fitting skirt and blouse. But she was still a journalist and the one thing he did not need was the probing nose of a reporter sniffing around. "What do you want?" he asked abruptly.

"To see you."

"Where's your sidekick?"

"Gary Mardoff?"

"Who else?"

"He's not my sidekick."

"Don't give me that crap. You called him your 'associate'."

"My, you're in a delightful mood. May I come in or are you going to punch me?"

Looking the woman up and down, he suddenly decided he needed company. Even a reporter's. He wanted to talk. Argue. Blow up. Purge the irritation. A reporter would be an ideal target. "Okay. Okay." He waved at the living room. "Suit yourself."

"I'll take my chances," she said, entering. She dropped down on the couch and placed the same brown leather embassy case he remembered from the *Ichi-riki* on the small coffee table fronting the sofa.

"Get some juicy pictures?" he asked sarcastically, grabbing his drink and sitting in the large easy chair.

She pushed a wisp of hair back of her ear and said, "I *did* get a few shots."

"You and Gary Mardoff of the fight?"

"Yes. He was there, but he's not my 'associate'."

"Then, what is he?"

"Nothing at all. I don't even like him—can't stand him."

"Those pictures will be quite a triumph for you and the tabloids will have a real field day. Why the 'Yankee Samurai' will crowd Princess Di and Prince Charles right off the front pages, bulimia and lovers be damned." He waved a hand skyward in a rainbow arc and his voice burned like acid, "I can see those headlines now: 'Yankee Samurai Assaults Helpless Demonstrator'; 'Yankee Samurai Mops Gutter With Helpless Man'; 'Yankee Samurai Performs Cosmetic Surgery on Man's Face With Bottle' . . ."

"Please stop it, Commander!" she said, face taut, eyes flaring. "I don't write stories like that." She waved at the window, "Why, there were other reporters down there. My God, don't lay it all on me or on Gary, for that matter." She waved at his glass. "Are you going to offer me a drink?"

"I only have scotch."

"Fine. With water, please."

He returned with two full glasses and sat. She took a large gulp and said, "I've only seen you twice, yet we've had two fights."

"The first one was with Mardoff, not you. He's a boor."

"Agreed. But right now you wouldn't win plaudits from Emily Post, you know."

"I'm not trying for 'Host of the Year'."

Chuckling softly she crossed her legs with studied carelessness, giving a glimpse of well shaped thighs that glistened under expensive panty hose. Then the expected modest pull-down of the skirt to just below the knees. Brent suspected she had done this many times, with many men. However, he had to admit, she did have spectacular, well-shaped legs. And then he ran his eyes over the other changes. It was like looking at a makeover on one of those awful American talk shows.

Her shimmering chestnut hair flowed almost to her shoulders, flat planes of her face softened by the clever use of cosmetics. And her eyes were different—highlighted perfectly by the touch of eyeliner and mascara. The thin lips were rouged full now, sensuous and soft. And her tight skirt and clinging blouse showed every curve and nuance of her well-formed body.

As if it had been dipped in water, her white silk blouse clung to surprisingly ample breasts that thrust their nipples against the tight material like large buttons. And her small waist was emphasized by a tight black belt. A great body completely hidden the first time under a baggy suit. It was like meeting a different person. Even her attitude had changed. He suspected the absence of the abrasive Gary Mardoff had an affect on her. No longer shy and reticent, she showed near aggressiveness and confidence. More like the archetype reporter popularized by American film and television.

The memory of his first impression of her in the restaurant came back, stark and confusing: hair swept up severely, drab shapeless suit, thick glasses. She bad been completely eclipsed by Gary Mardoff, who had dominated everything with his crude, drunken insults. The whole encounter had left her with little to do besides trying to mediate the terrible argument. He believed her when she said she didn't like Gary Mardoff. No one could. Now, a new appearance and a new attitude. A chameleon that changed dramatically at a whim; or was it a whim? No, it was all calculated and he knew it. She was up to something. He stared into her eyes which locked with his.

"Where are your glasses?" he asked. "They looked like you sawed them off the ends of Coke bottles."

"You've heard of soft contacts?" She smiled warmly and stared at him over her glass.

What was she up to? He hunched forward, "What do you want?"

"A story, of course. You're hot copy," she said simply. "And may I call you Brent?"

"Okay, Brent."

"And I'm Helen."

"No recorders."

She waved at the embassy case. "I won't even open it."

"What kind of story do you want, Helen? Most of my duties are classified and the media knows it."

"A personal interview."

"It's been done."

"Not for a couple years. You mentioned Arlene Spencer."

"And I told you I chopped her head off. Still interested?"

"The beheading isn't mandatory, is it?"

He chuckled for the first time. "No. Just a probability."

She threw her head back and laughed, a delightfully youthful sound. Then she held up her empty glass. "Please."

He walked to the kitchen and returned with the Chivas Regal, ice, water and soda on a tray and placed it on the table. Bending over the table, he refilled both glasses. She patted the sofa next to her. "Sit here, Brent."

He hesitated. She wanted a story. He didn't trust her. She was a reporter and the story was everything. They were all cunning and duplicitous. She'd probably come on to him just to try to get him to talk.

"Please, Brent," she persisted, "sit here." And then a wily smile, "I won't compromise you."

He looked at the body, the warm smile, the pleading eyes, and sat beside her.

She looked up at him, and for the first time he noticed her eyes were a deep blue-gray. She held him with them. "You were at sea for almost a month since I saw you last."

"Shakedown."

"The fishing boat?"

"Yeah, a fishing boat."

"There are rumors that it's really a small warship."

"We were at war with tuna. That's all. It's just a fishing boat."

"Then, why would one of *Yonaga*'s line officers shakedown a fishing boat?"

"And why do you ask such questions?"

"Because you're news and some strange violent things have been happening in the East China Sea."

"Oh, is that right?"

"Yes, that's right."

"Rumors. War is full of rumors."

"Maybe. But I think there's something to these."

"And maybe I just like to fish."

"Did you catch anything?"

"I hooked a big one."

"Did you land it?"

He was beginning to enjoy the game. Took a deep drink before he answered, "It got away."

"Too bad. The big ones always seem to get away."

"Yes, they do." He emptied his glass and began to feel very relaxed as a warm glow spread to every part of his body. He recharged both glasses.

"I would like to know more about your fishing expedition."

"Maybe, later."

"How much later?"

"We'll see."

She leaned close enough so that he felt a hard breast press against him and her breath on his cheek. "You were very violent in that fight with that thug. You wanted to kill him."

"Yes."

"The girl saved him."

"Yes. And some of the others helped."

She glanced at a small pad. "She was Sally Neverland of the 'Church of the Voice of God in Jesus,' located in Hollywood."

"That's what she told me."

He felt her hand on his biceps. "You can be a very brutal man."

"I lost my temper."

He looked at her. Her face was only inches away. It was flushed and excitement shone in her eyes. The sight of violence seemed to excite women, sexually arouse them. He had heard that during the London blitz many women become insatiable, and it was said that during the old Roman gladiator duels, the women were the most bloodthirsty. "Was your thumb down," he asked.

He expected her to be offended. Instead, she responded very quickly with a blunt, "Yes. He was a gangster." She leaned closer and would have brushed him with her lips if he had not turned away. "What's wrong, Brent?"

He felt tipsy. "I'm not that kind of boy. I'm saving it for my wedding night."

She laughed uproariously. "Sorry." She finished her drink and said, "Guess it's time for me to leave. But first . . ." She pulled his head down and kissed him full on the lips.

Brent felt the long dormant fuel ignite. It had been a long time. Their tongues met, twisted and searched each other. But he pulled away. He was convinced she would take him to bed for her sacred "scoop," her "hot copy." As desirable as she was, something ineffable brought it all to a stop. Maybe the whole thing was too cheap, too sordid even for a horny sailor. Or, somehow, Sally Neverland was involved. Rising, he said, "That's not necessary. There's no story, so you'd be wasting your time."

"You think I'd go to bed with you for a story?"

He felt the heat of anger displace the warmth of desire. "What in hell were you trying to do."

"Kiss you, that's all. I enjoy kissing handsome men."

He rubbed his jaw. "I'm sore, tired and dirty and you don't even know me."

"That's supposed to be my line."

"I know."

"You want me to leave?"

Brent almost bit his tongue when he said candidly, "Not really, but it would be a good idea."

She rose. "See you again."

He spoke honestly, "Why not?"

"I still want a story."

"We'll see."

She stepped close. Smiling, she ran a manicured nail gently over his cheek. "You're a strange, attractive man. Do you know that?"

"Thanks, Helen. And you do all right yourself."

"I'm staying at the *Shibu* in Kamakure. It's only a few miles from here."

"It's a *ryokan.*"

"Right, Brent, a *ryokan.* A small place run in the Japanese tradition. The rooms are in authentic Japanese style and it has a great cuisine. I love it."

She scribbled on a sheet and ripped it from the pad. "Here're my address and phone number." Her eyes searched his as if she were looking for a hidden signal.

"Yes." He rubbed his sore jaw gently. "Maybe in a couple nights? Dinner?"

"I'd like that, but not at the *Ichi-riki.*"

"Why not?"

"I don't like it. That waitress—ah, ah . . ."

"You mean Fumi?"

"Yes, Fumi. She has obscene designs on your body."

Brent chuckled. "Oh, I didn't know."

"I told you the *Shibu* has a marvelous kitchen."

"So does the *Kujaku.*"

"Call me, Brent?"

"Yes."

"Promise?"

"I promise."

She took him by the hand and led him to the door. She kissed him again, this time gently, not the deep, wet, hot kiss of before. For a brief moment she pressed her body to his as if she were trying to mold herself to him, prolong the moment. "You're a sexy bastard," she whispered into his ear.

"You do all right yourself."

Then, smiling, and holding his eyes she turned toward the door. He had a very hard time letting her slip from his grasp.

After the door closed, Brent shook his head and said, "Brent Ross, you're the biggest goddamned fool on earth. Time for a shower—a cold shower."

Peeling off his shirt, he walked to the bathroom.

Twelve

The Arabian Sea

Trimmed and level a hundred feet beneath the surface, SSN *San Jose* crept along at six knots. Standing on the periscope pedestal, Commander Richard Seitz felt no sensation of movement. In fact, the carpeted deck of the pedestal felt as solid as a slab of concrete. And the control room was very quiet despite the dozen men manning the rows of consoles, instruments and controls crowding the compartment. "Quiet" was the key word in this service—the "silent service." Nobody raised his voice, slammed a hatch, or even dropped a toilet seat.

Standing next to Seitz was the young OOD, Lieutenant j.g. August Lee. Behind Seitz were the nuclear submarine's two periscopes: the Type 2 attack scope to port and the Type 18 all-purpose scope to starboard. To Seitz's left was the submarine's Ship Control Station, Navstar GPS Receiver, and the ship's inertial navigational system (SINS). Fire control systems, Plotting Tools Racks were to his right, in line with the BSY-1 weapons consoles and control panel commanding the ship's sensors and weapons systems. However, to Commander Seitz's chagrin, some of the stations were unmanned.

The Navstar GPS Receiver was secured because the twenty-four satellites driving the navigational system had been destroyed by the Chinese SDI system. The same was true with most of the BSY-1 consoles and Weapons Control Panel which operated the twelve Tomahawk missiles, which were back in a warehouse in New London. They, too, had been rendered useless by the Chinese lasers. No jets. No rockets. Attack sub *San Jose* had had most of her teeth pulled by the Chinese who had screwed up the world's finest weapons systems. *San Jose's* only punch was in her Mark 48 torpedoes. That was it. All of it. Crappy new world.

Seitz was very bored. His submarine had been prowling off the Gulf of Aden for over four months. The Arab battle group of three carriers, three cruisers, and escorts had done nothing but conduct a few drills in the gulf and then return to base. Never had the Arab fleet appeared on his sensors as a full battle group. Only a few vessels at a time would sortie, conduct drills and then return to base. But that should change soon. Everyone knew that "Iron Admiral" Hiroshi Fujita was preparing to invade the Mariana Islands. Sooner or later, Kadafi would be forced to commit his fleet, or see his Pacific stronghold destroyed.

"Fire only if fired upon," his orders read. "Conduct reconnaissance and report any activity by any combat ships." Actually, the orders should have read "any Arab ships." Everyone knew the Arab fleet was the first priority.

Movements of Arab naval units had been carefully tracked by the nuclear powered ballistic and attack submarines of the U.S. Navy. *San Jose* was only one of at least thirty that were available for sea duty at any given time. Actually, the US was tracking *all* combat vessels; Japanese, British, Russian, Italian, French, even Indian and Indonesian. The one most versatile and durable power left the US was her reduced fleet of nuclear powered submarines. They were not rusting.

The Arab oil embargo had hurt the entire free world. It took all of America's Alaskan production just to keep Japan afloat. And the arrogance of the Arabs was unbounded. Most disturbing, one SSN, the *Shreveport*, had vanished under mysterious circumstances on this very station. "Overdue and presumed lost," had been the ancient epitaph of the submariner.

It certainly could have been an accident. No one was allowed to forget the losses of *Scorpion* and *Thresher*. *Scorpion* had been lost off the Azores after a mysterious internal explosion. *Thresher* never made it to back to the fleet after refit, sunk with all hands during rectification trials off Nantucket. It was fairly well established brazed piping joints in the engineering spaces had weakened during shock trials and *Thresher* was crushed by 1,400 fathoms of water. Seitz felt a cold shudder. It could happen to anyone, any boat, any time, at any place.

His mind dwelled on the special horror that haunted all men who served under the sea—death in a sinking submarine. Hull shrieking, cracking, collapsing. Water flooding in and compressing air spaces. Pressure and temperature soaring as in a pressure cooker, super-heating the air, rupturing your lungs and searing them, hemorrhaging and drowning you in your own blood before the sea could do it.

The deck trembled under his feet. The barely perceptible movement tore his mind from the reoccurring nightmare and he concentrated on his boat. It wasn't quite as stable as it should be. August Lee turned, threw a glance at the control station.

Usually, a submerged SSN gave one of the smoothest, stablest rides of anything afloat, or on land for that matter. Actually, *San Jose* was faster and smoother submerged than when on the surface. It was like being in the basement of a building. But, suddenly, the boat lurched and Seitz felt it yaw and drop a few feet. August Lee turned to the captain. "We've lost our trim, Sir."

Before Seitz could respond, the diving officer, Lieutenant Randall Turner, seated behind the two enlisted men at the ship control station shouted. "Mind your depth. What-in-hell are you guys doing, running a damned roller coaster?"

The two men operating the planes and the helm cranked their aircraft-style control wheels and studied the big circular dials of their instruments giving dive/bank angle, heading, and depth to keel. Turner was standing and staring at the instruments. "Must be a thermocline, Sir," planesman Neil Marz said. The helmsman, Quartermaster Roy Whitlow, nodded his agreement. Seitz felt one or both had become bored and careless. These were the submariner's greatest enemies, could lead to accidents, and a hundred feet beneath the surface the sea was very unforgiving.

The men needed a jolt and Turner provided it. "I don't care if we ran over a fat broad's ass. Hold her steady."

The boat leveled and Marz shouted out, "Depth 100 and holding, Mister Turner."

Turner said to Marz, "Speed six."

The planesman adjusted a small knob. "Speed six, Sir."

"Very well."

Seitz remained silent. Turner had provided the "jolt." He had seen these little dramas acted out a thousand times. Turner was handling it well. He was a little short on patience, but everyone was.

Seitz liked Randall Turner. Not only was Turner a fine diving officer and OOD, the big black man was his XO and best friend as well. Because he was so big and powerful, it was assumed by most people that the XO had attended the University of Pennsylvania on an athletic scholarship. Football or basketball like most of the poor blacks. Actually, a brilliant mathematician, Turner had graduated second in his class on an academic scholarship. When anyone asked about his sports, he answered, "Books and more books and Whitney Houston." He loved the singer and had an enormous collection of her

CDs and cassettes in a special section in his library. He spent many happy hours in his cabin while the singer soothed him through his earphones.

Seitz liked Turner for his brilliant mind, leadership qualities, and his fair-minded attitude toward race. He measured all men, regardless of color, on performance only. This showed in his impatience with the appellation, "African-American."

There were ten more blacks in the crew of eleven officers and 103 enlisted men. Once Seitz had heard one of the blacks use the term within earshot of the XO. The black skin took on a red hue and Turner bellowed, "You aren't a hyphenated anything: No Swedish-Americans, no Mexican-Americans, no Afro-Americans. You're Americans! Got it? Americans! This is an American sub, with American torpedoes, making this screwed-up world safe for American citizens. Do you understand, or do I have to stamp 'American' across your ass?"

"Loud and clear, Sir!" the terrified man had answered.

Seitz had chuckled. Turner returned to his cabin and to Whitney Houston.

With the deck level and solid again, Seitz's mind followed its inevitable course back to Hazel. His poor wife. She intruded at the damnedest times. Asleep or awake, she was always there. Alone at home for all these months. She had a great body and unbounded passion. It was torture to even think of her. And here, in the control room when his mind should be on business, he was thinking horny thoughts about his wife. But it was so great when he returned. They would go at each other like two starving people who had a feast set before them. But how long could she take this? She was an orgasm machine and she needed a man. Would she take a lover? The thought sickened him.

He banished the disturbing thoughts forcefully by bringing his mind back to his boat—the second great love in his life. *San Jose* was his first command. He had been the executive officer on board the "Boomer," SSBN *Ohio,* for two years. And now, finally, he had his own boat. He remembered the first time he saw *San Jose.* It was something like a new date; like seeing Hazel for the first time. Seitz chuckled. It hadn't been that good. But still impressive.

When he first glimpsed the SSN at the dock at Groton, he had been impressed by the straight and level sweep of the 360-foot hull. Actually, the hull was a series of rings, or barrel sections, welded together with hemispheric end caps welded onto the ends. In fact, for most of her length, *San Jose* was a perfect 33-foot diameter tube of three-inch high-tensile steel. One of the first things he had learned in class was that a long, thin tube can move through the water faster than any other configuration. On his first sea trial, *San Jose's* Westinghouse S6G high output reactor core drove her at an incredible 42 knots. He remembered how thrilled he had been. He could outrun destroyers.

Smiling to himself, he recalled the first time he stepped on the deck. He almost bounced. It was like walking on a thick rubberized carpet. "It's the new anechoic-decoupling," old Captain Barry Knowles, who was conducting the tour for Seitz, Turner, Lee and two other officers had said. "It absorbs active sonar signals and reduces the noise emitted by the boat's machinery." He waved a hand. "And note the detail work that minimizes the flow noise from the hull. Even the capstans are mounted on rotating plates and on the centerline." He pointed a finger and swept the length of the hull. "Cleanest damned shape this side of Betty Grable."

"Betty who?" Turner had dared.

"Why Grable, of course," the old captain had answered.

Seitz held his breath and had nudged Turner but the big man pressed on, "What about Whitney Houston?"

"Who's she?" To Seitz's relief, the captain seemed to be enjoying the exchange.

"An actress, a singer."

The old man indicated the boat, "Is she as well assembled?" The officers chuckled.

Turner had smiled broadly, "Like Madonna."

"She'll do," Knowles said grinning.

Everyone gave the captain an enthusiastic laugh, as if his pedestrian retort had been uproariously clever.

The voice of Sonarman Jim "Big Tooth" Smiley, coming through the small speaker above the captain's head, caught Seitz's attention. "Control room."

Seitz pulled a small microphone down from the overhead PA panel and threw a switch, "Control room, aye."

"Got something, Captain. Standing out of the gulf." Then he used the submariner's convention for the naming of a sonar contact, "It's a 'Sierra', Sir."

"Very well." Seitz turned to August Lee, "I'm going forward. Mind the store."

"Aye, aye, Sir. Steaming as before."

"Correct." The captain walked forward to the sonar room. Here four sonar consoles gave ears to *San Jose's* underwater world. All systems were in passive modes. It would be stupid to go active, to advertise *San Jose's* position by ripping the water with the 80,000-watt, low frequency pulses of the BQS-14 sonar in the bow. The fearful bellows of this brute could goose a killer whale right out of the water.

Seitz stopped behind Smiley and stared at the console. Analyzing data from the boat's new TB-23 passive 960-foot "thin line" towed array, the screen was showing its usual waterfall display like a greenish TV screen full of snow. At the moment it was showing nothing but the usual background noise. "Damn, it's gone, Captain," Smiley groaned.

"You're sure you had something."

"Yes, Sir. Might be behind Tamrida Island or temperature grading has caused a diurnal thermocline."

Seitz knew the young sonarman was making an accurate guess. The sound conductivity of the waters where the Gulf of Oman met the Arabian Sea was terrible. Stratified by layers of varying temperatures, the sea settled into isothermal sheets like a layered cake. Semipermeable barriers were formed when discrete layers of warm surface water from the gulf met colder water welling up from the depths of the Arabian Sea. An invisible block, this interface functioned as a reflecting shield, bouncing off acoustic signals. It could protect a sub or lead to its destruction. At this moment, Commander Richard Seitz was very frustrated. Even though he possessed the most sophisticated acoustical instruments on earth, *San Jose* was blinded by an accident of nature. "Damn," the captain muttered. "A 960-foot line of hydrophones should pick up a sardine's fart. But we aren't getting a damned thing."

"There it is, Sir." Smiley gestured at a thin white vertical line at the far left of his display. He studied the top of the display, smiled, showing the glistening rows of perfect white teeth that gave him the sobriquet "Big Tooth." "Bearing 250, range—ah, not close," he said. It was the closest thing to a range estimate Smiley could come up with. "Not close" meant anything over ten miles.

"Probably another freighter or tanker."

Smiley gestured at the vertical line. "Maybe, Sir. But that's a fast screw count—maybe a can. One of those Arab *Gearings*."

"One?"

"Not sure, Sir." He pulled an earphone over one ear, threw a switch and hunched forward.

"Well, Smiley, anything?"

Again the big flash of white. He always grinned when he had a solid contact. "High speed screws. Definitely surface vessels. Two cans at least, Sir."

"Very well. Call them 'Sierra 1' and 'Sierra 2'." Seitz leaned over the sonarman, "Are they towing arrays?"

Smiley pressed—palm to his earphone. "No, Sir. Can't pick up those sounds. Anyway, Captain, they're moving way too fast."

Seitz spoke to the other technicians, "Let's bring it all on line, the conformal array, the TB-16D and the WLR-9 receiver."

The man at the TB-16D console, Sonarman Jim Eberhard, asked, "All 2,600-feet, Sir?"

"Full length and all hydrophones," Seitz answered. "And put all data on 'data bus' and let's see if our computers can chew some information out of this. The whole Arab fleet could be standing out."

"Aye, aye, Sir," the sonarmen chorused. Smiley threw a switch, and Seitz felt new confidence as the incoming data was fed into the boat's racks of computers.

"Sir," Smiley said, one hand to his earphone, the other to a small wheel. "I think I know this guy."

"Sierra 1?"

"Yes, Sir. This is the one with the chip out of his port screw. Sounds like the springs of a wedding bed wrapped around the drive shaft, all humpin' and pumpin'."

"Put it on the speaker."

Smiley threw a switch and a bulkhead-mounted high-fidelity speaker came to life with hisses, crackles, and pops. But unmistakably, through the background noise, Seitz could hear the whining chirp of propeller cavitations. The thin screech of the damaged blade came through clearly over the low churning rumble and hissing of the destroyer's engines.

"*Gearing* Class, their usual lead DD, Sir," Smiley said. The smile looked like the keyboard of a Steinway.

Seitz slapped the young man on the back. "Good work, Smiley, I'll be in the control room. Keep me informed."

"Aye, aye, Sir."

A powerful ringing sound, like a sledgehammer striking a muted Big Ben pounded out of the speaker, stopping Seitz in his tracks. Then many more at precise intervals, rising and falling in frequency and strength. Sonar search. Unmistakable.

"Pinging, Sir," Smiley said. More ringing sounds. "Both of 'em. And those are big 'mothers', Captain."

"But they're not searching our sector?"

"Oh, no Sir. Standard beam to beam."

"Very well."

Seitz returned to his position next to Lee. He knew what was important now was patience and concentration. Now that the first sound lines had been established, all of the boat's passive sonar were concentrating on the contact. There was no automatic classification mode in *San Jose's* computers. It was up to the sonar technicians. But the sonar crew was familiar with the Arab ships, and they should have little trouble identifying the contacts. Jim Smiley had already proved that.

The contact had already been identified as two destroyers. Each of the different sonars in the suite had its optimum frequency band. If other, heavier ships were under way, the frequencies might fall within very narrow bands, and one sensor might be better at acquiring data on a particular signal than any of the others. In any event, the BSY-1 system could track all of them. Seitz sighed. He knew at this moment the four boys on the sonar watch team, not one of whom was over 24-years of age, were the eyes and ears of the boat. The safety of the boat and every man on board depended on just how efficient these young operators in the sonar room were.

Seitz heard the voice of Technician Carl Anselmo, who was manning the conformal console, the low-frequency passive sonar array mounted around the bow. "Captain, request we alter course ten degrees to port? It would give me a better window, Sir."

Seitz glanced behind him at the navigator, Lieutenant j.g. Joel Levinthal, who was hunching over one of the boat's two automatic plotting boards. "Depth under keel?"

"One-thousand-four-hundred fathoms, Sir."

"I want to come left to 330, speed six."

Levinthal moved his drafting machine, drew a line and nodded affirmatively. His response was precisely what Seitz expected.

"Good, Sir, for a couple of days running at this speed."

Seitz nodded at August Lee, who was still the OOD. Lee barked out, "Helm, left fifteen degrees rudder, come to new course 330."

"Left fifteen degrees rudder, aye." The helmsman turned the wheel. "Sir, my rudder is left fifteen degrees, coming to new course 330."

"Very well."

Under Turner's watchful eye, the planesman and helmsman worked their controls, and the boat settled slowly onto its new course. "Steady on 330, speed six, depth one hundred," Turner reported.

"Very well."

Smiley's voice: "We've got a lot of cavitations, Captain. Many DDs, three carriers and those three cruisers. The whole tamale this time, Captain. They're pinging like crazy."

Seitz came erect with new alertness. They had practiced tracking the Arab ships before in small groups, but never had the battle group sortied in full force. Something was up. He must track, observe and report. "You're sure?"

"Tracked 'em before, and our threat library confirms."

Seitz's reaction was automatic. *San Jose* must be put into a combat mode. "Put lead ship on Target Motion Analysis."

"TMA on, Sir."

"The point can? Sierra 1?"

"Right, Captain. Old 'chipped screw'."

He must assume there was a threat, and that it would come first from the lead destroyer. With TMA tracking, information was now being passed automatically between the sonar room and the fire control console. With the target already identified, the TMA would provide the fire control team with a usable fire control solution, target course, and speed and range.

Pulling the microphone down, Seitz said, "All hands Attack team man your stations. Battle lamps on."

Immediately the Control Room was flooded with red light and men changed stations, quickly but quietly. August Lee moved to the port side, where the manual plot team was huddled around its plotting boards and specially programmed Hewlett Packard desktop computer. Here, he would work on a separate TMA range analysis. With its special program library, the computer was interfaced with automatic systems, giving more intensive calculations and displaying instant ranges to the target or targets.

System after system backing up each other, checking and cross checking. If the threat was real, and they tracked carefully, a kill was almost certain. But Seitz did not expect this. Probably, just another dry run. Maybe the Arabs were standing out to practice with their air groups. In any event, the Arabs were providing a good exercise for the crew.

Randall Turner took his position next to Seitz as JOD while a young ensign named Rick Verlander sat in the diving officer's chair.

Smiley's voice, "Captain, we have three cans, Sierras 1, 2, and 3, closing on us."

"They haven't acquired us?"

"Right, Captain. They haven't."

"Very well."

Seitz turned to August Lee, who stood behind the attack team and their row of consoles. "Range and bearing of Sierra 1?"

"Range 17,000, bearing 280, Sir."

"Very well. Sierra 2 and 3?"

"Still astern of Sierra 1 by 2,000 yards, and almost same bearing," Lee said. "Can give you exact bearings, Sir."

"Not necessary."

"We have twenty more Sierras, Captain," Smiley's voice crackled through the speaker.

Seitz nodded. That figured. Twenty-two ships. *The whole tamale,* according to Smiley. "Continue to track them all."

"Aye, aye, Sir."

Seitz turned to Verlander, "Let's give ESM a sniff. Bring her up to periscope depth."

"Coming up to sixty-feet, Sir," the young ensign said. And then to Marz, "Up ten degrees, sixty feet and hold her."

Marz repeated the command and turned his wheel. Seitz felt the deck tilt and he stepped back behind the Type 18 periscope. He kept an eye on Verlander. The deck levelled and the ensign said, "Sixty feet and holding, Captain."

"Very well. Range to Sierra 1?"

"Ten thousand, Sir," August Lee responded.

"Up scope."

Quartermaster Whitlow released the search scope with a half-turn of the hydraulic ring control. The shaft slid upward from its well. Reading the calibrations on the shaft, Seitz shouted, "Stop scope!" while the lens was still below the surface. Bending almost double, Seitz unsnapped the handles and grabbed the scope in a full circle. A camera mounted above the scope flashed pictures of an empty sea on a monitor in front of Turner.

"Nothing, Captain."

"Good. Let's get an ESM reading. Up antenna."

Projecting above the periscope, an antenna array waved like a whip, monitoring radar and radio emissions. "Sir!" the technician at the ESM console shouted, staring at a warning display that had gone wild with flickering lights. "Many S-band radars. Pulse signatures of surface ships."

"Any aircraft?"

"No, Captain. Surface vessels."

"Very well. Down scope." Seitz was pleased. He was undetected by the ships, and apparently the Arabs were not searching with anti-submarine aircraft. He would remain at periscope depth and wait for the force to close to visual range. Then he would verify and report the sighting.

He turned to Lieutenant August Lee, who was hunched over the Hewlett Packard computer and staring at a display on his monitor. "Report, Lieutenant Lee."

"Sierra 1 course unchanged. Speed twenty-four. Sierras 2 and 3 have veered off to our port side. The whole force appears to be on a heading to port."

"But not Sierra 1?"

"Correct, Sir. Sierra 1 will pass very close to starboard."

"Range to Sierra 1."

"Six thousand yards, Sir."

"Let me know when he ranges five thousand yards." Seitz pulled the microphone down. "Sonar, report on Sierra 1."

"Still searching, but he doesn't have us."

"Very well." Seitz said a prayer of thanks to whomever invented the anechoic-decoupling that coated their hull. Without it, they would have been detected long ago. But the *Gearing* would pass very close. His sonar was powerful, and they were not immune. His back began to hurt.

August Lee's voice: "Five thousand yards, Sir."

"Very well. The rest of the force?"

"Five escorts in a column six thousand yards to port, six heavy ships in a column seven thousand yards to port, speed twenty knots . . ."

"Very well. Attack team concentrate on Sierra 1." He gripped the handles. "Up scope."

The lens broke the surface and he pressed his forehead

against the eyepiece. Immediately he swung the scope to starboard and caught the charging destroyer precisely where it should be. At its speed, the narrow hull cleaved the water like a knife, bow wave causing a white flurry of churning water and spray.

"A bone in her teeth," Seitz muttered to himself. With magnification fourteen, the periscope brought the ship very close; four gun houses, two stacks, torpedo tubes, a forest of AA guns, depth charges, clusters of crewmen smoking and lounging. A standard Arab *Gearing* with a slovenly Arab crew. He focused on the torpedoes. According to the Geneva Agreement, neither Japanese nor Arab torpedoes could contain guidance systems. But those depth charges contained a new Semtex-based explosive that gave them three times the power of TNT. Just one of them could snap *San Jose* like a twig. He felt a cold shudder.

"Down scope." He spoke to Turner. "Send the following, 'COMSUBPAC, Info COMYONAGA—Arab force of three cruisers, three carriers and sixteen DDs stood out Gulf of Aden at 1300 on a southeasterly heading. Speed twenty. Position' . . ." He turned to Joel Levinthal, who was bending over his chart table, dividers in hand. "Navigator, position?"

Anticipating his captain's order, Levinthal said, "Latitude ten degrees, thirty-eight minutes north, longitude fifty-eight degrees, fifty-five minutes east."

Seitz turned to Turner, "Log that into the message."

"Aye, aye, Sir." Turner scribbled on his pad and repeated the message back. He looked up, "Packet switching or BRT-1, Sir?"

Seitz reflected for a moment. He preferred packet switching because it was hard to detect. Messages were broken down into thousands of fragments, each with a coded address. His encoding computer automatically routed the "packets" over any free route in the communications network. On arrival, the addressees' computers reassembled the message. A powerful, almost foolproof method of transmission—but they must raise a HF antenna from their fin to make the transmission. For now, packet switching was out.

BRT-1 was nothing more than a buoy containing a cassette recorder and radio transmitter. He could release it at any time with a preset delay of up to an hour. At twenty knots, he could be anywhere in an area of 1,664 square miles. If the Arabs homed in on the transmission, they would find nothing but a buoy—if they were lucky. Then he could back up with packet switching, if necessary. The decision was easy to make.

"BRT-1, XO," Seitz said. The *Gearing* was so close, the sounds of his screws could be heard like a faint "chunking" sound. Why was he so close? An accident? Had they been detected? Seitz felt an amalgam of anger, fear, and frustration. He said to Turner, "But let's wait until this snooping bastard takes off—delay transmission for one hour."

"Aye, aye, Sir." Turner turned to the communications officer, "BRT-1 on my mark. One hour delay."

The communications officer muttered a command to a cryptologic technician. Quickly, a keyboard was fingered and characters ran across a tube.

Smiley's voice: "Captain, Sierra 1's passed us, Sir."

Seitz felt relief. "Very well. The other Sierras?"

"Holding course. Fading off our port quarter fast. Range to last Sierra, 17,000 yards."

"Very well." Seitz was about to turn to Turner to give an order to prepare to release the BRT-1, when Smiley's voice came back. "Captain, Sierra 1's turning, coming up on our starboard quarter at a high speed. Range 4,500, bearing 135 relative."

"Very well."

Was the Arab making a run? He had to assume he was. He shouted into the microphone. "All ahead emergency, collision stations." And then to Verlander, "Take her down! Fast!" *San Jose's* element was the depths. Only there could she find safety.

"Down twenty degrees," Verlander said.

"All ahead emergency, Captain," Turner said. The high whining sound of their two straining steam turbines filled the boat.

The hull began to vibrate with muffled ringing sounds: Pings, bouncing off the hull. The men looked at each other anxiously. Why? What was the Arab up to? *Shreveport* came back. She *did* disappear in these waters. Seitz felt a cold clutch of fear ripple up his spine. He gulped air. Shook it off.

Smiley's voice: "His sonar has us, Sir. He's ranging us."

"Passing 150 feet," Verlander said.

Seitz felt pressure begin to build against his eardrums. He shouted at August Lee the first of a mandatory series of commands to the torpedo room. "Make tubes one and two ready in all respects!"

August Lee repeated the command and added, "Tracking Sierra 1, fish in 'snap shot' mode for fast moving target, Sir."

"Very well. Let go four noisemakers." Seitz's tactics were simple. If the Arab was attacking, noisemakers, which were nothing but small gas canisters boiling out streams of noisy bubbles, could confuse the sonar. And if the Arab cheated and used homing torpedoes, the canisters mixed in with the turbulence of the submarine's wake—could distract the torpedoes homing devices.

Seitz to Lee: "Are the dots stacked?"

"Not yet, Captain."

Seitz glanced at the fire control computer, where the screen shoved the target's bearing versus time as a series of dots. The fire control technician was furiously pounding his keys as the computers fed in new data. The destroyer was moving so fast, its bearing was changing from second to second and he was having a hard time estimating the target's range and course. Only when the dots were arrayed in a straight column of dots stacked on the display would they have a firing solution. And that would be a low percentage snap shot. Seitz cursed to himself. Every element seemed to be conspiring against him.

Now the chugging of the destroyer was almost overhead. "Depth?"

"Passing 350 feet, Sir."

Smiley's voice froze everyone: "He's dropping depth charges—a whole pattern."

Seitz switched to "All Stations."

"Dog down all watertight doors! Stand by for depth charge attack!" Immediately, he heard hatches slam as watertight doors were closed and dogged down.

The chugging passed and began to fade. A blast a hundred yards astern shook the boat. Then another and another creeping closer.

"I have a solution, Sir," the fire control technician shouted.

"Match bearings and shoot!" Seitz shouted. August Lee pressed two buttons. There were twin jolts as the pair of 3,400-pound, Mark 48 torpedoes burst from their tubes.

"Torpedoes fired, running free and clear."

"Very well."

"Passing 450."

Seitz was beginning to feel a little more secure when the first thunderbolt struck. The initial shock knocked the submarine ten degrees to port and nearly deafened every man. Then three more battering rams knocked her nose down at over forty degrees and sent men tumbling from their chairs. Turner slid head-first across the deck until he smashed his skull against a shelf on the forward bulkhead with a cracking sound Seitz could hear. Seitz actually hung from the overhead PA unit, feet dangling above the canted deck.

There were screams of fear, the lights blinked. Then another flurry of explosions further ahead. But one, exploding ahead and below the boat, actually straightened her until Seitz could grab the periscope and balance on the deck again. They had been caught by the middle charges of the pattern, perhaps four or five depth charges. They were sinking fast—too fast.

"Damage report!"

The voice of Chief Torpedoman Weldon Shallenberger froze everyone. "This is the torpedo room, flooding in the forward crew's quarters. Missile room flooding!"

"Passing 550 feet, Captain."

"Blow negative, transfer water aft, all astern flank, full up on the planes." Then, into the microphone, "Chief Shallenberger, are you shipping water in the torpedo room?"

"Forward bulkhead secure, but the door's bent, and we have a ruptured gasket. We're shoring, Captain, but taking water."

"Increase your air pressure."

"We have, Sir. Our eardrums are killing us."

Verlander's voice: "Passing six hundred. I can't hold her."

Seitz: "Engine room. Give me more power."

"We're in overload now, Sir."

"I don't give a damn."

"We'll lose Number One turbine."

"More power, or we lose the boat."

The whine of turbines became a shriek. The boat vibrated. Shallenberger reported flooding stopped, but his men were suffering from the air pressure. There was nothing Seitz could do about that. His gut wrenched when he thought of his men in the flooded compartments. They must all be dead.

"Passing seven hundred feet," Verlander said.

"We're slowing."

"Yes, Captain, we're slowing."

"How much air pressure left?"

"Nine hundred pounds."

August Lee: "Presets on both fish holding, Captain. Wires running free and clear. Target acquisition complete."

With the destroyer moving at thirty-two knots, and the torpedoes at fifty-four knots and trailing a control wire ten miles long, the Arab was bound to lose the race. He did with two violent explosions.

"Right up his ass!" Lee shouted. Men cheered.

"But he got us," someone said.

"Not quite," Seitz said.

"Holding at 970 feet. We're over a hundred feet beyond our designed depth, Captain," Verlander warned.

"True. But we have our trim back and we're coming up." He spoke into the microphone, "All ahead two-thirds." Immediately, the whining dropped, but there were vibrations. Something was wrong with the main shaft or a bearing was burned out. He turned to Verlander. "Secure the blow, secure the pumping. We've got to get the pressure off the hull. Bring her up to sixty feet."

Everyone looked at him in shock. The entire crew expected an emergency surface. "Sixty feet, Sir?" there was incredulity in Verlander's voice.

"Yes, goddamn it, I said sixty feet."

"Aye, aye, Sir, sixty feet." Muttering, the men turned back to their consoles and controls. There was a new odor in the compartment. Not just sweating bodies, but the smell of fear seeping through the men's pores.

Seitz was grappling with his own fear, and every instinct told him to surface. But his training told him to make a thorough search first. Another destroyer could be lurking with everything shut down. Or, there could be aircraft. It was a matter of weighing chances and hazards against each other. He feared remaining submerged with a damaged pressure hull as much as anyone. It could all let go. But it did hold together at 970 feet. There should be plenty of reserve buoyancy at sixty feet he told himself.

Chief Shallenberger's good news helped sustain his decision and assuage the fear that gripped the men: "Torpedo room almost free of flooding, forward door holding, Captain," Shallenberger reported.

Seitz could almost hear the collective sigh of relief. "Very well. Reduce air pressure but watch that door."

"Aye, aye, Sir."

"Sixty feet, Sir."

Smiley's voice: "Breaking up sounds, Captain."

Seitz threw a switch and the speaker crunched out the sounds of the dying destroyer. There were bangs and thuds of collapsing bulkheads, the screech of tortured metal ripping and faint echoes of other far more horrifying sounds; the faint screams of trapped men dying in flooding compartments. The destroyer must be nearby. He turned the speaker off and switched to "All Stations." "Damage report!"

San Jose was badly damaged. The torpedo room was secure, but the compartments forward of it were flooded. Six men in the flooded compartments must be dead. Eight men had been injured, one with a broken arm. Number One turbine had burned out a bearing and the thrust block was out of line. The engineering officer recommended a speed of not more than five knots and that they surface. Seitz immediately reduced speed. Then he noticed Turner. He was very still. A hospital corpsman was leaning over him. The young man turned to Seitz. His face was very white and his voice thick. "He's dead, Sir. Fractured skull. Some bone fragments must have been driven into his brain."

"Oh, no. No!" Seitz pounded the periscope and then quickly became the composed captain again. "Sonar. Report."

Smiley's voice: "The DD has sunk, Sir. The battle group is not close—maybe thirty miles to the southeast. They must have read all the explosions as depth charges. Anyway, not one ship has altered course."

"Very well."

A quick ESM reading found all sectors clear. Then a look with the periscope found nothing but wreckage to the northwest, with a few survivors floating on rafts and wreckage. It was time to surface, send their report, make repairs, and head back to Guam.

He cursed the pull-back by American forces. Diego Garcia had been abandoned, and they would be forced to steam all the way to Guam for repairs. All ports in India, Burma, Malaysia and all of Southeast Asia were denied him. Fear of the Arab jihad and the threat of an oil embargo had whipped governments into declaring their ports "nuclear free." This effectively closed them to the all-nuclear American submarine fleet, while allowing the Arab diesel-electric boats free access. Lousy world.

Even more galling, some had closed their ports with undisguised hostility. Indonesia openly collaborated with the Arabs and the Philippines' new government had refused any nuclear-powered vessel access. There was a long, perilous journey ahead; across the Indian Ocean, the Malacca Straits, north into the South China Sea and then to Guam. But they had to steam all the way to Pearl Harbor before the boat could have a major overhaul.

He turned to Verlander. "Surface, Mister Verlander." The men cheered.

The diving officer shouted, "Surface! Surface! Surface!" sounded the horn three times, and *San Jose* rose slowly. Gripping the first rung of the bridge ladder, Seitz glanced at Randall Turner's blanket-covered body. His best friend gone. Killed by the great weight of his muscular body that had rammed his skull into a projecting steel shelf. A fluke, but he was still dead. No more big laugh, no more long conversations in his cabin, and one less Whitney Houston fan. And Whitney Houston would never know. It was so unfair. He felt the boat rock.

Verlander's voice: "Surfaced, Sir."

Seitz opened the hatch and climbed up onto the bridge and filled his lungs with fresh sea air. Quartermaster Whitlow handed him his binoculars. Staring at the misty horizon to the southeast, Seitz felt a great rage well up. The dead destroyer wasn't enough. Waving a fist, he screamed at the invisible enemy, "We're no *Shreveport*, you murdering bastards. I'm not finished with you. I swear you'll pay—you'll pay for Randall Turner and the rest of my men."

Quartermaster Whitlow stared at his captain silently. Finally the young man said, "Survivors, Sir." He stabbed a finger at the drifting wreckage where men were visible floating on bits of wreckage and filling a half-dozen life rafts. "Aren't we going to pick them up, Sir."

Seitz brought his binoculars up and focused on the wreckage. "Fuck the survivors!" he spat.

Thirteen

Flesh and the Devil

Commander Brent Ross found the first few days at the *Kujaku* Hotel pleasant enough. His injuries healed quickly, and he was able to enjoy himself playing poker with the other officers. As usual, the Japanese were the most clever and deceptive players. "Smart bastards, it's part of their bloody nature," he heard the Englishman, Commander William Sackville, growl once after losing a huge pot to a stony faced Japanese pilot.

Brent spent time at billiards, but enjoyed himself most in the well-equipped gym. Not as large as *Yonaga*'s, *Kujaku*'s gym could still give him all the work he could handle. There were Lifecycles, Stairmasters, Nautilus machines, free weights, and saunas where the exhausted man could soothe his aching muscles in 103-degree water. Two masseurs massaged and pounded out the aches the saunas couldn't reach. After the weeks of confinement on the subchaser, it was like opening the dam gates on an immense store of pent-up nervous energy. And the feeling of conditioning, of return to maximum strength and endurance did wonders for his morale. The papers did not.

Reports of his fight with the *Rengo Sekigun* thug were splattered across Japanese dailies. Some were candid, noncommittal, and tried to report the event without bias. But not all. With some, yellow journalism blazed as vulgar as the worst American tabloids, complete with photos. As he had expected, galling headlines appeared; "Yankee Samurai Beats Homeless Man Senseless," "Yankee Samurai Brutally Disfigures Starving Man," "Yankee Samurai Attacks Homeless Man with Bottle" were only a few of the most outrageous. And the pictures—pictures of him straddling "Flat Nose," bottle raised. It was so biased, unfair. He steeled himself for the deliberate lies and did his best to ignore them. After all, it had happened many times before. And he knew the "righteous" outrage would fade. But he *did* wonder if Gary Mardoff and Helen Whitaker had contributed to these stories and the pictures.

He phoned the *Shibu* but Helen Whitaker did not answer. Instead, the manager said he was to inform Commander Ross that Miss Whitaker had been sent to Tokyo on a special assignment. She would return in less than a week. Brent cursed in frustration. He wanted to see her. He wanted to know if she had a hand in the lies in the media. And who took the photographs splattered across the front pages? Of course, the American tabloids had jumped on it with relish, and smeared him from coast to coast. "Hot copy," he said to himself bitterly. "Really great celebrity."

And there was something else about Helen that was disturbing. He had seen her in two guises: the taciturn, coldly professional woman with the emotions of an IBM computer, and the sexy, flirtatious woman with the vibrant personality and hot eyes. Which Helen would he see next?

He knew which one he preferred.

The few moments they had had alone in his apartment came back. He couldn't forget the look, the body, the hot promise in her eyes, her lips. And her mind, clever, witty. And probably manipulative. She wanted some kind of scoop. Regardless of what face he saw, he knew she would employ any kind of subterfuge to get what she wanted. Try to dig confidential, even top secret bits of information out of him. In that, all reporters were the same.

He wondered about Gary Mardoff. Were they a pair? How could anyone stand him? She claimed she disliked Mardoff. But he had not seen Gary, either. "Must be a story, a big story in Tokyo, or, maybe, they were on a frantic sexual holiday. You can't trust women or reporters—especially women reporters," he told himself. His wait was not long.

On the morning of the third day, Helen phoned him. It was the effusive, gregarious Helen. "Hi, sailor," she said. "This is your favorite member of the Fourth Estate."

"Where are you?"

"In Tokyo. Didn't my manager tell you?"

"Yes. But what are you doing in Tokyo? We have a date."

"Do you think I've forgotten? The boss sent me here to cover a conference."

"What conference?"

"The U.N. Secretary General Boutros Boutros-Ghali is here to meet with a North Korean delegation. It was kept secret until the secretary landed at Tokyo International yesterday."

"Why the secrecy?"

"The North Koreans insisted."

"They're all paranoid."

"Right."

"Then why didn't he go to North Korea?"

"Because an American rep is here along with a Chinese wheel and an Indonesian, Indian, and I've heard a Pakistani. They insisted on a neutral site."

"Tokyo isn't a neutral site."

"It is to them—on this matter."

"What's it about?"

"They say trade and improving relations . . ."

Brent interrupted, "Bullshit! Nuclear bombs! Right?"

"You're very knowledgeable. That's the rumble."

"The North Koreans have been cheating."

"That's what I hear."

"When will you be back?"

"By the end of the week. Boutros-Ghali is due in Geneva at the beginning of next week."

Brent fumed for a moment. "Great pictures of me in the papers."

"None were mine."

"What about Gary Mardoff?"

"What about him?"

"The pictures. What do you think?"

"I don't know."

"He's not there?"

"No. I don't sleep with him."

"I didn't ask."

"But you've been wondering. I told you I didn't even like him, and I meant it."

"Can I phone you?"

"I'm at the Century Hyatt, room 732. But I won't be there very much. Try me at night if you get lonely."

"Okay."

"And Brent."

"Yes."

"Stay away from Fumi."

It was his turn to chuckle. "I can't promise anything. I'm nothing but a Neanderthal in long pants and a slave to my primal passions."

She laughed. "Well, chain it. I'll see you in a few days."

When Brent dropped the phone in its cradle, he was smiling to himself, but still wondering about this enigmatic woman.

The next day the officers were informed by hand-delivered messages that the Arab fleet was steaming for Indonesia, and that all liberties and leaves could be cancelled without notice. No one was permitted to travel further from the base than the suburbs of Yokosuka.

Then Washington released word of the attack on the SSN *San Jose.* The candid dispatch was succinctly bitter: "An unprovoked attack was made on the USS *San Jose* by an enemy destroyer on 29 September off the Gulf of Aden. Seven crewmen were killed and 10 injured. *San Jose* took defensive measures and reports her attacker destroyed."

Immediately, Radio Tripoli responded: "A cowardly attack was made on one of our destroyers by an ambushing American submarine. Our forces responded courageously, but one of our ships was sunk with a terrible loss of life. If these dastardly attacks continue, the jihad will respond with all the wrath of Allah. Allah *akbar!*"

"Strange," a young Japanese pilot named Atsushi Fukazawa said over the poker table that evening. As youthful looking as a high school freshman, Fukazawa knew far more about aircraft and poker than he did submarines. Everyone looked at the pilot while he shuffled cards and continued. "Kadafi didn't say a word about the fight until the U.S. Navy reported the damage to *San Jose.*"

William Sackville chuckled humorlessly, "Of course not, old boy. Those bloody Arabs thought the sub had bought it—didn't want to give their game away."

"Like *Shreveport,*" Fukazawa suggested.

"Ruddy well said, old man. Like *Shreveport*—probably did her in, too. Drive the Americans off the rails wondering what happened to their overdue sub."

Brent entered the conversation. "Exactly," he said, sorting his hand as Fukazawa slid the cards across the slick tabletop. "They have strings of seabed hydrophones like our SOSUS system. They know where our subs patrol—even their identities."

The fourth man at the table, a young French junior lieutenant, Francois Larousse, exclaimed, "SOSUS, *Commandant?*"

"Sound Surveillance System, Francois," Brent explained. "Every sub has its sound and magnetic signature, and by now the Arabs have most of them in their threat libraries."

"It's all Russian equipment," Fukazawa offered.

"That's right. Every goddamned hydrophone."

The next morning Brent's phone rang, and he heard a female voice. "You haven't called me, Brent Ross." At first he thought it was Helen Whitaker. It took him a moment to realize Sally Neverland was on the line.

"It's Sally Neverland!" he said.

"Right."

"Haven't called you?" Brent blustered. "Why, I thought you never wanted to see me again."

"But I do," she answered ambiguously.

Brent was silent for a moment, trying to fathom this strange female. "Why don't you answer, Brent Ross?"

"Do you want to see me or not see me? Make up your mind."

"See you, of course. Why do you think I'm calling?"

"You surprise me."

"Why? Because I want to see you?"

"Yes."

"The Lord works in mysterious ways, Commander."

"Please, don't try to launder my soul again. The last time we wound up in a fight."

"I don't mean to offend you."

Brent remembered the beatific face, the slender body, the hunger she had to feed her soul and her stomach. No doubt she still wanted to convert him. The thought repulsed him, but he was lonely. He needed female company—even that of a frigid missionary. Anyway, amongst all things, Sally Neverland was a challenge, and he loved challenges.

"I would like to see you," he said.

"Where?"

He thought for a moment, and the rebuke in the restaurant came back. He would square it. "In my room—tonight."

Silence. And then the unexpected, "All right. What time?"

Brent concealed his surprise, "Dinner at 1800 hours."

"Eighteen-hundred what?"

"Six o'clock. Okay?"

"Okay."

"Steak, lobster or both?" Sally's line fell silent. "Well, Sally, what would you like? Name it."

"Steak, please."

"Good. And there's something else."

"What, Brent?"

"I'll be a gentleman."

"You're different, then, aren't you." The tone was cursory, without a trace of sarcasm.

"Yes I am," was the quick retort.

"I'll be there at, ah—1800 hours."

Brent felt pleased, almost elated, "Four-oh, messmate."

She giggled, a little girl sound of pleasure, "Ten-four."

"That's cops . . . Old 'Highway Patrol' reruns."

"Oh!"

"Roger, wilco, and out."

"Roger and what, Brent?"

"Wilco—will comply."

"Okay. I'm complying. Out."

Brent had scarcely hung up the phone when the knock came. He opened the door and found *Yonaga*'s gunnery officer, Lieutenant Commander Nobomitsu Atsumi, grinning at him. "I have a two day liberty, Brent-san. Thought I would stay at the *Kujaku*. Admiral Fujita will not allow us to take liberty in Tokyo."

Brent ushered his friend in, and they sat on opposite sides of the small table in the living room. Brent nursing a scotch and soda, Atsumi sipping hot *saké*. Looking at his friend, he marvelled how well the Gunnery officer wore his years. A *Yonaga* plank owner, Atsumi was very much like Yoshi Matsuhara. Both defied time with strong physiques, black hair, and lean-boned, sun-beaten faces. However, only a faint spider's web of lines trailing off from the corners of Atsumi's eyes and mouth betrayed the inroads of time. If anyone disbelieved the preservative affects of over four decades of isolation, Atsumi was walking, breathing proof that it existed.

Brent respected Nobomitsu Atsumi because of his high intelligence and profound knowledge of the world's great religions. Although basically a Taoist, he was tolerant of all faiths. Actually, he practiced several religions. In the usual oriental's ability to entertain conflicting viewpoints simultaneously, the gunnery officer had no trouble accommodating Taoism, while still observing the nearly universal Japanese beliefs in Buddhism and Shintoism. To Brent, this made the lieutenant commander even more welcome company. His bright mind and complex religious convictions could provide many hours of delicious dialectics.

After toasting the Emperor, Brent began by mentioning the latest Arab communiqué. Politely turning the hotel's logo on his cup toward Brent, Atsumi said, "We decoded *San Jose*'s transmission four days ago. It was top secret."

"But the U.S. Navy released it, Nobomitsu-san."

Atsumi snorted over his cup, "They had to. CNN had most of the story."

"How in the world did *they* get it?"

The big gunnery officer shrugged. "Who knows? But intelligence reported a few Arab survivors were picked up by a fishing boat. We believe there was a CNN man in the crew."

"Not many survivors?"

"The sharks got most of them."

"Too bad."

"You are sorry for the Arabs?"

"No. The sharks. They must have indigestion."

Atsumi laughed, his big, deep sonorous rumble that had prompted some of the younger officers to give him the sobriquet, "Old Thunder Mouth." He was in fine spirits, the kind of elation he always showed on the eve of battle.

"I have some good news, Brent-San, some news that has made our friend Yoshi Matsuhara very happy." Brent looked at his friend expectantly. Nobomitsu continued, "After the attack on *San Jose*, the Americans released more aircraft to us."

"What aircraft?"

"A squadron of Grumman F7F Tigercats."

Brent thought for a moment. "A twin-engined aircraft—but big and heavy."

Atsumi nodded in agreement. "True. They have new, sturdier airframes, folding wingtips, and they are powered with the new Pratt and Whitney R-4360, Mark II engine."

"Those were the engines they used in the old Douglas Globemaster. They were huge transports and those were big engines."

"The new Mark II uses much more magnesium and titanium. Pound for pound it's the most powerful engine in the world."

"Horsepower?"

"Over 4,500."

Brent whistled. "What can the Tigercat do?"

"Nearly five hundred knots, with a service ceiling of 14,500 meters."

"That's over 40,000 feet, Nobomitsu-san."

"Right."

Brent took a drink and said with a big grin, "I'll bet Yoshi would trade his soul—ah, I mean his shiny karma for one of those engines."

Atsumi nodded. "I understand he's working on it."

"Put one in his Zero-sen? I was kidding."

"He's not, Brent-san."

"Soon, he'll strap himself to an engine, hold out his arms, and fly away."

They both laughed. "He's coming to that, Brent-san."

They talked of aircraft, ships and the mysterious trawler that *Edo* had fought. Latest intelligence placed it in Surabaya, where it was undergoing major repairs. "Our agents report she was so badly damaged, she was almost scrapped," Atsumi said.

"But she'll be back at sea."

"It looks that way Brent-san."

Brent pounded the table, "Cowardly, murdering bastards."

The Taoist broke through, "Remember, according to the *Kan-ying-pien* . . ."

Brent interrupted, "The *Book on Responses Evoked by Good and Evil Deeds.*"

"Very good, Brent-san." The gunnery officer stabbed a finger for emphasis and a new, intense gleam sparked his eyes. "Remember, evil deeds are repaid. This is guaranteed by the god *Tsao-shen,* who watches us all and reports our deeds to the Jade Emperor."

Brent nodded respectfully and weighed the close similarities to Christian beliefs. In a way, only the names were changed. "Yes, I know, Nobomitsu-san. The Jade Emperor will destroy the evil ones and consign them to hell, along with the devils of disease and misfortune." He pinched the bridge of his nose and grasped one of Atsumi's most salient beliefs. "And, Nobomitsu-san, I must conquer my inner demons, purge myself, if I am to become my own man."

Obviously pleased, Atsumi nodded and used words Brent had heard many times from Yoshi Matsuhara and Admiral Fujita. "You have been studying, Brent-San. You have a fertile mind. But do you believe?"

"I believe and disbelieve."

"Selectively?"

Brent tossed off his drink. "Sometimes I think it's random."

"Confused?"

"Perhaps."

Brent tapped his glass until it rang like a tiny chime. "It is very difficult to reconcile the humanism of the east with the authoritarianism of the west, Nobomitsu-san. Isn't this enough to confuse Confucius?"

"You are a very wise man, Brent-san. Even Ling Chang Tao-ling would hesitate to grapple with you." He finished his drink and began to rise.

"Stay, my friend. It's almost time for dinner."

"I know. I was going to return to my room, Brent-san. Maybe, pick up a game of *go* in the lounge."

"Stay here. Eat with me. You can play *go* anytime. I have a visitor coming, and I think you would enjoy meeting her."

"Enjoy meeting her?" He raised an eyebrow and stared at the American curiously, "And wouldn't I be in the way? You Americans like to say 'three's a crowd'."

"No," Brent laughed. "We wouldn't be a crowd."

"Why do you say that?"

"Because she's a Christian missionary."

Atsumi threw up his hands in an exaggerated defensive gesture. "Oh, no, Brent-san! How could you do that to a friend? They are the most obstinate, intolerant people on earth." He caught himself. "Sorry, Brent-san. No offense."

"Of course not. I'll need your help. I'll be outnumbered."

"One of them could outnumber an army."

"Please, stay Nobomitsu-san. Maybe we you can convert her to Taoism."

Atsumi's laugh was big and hearty. "And maybe we can reverse the path of the sun," he sputtered.

"Then, some other time, Nobomitsu-san."

"Yes, some other time, Brent-son."

The gunnery officer left hastily.

Sally Neverland arrived at 1800 hours, promptly. Again, Brent was struck by the pureness of her beauty, how she reminded him of an angel in a Botticelli painting. Although she was dressed in a loose-fitting blouse and long black skirt, her budding breasts still jutted out against the cotton fabric as if trying to break free from the prison of a tight-fitting brassiere. When she sat and crossed her legs, her well-formed calves and slim ankles shone like polished ivory. She wore no hose. Brent guessed she could not afford the expensive panty hose he had noticed on Helen Whitaker.

Looking at the chaste, fresh face, he was struck by the naiveté that shone in her blue-green eyes. Yet, as she sank back into the couch and stared at him, he sensed again the innate fear, a distrust of all things male. It was as palpable as a stone wall. Or was it his imagination? But he was sure of one thing: the tight brassiere, loose clothing, long skirt were all designed to hide her sexuality. In a very real way, she was trying to unsex herself. But this was not unusual for a missionary. Maybe, he was trying to read too much into the girl. And there was a gap. She was very young, a little more that half his age. She made him feel his years.

Her greeting had been warm enough, without a trace of the rancor of their first meeting. "Good to see you, Brent," she said, smiling as she entered.

"Glad you could come," he had answered, showing her to the couch while he took the chair opposite. He had decided in advance he would not sit beside her. He offered her a drink. She took tea. He brought the tea out in a ceramic service and poured two cups, despite his preference for scotch.

Her opening was blunt. Waving at her surroundings, she said, "You seduce women here?"

"I've never seduced anyone."

"Oh, you're a virgin?"

"No, it's always been mutual." He raised his cup and stared at her over the rim. "And you?"

"And you—what?"

"Seduce many men?"

Her face glazed over as if suddenly struck by a gust of Arctic air. It was almost as if he had asked her to describe a horrible nightmare. But she had made the *entree.* Let her answer. She backed out quickly, "I prefer not to discuss that, if you don't mind."

"You brought it up."

"Sorry."

"When your mind's not on God, it's on sex."

"The devil uses sex to have his way with us. He works in insidious ways. We who are born again must always be on guard." Her eyes bored into his, " 'From all the deceits of the world, the flesh, and the devil.' "

Brent knew her thinking. "The devil uses our flesh as a tool to claim our souls—right?"

"Yes, if man uses sex just to satisfy lust?"

"There must be love."

"Of course, if the union is beholden to the Lord, the devil is defeated."

He toyed with his cup, sliding it gently back and forth on the saucer. He had to satisfy a curiosity. "Your family?"

Turning her lips under, she looked away. Then she put her fingertips to her temples, massaging lightly and wincing—as if recalling the past had given her an excruciating headache. Her voice was so soft he could hardly hear her, "I'm from Hollywood."

"I know. Your mother—father?"

She took a deep breath and exhaled with a soughing sound like a breeze through autumn leaves. He expected her to take refuge in religion, but she answered frankly. "I never knew my father."

"And your mother?"

"She died when I was fifteen."

"And then?"

She looked at her hands. "I quit school, took odd jobs . . ." She jerked her head toward him so quickly her hair flew like a cloud. Eyes wide and misted over she said, "Please, it was hard. I didn't start living until I joined the church. Can't you see? That was my beginning. Then I was born. There was no life before that, I told you."

The anguish on her face made Brent wish he had never pried. "Yes, I understand, Sally."

To Brent's relief, they were interrupted by a knock. He ushered in two men. One was pushing a cart loaded with a covered meal. Brent began to describe his order, "Filet mignon, potato, broccoli, French bread . . ."

Eyeing the cart, Sally brightened immediately. "Please, Brent," she said, managing to smile. "I approve." They moved to the small dining area, where the two waiters began to serve the meal by placing two Caesar salads on the table. Brent waved them off. "Just leave the cart. We'll serve ourselves."

Looking at the girl and smiling knowingly, the men bowed and left.

Sally ate ravenously while Brent served and studied her. He was convinced she was still short of money. She obviously was not eating enough—perhaps, even suffering from malnutrition. That was probably why she was in his room—for the food. "Have you been receiving support from your church?" he asked casually.

"Oh, yes, I get a stipend."

"Enough?"

"Of course. And I have glorious news."

"Oh?"

She sat back and a look of unabashed joy limned her

face, "Reverend Ezra Freestone will arrive tomorrow. He'll personally assist me in my mission."

"The Church of God in . . ." He paused, failing the test of memory.

"The Voice of God in Jesus, Brent," she corrected.

"Oh, yes."

They finished the meal. Sally returned to the couch and Brent to his chair. He poured fresh tea and stared at the beautiful face. Some of the tension was gone. Clearly, she had been very hungry.

"You've had religious training," she said. "You told me you attended parochial schools."

"I went to Catholic schools until I was sixteen."

"Then you left?"

"Yes."

She nodded understanding and voiced the intolerance he expected, "You found the Church the work of the devil."

"Not really."

"Then, some priest molested you."

He felt a sudden warmth on his face. "Sorry to disappoint you. Most priests are fine people. It wasn't that at all."

"Then what was it?"

He placed his cup in the saucer carefully. "I had a slight disagreement with one of the brothers."

"A slight disagreement? Over what? Dogma? Tradition? Theology?"

"No. Sports."

"Sports?"

"Football. Father Domonic was a young priest, and he considered himself a real jock. He was our line coach. He was trying to show our linemen how to tackle me—I was a fullback. I told him to put on pads, but he wouldn't listen. Had to show everyone how macho he was. I broke his shoulder and cracked his right wrist."

"They threw you out for that?"

"I humiliated him in front of the team. He claimed it was deliberate, and that I used excessive force—attacked him."

"But you were never molested?" There was disappointment in her voice.

He winced at her intransigence and answered sarcastically. "Oh, you'd be surprised. Some Catholic boys are never sexually assaulted."

"But, you left the Church. You're reborn?" She raised her eyes and Brent knew what was coming, "Jesus said, 'Verily I say unto thee, Except a man be born again, he cannot see the kingdom of God'."

Brent shook his head. "Please, Sally, I have been exposed to too many religions to be convinced that there is only one way."

"Then what are you?"

"A bouillabaisse of beliefs—stir up a base stock of Christianity, throw in a bit of Buddhism, flavor with Shintoism, and spice with a touch of Taoism and you have Brent Ross."

Her laugh was airy. "You're all that?"

"Right. Remember, my closest friends are Shintoists, Buddhists, Taoists. In many ways they make sense, and they don't harangue me—try to convert me."

"How can you turn your back on Jesus?"

"But I haven't. There is room for understanding and tolerance in all men." He began to feel the frustration rising. "Remember, Christians have a hard time with Eastern thought because it's non-linear. It takes cultivation, and a good deal more discipline than Western logical simplification."

She nodded understanding, but the expected rejection came. " 'If any man be in Christ, he is a new creature'. Do you believe this, Brent?"

He gripped his hands together and rubbed his palms

until he felt the warmth. She watched him curiously. In time he answered candidly. "When I was young, yes. But now, I'm not sure of anything."

She beckoned to him to come sit next to her. He hesitated. She surprised him. "Please, Brent, I want to hold your hand."

He dropped down on the couch next to her. She took his big hand in both of hers. In a strange way, it was almost like sitting next to his mother. "My quote?"

"It was from Corinthians."

"Yes, Brent, the fifth chapter. I didn't finish it."

"You don't have to."

Ignoring him, she closed her eyes and spoke to the dim overhead light. " 'Old things are passed away, behold, all things are become new'."

She opened her eyes and fixed him with a gaze that gripped like a vice. There was fervor there, even passion. But for what? For him? For Jesus? She was maddeningly unfathomable. He couldn't stop the smile that crossed his face. She was so young, so beautiful, so earnest. "Sally?"

Her eyes never wavered. "Yes, Brent."

"Let's not turn this into a Bible quoting contest."

She laughed, the trilling sound of the little girl. "You want me to give up my mission?" She casually placed his hand, still gripped in hers, on her lap. He could feel the firm perfect thigh under the edge of his hand. It was not the thigh of an angel.

"You promised not to try to launder my soul again."

"You want me to change, Brent?"

"Just put it aside for a while. We'll never agree."

She sighed and tightened the grip on his hand. "All right, I know I can be persistent," she understated. "You could have become angry with me and you didn't. You're a gentleman."

"Thank you."

She brought his hand up and pressed it to her cheek like a little girl with her favorite doll. "I like you, Brent. You're very sweet."

"And I like you."

"If I could—ah . . ."

"If you could what?"

"If I could . . ." She blushed, stumbled a bit, and continued, "If I could ever want a man, want a man romantically—beholden in the eyes of the Lord, it would be a man like you."

"I'm flattered," he said sincerely. "But there isn't room for romance in your life."

Biting her lip, she looked away. "It isn't just that."

"Then what?" Silence. "You've known a man—a bad experience."

"You knew from the start. I could tell by the way you looked at me."

With a single finger to her chin, he gently turned her face toward him. A thin stream of tears streaked both cheeks. "No, Sally, I don't know and I don't need to know. I just feel you've been subjected to some of that abuse you thought I suffered."

She looked down at her feet. "There was a time when some terrible things happened . . ." Her voice broke.

"That's enough." Then slowly tracing his fingers over the fine satin of her cheek, "I'm not qualified to cast the first stone—no man is."

She turned to him quickly, "But I found the Lord, the forgiving, loving, merciful God."

Brent spoke sincerely, "I'm glad you did."

"I am not only reborn, I'm recreated," she said with breathless intensity.

"Good, Sally, good."

"And Reverend Freestone did it for me."

"I'd like to meet him."

"Oh, you will. I'll introduce you to him. He's the most

moral, honorable man I know. Truly, he lives in the grace of the Lord. You'll love him. Everyone does." She sagged back, just the thought of Reverend Freestone having a calming effect.

"I'm sure we'll get along."

She snuggled her head against his shoulder and he patted her head gently, as if he were stroking a kitten. It was like touching silk. They remained that way for a long time, silent and content.

"Brent," she finally said.

"Yes."

She shocked him. "I think I could fall in love with you."

He moved away, taking her thin shoulders in both of his hands and stared down into those great blue-green eyes. They were filmed over with moisture. His urge was to hold her, kiss her. But she was so young, so lonely, so vulnerable. It would be obscene. Instead, he said, "You can't."

"Why?"

"You don't even know me."

"But I do."

"You don't and you're a missionary. You love all of mankind."

"It isn't that."

"It is, and it's getting late."

"You want me to leave?"

"No, but it would be best." Brent couldn't believe his words. First he had rebuffed Helen Whitaker, and now Sally. He was repeating the same scenario. What had happened to him? New scruples? An innate sense of honor that had emerged with the years? Certainly, the memory of the butchered Ruth Moskowitz and Devora Hacohen would always be there. Murdered because they loved him. The guilt could never be erased. But, still, he was human, with all the desires and needs of other men. He was never destined to be a monk. Fujita had made that point. Sex with Helen would almost be a business transaction, while taking Sally to bed could destroy her. He had never been so confused, so utterly unable to fathom himself.

Sally came to her feet and, hand-in-hand, they walked to the door. She searched his eyes. "Hold me?"

He wrapped both arms around her and held her tight. She trembled. It was like holding a frightened sparrow. They stood that way for several minutes. He could feel her breath on his cheek, short warm gusts like a soft tropical breeze. Then she kissed him on the cheek and he brushed her brow with his lips.

"How are you going home?"

"There's a bus."

"To where?"

"Zushi. It's only about five miles."

"I know. It's a rough little town."

"I'm never alone. The Lord is always at my side."

"Even the Lord could be mugged there. It's late. I'll phone for a staff car and take you home."

She was objecting while he made the call. Then he shrugged into his tunic, led her into the hall and to the elevator. "This isn't necessary. I'll be all right," she insisted to his deaf ears. She did not stop until he pulled her into the elevator. Then, alone for the short ride, she stood very close, never releasing his hand until the doors opened.

Exiting the elevator and entering the lobby, they were halted by a hoarse voice that boomed from the large archway that led to the bar. "Hey, the big hero. Waddaya know?" Gary Mardoff was back.

Trying to ignore the reporter, Brent steered Sally toward the big double doors of the entrance. But Mardoff cut them off, stood glaring with bloodshot eyes, legs unsteady. "And 'Virgin Mary'. Been up to 'hero's' apartment?" He waved a single finger like a scolding schoolteacher, "My, my. Naughty, naughty!"

A few heads turned. The clerk and two assistants stared over the counter.

"That's enough," Brent said. With Sally tugging on his arm, he stepped toward the entrance. But Mardoff moved with him, still barring the way. His motion was quick, coordinated. Brent guessed the man wasn't as drunk as he wanted people to believe.

Mardoff stabbed a finger at Sally. "Found out about her. She's one of Freestone's girls. A whore. That's all she is, another Hollywood hooker." A half-dozen men came to their feet and stared at the trio. Three or four more left the bar, attracted by the commotion.

Brent felt the magma rising, muscles charging. Tension build in his sinews and nerves. His chest felt like it was constricted by a tourniquet and the taste of his meal was suddenly sour in his throat. "I said that's enough," he warned. "Shut up, damn you."

"Please. Please, stop," Sally pleaded. Everyone ignored her, and two spectators pushed her aside so that they could get a better view of the fun.

Mardoff sneered. "The hell I will. She has her own 'Walk of Fame,' put her little ass on more concrete than all the stars from LaBrea to Vine. Gives great head . . ."

Brent grabbed the reporter's throat hard. He pulled the man's tie tight like a garrotte. "Shut your goddamned mouth, or . . ."

"Or what?" he scoffed brazenly. Mardoff seemed immune to fear. The only emotion Brent could read in his eyes was hate. "Gunna scrape off my ear like that picketer—bite me, scratch my eyes out." He pulled back and slapped at Brent's hand. "Let go of me, you son of a bitch."

Brent brought an open palm around, while still holding Mardoff high with a grip on his tie and throat. With blurring speed, the big palm hit the reporter like a hawk striking a field rat. Open and flat, the slap caught Mardoff full on the cheek with the cracking sound of a bat meeting a ball. Mardoff's head snapped to the side, hair flew up like bent grass in a stiff wind, and spittle flew from his mouth. The crowd "oohed, aahed" and urged the men on.

Releasing the big reporter, Mardoff staggered to the side, face red, eyes wide and stunned. The slap was worse than a punch. Slaps were reserved for women and children. It was the ultimate insult.

Dropping into a crouch, he recovered with amazing speed. Lashing out with a foot, he took Brent completely by surprise. The foot caught Brent in the solar plexus, punching the breath out of him. Staggering backward, Brent hid behind his own smoke screen, deliberately reeling and wobbling unsteadily.

"Slap me, you prick! Now I'm going to show you, mighty Yankee samurai. The next one will be to the balls—if you have any."

"No! No!" Sally screamed.

Mardoff charged to exploit his advantage. Turning to the side, he brought his other foot around in a vicious circle. He had made a mistake. His adversary was not there. Instead, Brent stepped to the side lightly, completely controlled. Then he delivered a three-punch combination with all his power. His fists hit with the force of pile drivers; one to the eye, another to the mouth and the third to the kidney. The reporter crashed into a small end table, rolled onto a couch, and bounced to the floor. A reading lamp shattered on the hard tile.

Brent felt the old urge to destroy inflame him. He started forward, tensed and poised, to strike again like an arrow notched against the curve of the longbow. The small crowd urged him on. Everyone disliked the reporter.

The booming baritone of Chief Shin Kanemaru behind him stopped everything, "Commander Ross. Let me handle this."

"Yes! Stop! Stop!" Sally cried.

"That reporter started it," the clerk insisted.

"I know. I know," Kanemaru said. Followed by two of his men, the chief brushed past Brent to the fallen Mardoff. They leaned over the injured man. Brent suspected the chief had enjoyed the short fight, and had delayed his intervention until Mardoff had been humiliated.

Sitting up, Mardoff leaned back against the couch, rubbing his chin and trying to sniff the blood back into the streaming nostrils. His face was a brittle mask of surprise, like a man who had been blind-sided at an intersection by a truck running a red light. "Get you, motherfucker, get you yet," he muttered while spitting blood.

"My pleasure," Brent said. "Any time."

While the chief's men helped the reporter to his feet, Kanemaru said to Mardoff, "You'll be all right. Just keep that big mouth shut."

"Fuck you, Chief, and fuck your goddamned navy."

Brent and Sally walked out of the lobby to the waiting Mercedes SL 500.

The Mercedes staff car was driven by a seaman guard, while Chief Shin Kanemaru sat in the passenger's seat. Brent sat in the rear with Sally huddled against him. She clutched his hand as if it were a lifeline thrown to a drowning swimmer. For the first few minutes she sobbed into the sleeve of his tunic. He soothed her, assured her, never taking his hand from the silk of her hair. She kissed his bruised knuckles and seemed to find reassurance by pressing his hand to her cheek. Finally, she managed to choke out, "Horrible, horrible man."

"He has some problems."

"You hurt your hand," her voice still tremulous, but showing growing control.

"It was a pleasure."

"You could've been killed."

"Not by that cockroach," Brent snorted.

"I got you into it." She dabbed at her cheeks with a handkerchief.

"No, Sally. This started a long time ago."

"You know all about me. What he said was true."

"You told me in my apartment."

"I know, but Mardoff made my whole life so—so ugly."

"He's an ugly person. The world is full of them. That's why men like me can always find full employment."

Her voice cracked, "You—you'll never want to see me again."

He pulled her close. "Not true. I like you and I like your company."

"You don't care about what I did—what I was?"

"No. Only what you are."

"You like what I am?"

"You know I do."

"I'll see you again?"

"I would like that very much, Sally."

"I'll phone you tomorrow," she said brightening. "After Reverend Freestone arrives."

"Fine."

They fell silent as the Mercedes pulled up to the curb in front of a ramshackle, faded white building. A two-storey built in Western style. It was so old, so shaken by earthquakes, it looked as if it were collapsing right back into its foundation. One of thousands of cheap houses built after the great fire raids of World War II. Its porch sagged, the window and door frames twisted. Brent shook his head. Not a right angle was in sight.

Chief Kanemaru opened the door with, "This is the address you gave me, Miss."

"This is the place."

She took Brent's hand and led him up the short walk

to the front door. Standing in front of the door, she reached up and wrapped both arms around his neck. For a long moment she clung to him like a small child seeking a parent's protection. Hesitantly, she kissed him on the mouth, gently and tenderly. He sought no more.

Then she turned, opened the door, and was gone.

Fourteen
The Scoop

The next morning Sally phoned Brent just before noon. She was ecstatic. "The Reverend is here."

"Freestone?"

"Of course."

"You'll work together."

"Yes. We're going to Tokyo today—to the Ginza."

Despite Brent's efforts to choke it back, a chuckle sneaked through. "Well, you'll find a lot of souls to save there."

"But Brent, you should see our itinerary. We'll carry the 'Word' to Kawasaki, Nagoya, Osaka, Kobe, Okayama, Hiroshima, Nagasaki and more. We're even going to Hong Kong, Singapore and Shanghai—if the Chinese give us visas."

"I won't see much of you."

"I may be gone for months." She paused and her voice dropped. "I'll miss you, Brent. But the work of the Lord takes precedence over the needs of mere mortals."

"This mere mortal needs to see you."

"Thank you for that, Brent. And I want to see you so much it hurts."

"Keep me informed."

"I'll write. I promise. And when I return, we'll get together—just the two of us. Would you like that?"

"Very much."

"You're important to me Brent."

"And you to me, Sally."

"I'm glad."

"And be careful, you're going into some very tough neighborhoods."

" 'The good shepherd giveth his life for the sheep'."

"But not for the wolves."

She bubbled with amusement. "No, Brent. Not for the wolves. We will meet again."

"As sure as the wheel turns."

"The Wheel of Causality?"

"Of course."

"You're trying to convert me, Brent."

It was his turn to be amused. "Of course, and Sally, 'Do justly, love mercy, and walk humbly with thy God, but be wary'."

"Why Brent, you're the most confusing man. You're quoting the scriptures to me."

"Why not?"

"Then remember this, Brent—Jesus said to his disciples, 'If any man will come after me, let him deny himself, and take up his cross and follow me.' "

"All men have a burden to carry, Sally."

"And a prophet to follow. *Vaya con Dios.*"

"Vaya con Dios."

For a long while Brent sat quietly with his hand on the phone, goaded by the devils of impatience, doubt and anxiety. He longed for Sally. The thought that she had once been a prostitute was repulsive. But there was none of that in her now. In fact, she had swung to the opposite extreme. "Nothing's as pious as a reformed whore," was a favorite expression he had heard his old uncle use many times when he was a teenager. Maybe this applied to Sally. No doubt she *had* changed. The appellation, "Virgin Mary" had been well earned or the men wouldn't use it.

None of it made any difference. He wanted to hold her and hear that beguiling, insouciant voice of hers. He had only seen her twice, but she had grown on him like moss clinging to a rock. He chuckled at the simile. Was he her rock? Is that how she thought of him? She said she could love him. Could he love her? He shook his head. He was very much attached to her, true. But years ago he had decided there wasn't room for love in a world that marched to the drums of hate.

Whenever he thought of the war, he was touched by a sense of rue, a sense of being caught up in forces he could not master. He was rudderless, blown wherever the winds of war drove him. It would be cruel and selfish to drag a woman along with him. And there was something else. He had demons attached to his chariot. Lethal *kamis* that had killed all the beauty he had known. Could he unleash those demons on Sally, too? On anyone he cared for?

Sweet little Sally. So much in love with God. The high school cheerleader for Jesus who could plea for divine intervention like Tevya and actually expect it. She had found the family she had never known. There was a lot of that in her. He knew he had aroused her. Yet the way she had clung to him, found contentment in just clutching his hand, brought to mind the father she couldn't even remember. Here was the void, the hunger—the craving Freestone had helped fill, and, maybe take advantage. The old preacher had taken Sally off the streets, yet he disliked Freestone, sight unseen. Maybe he was jealous because the reverend had taken the beautiful little spirit from him.

But it was more than that. All cult leaders were suspect. They were licentious old men who lived luxuriously while their followers slaved and begged on corners to support them. And they all seemed to have insatiable appetites for young bodies. And looming over them like the Lord himself, they had no trouble filling their beds.

Brent cursed. Did the old reverend lust after Sally *that*

much, so much he had travelled halfway around the world? Could it be possible he was genuine? Could be possessed by a missionary zeal to spread the "Word" instead of legs? There had to be a few honest men in the profession—in the "calling." But he shook his head and dwelled on something he had heard Nobomitsu Atsumi say many times. "Some religions founder on deception, others are founded on it." The gunnery officer was very wise.

He sighed, a long, drawn-out explosion of air that sagged him back into the cushions of the couch. He walked to the kitchen, reached for the scotch, changed his mind, and poured himself a large mug of black coffee. Then he dressed, took the elevator down, and spent the rest of the day playing cards, pool, and working out.

Despite the full day's activities, that night he had a hard time drifting into sleep. Mardoff screaming, "Whore! Whore!" kept on intruding, and then Sally's sweet, tear-stained face. Finally, he watched old "Twilight Zone," "I Love Lucy," and "Get Smart" reruns—the only American programs on the hotel's closed circuit television—until he dozed off.

Helen Whitaker phoned him the next morning. She seemed bright and cheerful. She insisted that he come to her *ryokan* to enjoy the marvelous cuisine. The lively tone of her voice cheered him, pulled him out of his trough.

"And come early," she said. "We can talk."

Surprisingly, the prospect of seeing Helen did not excite him as much as it should. There was too much of Sally drifting in his mind. But he was lonely, felt he was existing in a desert of men. That had been his life. He felt the void ache.

He loved women because they were all the things missing from his world. He yearned for them, not only for the passion, for what they could do for him physically, but for their demeanor, the different mind-set, perceptions, and inherent compassion. He loved them for the smell of cosmetics, perfume, flavored lipstick, smooth skin, flowing scented hair, curves and planes of their bodies, sleek dainty clothing. And the lace—lace had been part of every woman he had ever known. He was starved for any woman's company, and Helen was one.

"All right," he finally conceded, more to himself than to Helen. "See you at five-thirty."

"Right. Five-thirty."

When the staff car dropped Brent at the *Shibu,* he was impressed by the sheer size of the building. Built like a large private home, the rambling inn was surrounded by gardens and stands of cherry, pine and maple trees. It was like being dropped on the edge of a forest. He could even hear the autumnal voices of insects making the air vibrate. A cool clarity presaged the coming of fall. The trees were lovely; the cherry trees beginning to don their fall gold, and a few of the maple competing with their own.

A special hospitality swept out the entrance the moment he stepped out of the car. As an act of purification and sign of welcome, the stones of the entrance had been ritually washed. They glistened in the declining sunlight. And a small, exquisite young lady waited for him at the end of the walk. Very youthful, she was dressed in an elegant silk *kimono* with a tight white *obi* showing off her tiny waist. Her shiny black hair was upswept and held in place with jeweled combs. It shone like lacquer.

"Commander Ross," she said bowing, "I am Mieko, Miss Whitaker's *jyochu.* With your permission, I will take you to her rooms."

"Of course," Brent said to the lady-in-waiting. She helped him out of his shoes and into silk slippers. With short, graceful steps of her white-gloved feet, she led him into the building.

Brent had been exposed to Japanese elegance and had

stayed in some of Japan's most luxurious hotels, but he was not prepared for the *Shibu.* It was like stepping into a Heian painting—or leafing through a Japanese book of art. In the entry they passed calligraphy prints, translucent *shoji* screens, and lacquered chests. All four walls were wall-papered with antique sheet music. Then Mieko turned down a long hallway, gliding past tranquil gardens, Korean chests, hand-painted screens, scroll paintings, and *Nõ* masks. Done in black ink on white paper, an astonishing display of landscapes by the ancient masters Jasoku, Sesshu and Sõami lined the walls. Brent caught his breath at the opulence.

Turning down another short hallway and then another, her feet padded softly on the dark wooden floor that glistened by candlelight. Brent chuckled wistfully. Without Mieko, he would have never found his way. In fact, the inn seemed to be built on the "conceal and reveal" principle and, although Brent suspected it was booked to capacity, no one else seemed to be around. Finally, they stopped in front of an elaborately carved solid oak door. Brent suspected that for privacy the Western-style doors were used instead of the flimsy *shojis.* Mieko knocked gently.

Helen opened the door, a broad warm smile of greeting on her face. Brent entered the room and Mieko vanished with the dexterity that would have done credit to the most accomplished Indian *fakir.* Taking his hands, Helen kissed him on the cheek and then waved at the suite. "Like it?" she asked.

Brent ran his eyes over Helen. Her skirt was short and tight, blouse plastered to her body as if she had painted it on. Her hair flowed to her shoulders and the blue-gray eyes were heightened by excitement. "I approve," he said.

She laughed with delight. "I meant my suite."

"Oh." Brent looked at the elegantly-ornamental entry foyer, which contained three modern chairs arranged for

Westerners. Taking his hand, Helen led him into the next room. "And my sitting room?"

It was very large. Covering the polished wooden floor were gold-bordered *tatami* mats, springy and soft. In the center was a black lacquered table and two chairs with bamboo backs and thick silk *zabutons*. In a concession to Western tastes, a plump sofa faced the far side of the table. It could be used for relaxation, intimate conversation and, Brent knew, very much more. He wondered if Helen had special-ordered it. Examining the rest of the room, he found no bouquets or elaborate flower arrangements, only a single orchid in an *ikbana* arrangement in a peaceful alcove.

Helen gestured at the alcove, "That's the *tokonoma.*"

"I know. It's used for meditation and prayer."

She gestured at a large sliding glass door, "Look at my garden. Isn't it beautiful."

Brent looked out on an immaculate garden of Japanese maples, ferns, bonsai, stunted black pines. A tiny lake of gravel lay next to mossy earth, black glistening stones and two stone lanterns carved from granite, were positioned at the ends of a miniature bridge. A stone cistern ornamented with adornments and designs was casually placed in a far corner. It held a bamboo ladle. In the usual Japanese fashion, everything had been trained, trimmed, pruned, immaculately swept and clipped. Brent could not find a stray leaf or twig anywhere. The only audible sound was that of a tiny waterfall that dripped more than ran.

"Isn't it beautiful, Brent. I love this place."

"Beautiful, and restful, and typically Japanese."

"Yes. The rocks, the plants are so perfectly arranged."

"It's more than that. The Japanese respect nature while we try to destroy it. They believe the fundamental elements of all things are found in nature and man is part of it and must fit himself into it. The rocks mean strength, the pine branches love."

She laughed lightly. "There's something else, my great big philosopher."

"And what's that?"

"The guests must have something beautiful to look at."

"Yes. Yes, of course, Helen."

"The rest of it is beautiful, too." She showed him the bedroom with its Western-style bed. "I ordered the bed," she explained. "Those damned *futons* are like sleeping on the floor."

"Once you get used to them, they can be quite comfortable."

"No springs," she said slyly.

He let the remark die in the air and gestured to a door.

"My vanity," she said, taking his hand again and leading him into a small room.

He nodded, looking at the polished copper wash basin, hair dryer, shampoo, body lotions and a scale. Wrapped in silver paper, even the soap was done with artistry.

"And in there, the bathing room, Brent." In the usual Japanese style, the bathing room was separated from the lavatory. It contained a shower and hand-crafted tub. Waving at the tub, Helen laughed. "The first time I took a bath I really blew it—broke a dozen traditions."

"You didn't shower first," Brent hazarded.

She laughed. "Right. I was scrubbing my hair when Mieko walked in."

"She must've been horrified."

"Ah, yes, but discreet. She tactfully told me I should scrub first in the shower and then soak in the tub . . ."

Brent interrupted her, "There to empty your mind of worldly distractions, meditate and come to know yourself better. It's the Zen in all Japanese."

"Yes. True. Except for one thing."

Brent chuckled. "The water was so hot you could cook a lobster."

"Right. I was parboiled."

"In the best Japanese tradition."

"According to protocol. But Brent . . ." She leaned close to him, so close her lips almost touched his ear. Her tone was conspiratorial. "I cheated."

"How terrible," he whispered back, catching her mood.

"I sneaked in some cold water."

"Good for you." They both laughed.

She gestured at the sitting room and led him to the sofa. A fine bone china carafe, with two cups, was placed on the table. "I'll be damned," he said. "It wasn't there a minute ago."

She smiled. "Mieko."

Brent shook his head. "A damned sorceress."

"She's very quiet and unobtrusive."

"Quiet and unobtrusive? She's a ghost. She can make herself invisible. She did it in the hall and she did it again."

She edged closer. "I can lock the door."

This remark was not allowed to die. "Not necessary," he said, matter-of-factly.

Ignoring the retort, she began to fill the two cups with hot *saké*. "You like my *ryokan* better than a hotel?"

"When it comes to the best hotels, it's like trying to compare Freud to Shakespeare."

"What do you mean?" she asked, turning with a full cup in each hand.

"It can't be done."

She grinned. "You're a very smart man, Brent."

He laughed. "Thanks, but remember I've lived in Japan for a decade."

"*Saké* heated to the temperature of blood," she said, handing him his cup and seating herself.

With his cup held high, he said, "And this is a *sakazuki.*"

She held his eyes with hers and toasted. "To us."

"Can't think of a better salute." They drank.

She smiled slyly, and touched his cup again, "To Gary Mardoff, may he recover from his injuries quickly."

Brent laughed. "You know about that?"

"Of course. Who doesn't?" She gulped her *saké.* "He's a strange man. I don't understand his attitude toward you."

"I don't need to understand."

"I hear you gave him a severe lesson."

"He knew *karate,* but not enough."

Her mind changed direction, like a flipped card, to a subject Brent expected. "The Arab fleet's headed for Indonesia."

"The whole world knows that."

"Admiral Fujita will have to stop them."

"If they move north, Helen."

"They will, when you invade the Marianas."

"You're walking on egg shells again."

"Come, come, Brent. The whole world knows that, too."

He emptied his cup and dropped it into the saucer with a loud clatter. "It's not a subject for casual conversation."

"Sorry." She refilled both cups with the hot, spicy rice wine.

He drank half of the cup, and felt the welcome spread of warmth begin. Relaxing back into the cushions, he studied her. "What about you? You know all about me."

She drained her cup and refilled it. She seemed to be bracing herself. "I was born in Boston, into a perfectly normal, all-American family," she answered, her words edged with sarcasm and slippery with the effects of the *saké.*

"Normal American family?"

"Right."

He played the tease. "No offense, but if it was a normal American family, you're mother hustled or you're father was an alcoholic, or both."

Her smile was polite but tight. His humor had obviously missed the mark. Now they were both on egg shells. "Wrong. It was my father and he had other problems."

He stared at her silently. She continued, "He ran off with his secretary when I was sixteen."

"Normal enough," he said, feeling the *saké.* He recharged his own cup.

"His secretary was a guy."

"Oh."

Then it poured out of her. Her mother working long hours as a legal secretary to put Helen through Boston College. An affair with her history professor, a man twice her age. His divorce and abandonment of his wife and four children. Their marriage. His drinking. His new affair with an eighteen-year-old freshman. Her divorce. Transfer to Penn State, where she finally got her degree in journalism.

"And then you went to work for the United American Information Service?"

"Oh, no. First I worked for one of those tabloids you love so much."

"Which one?"

"The *International Inquisitor*—'The magazine for inquisitive minds'."

"Inquisitive minds?" Brent said incredulously.

She laughed. "You have another opinion?"

"I could suggest another slogan, yes."

"For twisted minds? For polluted minds, Brent?"

"You said it."

She stared at the intricate cherry blossom design on her cup. "You know Brent, reporters take a helluva beating."

"Oh?"

"We're one of the most despised groups on earth."

"Really?"

"We can't satisfy everyone and sometimes, anyone." He remained silent while she sipped. "I've been accused of writing outright lies, half-truths, curlicues, periphrases, concealment by silence, spurious candor, feigned openness . . ." She drank some more, "And just producing nothing but literary noise."

He laughed. "Nothing but foam whipped up on the river of facts, right?"

"You have a way with words, Brent. You should've been a reporter."

Brent almost slapped down the remark, but then took it for the compliment intended. "Thank you," he said simply. "And speaking of reporting, what did you find out in Tokyo at the conference with Boutros Boutros-Ghali, the North Koreans and—ah . . ."

"Indonesians, Chinese, Indians, Pakistanis and even a Sri Lanka delegation was there."

"Right, on nuclear bombs." He smiled wryly. "They all lied, didn't they."

"Through their teeth. The only honest man there was Boutros-Ghali."

"Face it, Li Penga and Kim Il Sung won't give up their bombs. If they get the chance, they'll throw them like marbles."

"Screwed up world, Brent."

"Now you're the philosopher."

She chuckled and they both drank and remained silent for a moment. "Gary Mardoff was there, too," Brent said.

She shook her head. "He was in Tokyo, but on another story." He looked at her quizzically. She continued, "He was doing a bit on missionaries." She smiled, a crooked kind of smile that made him uncomfortable. "He found out a lot and faxed me his report." She raised an eyebrow, "Would you like to hear what he reported? I'll get you his fax."

He waved her off. He already knew the contents and felt he was being baited. "Not necessary."

She sighed, took a deep drink and segued out of the awkward subject. "These cups don't hold much," she said, refilling both.

"Great stuff," he said, taking a small drink.

She moved closer. "You're great stuff, Brent Ross."

He stared down into the blue-gray eyes. They had changed, glowing as if backlighted by warm lamps. The look was so intense she seemed to be boring through him. She offered her lips. He hesitated and then leaned toward her. Then came the knock.

Helen sighed. "It's Mieko with our dinner." She moved so close her lips brushed his ear. "I can send her away."

"No. It's all right."

"You're hungry?"

"Famished."

Helen opened the door and Mieko pushed a cart into the room. Brent and Helen squatted down on the *zabutons.* "I don't see how you can squeeze those long legs under this table," Helen noted.

Buoyed by the prospect of food, Brent laughed boisterously. "I've had a lot of practice."

Mieko began to lay out the meal. It was in the *kaiseki* style of cuisine that had evolved in Kyoto and was elaborate by any standards. They started with *yudofu,* snowy cubes of bean curd in hot water. Then a seaweed-based broth filled with carefully carved shell fish. In all there were ten different dishes—seafood, rice and vegetables—served on wood, lacquer, pottery, ceramic, porcelain, bits of leaves. Brent shook his head in awe. No two were alike. All were beautiful.

Throughout the meal, Mieko moved like a wraith, sometimes standing, other times kneeling next to the diners. Each portion was offered as a gift, making the usual room-service attendants seem like amateurs. Finally, the dessert came; beautifully peeled grapes on a lacquered platter.

As the diners moved to the couch, Mieko swiftly cleared the table, loaded her cart, and exited smiling. Then Brent noticed a fresh carafe of *saké* was on the table. Helen poured.

"Satisfied?" she asked with obvious double entendre.

He chuckled into his cup. "Yes. That was wonderful."

She moved so close he could feel her hip nudge him. "A little special dessert to make it complete." Pulling his head down, she kissed him full on the mouth. Her lips were parted wide and her tongue touched the tip of his, then circled it, toying, tantalizing, traced his gums, the inside of his lips. It was maddening. Inflaming.

The dormant fuel ignited. It had been a long time. He pushed her back and ran his hand up to a hard breast. Her breathing quickened, but she pulled back and spoke into his lips, "Brent, that big one that got away."

"What the hell? What got away?" he asked, surprised and puzzled.

"In the East China Sea?"

Sitting bolt upright, he stared down at her. He couldn't believe her words. "What about it?"

"It was a trawler—it's in Surabaya being repaired."

"So what? And why now?"

"Because I want to know."

He dropped his cup, spilling some of the *saké*. "I can't believe you." He waved, an encompassing gesture. "All this. All this for a story?"

"No. No, I like you."

The heat of passion began to turn to anger, and he felt the flash point coming on, "Bullshit! You're working on me. The story! That's all it ever was, the story!"

"You don't understand. You said next time . . ."

His anger was unquenchable. Her words seemed to add fuel. He couldn't understand the firestorm that seemed to be sweeping him. It was Sally, guilt, disgust, frustration—all of it, a meld of emotions that burst through the dam. "I don't give a damn what I said. And I understand. All you can think of is a story. You have no morals, no scruples. You're not foam on facts, you're shit in a cesspool."

He began to rise but she pulled him back. His words

had stung. "No morals, is it? Shit, am I? Maybe you miss that little whore of yours. Do you want to know what Gary found out?" She tugged on his sleeve.

"No. I won't wallow in garbage. I don't want to know what Gary found out."

A malevolent grin wiped away the beauty and warped her face into a mask of anger and jealousy. Her voice was deep, harsh, and filled with spite. "She was arrested twenty-seven times for soliciting and . . ."

"Shut up and get your goddamned hands off me."

But she rushed on. "She was giving blow jobs in Hollywood alleys when she was fifteen for a snort of nose candy. Fucked a hundred johns by the time she was sixteen and used every kind of dope known to medical science—and washed it down with booze!"

"Shut up, I said."

She seemed not to hear him. "She shacked up with perverts that could even sicken Hollywood. One was Howard Cook, another was Nicholas Vance, the kinkiest sex maniac who ever lived. You name it and she can do it. Why, she could rewrite the *Kamasutra.* She'd make 'Deep Throat' look like Mother Teresa . . ."

The slap was almost a duplicate of the one that stung Gary Mardoff. Her head wrenched to the side with the sharp blow and the long hair flew out like a brown cloud. Crying out, she half fell, half hurled herself way from him, back down on the couch. Clutching her reddened face with both hands, she shouted into her palms. "Damn you! Damn you, you son-of-a-bitch! Leave! Leave, before I have you thrown out!"

Rising, he glared down at her. "Who's the whore? You'd fuck the devil for a story. At least Sally's honest about it—not a fuckin' hypocrite like you."

"I wouldn't fuck you if this world ran out of men. Go back to your little slut." Sitting up, she dropped her hands and grinned again—an evil smile burning with anger and vindictiveness. "Before you bang her, you'll have to pull Freestone off of her. There won't be room between her legs for both of you. Maybe you could try a *ménage á trois*. She'd be good at that."

Her laugh was wild and mirthless, like a wind born in the bowels of hell.

He grabbed his hat, punched his way through the door, and stomped down the hall. He could hear her laughter echoing behind him.

Fifteen
Reaching Cessation

"You have returned early from your leave, Brent-san," Admiral Fujita said from behind his desk.

"Yes, Sir," Brent said, shifting his weight in the chair and stretching his legs. "I felt I could be of service in the preparations for the assault."

"I understand you were involved in a few assaults of your own."

Brent pushed down on his armrests with his elbows and straightened his back. "Ah, yes, Admiral. I had some minor disagreements with a *Rengo Sekigun* and a reporter."

"Somewhat understated, Commander." The old man picked up a yellow sheet. "According to this police report that *Rengo Sekigun* was an American named Tobin O'Brien, and you seriously injured him—knocked out four teeth, lacerated his mouth, scraped off his ear and part of his cheek, broke his jaw, cracked three ribs."

"O'Brien attacked *me.*"

"Not according to this policeman," he glanced at the bottom of the report, "Lieutenant Yohei Kono. Lieutenant Kono claims you were trying to kill a harmless demonstrator."

"Kono didn't see it, Sir. He hates us. O'Brien is nothing but a filthy terrorist. He attacked me. I defended myself."

Sighing, the old man sagged back into his tunic that

appeared to be on the verge of swallowing him. "Brent-san, when are we going to learn to control that temper?"

Brent resorted to the most potent defense. He tilted his head toward the *Hagakure* at the admiral's right hand. "Sir, if a samurai is attacked, he is obligated to defend his honor by every means available."

"You teach *me* bushido, Brent-san?"

The young man tapped the tang of his Konoye blade. "I respect it, study it, Sir."

A slight smile cracked through the wrinkles, "But what about this reporter, Gary Mardoff? This is the man you warned me about. Was he attempting to kill you, too?"

"No, Sir. Worse. He insulted a woman. I slapped him. I would not dignify him with my fists."

"And then he kicked back?"

"Correct, Admiral, and then I took appropriate action."

"Appropriate action was a thorough beating."

"Negative, Sir. I only hit him three times."

"Unusual restraint."

"Contrary to what may be said about me, I do try to restrain myself."

"We investigated Mardoff. We have found no evidence that he is pro-Arab. Only that he can be a very abrasive investigative reporter."

"Abrasive, sir? He can come on like a mad dog. I feel he hates us, Sir. He deliberately antagonizes."

The old man raised his bony shoulders and let them drop again. He tapped a report. "His style, Brent-san." He turned his thin wrinkled lips under and leaned forward. "And the other reporter, Brent-san?"

"Other reporter, Admiral?"

"Yes. Helen Whitaker. Did you have a 'minor disagreement' with her, too?"

Brent was stunned. The old admiral had eyes and ears everywhere. But at the *Shibu,* too? Unbelievable. "Ah, yes, Sir. She was very insulting and I slapped her."

"You have delivered a number of slaps to the 'Fourth Estate'."

"Two, Sir. Both well earned."

"Perhaps it is wise you cut your leave short."

"Yes, Sir."

"Before you are killed."

Brent gestured at some other papers. "You have some other reports, Admiral."

"Yes. From Commander Matsuhara and Chief Kanemaru. They substantiate your claims." He picked up a pair of documents and waved them, "But I would expect that."

"They speak the truth, Sir."

"Of course, but I wanted to hear it from you, Brent-san."

"Militarily, I would expect that, Sir. I hope you are satisfied, Admiral."

"You know I do not hold reporters in high regard." Brent was forced to tighten his jaws, gulp hard to block the laugh that was trying to force its way to the surface. He had just heard the understatement of the century. The old man hated reporters almost as much as he hated politicians and Arabs. Yet, as the commanding officer, he was obliged to investigate the conduct of a member of his staff who had been in three fights in less than two weeks. Fujita continued. "But I must hold my officers to a high level of conduct." He smiled and quoted an American axiom, "Officers and gentlemen—is that not correct, Brent-san?"

Brent smiled back, "Correct, Sir. I strive to be a credit to *Yonaga,* Admiral."

"You are, Brent-san. I consider this matter closed."

"Thank you, Sir. Am I dismissed?"

"Negative." Thoughtfully, he ran a hand over an eroded cheek, gathering flesh like wet parchment, and then letting it droop back again. In time he spoke. "This woman who was insulted by that reporter, Mardoff?"

"Yes, Sir."

"She was that missionary woman—ah, Sally . . ." He scratched his head as if attempting to free a blocked thought."

"Sally Neverland, Admiral."

The old man pawed through some papers. Brent wondered how much he knew about Sally. After all, he had detailed information about Gary Mardoff and Helen Whitaker. Did he know all about Sally, too?

"Chief Kanemaru reports she represents some Christian splinter group, a cult."

Brent nodded. Apparently, this was one area where the old man had not been thoroughly briefed. He was certain that if Fujita had considered the matter important, he would have had a complete dossier on the girl. Quickly, he explained Sally's affiliation with "The Voice of God in Jesus" church. Her naivete and vulnerability. Her near starvation. The attack on her by the *Rengo Sekigun* woman. How he had fed her and protected her from Mardoff's insults. He avoided describing her years on the streets; not to protect her, but because it would have degraded Fujita's dignity to openly discuss such sordid matters without the old man first indicating he desired the information. And obviously, the C.O. was not interested in the girl's past—only what she was now, and how much she meant to Brent Ross. "Gossip is for women," Brent had heard the old sailor say many times. And Sally's past would be gossip.

The old sailor sat as implacable as a stand of petrified wood. Finally, he repeated an old sentiment. "These missionaries are as fanatical as *Rengo Sekigun.*"

"True, Sir. That is one aspect of my Christian background that embarrasses me."

"I did not mean that, Brent-san."

"I know, Sir. We have discussed this before." A fleeting riffle of confusion eddied across the old man's face. Had he forgotten? Was his memory slipping again? Brent had noticed a recent tendency to ramble, to repeat himself, to recall ancient events vividly, and sometimes completely forget yesterday's conversation. The erosion of age. A natural concomitant of the years? Certainly, they had discussed the inflexible, obstinate missionary zeal of Christian missionaries several time. Had the admiral forgotten it all?

"Ah, yes, I remember," the old man managed unconvincingly, as if aware of his own failings. And then with quickly regained composure. "You—ah, you are fond of this Sally Neverland?"

"I am concerned about her and she is important to me. Nothing more."

Fujita deflected the remark. "Nothing could come of this, Brent-san. She is a missionary. This could drive a man mad."

"I know, Sir. As I said . . ."

"Where is she?"

Brent sighed at the old man's intransigence. He was out to pursue a point, moot or not. He answered simply, "Traveling throughout Japan, Admiral."

"Saving souls?"

"Yes, Sir."

"Irrevocably dedicated to her cause." It was a statement, not a question. Brent remained silent while the old man changed his tack in his usual eccentric fashion. "You know, Brent-san, I see this fanatical dedication as a flaw in the western mentality."

Brent rose to the challenge. "A weakness, Sir?"

"As an example, the rise of Nazism was an outgrowth of this absolute devotion to one's cause."

"What do you mean, Sir? And what does this have to do with Sally Neverland and others like her?"

"Everything, Brent-san. Be it dedication to any cause you can suggest—Christianity, fascism, family, communism, obtaining wealth or converting the heathen," he smiled. "We heathen, I mean, the true believer is convinced that the true belief itself guarantees him salvation."

Now Brent was caught up in the old man's thinking. "Regardless of the nature or consequences of his actions, Admiral."

"Even if they lead to Dachau, Treblinka, Auschwitz, Babi Yar, the Gulag, Lubyanka, 'ethnic cleansing'." The old man let air escape through his pursed, wrinkled lips with a soft piping sound. "With this mentality, you can never expect this missionary to lose her zeal, Brent-san."

"I do not wish to change her, Sir. I am not trying to set up a liaison of any kind," Brent explained in near exasperation.

The old man was not convinced. "Regardless of what you say, I can see you prize this Sally Neverland, and you are young and you need a woman."

"I am fond of her, enjoy her company," Brent admitted. Then he shook his head, "But nothing can come of this, Sir." He pinched the bridge of his nose thoughtfully. "There is something else, Admiral, that has nothing to do with Sally's or any other woman's 'flaw'."

"And what is that?"

"My own fatal flaw. Evil *kamis* follow in my wake, Admiral, like hungry sharks. I must consider this in my relationship with any woman."

The old man clasped his hands behind his head and stared at the overhead. The eyebrows lowered and the forehead wrinkled. Again, the mercurial mind was off on another track. "Brent-san I know you have studied Zen. Have you ever reached suspension—cessation?"

Brent was taken by surprise, but was not unprepared. "The transcendent state of non-feeling? What does this have to do . . ."

The old man waved him off. "Yes. In this state, a man can realize his essential identity with ultimate reality."

Now Brent had picked up the thought. "The Zen of the monk Dōgen?"

"Very good, Brent-san. You always have a book open."

"I try."

"Then you know Dõgen understood the samurai, the problems of the warrior, the necessity to push your consciousness beyond the meaningless chaos of material life."

Brent nodded. "And, Sir, finally meditate oneself into the state where feeling is denied, obliterated for as long as the transcendence of meditation lasts."

Beaming, the old man expanded the thought. "True, Brent-san. Through transcendence a man can uncover the reasons for everything. Why red is red, and black, black. Why the human eye sees only the colors that objects have rejected. To grasp what lies beyond reason, beyond the perceived world."

"And to know my evil *kamis,* grapple with them, Admiral?"

"More than that, Brent-san."

"What, Sir."

"To vanquish them by knowing yourself."

Brent sagged back, almost in a concession of defeat. "I have tried, Sir."

"You must continue, Brent-san. You will reach it. I have."

Before Brent could respond, a knock interrupted. He opened the door and Rear Admiral Whitehead and Colonel Irving Bernstein entered. It was obvious from the expression on their faces that something of grave importance had happened. After greeting Brent and bowing to the admiral, the pair seated themselves. Whitehead spoke. "Admiral, Arab radio has gone mad—there has been a raid on a Libyan target by a B-24 Liberator . . ."

Brent interrupted, all thoughts of Zen banished. "That Liberator was *Shady Lady*?"

Bernstein fielded the query, "Yes. It was *Shady Lady.* That's the only B-24 we have."

Brent was transported back almost a year. *Shady Lady,* his Liberator. His mind's eye brought the crew back, tough, courageous fighters. The jolly, bombastic master pilot, J.R. "Bull" Ware; Devora Hacohen, copilot, Brent's lover who was murdered in her own shower; bombardier, the Englishman Horace Burnside; navigator, Kinnosuke Torisu; engineer, Michael Shaked; gunners, Philipe D'Meziere, Efrayim Mani, Oren Smadja, and Roland "Rollie" Knudsen. He remembered the flight from Tokyo to Israel, over 240 degrees of longitude. How the crew welded together, became a team, the genuine affection that grew with the approaching danger. The attack by Rosencrance, Stoltz and the killers of the *Vierter Jagerstaffel* over the Mediterranean, Knudsen's arm shot off, Smadja's brains blown all over the waist, *Shady Lady* severely damaged. How he agonized, screamed out his anguish into the slipstream and pounded the breech of his Browning until his fists hurt. Yes, it all came back. Vivid. Too vivid. And now *Shady Lady* had made her raid. He should have been aboard.

"Right. Your old crew, Brent," Whitehead said. "*Shady Lady* pulled a surprise raid on the nerve gas works in Libya." He fumbled with his notes.

Bernstein slipped in with the usual Mossad efficiency. "At Garyat az Zuwaytinah. Mossad reports she put in three tons of H.E. right down their throats. Uncanny accuracy with 'dumb' bombs. Completely wiped out the facility."

Brent could hardly contain himself, "*Shady Lady*—casualties?"

The Israeli became grim and his voice sank. "The copilot was wounded, the navigator and a gunner killed." He shook his head. "AA was very heavy and accurate. The Russians have been selling their best radar to anyone with the money."

"Colonel Ware?"

The Israeli smiled. "Not a scratch. In fact, he's planning his next mission."

Brent sighed out his tension. "Fighters?"

" 'Rosie' Rosencrance? His *Vierter Jagerstaffel*—Fourth Fighter Squadron? You want to know about him, Brent?"

"Of course."

Bernstein said to Brent, "They did not engage *Shady Lady*. In fact, Mossad reports the *Vierter Jagerstaffel* no longer operating in the Mediterranean theater. We have strong evidence they are based in the Marianas."

Fujita entered. "Of course. Tactically, it makes sense to place your best units where the danger is imminent."

Whitehead said, "Commander Matsuhara will be glad to hear this news. He has a personal score to settle with that butcher, Rosencrance."

"Willard-Smith shot in his chute," Bernstein recalled.

"And he butchered Munakata the same way," Brent reminded the Israeli.

Whitehead said, "Kadafi claims two schools destroyed by the raid and over a hundred children killed."

Everyone laughed. Fujita broke through. "Since when have we ever hit any target in Libya that was not a school, hospital, mosque or helpless civilians huddled under their beds?"

"And there is something else, Admiral," Bernstein said. "We have learned that Admiral Otto von Hanfstaengl is in command of the Arab battle group."

"Von Hanfstaengl," Fujita mused. "He was captain of *Daffah* when we sank her off Gibraltar."

"He is experienced and very capable."

"Not capable enough. We sank him."

"Right. But *Daffah* fought well."

"Indeed it did, but Hanfstaengl is impetuous and a gambler."

The Israeli stroked his spade-like Van Dyke beard. He was not convinced. "Ah, yes. But sometimes he can be very cautious. We saw this when he was a cruiser captain. He would fight and run—punished our escorts back in eighty-four in the 'Med', and again in the South China Sea. At best, Admiral, I would evaluate him as unpredictable."

"He served in the German Navy during World War Two and is an unrepentant Nazi," Whitehead said.

The Mossad agent glanced at a document. "Right, Admiral, joined the Hitler Youth in 1940, the navy in 'forty-two when he was sixteen and served on battle cruiser *Gneisenau* until the end of the war. He is quite bright and ended the war as assistant gunnery officer. He was officially 'denazified'—which is a lot of nonsense—and then served in the West German Navy until he retired in 1981."

Fujita said, "Then, when the Arab wars began, he joined Kadafi's forces."

Bernstein nodded agreement. "He's a classic Jew-hater and has adopted the Five Pillars of Islam. He's become a fanatic Muslim, prays five times a day, eats according to Arab laws, no smoking or drinking, and has added 'Hajj' to his name."

"So he's made the *hegira,* the pilgrimage to Mecca," Brent observed.

"Right."

"But he likes whores, Irving," Whitehead said.

"Of course. They all do."

"Fits all the parameters, all right," Whitehead said. "No shortage of hypocrisy." Chuckles filled the room.

"He eats, drinks, dresses and thinks like an Arab," Bernstein added. "Has accepted Kadafi as his Mahdi and is more fanatic than the most zealous Hezbollah. Why, he even has four wives."

"Four wives?" Whitehead said incredulously. "That's enough to derange anyone." Everyone chuckled.

Bernstein said, "More Arab than Mohammed. In fact, Kadafi has given him the Muslim name Hajj Sami Musallam. But, I understand, Hanfstaengl still prefers his German name—only uses Hajj Sami Musallam for ceremonial purposes."

"Regardless of this man's name, Kadafi has promised vengeance," Whitehead reminded everyone. "He promises a massive attack by his fleet."

Running a hand over the Hunnic contours of his shriveled pate, Fujita startled everyone. "This may be what we have been waiting for."

"What do you mean?"

"Let this Mussalam-Hanfstaengl move imprudently before we attack with our amphibious forces—before we are forced to protect our transports while engaging his battle group."

"He wouldn't attack us here, in Tokyo Bay—he wouldn't be that foolish," Whitehead observed.

"The Arab mind, Admiral, and Hanfstaengl thinks like one," Fujita said. "There is no affinity for rationality there. They would charge the gates of hell if their Mahdi ordered it. Again and again we have seen their bombers press home their attacks against *Yonaga* in the face of certain death." The peering nimble black eyes flicked to Bernstein and then to Brent. "Both of you have seen this in the desert again and again, at *Bren ah Hahd*, Zabib Pass. The human wave attacks, the reckless charge of tanks against emplaced artillery. We must remember, gentlemen, fanaticism is never allied with reason."

"Yes, yes, Admiral Fujita. We can expect the unexpected—but an attack on Tokyo Bay?"

"An overt move of some kind. It could be a sortie in force to attack our base on Iwo Jima, our fields on Kyushu." He fixed Whitehead with an unwavering stare. "And, yes, an attack on our home islands is not out of the question."

Whitehead shook his head. "Poor politically, Admiral Fujita, and Kadafi is a political animal. An attack on the home islands would finally unite Japan against him, force the Diet to support us directly instead of," he patted his

DOP—Department of Parks—shoulder patch, "calling us a public park to wangle appropriations."

Fujita pinched his thin lips. "Reasonable thinking, Admiral Whitehead. The old women of the Diet could be frightened into giving us the support we need without all this maneuvering and subterfuge. I dislike being a public park as much as you do."

He shook his head negatively, as if disagreeing with himself. "But, again, you are using the rationale of a sane mind. If we are to anticipate our enemy, we must throw out the logical and think like lunatics possessed by a mad religion—a religion based on 'The Five Pillars of Insanity'." He thumped the desk with knuckles like knobby raised roots. "Have you forgotten how this all began? How that Libyan DC-3 invaded our air space and Commander Matsuhara fired on it, punching a few holes in the wing?"

Whitehead nodded. "Of course I know, Sir. It was over ten years ago."

The old Japanese continued. "Then how rational was Kadafi's reaction?" The voice became bitter, "He massacred over a thousand people on the *Maeda Maru.* Have you forgotten the cruise ship slaughter? Embargoed oil. Started his jihad. Brought on this war. All over a few holes in the wing of an airplane." He threw out his arms in a gesture of frustration. "Madness! Madness! How can you anticipate such warped thinking?"

Whitehead looked at Bernstein, and then at Brent. Finally, he returned to Fujita. "You can't, Sir, you can't." Brent and Bernstein nodded and remained silent as Whitehead continued. "Then, Admiral, you believe we may engage much sooner than we first anticipated."

"Yes. We may have no more time than it takes the enemy battle group to fuel and take on stores at Surabaya."

"Could be a few days, maybe two weeks at the outside."

"Correct, Admiral Whitehead."

The old man came erect and a new gleam enlivened

the narrow eyes like shiny black currants. Fujita had caught the scent of battle. Brent saw it. He had seen it before. The old man was cranking up his emotions with the thought of combat.

"All leaves are cancelled and liberties restricted to the Yokosuka area. All ships are to be brought up to combat readiness." He stabbed a finger to the south. "Let them come. There is nothing I would welcome more."

"Hear! Hear!" Bernstein shouted. Brent added his, *"Banzai!"* Whitehead remained silent.

Fujita leaned back and smiled.

Sixteen
The Bait

The next two weeks were hectic. Reports of the enemy ships loading, fueling, and obviously preparing for sea propelled Fujita's preparations into a controlled frenzy. The media was alive with Kadafi's bellows of rage at the "barbaric attack by the enemy Liberator on our helpless women and children." The threats of retaliation were incessant. And the sinking of one of his *Gearings* by submarine *San Jose* was not forgotten. He promised vengeance for "this act of barbaric piracy," too. The American forces on Guam were brought to full alert, and work on *San Jose* was accelerated. Yet, despite threats and counter-threats, both the Arabs and Americans avoided open hostilities. Kadafi had his hands full with the Israelis and Japanese, the Americans were hard pressed to keep their allies supplied with oil. The hands on the oil spigots controlled the world and Kadafi had a firm grasp on the largest.

Brent was not only busy supervising the installation of new ESM equipment, but was called on by Lieutenant Commander Atsumi to help expedite the delivery of 25-millimeter shells for *Yonaga's* batteries of triple mount AA machine guns. Apparently, the two manufacturers were short of brass for the casings and delivery had fallen short. A contract had been let to the American Colt Firearms Company, but the shipment had not arrived.

He received letters from Sally Neverland almost every other day. She always told him she missed him and looked forward to seeing him again. And she praised Reverend Freestone's work "for Jesus" in every letter. She always closed with an accounting of the number of souls saved.

"Twenty-seven souls saved in Osaka." "Thirty-two souls saved in Kobe." Brent laughed out loud at the gullibility. What Sally and Freestone failed to realize was that the Japanese were born con artists. Most of these "saved souls" were chuckling behind the missionaries' backs. And those who were "saved," just added the Christian God to their pantheon of Eastern gods. Brent had actually seen the Virgin Mary and the crucified Jesus crammed into shrines with squat little Buddhas, the god of war Hachiman San, the god of the sea Watatsumi-no-Mikoto, Tora the Resolute Tiger, and a potpourri of icons, charms, and lucky talismans.

Brent was amused by the earnest naivete. And he wondered about Ezra "The Word" Freestone. There was no hint in Sally's letters that the reverend had made any advances on her. Maybe he was wrong, maybe Helen Whitaker had been wrong, too. And he did not hear a word from Helen. He knew she and Gary Mardoff had been snooping around Tsuchiura, Tokyo International, Maritime Self Defense Force headquarters in Tokyo and even Yokosuka. Something big was brewing and everyone knew it. Usually, the reporters were not seen together. However, he despised them both and gave little thought to their relationship, if there was one. Both were unscrupulous, unethical, morally bankrupt and were beneath his contempt.

Three weeks passed and the Arab fleet did not move. The 25-millimeter ammunition arrived. All ships were topped off with fuel and their magazines were filled. The fourth week passed and the Arabs were still lashed to their docks. Then, inevitably, impatience set in. The men became irritable. The pistol was cocked and primed, but the trigger was not pulled. War is an ordeal of waiting, and the inevitable frustration that comes with it. Men become bored, anxious for a break in routine that is sterile without the threat of the enemy. Hunger to break the routine grows. Battle, where the risks are mortal, becomes a welcome option.

But the delay also worked in Fujita's favor. Thirty-three troop transports, two command ships, ten LSTs, and twelve attack cargo ships were nearly ready for operations. Angered by Kadafi's threats and alarmed by the Arab bases less than two hundred miles from Guam, the U.S. Navy expedited the delivery of eighty-seven LCMs, instead of the grudgingly promised fifty-seven. In addition, two thoroughly reconditioned LSDs manned by "volunteers" steamed into the Inland Sea.

Everyone was elated by the LSDs. Of the old *Thomaston* class, the big 12,000-ton ships were each capable of landing twenty-one Abrams tanks with their LCMs, and still carry thirty LCVPs on their upper deck. They provided the mailed punch any amphibious force required. "Hah. Now we can land a full corps and armor," Fujita chortled. But everyone knew troops need months of training, practice landings on friendly sands before they could be blooded on hostile beaches.

And the Americans quickened the delivery of aircraft. A joyous Yoshi Matsuhara welcomed the promised twelve new Douglas AD-4 Skyraiders, and a full squadron of Grumman F7F Tigercats. Training was escalated, and the thunder of engines could be heard over most of Honshu, the eastern reaches of the Pacific, and the Inland Sea. Training missions were even flown over the Sea of Japan and Shikoku. Every man was bolstered by the booming new power overhead. Notwithstanding, the enemy remained tied to his docks.

Finally, after two months had passed without the enemy

budging from his wharfs, an exasperated Fujita realized he had misread von Hanfstaengl. He was faced with the cautious Hanfstaengl, not the impetuous fire eater. Militarily, it appeared von Hanfstaengl had made a wise decision. Because the amphibious forces posed the greatest threat to the Arab presence, he would not budge until the Japanese landing force was under way. And, in waiting, he would gain another crucial tactical advantage: Fujita would face the complex problem of protecting his transports, softening up the beaches for his landing craft with his big guns and bombers, and engaging the enemy fleet at the same time. An uneasy Fujita called a staff meeting.

Seated at the long table next to Yoshi Matsuhara, Brent was elated to see the white-haired, bull-necked escort commander, John "Slugger" Fite in his chair. With the exception of a slight limp, the hulking captain appeared completely recovered from his wounds. Also returning after nearly a year of mysterious duty, "somewhere in the eastern hemisphere," was the young CIA agent Elliot "Ellie" Amberg. Seated in a far corner, he studied some documents through lenses as thick as window panes.

Captain Paul Treynor, the C.O. of carrier *Bennington* and Captain Justin McManus, captain of *New Jersey*, were also present. McManus had brought an aide, a young gunnery officer, Lieutenant Walter Hoffman, with him. The other places at the long walnut table were occupied by the faces of the usual staff members.

Two strangers occupied chairs to Fujita's left. Both wore the uniform of the Self Defense Force. Fujita introduced the officers.

The first was Lieutenant General Ichiro Sago. A big-bodied, rugged-looking man, he had a bullet head, fleshy visage and hard, ruthless eyes that rummaged the face of every man in the room. Although he appeared to be in his mid-sixties, he carried himself with the rigid, military manner of a man twenty years younger. The second, Sago's aide, was Captain Gorsuko Uchimura. Less than half the general's age, the youthful captain was the antithesis of his senior, appearing awed and ill-at-ease in the presence of the fabled "Iron Admiral" and his legendary staff.

After introducing the two newcomers, Fujita addressed the staff. "General Sago is a career infantry officer and imminently qualified to lead our expeditionary force against the Marianas. He feels some mistakes were made in the attack in 1944 and has assured me he will avoid them. I have given him a free hand in planning the invasion and, like you, have yet to hear his plans." His eyes moved from man to man and the old face became very grim. "He is intimately acquainted with the invasion of 1944."

Nobomitsu Atsumi spoke out. "Intimately acquainted, Sir?"

"Yes, he was a sixteen-year-old private stationed on Tinian when it was invaded. He was an artillery observer."

The older Japanese looked at each other. Captain Mitake Arai blustered incredulously. "You fought on Tinian and you survived?"

Sago's jaw hardened. It was clear he was unintimidated by the mass of gold braid, staring faces, and legends. The surly twist of the lips, the mocking gleam in the eyes exposed a mammoth chip on his shoulder. Eyes boring into Arai's, his voice stormed out with enough force to fill the Imperial Kabuki. "Obviously, Captain, that is true." His diction was strangely guttural and he had trouble with his "t" sounds.

The ancient scribe, Commander Hakuseki Katsube, jerked erect and spoke out in a spray of spittle, "If you were defeated, why did you not take your life?"

The general swung to the scribe, acidly, scoffingly. "Have you ever been blown up by a sixteen-inch shell, Commander?"

"A sixteen-inch shell?"

"The *Colorado* took my battery under fire at Sunharon Bay. We were emplaced in a cliff east of Tinian Town, and I was posted in an observation bunker on the crest. A full broadside blew the whole cliff over and most of it slid into the harbor. I was knocked senseless. Woke up days later on the American hospital ship *Solace.*" He stabbed a finger. "Now, do you understand?"

"You did not attempt *seppuku?*" Arai taunted, revealing his own perennial chip.

"Of course I did," the general hissed back. "But the Americans were very watchful. I was not allowed to kill myself. They put me in restraints when I tried to hang myself."

"You could bite your tongue." All of the Japanese chuckled.

"I did. That is why my speech is impaired."

The men looked at each other. There were nods of understanding exchanged by the Japanese, uncomprehending looks by the others. Then Arai posed the question that was on everyone's mind. "Your plans for the attack. You would duplicate the American's invasion?"

Again, the ruthless disregard for the dignity and self-respect of others. "No. I do not duplicate stupidity."

Every American in the room straightened at the spiteful remark. Even Amberg looked up from his documents. Brent expected Fujita to intercede in a situation that was rapidly deteriorating, but the old man remained silent. He would let the arguments run, expose the old hates and prejudices to the fresh air of reason and hope they would wither and, perhaps, die away. And, anyway, Brent was convinced the old man enjoyed watching the heated dialectics. In fact, a slight smile twisted the pencil-thin lips. Brent had seen this look many times before. The belligerent general would remain unleashed and the vitriolic arguments would roll on.

Whitehead picked up the gauntlet, immediately igniting a fierce smoldering chemical reaction between himself and the general. "I was in the campaign with Task Force Fifty-eight, saw the planning, General. We took the islands, didn't we? What's stupid about that?"

"And threw away thousands of lives uselessly, Admiral. That is stupid."

Whitehead's eyes flashed cold blue light, like arcing electricity. His lips drew into a grim line and the rims of his fleshy nostrils flared and turned as white as sun-bleached bone. "And how would you improve on our attack?" he hurled back angrily.

"That is obvious. Take Tinian first, Admiral."

Everyone gasped, and a murmur swept the room. "Tinian first, General," Whitehead said. "But why?"

"Why did you assault Saipan first?"

"That's obvious. Because it was the tougher."

"And, obviously, that is precisely why I will attack Tinian first." He pointed to a chart of the Marianas on the side bulkhead and said to Fujita. "With your permission, Sir."

Fujita nodded his approval and the general walked to the chart, as rigid and stiff as a marionette. Stabbing a pointer at the chart, he showed everyone he had his own effective intelligence unit and had done his homework. "According to G-Four, the Arabs are expecting a repeat of the battle of 1944. Major General Ibrahim Mohammed Awad is in command of all forces in the Marianas, and his headquarters is in Garapan."

"We know that," Bernstein said. "Awad's stubborn, tenacious, and is quite willing to sacrifice his men in wholesale lots on a tactical whim, or to settle a grudge."

Sago nodded accord. "True, Colonel. He has the demeanor of a bull and the imagination of a barroom brawler." He circled Saipan with the rubber tip. "He has a formidable force. The Sixth Infantry Division, an armored regiment—fifty to sixty tanks—at least four batteries of 122-millimeter guns, and four or five 152-millimeter pieces covering the landing beaches fronting Charon Kanoa. They are dug in, hidden in caves, and some are in concrete emplacements. And you must remember Saipan is a natural fortress, mountainous with its best beaches protected by reefs. And here," the rubber tip struck the chart with a thump. "Mount Tapotchau is an ideal observation post. It's over five-hundred meters high . . ."

Fujita interrupted. "The language of our force is English. Use English units, General."

"Of course, Admiral." He looked at the Americans, "Over fifteen-hundred-feet high." He moved the pointer south across the narrow straits to Tinian. "But Tinian is flat and defended by only a brigade of infantry, two companies of combat engineers, and, perhaps, six batteries of field artillery. Most of the terrain is ideal for tanks. You Americans lost less than four hundred men taking it." Dropping the pointer, he stared at Whitehead and scoffed. "You should have taken Tinian, established your airfields on the kilometers—ah, acres of flat land. Emplaced your heavies and neutralized Saipan without throwing away over three thousand American lives and," bitterness stole in. "Over twenty-thousand Japanese." Whitehead remained silent, glaring and sullen. Sago had made sense.

Colonel Bernstein looked up from his documents. "General, Mossad reports a company of tanks has been shipped to Tinian—maybe eighteen Russian T-62s."

"We had suspected this."

"It's definite, General."

"The dive bomber commander, Lieutenant Oliver Y.K. Dempster, narrowed his strange almond eyes and spoke. "You said 'neutralize Saipan', General?"

"Of course, Lieutenant. A page out of your own General MacArthur's book of tactics. He was sickened by the hideous waste of lives on Saipan." His eyes moved from American to American, paused on each face, bored into each man. He continued. "His tactical vocabulary contained hateful words to us Japanese—'leap-frog', 'wither on the vine'. But he taught us a lesson and now we will use it. We will let the Arab garrison on Saipan starve and die under our bombs and artillery. We will not throw away one life uselessly." He thumped the table with coiled, pudgy fingers and leaned very close to Whitehead. "You derided our attacks, called them *'banzai* charges'. Ha! How do you think your Marines attacked us? Sometimes they came on without artillery preparation—straight into our Nambus and artillery."

The silence of swirling ashes filled the room. Staring at Sago and Whitehead, the men preserved it for an awkward moment. Finally, Whitehead spoke softly, voice ominously low and trembling with rage, "Don't you ever talk into my face like that—in that tone of voice!"

Everyone stared at the admiral. Fujita stirred, but remained silent. To Brent he seemed almost inattentive. Was the old brain somewhere else? Was it finally yielding to the years? And there was something wrong with the entire debate. They were not ready for an amphibious assault. Weeks of training still lay ahead. Certainly the senior officers knew this. But everyone in the room seemed caught up in this debate, as if the landings were to be made the next morning.

Sago came erect. "I will do whatever is necessary to achieve victory and conserve the lives of my men, Admiral Whitehead."

Whitehead sat fuming, face crimson, cheeks puffy as if the pressure were building up within his skull. *Vesuvius is about to blow,* Brent said to himself. But the old rear admiral had remarkable control.

Captain Justin McManus spoke out for the first time, "Tinian is not an easy place to invade, either, General. I was there on the *California* when she shelled the northern landing beaches—White Beach One and Two. They are narrow, very restricted landing sites." He stabbed a finger at the chart and spoke from experience. "Tinian breaks off into the water in a series of jagged cliffs, some one-hundred-fifty-feet high. Most are faced with coral, which can rip a man like knives. There are very few beaches suitable for LCVPs, LCMs, and tracked vehicles. The best are in Sunharon Bay in front of Tinian Town, but these are too obvious and easy to defend." Sighing, he shook his head. "In the northern half of the island, the coral drops off to about three to eleven-foot heights at the water's edge. There are a few narrow landing sites here, White beaches One and Two were two of them. We got a foothold there."

"I know, Captain. My staff is well aware of the tactical problems. We have spent months studying your invasion. Your own Navy Department has sent us thousands of documents. We have planned . . ."

Whitehead finally exploded. "You don't know what-in-the-hell you're talking about," he hurled across the table, rudely interrupting. "You're nothing but a goddamned loser and amateur playing soldier . . ."

Brent was astonished by Whitehead's outburst. He was usually controlled, discreet and diplomatic. The old warriors, the old hates. Old men never forget. He had seen it many times in this room. And now the same scenario had been played out. And he knew another element had entered: the massive egos of those who command were in collision. Hubris that had driven men like Douglas MacArthur, Irwin Rommel, Bernard Montgomery, George Patton, Chester Nimitz, Wilhelm Keitel, Hermann Goering, and dozens of others permeated the room with a palpable force. Prestige and pride were at stake. Nothing was more important to men who command men. It was time for Fujita to act.

And Fujita did finally intervene, stopping the American admiral with a raised hand and voice. "Gentlemen, enough! We are not here to open old wounds. The Greater East Asia War ended almost a half-century ago. Now we have a common enemy to kill before we kill each other."

"Hear! Hear!" *"Banzai!"*

While Whitehead fumed and knotted his fingers together in his own personal turmoil, Sago returned to his chair and looked at Admiral Fujita. Ignoring Whitehead, the general said in an even, collected voice. "I need at least three months to train my troops in amphibious warfare. Some have never even ridden in a LCVP before. Integrate the LSDs into my order of battle. Coordinate the armor with my assault troops. We have new Abrams tanks, but some of my crews have never seen a LCM. We must work on our communications—why, my Beachmasters have never made a landing under fire before." He waved. "I know nothing of my fire support. Will *New Jersey* support us? How many destroyers will bombard the beaches, and . . ."

Fujita halted him with a perfunctory wave. "We are not here to discuss an invasion as our next strategic move."

The men looked at each other in astonishment. Sago appeared stunned. "But Admiral, after all this? Why did you let me . . ."

"I let you discuss these plans because every man on this staff must be aware of your plans—your tactics for the invasion."

"But not the details, Admiral?"

"Yes, General. Those unit-by-unit, objective-by-objective plans will wait for our second sortie."

"And the first?"

"We will get underway in a week, seek out and destroy the Arab fleet if we have to steam into Surabaya to do it."

"Banzai!" echoed throughout the room, punctuated by "Hear! Hear!"

"Then you won't need me."

"On the contrary. I am delaying a week so that you

can load your transports. I want thirty-three troop transports, eight attack cargo ships, two control ships, both LSDs, and all ten LSTs to put to sea."

"Only thirty of my troop transports are ready for sea."

"So be it. That will be enough."

"But why? We are only partially trained, Admiral. We have the equipment now, but we are not ready!"

"The enemy does not know this and if you will remain silent, I will explain my plan, General."

Rising, Fujita straightened slowly, as if his spine were made of rusty metal. He picked up the pointer and stabbed a chart of the Western Pacific. "Your forces are training here, in the Inland Sea." Sago nodded. Starting at Tokyo Bay, Fujita traced a line southward. "Since the battle group must steam over thirteen-hundred miles south to rendezvous with you off the Bungo Suido, you will put to sea three days after the battle group clears Tokyo Bay. We will call this our H-hour. Then, with the battle group leading, we will cut a course southeast. When enemy reconnaissance spots your transports, von Hanfstaengl will have no options. He must put to sea and fight his way through us to reach you. This was the problem the Imperial Navy faced in 1944."

Brent rubbed his temple and nodded. So, the old brain still functioned like a computer programmed for war games. And, obviously he had been studying the lessons of 1944. A young, drunk Lieutenant Tokuma Shoten had once enthused after one of their greatest victories in the Mediterranean, "The old man is a military genius. He's an Alexander, Hannibal, Genghis Khan, Tamerlane, Napoleon, Lee, von Moltke, von Clauswitz, and Rommel rolled into one. He could teach them *all* lessons." Several of the officers had chuckled at the exalted company, but no one had tried to argue with Shoten's analogy. Despite the overload of *saké,* there was some truth in what he had said.

"I could take heavy losses," Sago insisted.

"Negative. You will retire after Hanfstaengl is committed."

"Committed?"

"Within range of my bombers, General."

Sago still appeared disconcerted. "But embark my divisions? My tanks?"

"Correct."

"But, they are going nowhere. Only into harm's way for nothing."

"Not for nothing."

Sago showed his backbone and his concern for his command. "Why not send the transports out empty, Admiral? Not risk my men. We could march them aboard in the daylight and off-load them at night."

The old man shook his head in rejection. *"Rengo Sekigun* spies watch your every move, and the empty transports would ride too high. This would be noticed by the trained eye. We must make this ruse as authentic as possible. Do not forget, they even use night glasses. They would spot your ruse. You will carry full combat loads."

"My men will be taking a terrible risk."

"When has there ever been a war fought without risk?"

"Then all this," he raised an arm that included everyone in its sweep. "All this was for nothing. You just wanted to tell me you would use my forces as bait."

This time Brent expected Fujita to add his explosion to Whitehead's. But the old man retained his composure. Apparently, he liked Sago's panache and élan as much as Whitehead and Arai despised it. "That is correct. Bait, but not for nothing. You will give Admiral Otto von Hanfstaengl no choice. It will appear to him that a full scale invasion is underway. If he hesitates, Kadafi will order him into action, anyway. Then, when the Arab fleet sorties we will destroy it in the great final battle all samurai seek."

"Banzai!"

Sago did not join the celebration. He was still disconcerted. "My escorts? I have not seen a single destroyer in the Inland Sea."

Fujita gestured to John "Slugger" Fite. The big, round escort commander came to his feet. "I have twenty-seven destroyers, twenty-six *Fletchers* and *Haida*. We also have two survivors of the Maritime Self Defense Force, cruiser *Ayase* and destroyer *Yamagiri*. I will detach fourteen of my command to escort you."

"Air cover?"

"Fighters from *Yonaga* and *Bennington*," Fujita said.

The general was no fool. "If you engage, we could be left uncovered, vulnerable to Mohammed Awad's bombers in the Marianas."

Fujita indicated Commander Yoshi Matsuhara. The air group commander stood, and then walked to the chart. Picking up the pointer, he stabbed an island of bitter, bloody memories to everyone in the room. "I have two of my best squadrons of long-range Zero-sens based here on Iwo Jima, about five-hundred miles from the Marianas. They can give you cover. Also, I will send our new squadron of Grumman F7F Tigercats to join them."

"Then I will have a continuous CAP?" Sago asked.

"Continuous, *and* coordinated with the battle group's fighters," Yoshi assured him.

Captain Mitake Arai threw Yoshi a puzzled look. "Why not fly those Tigercats from our carriers. It would add great firepower and durability to our fighter squadrons."

"It is a big, heavy plane with two engines and I will not have time to adequately train the squadron in carrier operations."

"How heavy? How big?"

"Almost twelve-thousand kilograms—that is, about twenty-five-thousand pounds, and it has a fifty-one foot wingspan."

Arai pulled on his flat nose. "That is a big—a big aircraft for our deck crews and equipment to handle."

"Yes," Yoshi agreed. "When you consider my heaviest fighter is the Hellcat, at about thirteen-thousand pounds."

Lieutenant Commander Nobomitsu Atsumi entered. "And we have had accidents with our arresting gear hooking up to the Hellcat. We would have to refit to handle this monster you call 'Tigercat'."

"True, Commander," Yoshi said. "But we are expecting new arrester gear from the Americans to arrive any day."

"Commander Matsuhara," Fujita said impatiently. "What is the range of this Tigercat?"

"The new Pratt and Whitney is a miser. With its huge drop tanks, more than two-thousand miles."

There were whistles and excited rumbles.

"Then this Tigercat could support the battle group after the transports have withdrawn to the Inland Sea."

"TOT would be as long as our carrier-based fighters."

Katsube sprayed, *"Banzai!"* Then his head dropped to the side, as if his shriveled neck had been broken. Atsumi propped him up with a single hand to his shoulder.

Sago interrupted. "Admiral, may I be excused? I have much work to do to meet your H-hour."

"No, General. Every matter discussed in this room affects your forces. You will remain."

"But, Admiral, there is too much . . ."

Fujita's voice had iron in it, "You will remain!"

"I protest." There was no fear, no intimidation.

"Protest all you like, General. Remain in your chair."

Incensed, Sago glared at Fujita with eyes burning with resentment. He glanced at his aide, Uchimura, but remained silent. Whitehead and Arai, reveling in Sago's embarrassment, exchanged a gloating look.

Brent looked at Matsuhara and whispered in his friend's ear. "Sago's a tough old bird."

"Got backbone. A hawk, a real hawk."

Fujita turned to lieutenant Oliver Y.K. Dempster, and opened a new subject. "Your dive bombers, Lieutenant?"

"All are powered up with the new *Sakae Arashi,* and all aircraft are equipped with a single rear-firing 50-caliber Browning machine gun," Dempster said. He licked his lips like a hungry man looking at a gourmet dinner. "The twelve AD-4 Skyraiders, Admiral. They will fall under my command?"

Instead of answering Dempster, Fujita turned to Yoshi, "The range of this Skyraider, Commander?"

"Fifteen-hundred miles, with a full load."

"Take off weight?"

"Seventeen-thousand pounds."

Fujita returned to Dempster. "Does that answer your question, Lieutenant?"

"It's too heavy."

"Correct. And with its range, we would be foolish to use it as a carrier-borne aircraft, off-load twelve of our own bombers to make room for them. The Skyraider squadron will fly from Iwo Jima."

"Banzai!"

Dempster waved at Captain Paul Treynor. "*Bennington* operates six Skyraiders."

Treynor answered, "You know I operate the AD-1, Lieutenant. It's lighter than the 'Four' and remember, *Bennington's* arrestor gear is built for much heavier duty than *Yonaga's*."

Dempster scowled, nodded and remained silent. There was no argument. Fujita turned to Yoshi Matsuhara, "The crews of these new bombers?"

Matsuhara said, "They are all manned by volunteer American crews. Ultimate professionals. Some of them flew in Vietnam."

"Five tons of ordnance each?"

Yoshi smiled, "With the new engine, six."

There was a babble of excited voices. "That's more than the old B-17 could carry," Fite said in awe.

Fujita moved on to another area. "Torpedo bomber commander."

Lieutenant Akira Terada answered. "All of my Nakajima D-3As are also ready with the new twenty-five-hundred horsepower *Arashi* and all aircraft are armed similar to our dive bombers."

"Very good."

"Admiral," Terada said with a troubled look. "I need a more modern aircraft. My D-3As are slow and easy targets for fighters. The Americans have a new torpedo bomber based on the Grumman AF Guardian. I understand both Grumman and General Dynamics have started production. It is a big plane, fast, heavily armed, and a great attack aircraft. The original design could carry two torpedoes or two tons of ordnance. The new model must be a much more formidable aircraft."

Matsuhara spoke up. "I have been in contact concerning the Guardian. The Americans are short of torpedo bombers for their thirteen carriers." He turned up his hands in a hopeless gesture. "We will have to wait."

"And my men will die."

"And so will mine, Lieutenant Terada."

This time Admiral Fujita nipped the budding argument before it could erupt. "The argument is academic. We will engage the enemy with our current equipment. After we destroy the enemy, we will pursue this matter further." He thumped the table impatiently and said to Whitehead, "According to latest intelligence, the enemy has some new aircraft based in the Marianas. Does NIC have any more intelligence?"

Whitehead, still flushed but apparently composed, nodded at the taciturn CIA agent, Elliot Amberg. Amberg sat so unobtrusively, Brent had forgotten he was in the room.

"Mister Amberg has the latest information from the CIA," Whitehead said.

Self-consciously, the small, pale young man stood. Looking at Amberg, Brent almost laughed. Nervous green eyes, skin as pale as an Alpine ski slope, electrified yellow hair that sprang out like Don King's. The man was the antithesis of the secret agent, an embarrassment to the image created by Sean Connery's 007. But he was efficient and, it was rumored, a ruthless killer.

Adjusting his glasses with short jerky movements, he spoke in the high piping voice of the high school senior. "We have reports," he glanced at a document. "That a single squadron of that deadly little Focke Wolf 190 is based in the Marianas. Also, we count three squadrons of ME-109s, two squadrons of JU-87 Stukas, an assortment of North American Texans. And, just delivered, a new squadron of Heinkel He-111 bombers. All of these aircraft are dispersed on both islands, most in concrete revetments."

Bernstein snickered. Brent expected the perennial Mossad-CIA competition. He was not disappointed. "Not quite accurate, Elliot. There are ten, not a full squadron of twelve Heinkel 111s, *and* we have reliable reports that a half-dozen Fairey Barracuda torpedo bombers are ready to fly against us."

Groans and angry oaths.

"International arms dealers," Fujita muttered. "The pariahs of civilization. If you have enough money, you can buy anything."

"True, Sir," Amberg said. He looked at Bernstein. "We also picked up a rumor that the Heinkel 100 fighter has been shipped to the islands."

Brent looked at Whitehead, and stared into a face as surprised as his. But Yoshi Matsuhara was not surprised, only angered. "Are you sure?"

"A highly reliable source."

"How reliable?"

"An agent on the island."

Yoshi nodded. "This Heinkel fighter was designed to be the successor to the Messerschmitt Bf-109."

Fujita showed his encyclopedic mind. "A very formidable fighter. Held the world absolute speed record of four-hundred-sixty-three miles per hour as early as 1939. But, Hitler favored Messerschmitt, and the Heinkel 100 died in the morass of Nazi politics. The Allies were fortunate, indeed."

More murmurs. "Another brilliant decision by Adolph Hitler," someone at the end of the table muttered.

Amberg continued. "It's small, like the FW-190. This new version has a Daimler-Benz, DB-601R engine, top speed is four-hundred-ninety miles-per-hour, and is quite maneuverable."

Everyone stared at the young man silently. Even the usually well-informed Bernstein did not challenge the CIA man. Despite his obvious triumph over Mossad, Amberg's face remained as placid and composed as a block of ice.

"How many?" Yoshi asked.

"Probably eight or ten. Production is very slow."

"We will kill them, too," the air group commander muttered.

"Banzai!"

Captain McManus broke his silence. Like Amberg, he had sat through most the meeting like a spectator at a sporting event. "Admiral Fujita," he said. "I'm a battleship sailor, have spent my life firing big bullets and know very little about carrier warfare." He glanced at some figures on a pad before him. "But, Admiral, I count fifty-eight enemy fighters and fifty bombers, minimum, based on Saipan and Tinian."

"Correct."

"That's like facing another carrier, Sir. Another carrier that can't be sunk."

"Good analogy, Captain McManus. What is your point?"

The captain tapped his pad with the point of his pencil. "My point is this, Sir. We will face three carriers that must carry over two hundred planes, and at the same time we must engage over a hundred land-based aircraft. We'll be outnumbered."

The staff exchanged glances, and then every eye was focused on Fujita. The same question had troubled all of them, but a battleship sailor was the first to articulate it.

"Captain," Fujita said, "we will not engage both forces at the same time."

Terada came to his feet, stabbing a finger at the chart. "But how can we avoid . . ."

Fujita halted him. "Please find your seat, Lieutenant!" Fuming, Terada dropped back into his chair. Fujita moved slowly to the chart, as if every joint was creaking and rubbing like sand paper. Stabbing with the pointer for emphasis, he said. "We will lead our transports on a wide sweep, here—to a point northwest of Eniwetok Atoll. This will keep us over six-hundred miles from Saipan and Tinian."

"Out of range of the Marianas aircraft?"

"Correct, Captain McManus. And remember, the enemy abandoned his base in Tomonuto after our last raid. So there will be no threat there." He pulled thoughtfully on the single white hair hanging from his chin. "The Heinkel He-111 is their longest ranged bomber. But it was designed for European distances, and its range is under a thousand miles."

Whitehead injected. "Admiral they have some LRAs—a Globemaster and a DC-6 or two. They will spot us."

"I know. I am counting on being spotted by their LRAs or submarines."

"Then von Hanfstaengl must act," Whitehead said.

"Correct. I do not want to engage in the narrow waters between the Celebes and Java."

Sago came to life. "You would steam that far south?"

Fujita drew another line. "If necessary, we will steam south and west through the Carolines, leave Truk and Tomonuto to port and split the waters between Palau and Yap."

There was an excited babble of voices. Sago's voice snapped through with disbelief. "With my transports astern?"

"Yes."

Sago slapped his forehead. "But Admiral, why? Why?"

Fujita fielded the challenge calmly. "Because Von Hanfstaengl will not know if we intend to turn on the Marianas, or make an assault on his fleet in Surabaya, or both. In any event, he cannot afford to be caught at his moorings. He will be trapped in the dilemma of trying to decide what we will do, where we will land. He must consider an amphibious attack on Surabaya and the threat to oil production on Borneo as not being out of the question. We would be justified. The Indonesians have been openly hostile to us."

He halted, as if to catch his breath like a long distance runner nearing the finish line. Sago stared silently.

Leaning with his back against the bulkhead, Fujita continued as if he were having a dialogue with Sago. "You need not be concerned about taking your force so far south. Hanfstaengl is a clever commander and will never allow us to approach his base so closely. In any case, he must put to sea and I anticipate he will sortie long before we make our southern sweep. I expect him to give battle when we approach Eniwetok."

He tapped the table as he spoke. "Then, your transports will retire and we will fight him on our terms."

"Banzai!" "Hear! Hear!"

McManus spoke up. "Destroy his fleet, and then attack the Marianas."

The old man dropped the pointer, missing the tray. The long stick clattered on the deck. Fujita looked too fatigued to even bother with the pointer. Brent wondered if the old man could bend enough to pick it up. Quickly, Brent scooped up the pointer, placed it in its tray and returned to his chair. Fujita walked unsteadily to his seat and seemed to collapse in it. The fire generated by the impending battle was gone. The bright, almost feverish glint snuffed from his eyes. Age had caught up with him. It seemed to be overwhelming him.

Uneasy and concerned, every man stared at the admiral. He sat quietly for a moment, head down, hands in front of his chest as if he were holding a ball. Nothing but the rumble of auxiliary engines, the faint pounding of shipwrights two decks below, and the whine of blowers could be heard. Finally, the old man looked up and dropped his hands to his sides. The closing prayer was mandatory and everyone knew it. They must wait. Whitehead coughed, Sago and Uchimura fidgeted. The rest of the men sat like slabs of marble.

Finally, struggling out of his chair, Fujita faced the paulownia wood shrine on the opposite bulkhead. The shrine—built like a tiny log cabin that had been sliced in half by a berserk samurai—contained some new icons. Now, keeping company with the mandatory gold Buddha were the god of wealth, Daikoku—who was seated on rice bales—and the god of good fortune, Ebisu, holding a fish. The tiger, who was admired for wandering far, making his kill, but still returning to guard his home ground, was represented by a glistening black cat, crouching as if ready to leap.

Everyone stood. Fujita clapped twice to attract the attention of the gods. The Japanese and Brent also clapped. Fite, Treynor, McManus, Sago, Uchimura, and Hoffman stared at Brent curiously. Whitehead shook his head. Amberg's face was blank. Bernstein and Yoshi grinned.

Calling on the great power of Shinto, Fujita spoke in a gravelly monotone. "Oh Izanagi and Izanami, whose love gave birth to our islands, earth, sea, mountains, woods, nature herself, join with your descendant, Emperor Akihito, to anoint our arms in the struggle to come." Then the homage to Buddhism. "Let our cause polish our karmas through energetic striving, pure motives, and inner serenity." He arched an eye toward Brent. "Let us find the highest level of tranquillity by eradicating desire, passionate craving, and attachment. Let the turning of the Wheel of the Law bring victory to our arms." He glanced at Bernstein.

Standing, the Israeli placed a yarmulke on his head. He quoted Exodus with centuries of bitterness in his voice. " 'He that smiteth a man, so that he die, shall be surely put to death. An eye for an eye, tooth for tooth, hand for hand, foot for foot'." He stared up at the overhead and implored. "Give us the courage of David, the wisdom of Solomon, the vision of Moses and let the tyrant know this—he cannot escape the vengeance of God for the fire and brimstone will rain on him, wherever he may hide." The Jew sat.

Fujita nodded at Rear Admiral Whitehead. Whitehead spoke solemnly. "Oh, Lord, help us in this moment of trial. Show us the way to defeat this unholy enemy, who would drag mankind into the depths of hell. In the name of the Father, the Son, and the Holy Ghost."

A chorus of "Amens" filled the room. Brent added his and several confused looks were cast his way. Yoshi chuckled under his breath. Whitehead concluded with the Lord's Prayer. " 'Our Father which art in . . .' " All the Christians joined him including Brent.

When the prayer was finished and the Christians had found their seats, Fujita said wearily, "Gentlemen, it is time to close this meeting. Return to your duties and be prepared to get under way in seven days." He stared at Lieutenant General Sago for a long moment. Sago stared back unflinchingly. The old man let air escape from his lungs in a low sighing sound and said, "You are dismissed."

Sagging with his head down, the old admiral sat with his hands clasped on the table. Quietly, the officers stood, bowed, and filed from the room. Sago was the first man out, with a distraught Captain Uchimura on his heels.

Fujita seemed unaware.

Seventeen
The Son of Heaven

The next week was hectic for Brent Ross, as last minute preparations were made for getting underway. Distracting him was a steady stream of letters from Sally Neverland. She and Freestone were hard at work for the Lord. Apparently, legions of souls had been saved in Okayama, Hiroshima, Fukuoka, Miyazaki and Kumamoto. At least Sally was convinced of this.

"We'll be in Yokosuka soon," she wrote. "There are many lost souls amongst the sailors who dwell there." Brent chuckled. There was certainly truth in that statement.

As her mission progressed, her ardor seemed to grow. She was still anxious about the status of Brent's salvation. Her letters repeatedly stated her concern for, "lost souls," including his. She promised to show him, "The one true way" the next time she saw him. There was no shortage of the Biblical quotes she loved, her last letter concluding with a verse from Ephesians: " 'One God and Father of all who is above all, and through all, and in you all.' "

Obviously, there was no change in her attitude, and she was still consumed by her sacred calling. Still, he was uneasy with Freestone. "Too damned many charlatans in that business," he told himself. But his concern for the girl was overwhelmed by the demands of his duties.

He spent most of his time in CIC. Here Rear Admiral Whitehead and Lieutenant Giovanni Castagnini joined him, supervising the installation of new equipment and training personnel. And there was a problem with their basic code. It was feared "Green Alpha," the computerized fleet code used for top secret transmissions, had been broken by the Arabs.

Breaking a computerized code was an arduous, complex procedure. But any code developed on a computer could be broken, in time, by other computers if they could "chew on it" long enough. Mossad repeatedly warned Arab main frames in Tripoli, Alexandria and Damascus were on the verge of breaking through "Green Alpha." It was suspected some Russian brutes were also attacking the code. "You can never trust Moscow, regardless of who is in the Kremlin," Bernstein had warned. It was time to change.

A new "Purple Alpha" code was developed by the Israelis and the CIA. Only Rear Admiral Whitehead, Brent Ross, Giovanni Castagnini, and Colonel Bernstein were conversant with the new code. Well masked, it was computer generated, expressing the English alphabet as a ten-figure sub-routine which, in turn, was based on random combinations and permutations of a twelve-figure master. The master would be changed randomly to confuse the enemy.

Decoding was made painfully complicated. The cryptographer needed an eight-figure digital control code governed by the moon phase, a base key-number which changed daily, and Greenwich Civil Time of reception, minus two, before he could even begin his search for the sub-routine and the twelve-figure master. It was complex and very formidable. Still, with time, "Purple Alpha" would be compromised. "That's the facts of life," Whitehead had muttered one afternoon in the eerie yellow-red glow of CIC. "Then we change the whole goddamned thing again."

"Si, si," Castagnini agreed. *"Brutta bestia."*

Whitehead, still in a vile mood after his argument with Lieutenant General Ichiro Sago, blistered. "What the hell was that?"

"Ugly damned animal," Brent translated.

"Why in hell don't you say so Castagnini, and stop talking in your own damned code?"

"Si, Ammiraglio—ah, yes, Admiral."

Whitehead slapped his forehead with an open palm, "Jesus Christ, a man's got to be a linguist and a mind reader to serve on this goddamned ship."

The Italian hung his head like a dog that had been kicked for leaving something naughty on the living room floor. Later, Brent patted him on the back and said. "You're doing okay, shipmate. Okay."

Castagnini had smiled wistfully, "Okay, *si?*"

"Okay, yes."

Purple Alpha software and "hard-wired" encryption boxes had to be delivered by an officer/messenger to all ships in the flotilla. This job was assigned to Castagnini and Brent. Escorted by four seamen guards armed with M-16s, Brent delivered the equipment to *New Jersey* and a dozen escorts. Whitehead flew to Hiroshima to personally hand the equipment to Lieutenant General Sago, and no doubt, continue his personal war.

While Whitehead was in Hiroshima, Admiral Fujita was summoned to an audience with Emperor Akihito. He left early in the morning. Rigidly erect and wearing his old-fashioned dress blues, that dated back to the old Imperial Navy, the old man marched proudly from the elevator to the quarterdeck. Staring straight ahead, he stepped as briskly as his arthritic joints would permit through ranks of officers and men.

Standing at attention between Castagnini and Atsumi,

dressed in his number one blues with white gloves and sword, Brent watched the old sailor approach. Only on three other occasions had Brent seen the admiral dressed so splendidly. The first two were when he was summoned by Emperor Hirohito, and the third was just after Akihito assumed the throne, and he had his first audience with the new Emperor. These were the only times he had left the carrier in fifty-three years.

Watching Fujita pass, Brent noted everything was correct for 1941; for an era long dead, a navy rusting on the bottom of the Pacific. In fact, the uniform would have been appropriate for a figure in Madame Tussaud's Wax Museum. Single breasted, the tunic had five polished brass buttons that glowed like gold, slash pockets and hook and eye fasteners. The stand collar was wide with black lace trim and a single gold stripe. Black lace was repeated on the front and skirt of the tunic and pockets. More heavy folds of lace layered the cuffs, with four cherry blossoms designating admiral's rank. The shoulder boards, too, boasted four cherry blossoms. Three gold lace rings circled his field cap, and a large gold sixteen-petaled imperial chrysanthemum, which was worn only by *Yonaga's* officers, sparkled proudly on the cap's badge. His black boots were polished to mirror-like intensity. To complete the recondite aura of the samurai, the admiral's right hand pushed down on the tang of his sword with just enough pressure to give the blade the correct parade-ground angle.

Followed by his executive officer, Captain Mitake Arai, Fujita stepped as briskly as his stiff joints would permit through the ranks of seamen. He stopped at the head of the accommodation ladder. At that moment, two-hundred booted heels clashed together with a report like a pistol shot as seamen guards, in dress blues and flat hats, presented arms. Then the tweet and squeal of boatswain's pipes, the low beat of ruffles from a pair of drummers working their sticks like staccato gun blasts. Completing the cacophony of pomp and circumstance were the flourishes of a quartet of trumpeters. The whole spectacle smacked of Cecil B. DeMille hamming up a script by C.S. Forrester.

Yet, Brent found nothing amusing in the Byzantine ceremony. Gazing at the little admiral, he was forced to choke down an Adam's apple that was suddenly as large as a rock, and blink the mist from his eyes.

He heard Castagnini mutter, *"Dio mio, veramante magnifico."*

Brent nodded. "Yes, Lieutenant. *Yonaga* still knows how to put on a show."

Brent watched as the duty officer bowed to the admiral and Fujita nodded back. Then the mandatory turn aft, a quick salute to the colors, and the old man stepped onto the accommodation ladder. There was more screeching of boatswain's pipes, ruffles and flourishes. And then, *"Banzai Fujita!"* was thundered by hundreds of throats three times in succession. The old man nodded, turned and started down the ladder. Stumbling, he gripped the rail. Atsumi stepped forward and offered a hand. Fujita refused it, and managed the ladder by himself. Then, flanked by seamen guards, he walked to the waiting limousine.

Preceded by a truck-load of seamen guards, and followed by two more, the car drove off. All escorts had red lights and sirens. Suddenly *Yonaga* rumbled, as if an explosion was building in her magazines. It was the sound of thousands of boots striking steel decks. Then two thousand crewmen lining the rails, and AA gunners standing by their weapons, began screaming. *"Banzai Fujita!"* This was spontaneous, a pledge of homage, veneration, affection unleashed. The cheering did not stop until the limousine vanished in the maze of warehouses and shops. Only then, the tumult faded and the ranks melted away.

"Viagie—ah, the *ammiraglio* travels *elegante, Commandante,"* Castagnini muttered in admiration.

'He's the consummate samurai," Brent said.

'As long as he lives, bushido lives," Atsumi said.

"Vero parolae," Castagnini said.

Brent chuckled. "Amen."

The three officers walked to the elevator.

The next day Brent was summoned by Admiral Fujita to give a report on the state of readiness of the CIC. Brent expected him to be euphoric, in a state of elation after his visit with the Son of Heaven. Instead, he was reserved, stiff, and far more formal than usual. Brent wondered what had transpired at the meeting, why the admiral appeared almost dejected.

While Brent proceeded with his report, the admiral listened attentively. One of his telephones rang. Fujita put the instrument to his ear. "Have them report to me," he said, and then dropped the phone back into its cradle.

He looked at Brent. "You can complete your report later."

"Am I dismissed, Sir."

"No. I wish you would remain and meet them."

"Meet whom, Sir?"

"The reporters."

Brent was surprised. "You're giving an interview?"

The old man shook his head. "No, Brent-san. You know I saw the Mikado yesterday." Surprisingly, there was no joy in the voice, no enthusiasm. It was lifeless.

Brent was concerned. True to samurai tradition, Fujita was an avowed Shintoist. According to Shinto, Akihito was the one-hundred-twenty-fifth direct descendant of the sun goddess, *Amaterasu-O-Mi-Kami.* Shinto, also, ordained the doctrine of *Kakutai*—the belief that the Emperor and Japan were one, and that the national essence was embodied in this man-deity. In this, Fujita believed with every fiber of his being. Thus, to just be in his presence should have been a supreme moment in the admiral's life. Yet the joy he had seen after previous meetings with Hirohito and the first with Akihito was missing. Something indecorous had happened yesterday. Something was definitely wrong.

Brent remained silent while the old man clasped his hands together, weaving his fingers, clenching and unclenching. He had never seen him so distressed. In time, Fujita said, "I had a long audience. The Emperor is concerned about the coming battle."

"Of course, Sir."

"He is also disturbed by the hostility in some of the media, and the 'peace' demonstrations outside his palace."

"Rengo Sekigun swine, traitors, terrorists."

"True, but they are making an impact, Brent-san."

"And he is having trouble maintaining support in the Diet. Right, Admiral?"

The old man nodded. "You are very perceptive."

"They are frightened women," Brent spat.

Fujita dropped his hands to the desk, and for the first time his face was creased by a faint smile. "We are in complete accord there, Brent-san." He drummed the desk top. "There is something else."

Now, it was coming. Brent waited expectantly while the old man shifted his weight. He was so thin, one wondered how he could ever be comfortable seated for any length of time. He continued. "You gave that Gary Mardoff quite a beating."

"The Emperor knew this?"

"His news agency complained directly to the Imperial Palace."

"I'll be damned."

Fujita swallowed with difficulty, as if his mouth were filled with a foul acid. "The Emperor feels we should attempt to cultivate better relations with the media."

So that was it. They had to be pleasant, show hospitality

to some of the most repugnant people on earth. Brent could not restrain himself. "With due respect to the Emperor, Sir, jackals, rats, politicians and reporters are of the same species."

Fujita chuckled. "Well said. But we must honor the Emperor's request."

"His request, Sir?"

"Yes, the Son of Heaven insists we allow four reporters aboard for this operation."

The American was taken by surprise. This was unprecedented. Never had the Admiral even considered allowing reporters to sail into combat. The only civilians ever permitted to sail with *Yonaga* had been CIA agents. Only the Emperor could break through this barrier. Apparently, this was precisely what had happened. Barely able to conceal the shock in his voice, Brent said, "I honor the Emperor, Sir, but that is not a good idea."

"I agree, Brent-san. I argued against it, but Emperor Akihito insisted we take seven reporters aboard. I persisted and finally was able to reduce the number to four.

"But why?"

"As I told you, he feels too much of the world's media is unfavorable to our cause—that by taking a few reporters we can cultivate a better atmosphere—let them see first-hand our war, perhaps better appreciate our cause."

"And the cost."

"Especially that." The thin lips formed a grim straight line. "That, I want them to see, feel, smell. They write, criticize, gloat, scheme, hiding behind their typewriters and word processors. Let them know our war, and maybe even bleed."

"I still don't like it, Sir."

"Neither do I, Brent-san."

"They are civilians. Could lead to complications. Could be killed, picked up by enemy ships, even executed, Admiral."

"I made that point with the Mikado." He absent-mindedly ran five fingernails over his pate to comb hair that had vanished decades ago. With a trace of bitterness he said, "They call themselves war correspondents. One, an Englishman, served in Vietnam with an American infantry unit. All claim they are prepared for the risks—welcome them." He chuckled and shook his head.

"We lost one civilian." Brent reminded the Admiral of Lieutenant Oliver Y. K. Dempster's father, the CIA agent Frank Dempster, who had the top of his head blown off in the South China Sea.

"Yes. Yes, I warned the Emperor of the risks, Brent-san." He shrugged. "But he was inflexible—adamant."

There was a knock. Brent opened the door and was almost shocked off his feet. Helen Whitaker, Gary Mardoff, and two strange men were in the passageway. Helen smiled sweetly, Mardoff sneered, and the two strangers stood patiently. Brent waved them in.

Looking up from a document, Fujita's eyes leaped from reporter to reporter, finally stopping on the woman. "You men seat yourselves," he said. "But you," he pointed at the woman, "you, remain standing."

"Why?"

"Close your mouth."

"I don't get this," Helen said, face taut with mounting anger.

"Get off my ship!"

Helen showed her guts. "Why?" she snapped.

The tiny fist thumped down hard on the oak. "A warship is no place for a woman. You are leaving!" His finger pushed a black button.

Helen glanced at her companions. "Welcome to the nineteenth century." The men stared silently. No one dared challenge the admiral's mood. The door opened, and two burly seaman guards stepped in.

"Escort this woman off my ship, immediately!"

Helen did not budge. "I'm here because of the orders of your very own 'Son of Heaven'."

The seamen guards moved forward. Fujita halted them with a raised palm. He was not finished with the woman. "I agreed to take four reporters. That is all. Not a woman. No woman will ever sail on *Yonaga.*"

"We're bad luck," she scoffed, voice filled with sarcasm.

"Yes. The first true words out of your reporter's mouth." Mardoff and the two other men looked at each other with wide-eyed apprehension. Fujita gestured to the guards. Each man took one of Helen's arms.

"All right. All right," she said, trying to pull away. "You can call off your goons. I'll leave peacefully." She smiled, a wicked, twisted grin. "I won't sink your precious boat—honest to God."

"Out!"

While the guards eased her toward the door, she said over her shoulder, "I'll go home, have babies, wash dishes and walk four steps behind my lord and master." She hacked out a harsh, sarcastic laugh. Then, as she passed Brent, she brushed against his crotch with a firm hip and shocked everyone. "Be careful out there, you big stud. Be a big loss to my gender if you had it shot off."

Brent could feel the temperature of his face race up to boiling. He said nothing. His words could only exacerbate an impossible situation. Helen was having her moment—a vengeful, hateful moment.

Shaking off the guards, she walked through the doorway, head high, seamen on her heels. She had shown pride, courage and had enjoyed a minor victory. Brent could hear her laughter as she was escorted out of flag country.

Calm and collected, Fujita addressed the three reporters. "You are here because the Emperor specifically ordered me to take you aboard. You must understand, I dislike having civilians on *Yonaga.*" He scanned the three men. "Which of you is Gary Mardoff?"

Mardoff raised his hand, "I am, Sir." He was respectful and obviously on good behavior.

Fujita inclined his head toward Brent, who had returned to his chair. "I understand you and Commander Ross had a disagreement—a rather violent disagreement."

Mardoff brushed back a lank of hair from his forehead and glanced at Brent. There was contrition in the timbre of his voice. "Ah, a minor thing, Sir."

"Minor, hell!" Brent shot back. "You insulted a woman—a young girl."

"Of questionable background."

Brent came half out of his chair. "A young, helpless girl."

Obviously trying to impress the admiral, the reporter raised and dropped his shoulders and turned his palms up in a hopeless gesture. "A misunderstanding, Admiral. I am truly sorry."

Brent knew the man was acting, lying. He shook his head. "Just stay out of my way."

"Of course."

Fujita turned to the other men and spoke to a tall, patrician, natty man of about fifty. "You have been on board before?"

Pleased by the recognition, the man smiled and spoke with a crisp British accent. "Right you are, Sir. Alistair Cunningham of International Reporting. Came aboard in '92 and witnessed the *seppuku* of Lieutenant Jimpei Yashiro?"

Fujita acknowledged with a simple, "Yes, yes, a glorious samurai death." He turned to the third man.

Stocky, he had a slight belly, thick shoulders and chest, and a huge round head that reminded one of a billiard ball with a happy face painted on the front. "I'm Loren Hobel of the Associated World Press," he said with a flash of wide, white teeth. "It's an honor to be on board, Admiral." He glanced at his companions. "Speaking for all of us, I can assure you we will not be underfoot, or, when this is all over, report anything that is not true."

"That is a very broad statement," Fujita said. "Truth depends upon the observer, and the lenses he wears. Some eyes twist truth like light through melting glass. Is that not true?"

Hobel responded. "The unbiased journalist reports facts, only, Sir. Personal prejudice should not enter, be bent by those lenses."

Fujita's laugh was humorless. "I know all about unbiased reporting." He scanned the reporters silently. "You will be assigned to a cabin in 'officer country' and be given officer privileges. You will be given the freedom of the ship, except for certain sensitive areas which my executive officer will designate."

"Sensitive areas, Sir?" Mardoff asked.

"Yes. Magazines, fuel bunkers, the hangar deck when we are arming and fueling for a strike, CIC where your presence could be disruptive."

The reporters nodded understanding.

"Each of you will be assigned a seaman guard who will act as an escort and guide."

Cunningham said, "When we engage the enemy, Sir, will we be given specific station, or can we be at large?"

"I will see to it you are somewhere on the bridge. Here you will have the best view."

Brent came into the conversation. "It's also a very dangerous place. It's the command center, the brain of the ship. Arab suicide planes have even rammed us. You'll be very exposed."

Mardoff stared at Brent. "No problem, Commander. No problem at all."

"Hear! Hear!"

Rubbing the afternoon stubble on his chin, Brent stared at Alistair Cunningham. "You came on board with Lia Mandel and Arlene Spencer?"

"Right you are, Commander. Arlene Spencer of the Nippon Press and Lia Mandel of United Information Service."

Fujita picked up the thread with relish. "We executed both of them."

The reporters exchanged a sober glance. Alistair said, "We know, Sir. They were spies—bloody traitors."

"I hanged their friend, Horace Mayfield, from the yard-arm."

Mardoff spoke up. "He conspired with them—fed them information, Admiral."

"And they gave it to the enemy, cost us heavily in casualties over Rabta," Fujita added bitterly.

"You have no worry about us, Admiral," Loren Hobel said.

The old man's smile crinkled his wrinkles into a menacing leer. For a moment he looked like a death's head. "The lesson has been taught. Learn or die. I will not tolerate loose tongues or even careless reporting. My yard-arm is very wide."

The silence of the grave filled the room. Finally, Fujita said, "Do any of you wish to withdraw from this assignment?"

The reporters looked at each other. There was a shaking of heads and Cunningham spoke for himself. "I for one, Sir, am keen to carry on."

"Then you will remain."

"Yes, Sir."

Mardoff and Hobel both nodded concurrence.

"So be it. But remember Mandel, Spencer and Mayfield."

"Yes, Sir," the reporters chorused.

We shall see, Brent thought. *We shall see.*

Eighteen
The Sortie

The morning *Yonaga* stood out of Tokyo Bay, there was still no real dawn, but the sun was awake and the sky was changing color. As the great carrier cleared the Uraga Straits, Brent Ross leaned on the windscreen of the flag bridge. Over the bow, the gray mist and black sea blurred into each other, endless, changeless, featureless. Then, slowly, he swept his binoculars over the pulsing lights of Kurihama to starboard, and the dark wooded shore of the Boso Hanto to port. The darkness of the moment matched the depths of his mood.

How many times had he followed this path on his way to challenge the gods of war? How many times had he felt cheated, forgotten, even betrayed by those who remained safe under those guarding lights, secure in their homes in the sheltering woods with their families? Would he ever know this? A wife, children, security? Again, he felt locked in, trapped by the bars of a cage he could never break. Was he doomed to repeat the exact same events until he was destroyed by the cycle itself?

Again, the apprehensions and resentments of the fighting man returned. All men, on the eve of battle, feel the helplessness of the pawn manipulated by faceless players, playing their games in opulent war rooms in the far corners of the world. It had always been this way, since the first chief sent his tribe into battle. While thousands of men died horribly, other men in splendid uniforms counted objectives taken, decorated each other, and raised replacements. Smug, thick-bellied men who used such phrases as "search and destroy," "occupy and hold at all costs," "damn the casualties, take that hill!" Men who counted dismembering deaths as impersonal ciphers. Who measured war in cold statistics, and could only search for the bottom line like greedy investors scanning financial statements. Callous men who had never seen battle, the smell of death, the blood of friends. Men who never felt the devastation of loss. War was as impersonal as a game of chess to them, or colored pins in a grid map.

The wheel of chance whirled in Brent's head like a macabre roulette wheel spun by the angel of death. He had defied this specter dozens of times: in the desert, on the sea, under the sea, in the air. How many times could he spin the wheel without coming up a loser? To have his chips swept from the board was inevitable. His time would come. Every fighting man knew this. The angel of death was patient. The game was wired, his finger was on the button.

The voice of Quartermaster Rokokura Hio broke through his musings. "Nojima Zaki bearing two-three-zero," a pause while Hio spun the bearing ring around on the gyro repeater to the first island of the string called Izu Shichito. Squinting through the peep sight, he said, "Tangent on O Shima, zero-four-zero."

"Very well," Captain Mitake Arai said, leaning over the chart table and clacking his parallel rules across a chart. Although modern navigational methods were available—Loran, Inertial Guidance Systems—Fujita distrusted machines. He insisted, over the objections of his senior staff, on keeping the old method of sextant, chronometer and an accurate DR (Dead Reckoning) track. Fortunately, *Bennington, New Jersey* and the escorts were not encumbered by this outmoded thinking. On previous voyages, Brent had always been relieved when, after morning sights, *Yonaga* exchanged position reports with the rest of the flotilla by flag hoist. Inevitably, *Yonaga's* navigation was almost as precise as that done by radio and electronics. Fujita would chuckle. "Tubes and transistors can burn out, gyros can break. Our sextants and our chronometers go on forever."

Arai, the official navigator for special sea detail, turned to the admiral. "Suggest course one-eight-zero, Sir. Should put us in the center of the channel."

"Very well." Fujita bent over a bank of voice tubes and shouted into one. "Pilot house!"

"Pilot house, aye."

"Right standard rudder, steady up on one-eight-zero, speed twelve."

The tinny voice repeated the command, and the bow of the great warship swung ponderously to the right. Beneath his feet, Brent could feel the vibrations of the four great engines increase their beat.

"Steady on one-eight-zero, speed twelve, sixty-two revolutions, Sir," came up the tube.

"Very well."

Cunningham, Mardoff and Hobel were huddled together on the aft part of the bridge. Cunningham and Hobel had camcorders slung over their shoulders, Mardoff was burdened with a camcorder and a 35-millimeter camera. Fujita had given permission for the photographic equipment with one proviso. "We will examine every millimeter of film before you can release it." The reporters had beamed happily. They had been granted far more freedom than they had ever anticipated.

Brent turned to Rear Admiral Whitehead, who was close to his side, and jerked a thumb at the reporters. "Wait till we hit the North Pacific swell. They may have their breakfast again."

Whitehead grinned. "Once down and once up."

They both laughed.

An hour later, speed had been increased to eighteen knots and the sunlight, full-bodied and strong, had begun to warm the drab colors of daybreak. The sea, which had been a vast counterpane dyed in black and purple, brightened to indigo and deep blue. The crests of the small chop received the sun and turned it back again, in brittle sparks of light. To Brent, it looked as if broken bits of mica had been dusted over the sea.

And there was beauty overhead, too. In the north the clouds piled up like gray-and-white cotton candy balls thrown by a mischievous child. To the south, stringy, flat clouds lay against the sky like an abandoned theatrical backdrop, tarnished and yellow. Only in the east did the sky show any menace. Here a leaden thunderhead raised its mushroom head, like the yield of an enormous nuclear blast. The sun played with it too, brushing with mauve, purple, and deep grays that darkened to black in the chasms and fissures. Now and then it blinked with internal lightning, as if Susano were proudly photographing the whole vast vista of his work.

Looking around, Brent's spirits rose with the rising sun. "Watatsumi-no-Mikoto is putting on quite a show," he said to himself.

Cunningham, who had moved close to his side, asked, "Who's that blighter?"

Brent chuckled, "The god of the sea?"

"By your leave, Commander, do you believe in that?" Cunningham asked. "In Shinto?"

"Why not? It's not any more rot than the Anglican Church."

Cunningham's nervous eyes darted over Brent, like a man convinced he had committed a gaffe. "I didn't mean to infer that, Commander. No offense?"

"Of course not."

Relieved, the Englishman continued the patching. "Daresay, it's as good a show as any. To each his own. Right, Commander?"

"Right you are, you bloody bloke," Brent mimicked good-naturedly. They both laughed. He was beginning to like the Englishman.

Three hours later, Brent was still on the bridge. The special sea detail had been secured and the port watch set. Fujita, ever cautious, had set a Condition Two of Readiness, manning one-half of the ship's armament. Although the navigation was officially moved to the navigation bridge and Arai had left, Rear Admiral Whitehead took periodic sights and penciled in the DR track. Fujita maintained the con and the three reporters still remained on the bridge, fascinated by the details of the operation of the great warship.

Whitehead turned to Admiral Fujita, "Thirty-seven miles from Point *Kaji,* Sir."

"Very well."

Cunningham said to Brent Ross, "Point *Kaji?*"

"Point Fire. A rendezvous point. We'll take aboard our air groups there." He took Cunningham by the sleeve and led him to the chart. Tapping the chart south and east of Mikura Jima, the last island in the Izu Shichito chain, he said, "Latitude thirty-three degrees, fifteen-minutes north, longitude one-hundred-forty degrees, fifty-minutes east."

"That's your road sign, Commander."

"Right. That's the intersection. We'll make a sailor of you yet."

"Right-oh."

Cunningham returned to Mardoff and Hobel. Gesturing at the chart, he gave them the information. They all seemed as excited as schoolboys at their first baseball game.

Watching the reporters talking and gesturing, Brent

said to himself, "When you're tagged out in this game, you're buried."

Then, studying Mardoff, he assured himself the reporter was no Mandel or Spencer. Although he was thoroughly dislikable, placing himself on *Yonaga* on the eve of battle would be the worst place for a spy. If he did learn of Fujita's plans, there was no way he could communicate with the enemy. And there were few secrets, anyway. Thousands of people had seen the battle group stand out, and millions had seen the air groups practicing over the most heavily-populated areas of Japan. The types and numbers of aircraft were well known. And the man had put himself in mortal danger. It was the drive to "get the scoop," "the perfect shot." To make a career with one big story. Become another Tom Brokaw, Peter Jennings, Dan Rather, David Brinkley overnight. In that way, Mardoff was just like the rest of them. Basically, he was driven by ambition—spiced by no small measure of greed.

While *Yonaga* nudged her nose further out into the vast wasteland, the freshening wind backed off to the southeast and the usual North Pacific swell came with it, taking the great carrier on her port bow. *Yonaga* showed her disdain for the puny attack by bulldozing her way through the endless ranks of swells, slashing the seas aside and leaving a wide wake frosted with white. But the effort cost her stability, and some of her crew's stomachs. Her bow rose and dropped, she rolled gently from side to side. Mardoff and Hobel both gulped frantically, turned a beautiful green-yellow, and hastily excused themselves from the bridge. Whitehead, Brent, and the admiral all chuckled.

Cunningham was made of sterner stuff. He remained unperturbed at Brent's side. In fact, he drank black coffee and ate a sweet roll when a rating brought a snack to the bridge. Then came the report from radar: "Many aircraft, approaching from three-five-zero true. One-hundred-sixty miles. Low. IFF indicates friendlies."

"Very well."

Then the radio room: "We have Air Group Commander Matsuhara on the fighter circuit."

The talker, Seaman Naoyuki, turned to Admiral Fujita. "Should I switch on the speaker, Admiral?"

"Affirmative. Channel Six, Naoyuki."

Brent gestured at a microphone and the admiral nodded his approval. At the same time, the talker threw the middle switch in a panel of eleven. Matsuhara's voice came in loud and clear, calling *Yonaga* with the code word for Icebreaker, "*Saihyosen, Saihyosen,* this is *Yubi* Leader." Every head turned toward the speaker. Brent pulled the microphone to his lips.

At six-thousand feet, Commander Yoshi Matsuhara had a horizon of nearly ninety miles. Beneath him, he could see the islands of the Izu Shichito stretching out to the south and west like a road sign pointing to the battle group. He switched on his microphone. "*Saihyosen, Yubi* groups one-hundred-sixty miles from Point *Kaji.* ETA fifteen-thirty hours."

"*Yubi* Leader, this is *Saihyosen.* Roger, I read you loud and clear." Yoshi recognized Brent Ross' voice instead of the usual rating. "Bring all your friends."

Yoshi chuckled. "We're all invited to the party?"

"Your table's reserved. See the maitre d'."

"Roger."

Except for the faint hissing of the carrier wave, Yoshi's radio fell silent. He looked around at his groups. Hundreds of aircraft were within view, like a vast flight of migratory birds in winter. Just off his elevators his wingmen crowded close. To port, the cheeky street-tough Cockney, Pilot Officer Elwyn York. To starboard, the urbane, aristocratic Flying Officer Claude Hooperman. Although as diametrically opposite in temperament and demeanor as

Dog Island and Hyde Park, they were two of the finest pilots Yoshi had ever seen. They were flying Hawker's new version of the magnificent Sea Fury.

A vast improvement over the Seafire, the Sea Fury's fuselage was built with a distinct slope forward of the cockpit, so that the pilot had a nearly unobstructed view over the nose during carrier landings. This, the Seafire lacked. Hinged outboard of the cannon, the wings featured power-folding. Another distinctive feature was the radiator, which was mounted on the leading edge of the port wing.

The Sea Fury was powered by the eighteen-cylinder, Bristol Centaurus radial engine, boosted to 3750 horsepower. This great power plant turned a five-bladed Rotol propeller that could drive the fighter through the air at 480 miles-per-hour. Four short-barrelled Hispano Mark 5, 20-millimeter cannons gave the Hawker its devastating punch. So formidable was this aircraft, during the Korean War it had several kills of MiG-15 jets.

York and Hooperman fit the fighter perfectly. Yoshi knew they would deliver its cyclone of metal and explosives with typical British zest and panache. Already, with the inferior Seafire, Hooperman had eight kills, York eleven.

Pivoting his head and glancing into his rear view mirror, Yoshi checked the rest of his fighter squadrons. He caught Commander Steve Elkins leading his twelve Grumman F6F Hellcats far to starboard. As usual, the stubby fighters were flying in the American style of two fighters in an element, two elements a flight, and three flights forming the squadron. Trailing Elkins and slightly below were the six Seafires. These fighters were not as fast as the Sea Fury, but were very maneuverable and had the same firepower. All were piloted by British volunteers.

High, above and last in the armada, were his beloved Mitsubishi A6M2, Zero-sens. With the new *Sakae Arashi* 2500 horsepower engine, the completely rebuilt fighter could still hold its own in a dogfight with the enemy's best.

"Nothing in the world short of a humming bird can turn with me," he had heard one of his pilots boast. The truth, indeed. However, it was slower and lacked the diving speed of the Arab fighters. It could be victimized by the dive and run tactics of the heavier enemy aircraft. And, with its low horsepower, it lacked adequate pilot armor and still had a nasty proclivity for blowing up when hit in the fuselage fuel cell—despite new American self-sealing tanks.

Moving his stick with a bare touch, Yoshi dropped his starboard wing and peered over the combing. Far below, Lieutenant Y.K. Dempster and Lieutenant Akira Terado led their bombers. The old Aichi D3As and Nakajima BSNs looked slow and vulnerable despite their new engines and the long barrel of the American 50-caliber machine gun jutting upward from their rear cockpit. In all, there were 52 dive bombers, 54 torpedo bombers and 51 fighters in his groups. An enormous number of planes for one carrier to operate. *Yonaga* was the only carrier on earth capable of doing this.

Yoshi tugged his mask away from his cheek. The plastic always seemed to glue itself to his face, and inevitably his whiskers fought back with a maddening itch. Scratching his cheek, he sighed with relief. It had been his own orders that had added this torment to the patrols. Because men were more alert on pure oxygen, he had ordered all fighter pilots to be on oxygen from the moment they took off. Bomber crews had the option to go on at 12,000 feet, or when engaged. Oxygen could make a man a fraction of a second faster, even at low altitudes where dogfights often drifted. That fraction of a second could be the difference between life and death. Yet, he knew some of his pilots cheated, including his Englishmen. He couldn't fly in each cockpit with every man.

He searched the sky to the south. Although his uncanny eyes often felt dry and throbbed with a dull ache, he could still focus to infinity like a fine range finder. It just took him a little longer. Then he spotted the swarm of insects low on the horizon. *Bennington's* air groups, strung out in loose formations. Leading and at six-thousand feet was a squadron of fierce little Grumman F8F Bearcats. Even from ten miles, Yoshi could see the elements were too far spaced and the formation sloppy.

He switched to *Bennington's* fighter circuit. Immediately his earphones were filled with the gruff voice of Group Commander Emmitt Hopp. The gnarled old professional was shouting at his squadron. "Madonna Flight, this is Madonna Leader. Close up, goddammit. Quit playing grab-ass with your wingmen and tighten up. I want this squadron as tight as a virgin pussy or I'm going to send your butts back to 'Primary'!"

There was a series of "Rogers" and the squadron tightened into a perfect "v" of six "top guns" trailed by wingmen slightly below and to starboard.

"That's better," Hopp grumbled. "You'd better remember this when we begin our fun and games with our Arab friends—if you don't want a twenty-millimeter up your ass."

Chuckling, Yoshi ran his eyes over the seventy fighters and bombers of *Bennington's* groups. He could not help but feel a surge of pride and confidence. Twenty-four Bearcats, twelve F6F Hellcats, twelve Vought F4U Corsairs with their strange gull wings, ten Douglas A-1 Skyraiders, twelve Curtiss SB2C Helldiver dive bombers, and a squadron of Grumman TBF torpedo bombers. Not one of the lumbering, vulnerable Douglas SBD Dauntless dive bombers was in the groups. All had been destroyed or retired.

All of *Bennington's* aircraft had been powered up with new engines. Most of the fighters in both *Yonaga's* and *Bennington's* groups were capable of speeds in the neighborhood of five-hundred miles an hour. The limiting factors were the durability of the airframes and the strength and stamina of the pilots. However, the wall that faced them all was the turbulence and vibrations that set in when the propeller tips approached the speed of sound.

He smiled to himself. There were great fighters all around him. There were great fighters based in the Marianas and on the enemy carriers. But no one had a fighter like his completely rebuilt Zero-sen. Brent Ross, Nobomitsu Atsumi, and Steve Elkins thought he was mad when he and his crew chief, Shoishi Ota, bolted the great 3,500-horsepower Sakae, *Taifu* (Typhoon), to the nose of the Mitsubishi. Actually, the engine was a Nakajima version of the old Wright Cyclone R-3350 engine that had powered the Boeing B-29 Superfortress. The R-3350 had eighteen cylinders in two banks, and a pair of turbo-superchargers.

"It'll fall apart," Nobomitsu Atsumi had warned him. "Aerodynamically, its a freak," Elkins had commented. "The engine will take off and leave you on the deck," old Chief Engineer Tatsuya Yoshida had grumbled. A disbelieving Brent Ross had chided, "all the Emperor's horses and all the Emperor's men, won't put Yoshi back together again." Fujita had soberly added his admonition. "The A6M2 is built for a nine-hundred-fifty horsepower engine, Yoshi-san. You would multiply that engine many times over. Do not kill yourself in this mad quest for horsepower."

But he had assured the admiral the entire aircraft would be rebuilt. Actually, the original Zero was nothing more than a template for the new fighter. It was rebuilt from spinner to tail hook. The skin was stripped and the main wing spar, ribs, longerons and formers replaced by titanium-aluminum alloy members. The flimsy control cables were removed and replaced by heavy-duty lines. Control surfaces were strengthened to compensate for the enormous torque and high speeds. New stressed steel hinges were installed on ailerons, flaps, elevator, and the rudder. Because the new power plant was two hundred pounds heavier than the old Sakae, a bigger fuel tank, and pilot armor were positioned behind the cockpit to counterbalance the huge engine.

Despite the ominous predictions, it flew like nothing else in the air. No one had a fighter like his. Its performance was mind-boggling. It could stand on its tail and climb like an old jet, yet, its low wing-loading allowed it to maneuver and turn almost as sharply as the classic Zero-sen. Actually, Yoshi did not know its top speed. He had exceeded five hundred knots in level flight, and the engine had begun to overheat. Also, although he would not admit it, he was afraid to put the plane in a full, all-out power dive. He had visions of his wings peeling off like scraps of paper, or the g-forces blacking him out when he tried to pull out.

Suddenly, his attention was caught by a ship on the horizon. The unmistakable pyramidal silhouette of a *Fletcher.* He was coming up on the battle group. Soon, the huge array of capital ships and escorts began to fill the sea to the southeast. Finally, *Yonaga* loomed, led by *New Jersey* and surrounded by her destroyers. Cleaving the sea at high speed, the ships all left white signatures on the surface like scratches on blue glass. At least ten miles to the south, *Bennington* steamed with her escorts ringed about her. Both carriers were turning into the wind.

Despite her length of 1,050 feet, 180 foot beam, 84,000-ton displacement, a seven storey island, and a four-acre flight deck, *Yonaga* looked as small as a book marker. The biggest carrier in the world, she was still a very small airport. Tokyo International had 10,000-foot runways. *Yonaga's* landing area was only about 750 feet. And he must bring his fighter down in almost the same spot every time. Flying too low, he would splatter himself against the carrier's stern. Too high—even only 4-feet—meant "boltering"—missing the four arresting wires. This would lead to a "wave off" or being snared by the steel-mesh barrier. And this game of inches meant beating the clock.

Yonaga could land a plane every forty seconds, if all went well. With her huge air groups, this was an absolute necessity. Wrecks were ruthlessly pushed over the side.

Yoshi saw Pennant Two two-blocked at *Yonaga*'s yardarm. Then the voice of the Landing Signal Officer, Commander Masanobu Yada, crackled in his earphones. "*Yubi* Leader, this is *Saihyosen.*"

Yoshi could see the white-shirted officer standing on his platform on the port quarter of the ship. A headset was strapped to his chest, microphone curving up to his mouth. "*Saihyosen,* this is *Yubi* Leader. I read you loud and clear."

"*Yubi* Leader, you are cleared to land. Speed of carrier twenty-four knots. Wind force six down the center line."

Yoshi could see the steam from the carrier's bow vent streaming down the yellow center line. As usual, Fujita was handling *Yonaga* perfectly, holding the ship head-on into the wind. And there was no aircraft control officer to direct takeoffs, landings and the movement of planes on the flight deck and in the air around the ship. Usually, a former squadron commander did this. But not on *Yonaga.* Fujita took this responsibility, too.

Yoshi acknowledged, and barked out landing orders to his groups. Immediately, the squadrons followed him in a five-mile circle to the port side of the carrier. The first Aichi began its descent two miles astern of the ship. From this moment on, the entire landing procedure would be done visually, with the Landing Signal Officer only shouting instructions into his headset in case of a sloppy approach. To the south, *Bennington* was following the exact same procedures. Actually, the landing procedures of both ships had been modified, incorporating both Japanese and American practices.

The Aichi caught the second wire and was jerked to a halt by the twenty-four millimeter, wound-steel cable. Immediately, brown, red and green-shirted handlers rushed to the bomber. Within seconds, she was unhooked and taken under tow by a tractor. In less than forty seconds, the second Aichi touched down. The procedure was repeated, and then a steady stream of bombers made their landings.

All went well until the fourth Nakajima B5N torpedo bomber made its approach. Yoshi, on the inside of his orbit and close to the ship, heard Yada warn. "Too high. Too high. Abort! Abort!"

Either the pilot did not hear, panicked, or the engine did not respond to the throttle. The bomber dropped, then bounced high, caught the last wire, and was yanked down with so much force its landing gear collapsed. Sluing off to the side, its starboard wing scraped the deck and was bent up like wet cardboard. Immediately, white-clad fire fighters swarmed out and sprayed foam on the wreck, while a tractor crew attached cables and dragged the Nakajima toward the bow. Three crewmen jumped from the plane and raced toward the island. Yoshi cursed. They had lost at least three minutes and the entire training procedure he had planned and put in place now appeared questionable. All because of one pilot's poor judgement.

Luckily, the remaining aircraft made their landings without incident. Then, after every bomber had landed, came the fighters.

One after the other, the sleek killers streaked in for their landings. Yoshi watched with pride, until only his Zero and the two Sea Furies of his wingmen were left in the sky. He heard Elwyn York's voice calling Hooperman. "*Yubi* Two, let's bugger the old girl."

"Bully for you, *Yubi* Three. I'm on your arse, you son of Dog Island," Hooperman whooped.

Before Yoshi understood what the Englishmen had in mind, York followed by Hooperman peeled off and roared just a few feet off *Yonaga's* starboard side at over four-hundred-miles-an hour. "*Yubi* Two, *Yubi* Three! Negative!

Negative!" Yoshi shouted into his microphone. But he was too late. The exuberant Englishmen would have their day.

Screaming past the bow, both fighters broke left in sharp turns so that their port wingtips were pointed down at the sea only eight-hundred feet below. Yoshi shuddered. He knew the Englishmen were pulling four to five g's. A slight misjudgment would splatter them over acres of the Pacific.

The turns slowed the planes, which straightened a mile to port and headed in the opposite direction. Then they raced past the stern, turned again, and York landed while Hooperman made a quick, low-level circle that kicked water from the crests of the chop. Then the second Sea Fury landed with gusto and an arrogant flair.

Instead of feeling anger, Yoshi laughed out loud. Touched by the exuberance of the Englishmen, he was suddenly a young pilot again, fresh out of Eta Jima. Maybe it was the oxygen. Too much made him giddy.

"Good show, you bloody blighters," he mimicked with his microphone off. Then with a mixture of English and Japanese expletives, "What the hell, Watatsumi-no-Mikoto, let's do our bloody bit." He duplicated his wingmen, racing down the starboard side, pulling up and over into a sharp turn that left him hazy, and then down the port side, throttling back to make his final approach down the center of the carrier's wake.

But his head had not cleared. The tally of his years was reaching for the eighth decade. The exhilaration was gone. Shaking the haze from his brain, he raced through a routine so deeply ingrained it was almost as if his hands and eyes were managed by his subconscious. Landing gear selector level to "down," whine of hydraulics, double clunk as the wheels locked, green light on; canopy back and locked open; fine pitch; full rich; full flaps; airspeed 150 knots and falling. And last, a tug on his harness assured him it was securely locked.

Reducing throttle gradually, with a feather-like touch, he focused on the Landing Signal Officer, who held his paddles extended as if he were preparing to fly off his platform like a bird. For the next few seconds the officer and the rushing deck commanded Yoshi's vision; his total concentration. Suddenly, the paddles crossed at the knees. He eased the throttle back, almost to the last stop. With its manifold pressure dropping toward zero, the Mitsubishi lost air speed. His controls felt heavy. Instinctively working his stick and rudder pedals, he kept the nose pointed directly down the yellow center line and into the steam vent, while his peripheral vision caught the white broken lines to each side. He was perfectly aligned.

Then the usual blur of impressions—the stern flashing by only fifteen feet below, the pale faces of AA gunners looking up, the deck filling his windshield, rushing toward him, the lines of teakwood decking, splotches of oil from the wrecked bomber, black streaks of burned rubber, the four steel wires, glinting glass on the bridge, more faces staring down, the brown, purple, red, and green-shirted handlers staring from their galleries, white-clad fire fighters standing by their tiny wagon, medical orderlies with their big red crosses on their chests, white broken lines flashing past to each side.

Pulling back on the stick, he watched the huge engine come up slowly—too slowly. A bolt of panic shot through him. With a hard tug, he pulled the stick back into his stomach. Suddenly, the engine was up, blocking his view of the deck. He cut throttle and dropped like a high-speed elevator. He hit on three points, hard. He was late. Very late.

There was a bump, screech of rubber on wood and the powerful shove forward against his six-point military harness as his tail hook caught the third wire. The fighter bounced off the deck and was jerked down again with a vicious jolt that made his teeth click. In less than three-hundred feet, the bounding 8,500 pound aircraft was dragged to a halt. His hand found the switch and the idling engine gasped before it died, the four bladed propeller jerking stiffly with each gasp until it, too, stopped. Numbly, he sat for a moment, listening to the hissing and ticking of the cooling engine. Then a deep sigh emptied his lungs and he sagged back into his bucket seat. He smiled. He was down and alive. After all these years and countless landings, he still felt it. He would never change.

"Anytime you can walk away from it, it's a good landing," the Americans liked to rationalize. He snickered grimly. Then, he had made a good landing. But deep down, he knew he had slipped a bit. The landing was sloppy, not up to his usual standard. He knew the *Taifu* was heavy. Why didn't he compensate? Admiral Fujita would have a few choice words to say to him. That was inevitable.

Quickly, he stirred himself from his lethargy, unhooked his oxygen and radio leads and pulled off his mask. Luxuriously, he filled his lungs with sea air that smelled sweet after hours of pure oxygen. The metallic taste was still in his mouth and would be until he ate or drank something. There was a bump, the aircraft rocked and the familiar face of Crew Chief Shoishi Ota peered down into the cockpit. Smiling, the old chief reached in and unlocked the single lock on Yoshi's harness. "Welcome aboard, Commander." He patted the Perspex canopy affectionately. "Brought her back home, Sir."

"Still a little heavy in the nose, Chief."

Ota waved at the tail. "We can adjust that out, Sir."

"Right. I'll see you in the hangar deck in a hour."

"Game of *Go* tonight, Sir?"

"Why not, Chief? It's been a boring day."

Nineteen
The Snooper

"Commander Matsuhara, you and your wingmen demonstrated a distinct lack of discipline in your landings today," Fujita said from behind his desk.

Standing between Hooperman and York, Yoshi stared down at the little admiral. All three pilots were still dressed in their brown flight suits, faces darkened around the white ovals of their goggles like night creatures of the forest. Before Yoshi could answer, York did. "Respectfully, Admiral, I's the one who's the dirty deuce. I begun the whole rotten lot."

Hooperman broke in. "Tommy rot, old boy, let me set the matter right . . ."

Fujita stopped him with a downward motion of his tiny hand like a karate chop. *"Enough!* The senior officer is responsible."

"Of course, Admiral," Yoshi said. He looked at his wingmen. "You know by military protocol of any nation, I am responsible for those under my command."

The Englishmen tried to speak, but Fujita preempted them. "There is no other option. Commander Matsuhara is culpable and accountable." The eyes moved from man to man. "All of you know good fighter pilots are hard to find, to train, to keep alive." The pilots winced. "You took undue risks today in your high-speed, low-level turns about the carrier." And then an inadvertent compliment. "I could have lost my most valuable pilots for nothing." He patted the *Hagakure*. "The book tells us, 'There are as many ways to die as the hairs on the leg of a three-year-old calf.' " Two little fists came down on the desk, "Do not invent another demise through recklessness and poor judgement! If there is a repetition, I will ground all of you."

Again, the burning black eyes flashed from man to man. "Is that clear?"

The flyers seemed relieved. For Fujita, the disciplining was very moderate, indeed. It only amounted to a warning. "Aye, aye, Sir. We understand, Sir. It won't happen again, Admiral," the Englishmen chorused.

"Pilot Officer York and Flying Officer Hooperman, you are dismissed." He nodded at Yoshi. "You will remain, Commander."

After the Englishmen exited, Fujita waved the air group commander to a chair. Yoshi knew what was coming. It was a familiar refrain and Yoshi's ears were attuned to it. "You are advancing through the years, Yoshi-san," the admiral said. "Do not try to fight time by acting like a foolish young pilot."

"I deeply regret my conduct, and the actions of my wingmen." He ran a hand over his temple and forehead, picked up some black residue from burned petrol and oil, glanced at his hand, and wiped it on the leg of his stained flight suit. "I realize that I am considered the oldest fighter pilot in the world, Sir. But I am still capable of punishing the enemy."

"The 'Geriatric Killer', Yoshi."

"I know, Sir."

"You were trying to prove something with that little demonstration?"

Yoshi shifted uneasily. "I can fly with the best of them."

"That was not one of your best landings. You are losing

your touch. Perhaps it is time for you to direct your groups from the carrier."

"But, Sir . . ."

Fujita pressed on. "You know, I assumed the duties of the Aircraft Control Officer when Commander Masayasu Omura was killed."

"Yes, Sir. Omura was a great flyer and control officer."

"It's been ten years now, Yoshi-san."

"I know, Sir."

"When we first commissioned *Yonaga*, Masayasu Omura was one of my best squadron commanders. But he grew old, slow. Took on the duty of the Aircraft Control Officer. A pilot should have this duty. The Imperial Navy regulations stipulate this. Obviously, a pilot has a better grasp of the problems in the cockpit. It would be no disgrace . . ."

"Respectfully, Sir, I am not ready for ground duties. My men need me . . ." He stabbed a finger upwards, "up there with them."

The old man sighed. "To die in the realm of the gods, Yoshi-san. That was how you put it the last time we discussed this matter."

"Yes, Sir." He indicated the *Hagakure*. "In the book, Lord Matsudaira told his retainer, 'In preserving the Way of the Samurai, one will throw away his own precious life in attacking the enemy.' "

The old man stared at Yoshi. It was an unblinking look, the cold look of a man with a monolithic ego that seldom yielded to a contrary view. "Not throw it away in a useless crash."

"Of course not, Sir."

"Or because one's senses and reactions are dimmed and slowed by the years."

"Not true, Admiral."

"Again, Yoshi-san, I insist—you made a poor landing today."

"Not perfect, Sir, but adequate under the circumstances."

"What circumstances?"

"My Zero-sen is still a little heavy in the nose. Chief Ota and I will correct that tendency this afternoon."

The old man shook his head. "Are you not a little heavy with the years?"

"No, Sir." The pilot hunched forward. "I promised you that I would ground myself if I ever felt I was a burden or a danger to my men."

"True."

"On my word as a samurai for *Tenno*, the Son of Heaven, I will ground myself immediately."

Fujita was still skeptical. "Not so easily this time, Yoshi-san." Matsuhara's heart fell. "You must report immediately to Chief Eiichi Horikoshi for a complete physical examination."

"I just had one two months ago, Sir."

"I know. You are due for another. You are dismissed."

"Well Commander, your lungs, heart, blood pressure are all normal," Chief Hospital Orderly Eiichi Horikoshi grunted, pulling the ear-pieces of his stethoscope free. Then, with a baneful grin, "In spite of your years." The chief chuckled and nodded so that the last few score of white strands of hair remaining on his polished pate stirred like sea growth in a current.

"Good," the pilot said, staring into the watery eyes that seemed shrunken into their cavities like a skull. He had known Horikoshi since the day they both reported aboard *Yonaga* in 1941. The dislike had been instantaneous and mutual.

A brilliant student of medicine, Horikoshi soon graduated from assisting in operations to actually performing them in emergencies. He devoured the medical literature, studied the surgeons, and often entered into heated debates with them. Soon, he exceeded them. After all of *Yonaga's* doctors had died off during the entrapment in Sano Wan, Fujita had offered him a commission. Horikoshi refused. He never told the admiral his dislike for officers was so intense he could never bring himself to wear their gold. Nevertheless, he bowed to no one regardless of rank, except Fujita. He wore his arrogance with high panache and was pointedly rude to officers; especially Commander Yoshi Matsuhara. He feared no one, no reprisal. He was one of Fujita's favorites, and to the admiral his presence on *Yonaga* was absolutely essential. The four new doctors, all commissioned, feared him as if he were an evil *kami* come from the depths to flagellate them.

He brushed the stethoscope through the mat of hair on Yoshi's chest. "Getting a little gray there Commander." He grinned wickedly. "Becoming forgetful, slowing down in your reflexes?"

"I had five kills in one dogfight the last time we met the enemy." He brushed the stethoscope aside. "Does that answer your question?"

"Your prostate's enlarged."

"I'm quite aware of that."

"Piss in your pants yet?"

"My fighter has a relief tube."

"If it ever freezes up, you'll burst your bladder."

"I don't piss the enemy out of the sky, Chief."

Horikoshi leaned back in the chair with his arms folded across his chest. "Your eyes? Need bifocals yet?"

"Check them. That's your business."

Quickly, Horikoshi tested the pilot's eyes. "They are acceptable," he conceded grudgingly.

"They're perfect," Yoshi corrected him. "I'm cleared for flight duty?"

"You are healthy enough to be killed, if that's what you mean." He drew back disdainfully and gave a soft, scornful chuckle, as though he had given up on a dull and stubborn child.

Yoshi began to shrug back into his shirt. He would not push the chief further. He had what he wanted. More talk could only lead to more opportunities for Horikoshi to taunt him—and perhaps ground him.

Horikoshi watched him button his shirt with those rheumy black eyes. "You have slowed down, Commander. Soon the gods will desert you and you will become fish food. Remember this."

"You cleared me for flying duty."

"True. But I cannot cure the inroads of time. You are quite capable of flying and dying. If you are still *shinigurai,* you will soon be granted your wish."

"Then why don't you ground me?" Yoshi dared.

The answer was harsh and blunt.

"Because I dislike you."

After three days of steaming a southerly heading, the battle group rendezvoused with General Sago's amphibious force off the Bungo Suido. From the bridge, nothing could be seen of the huge flotilla of transports, LSTs and LSDs. The only indications of Sago's presence was increased activity in the radio room and the detaching of twelve *Fletchers,* cruiser *Ayase* and destroyer *Yamagiri.* Then, as the force turned eastward toward Eniwetok, six Tigercats from Iwo Jima streaked high overhead, turbo-chargers screeching like children's whistles.

Standing on the bridge as officer of the deck, Brent said to Admiral Whitehead, "I was at an air show once when a P-38 Lightning flew over. It made a sound just like that."

Whitehead nodded and smiled. "Right, Brent. The Germans used to call it 'the whistling death'."

Brent waved after the quickly vanishing fighters.

"Those Tigercats are the 'screaming death'. They should calm Sago's nerves."

Whitehead nodded. "And he has a squadron of our Zeros, too."

"Good for his morale, Admiral."

"He's a mighty nervous soldier and an obnoxious boor. Got his facts about World War Two all fouled up."

Brent caught and held the admiral's eyes. "I've known you for a long time, Sir."

"Since you were ten."

"Off the record?"

"Why?"

"Please, Sir. Off the record."

The old man expelled his breath noisily. "Okay. Off the record."

"Thank you, Sir." Brent fingered his glasses and then said, "Let it die, Sir. The war's been over for half-a-century."

The old man's eyes narrowed, increasing the depths of the creases trailing off from the corners. He spoke with unusual harshness. "That's none of your business, Brent."

Brent was not accustomed to backing down to anyone, regardless of the abundance of gold braid. "Respectfully, it *is* my business. We are on the same team now. We can live or die on the other man's decisions—his state of mind, on our rapport."

"I don't need a lecture."

"I should stay in my place?" Brent challenged.

"I didn't say that." A gust of wind sent his hands to his cap. He pulled it down almost to his ears. "You have a good point, Brent," he conceded. Brent remained silent. "I am concerned with morale." He waved over the stern, where Sago's invisible force plodded in their wake. "I'll get along with him—if he'll give me half a chance." He smiled thinly. "I decided this before your lecture." A roar distracted him. They both raised their classes as Elkins led six of his Hellcats in a wide sweep over the force.

"Good man," Whitehead muttered, deliberately changing the subject.

"One of the best."

They were interrupted by a click, and then a hissing from the bridge speaker. Admiral Fujita's voice sounded as if it were coming through a tin horn. "Men of *Yonaga*. I have just received a report that the Arab fleet has been sighted by an American submarine steaming northeast between Mindanao and Halmahara. The submarine reports three carriers, three cruisers and at least fifteen escorts. Our combined closing speed should permit us to engage within two or three days." He paused. Silence, like the dust of cremated souls, swept through the carrier. Not one man could look at another. Their mortality had been committed.

The metallic voice continued. "This is our opportunity. This is our chance to engage the enemy in the final climactic battle all samurai seek. If von Hanfstaengle gives battle, we will destroy him, and then we will invade and destroy Kadafi's bases in the Marianas. Only then can our sacred homeland, and all of the free world, be unfettered from the tyranny of oil and the depredations of terrorists." A short pause and then, *"Tenno haiko banzai*—Long live the Emperor!" echoed through the speakers.

"Tenno haiko banzai!" was shouted back.

Fujita began to sing. Brent recognized the Naval Lament of the old Imperial Navy. "Corpses drifting swollen in the sea depths." Thousands of voices, including Brent's, joined in. "Corpses rotting in the mountain grass. We shall die, we shall die for the Emperor. We shall never look back."

To the man, every Japanese in the crew screamed out *"Banzai!"* Hard leather boots pounded the deck. Finally, the shouting and stomping faded away like the dying winds of a typhoon. The foreigners looked at each other in awe.

"Von Hanfstaengle's taken our bait," Whitehead said.

"Or have we taken his?" Brent asked.

Whitehead smiled wanly. "Well said, Brent." He shrugged. "We'll know in a few days."

With the slower transports lagging further and further behind, the force swept to the south and east, maintaining a range of over 700 miles from the Marianas. Scouting aircraft were in the sky continuously, searching every quadrant. But the Arab force had mysteriously vanished somewhere in the Philippine Sea. Fujita doubled the number of scouts, using *Bennington*'s Skyraiders, but to no avail. Two of the aircraft failed to return. Tension became as palpable as a spring nearing the breaking point.

Everyone knew Arab LRAs would be patrolling, too. Admiral Otto von Hanfstaengle needed intelligence as well as Fujita. In carrier warfare, he who sights the enemy first has an enormous advantage. Without a doubt, long range aircraft from Saipan and Tinian would be making their searches, along with von Hanfstaengle's carrier-borne scouts.

Yonaga was just south of the Tropic of Cancer and 600 miles northwest of Wake Island, when Elwyn York spotted the enormous aircraft. "*Yubi* Leader, this is *Yubi* Three. There's a bloody big goose stoogin' aroun' at ten o'clock low."

"Oh, rather," Hooperman answered. "Got the bugger."

"Oh, rather, your nibs. Tally-ho!" York taunted.

Then Yoshi saw it. A huge, four-engined aircraft painted blue with Arab markings. Deep, double-deck fuselage, radar in a thimble radome, wing tip combustion heaters, clamshell nose cargo doors. No doubt about it. It was a Douglas C-124 Globemaster, which had just come out of some billowing cumulus-nimbus to the southwest of the battle group. He knew the Arabs had one C-124, maybe more. They had found it and it had found them. To the east, the entire battle group was visible. Why hadn't radar picked him up? Could have been interference from the rain storms. But *some* of the ships should have had him. It was rumored the Arabs had some radar deflecting coatings. But how could a 90-ton aircraft with a 174-foot wingspan be made invisible? Regardless, it was there, and it was there to be destroyed.

"*Yubi* flight, this is *Yubi* Leader. I see him."

Hooperman said. "He's getting his bloody eyes full."

York came in, "Bugger all, Hooperman. Let's splash the sod, or ain't that cricket, your lordship?"

"Up your bloody arse, York."

"Radio discipline!" Yoshi shouted. "I'll decide when we attack." He was angry, not only at the lack of discipline. He was irritated with himself because York had spotted the intruder before he did. He spoke into his microphone, calling the carrier. "Enemy reconnaissance aircraft at twenty-thousand feet, bearing two-three-zero true from you. I am engaging."

"Very well, *Yubi* Leader. Sending support."

"We don't need none," York growled.

"*Yubi* Flight. Clear your guns!" Yoshi said.

Yoshi flipped the safety cover from the firing button and fired a short burst. He saw squirts of tracers race past from the Sea Furies. After both wingmen reported their guns were armed, Yoshi said, "We'll gut him. Follow my lead."

York whooped, "Got me cock up."

Yoshi's hand flew through a familiar ritual. Fine pitch, full rich, full throttle, electric sight on. He pushed the stick forward and to the left, so that he dropped his port wing, curving into his dive. Turbo-chargers screaming, the Nakajima *Taifu* vented its 3,500 horsepower in a burst of unleashed savagery. Banking ponderously, the Globemaster was trying to flee to the questionable safety of a thunderhead. But the big plane was only capable of about 300 knots, and was flying right into Yoshi's line of interception. A glance at his instruments told him his air speed was almost 470 knots, cylinder head temperature a safe 240 degrees. No worry there, yet. Not unless he opened all the way up to overboost, which was highly unlikely.

As usual, he began to pull away from his wingmen. Nothing could stay with him. Grinning, he brought the glowing pink one hundred-millimeter glowing reticle of his reflector sight to the big target. As he expected, the wingtips had not yet reached the sight bars. Then he saw them. Two, not one, fifty-caliber twin mount dorsal turrets. In addition, a tail turret was also training two machine guns on him. Six weapons could track him. Too many. Why take the risk?

Pushing the stick forward, he nosed into a steeper dive that would take him below and behind the Globemaster. He wanted the tail turret—then the others. Pulling back on the stick and balancing with rudder, he brought the pip of the gunsight directly onto the huge tail. But the tail bounced and bobbed in his sight as the great aircraft's slipstream caught the Zero and lashed it about like a kite. Yoshi eased slightly above the Douglas and out of the turbulence.

He nodded with satisfaction. The analytics of the gunnery problem were nothing more than the intersection of straight lines. No frantic acrobatics. Completely linear. Zero deflection. Simplest of attack problems, if the tail gunner didn't kill him. Still out of range. He dropped the pip until it rested on the turret. Yellow flashes blinked. Tracers smoked toward him but dropped off far below.

"Out of range, you amateur," Yoshi snorted. But within seconds, the tracers began to reach for him, some actually tearing past just over his wings. Looking at nothing but the target, he kept his wings level with the enemy's. There were no evasive maneuvers. The Globemaster's only chance was to reach the cover of a nearby rainstorm.

At 400 yards the great wings reached the second sight bars. He pressed the button. The massive recoil of the two twenty-millimeter cannons and the two 7.7-millimeter machine guns shook the airframe and slowed the fighters by at least 20 knots. The vibrations sent tingles up his arms, all the way from his grip on the stick. He had aimed a little high to compensate for bullet drop, and his calculations had been perfect. There were flashes as shells chewed chunks of aluminum from the tail and rear fuselage. He closed the range quickly. Then harmonized for 200 yards, his guns hurled a cone of death into the enemy. At least four shells hit the power turret. There was a hail of Plexiglas reddened by bloody detritus that streamed back into his prop and bounced off his wings. The gunner had been blown to pieces, along with his turret.

He cursed. He, too, had made an amateur's error. He should have fired from further above or the side to avoid the flying debris. Pulling back on his stick was out of the question. He was too close. He would expose his belly to the two dorsal turrets. He'd continue his run despite the flying debris.

Raising his nose slightly, and then dropping it, he brought the pip back down on the huge target. The target fired back. But Yoshi's speed was so great he flashed past the giant before the gunners could track him. In return, the Japanese kept his button depressed and raked the Globemaster from tail to cockpit. But speed defeated Yoshi, too. There were only a few flashes from perhaps two hits from his cannons. Not one shell hit the turrets or cockpit. He pulled back on his stick and shot skyward, airframe groaning, tracers from the nose turret floating by like burning embers. His gut pushed against his pressure suit and a thin fog swirled behind his eyes. He shook his head and gulped oxygen.

Now Hooperman and York struck. Hooperman from the right side, York from the left. At slower speeds and without the tail turret to challenge them, they had more destructive runs. The devastating power of eight twenty-millimeter cannons struck the fuselage of the transport like a tornado ripping an old barn. Both dorsal turrets were shot to pieces, and huge chunks of aluminum were blasted into the slipstream. Then, flashing past and climbing, the two Sea Furies followed Yoshi. Tracers from the nose turret hounded them, but there was no apparent damage.

Banking for another run and looking down, Yoshi was stunned. The great Douglas still plodded along without reducing speed a knot, despite a damaged tail and hits that had exposed the ribs, longerons and formers of her fuselage. He shook the last of the fog away and spoke into his microphone. "*Yubi* Flight, this is *Yubi* Leader. Let's hit her engines on this run."

"Bully, old boy. She's as durable as a Soho whore," Hooperman said.

York's voice, "Bumf, your lordship. Get your finger out of your chuff and let's bullock the pisser."

"Follow my lead!"

Yoshi jammed the stick to the left and forward and split-essed into a dive. Again he curved toward the Douglas' tail. Now, if he attacked from the rear and above, she had no guns that would bear. This time he throttled back for a slower run. He brought the pip to the starboard wing and pressed the button at 500 yards. His shells blasted into the outboard engine, blowing off the cowling, exhaust collector ring, and ripping the oil tank. Instantly, a black ribbon of smoke began to unravel behind the great plane. "Too old, am I!" Yoshi shouted as he pulled up and curved away from the Globemaster. But the big plane still plodded along. The rainstorm was only a few miles away. She might make it.

Then the Englishmen struck. Their shells shot out another engine, blowing the turbine of a turbo-charger into the slipstream like a thick gray saucer. More smoke. York banked gently to the left and sent at least a half dozen shells into the cockpit and nose of the Douglas. Now, with two engines burning and a dead flight-deck crew, the transport began a gentle curve toward the sea. The giant was dying.

Yoshi had seen hundreds of planes destroyed. Some shot to pieces, others exploding like supernovas, others shedding wings and flipping and gyrating like insects burned by a candle's flame. But not the Douglas. It was dying proudly, headed for its grave with dignity that defied the inescapable.

"I jig-a-jigged the bloody bugger," York chortled. "My kill."

"Your kill my arse!"

"*Yubi* Flight, form up on me," Yoshi snapped. Silently the two wingmen assumed their stations off their leader's elevators. Looking down, Yoshi saw the great Douglas' dive had steepened until it had become nearly vertical. At a tremendous speed it struck the ocean, shattering as if it had hit concrete pavement. The stateliness vanished in a towering geyser of water that shot a hundred feet skyward, speckled with ripped blue aluminum and glinting bits of Plexiglas. A wing, with two burning engines, flew off to the side and landed at least a hundred feet from the wreck. The huge Douglas had just added 90-tons and ten corpses to the garbage of war.

Circling, Yoshi watched intently. Within minutes, the sea had calmed the ripples from its face and a thin wisp of smoke was blown to infinity by the wind. Yoshi felt a little sad. A great machine of the sky had died. Its only epitaph, the column of black smoke which had already been obliterated by the wind.

He felt nothing for the men.

Twenty
The Road to Glory

The battle group was about one hundred miles southeast of Eniwetok Atoll when an old Nakajima B5N scout sighted the enemy force. Admiral Otto von Hanfstaengl's flotilla was steaming northeast between Truk and the Mariana Islands. This placed him between the attacking Japanese forces and their targets. It appeared he had bought the ruse of the amphibious attack and had taken a blocking position. "He is ready to give battle," a delighted Fujita cried out.

"He's out of range of his Marianas' bases," Whitehead said. "That doesn't make sense."

"We'll sink him. That makes sense," Fujita countered.

After detaching Sago's amphibious force, Fujita did not steam directly for the Mariana Islands. Instead, he swept to the south and west, hoping to cut off von Hanfstaengl's line of retreat. He sought the final climactic battle and apparently the enemy was willing to give it to him.

The force was nearing launch point when an AD-4 Skyraider from Iwo Jima discovered von Hanfstaengl was springing a trap of his own. He had split his forces. A second force, a carrier and a cruiser with six escorts, was steaming under forced draft on a northerly heading through the Philippine Sea. When sighted, they were just to the west of the Marianas, within easy range of their own aircraft based in the islands. Apparently, he had anticipated Fujita's ruse and was determined to cut off the retreat of Sago's ships. The entire amphibious force was in danger of being slaughtered.

Fujita detached *Bennington* and five escorts to intercept the enemy's second battle group, and Sago's transports were sent on a northeasterly retirement away from the impending battle. But they were slow, very slow. They could be caught. The squadrons on Iwo were alerted and continuous patrols in squadron strength were flown north of the Marianas, where the enemy would be expected to appear if he were to intercept the transports. Enemy fighters from Saipan and Tinian were encountered, and the first air battles of the campaign were fought. *Yonaga, New Jersey* and twelve *Fletchers* remained to give battle to two carriers, two cruisers and at least ten destroyers of von Hanfstaengl's main force.

Not everyone agreed with Fujita's tactics. The most vocal critic was Rear Admiral Byron Whitehead, who had survived twelve carrier battles during World War Two. The argument broke out over the chart table on the flag bridge. Brent Ross, Loren Hobel, Alistair Cunningham and Gary Mardoff all stood silently while the two admirals clashed.

"You should take your whole force north and protect those transports, Admiral," Whitehead said, pounding the chart. The reporters were shocked that the American admiral would challenge Admiral Fujita so openly.

Instead of exploding, Fujita said casually. "Let us plot the problem, Admiral."

While the two admirals worked parallel rules across the chart in short jerky movements, plotted course lines and calculated ranges, Brent explained in hushed tones Whitehead's background to the reporters. "Admiral Whitehead is one of the world's most experienced carrier officers, and Admiral Fujita expects and respects his opinions." He did not express his own view that, in a way, Fujita used

Whitehead as a sounding board for his own tactics and strategies.

"I hear Whitehead was sunk six times," Loren Hobel said.

"True. He saw a lot of combat."

"They used to call him, 'Deep Six Whitehead'," Mardoff scoffed.

"One devilish roll of luck," Cunningham added.

Fujita's voice, with the honed edge of a sword, cut off the exchange. Whitehead had said something to him that no one had overheard. He was upset. "Nonsense!" he said to Whitehead, stabbing a pair of dividers at the chart. "See for yourself. We have von Hanfstaengl almost in range." And then referring to Admiral William F. "Bull" Halsey's infamous run north with the cream of his carriers and battleships during the Battle of Leyte Gulf. "I have told you before, I will not repeat the 'Battle of Bull's Run'. It was a stupid blunder."

"And risk a whole corps? Our chance for final victory?"

"Yes. Find me a war without risk and I will be happy to fight it for you." The little Japanese drummed the chart. "We will have von Hanfstaengl in range within the hour. Destroy these two carriers, and then we can sweep north and catch his second force on an anvil." He turned, face only inches from Whitehead's. "We have a chance to wipe the enemy's battle force out. Sink them all."

"His second force has an umbrella of fighters and bombers from the Marianas."

"And they are in range of our squadrons on Iwo Jima."

"Still, Admiral, our amphibious force could suffer heavy casualties."

"If we destroy his carriers, no price is too high. Without them his war is lost. They are my first priority."

"You'd let the troops be slaughtered in their holds."

"They accepted the risk when they volunteered."

"That's a terrible way to die."

"Show me a pleasant way!" Fujita's bent finger touched the American's ample chest. "And remember, they are samurai. To them death is as light as a feather."

The American recognized the old Meijian rescript. "Yes, yes, I know, Admiral. And duty is as heavy as Fuji-san."

"You are learning, Admiral Whitehead."

The reporters and Brent Ross stared at the two old men. No one said a word. The argument was concluded.

The old Japanese fidgeted over the chart table for a few minutes, looked at the sea and the sky, asked for an anemometer reading and finally said to the talker. "Aircraft launching details report to your stations. All hands, stand by to launch."

Within minutes, the flotilla had turned into the wind and the command, "Pilots, man your planes!" given. Then the first fighter rocketed off the flight deck. It was Commander Yoshi Matsuhara's strange, crossbred Zero-sen.

Rear Admiral Byron Whitehead shook his head and stared into the glare of the distant horizon.

Commander Yoshi Matsuhara's head turned ceaselessly, as if his neck was on a swivel. Alert, always alert. A fly speck on your windshield could turn into a fighter in the time it took to scratch your jaw. A little smear on your goggles could hide the enemy racing in to kill you. Quartering the sky, he examined it section by section. Wing tip, cowling, wing tip, rearview mirror, up and down. And then all over again. What made it wearying was the utter absence of anything to look at. His aging eyes were laboring to focus on an object that wasn't there and the drudgery was tiring. His eyeballs ached. But he never relented. Years of fighting had taught him one moment's slackness could be your last.

The fighter pilot who was not continuously on guard, soon became a boasting enemy's kill—another Japanese flag on an Arab fuselage. And in his case, a million-dollar bounty. He was a popular target, indeed. And he was easy to identify. Huge, out-sized engine, red cowling, green hood and white fuselage. He snickered to himself. He wanted them to see him, know him. The 72 Arab flags painted on the side of his fuselage like a checkerboard galled the enemy even more and fed his hatred.

Then his mind settled on the renegade American Kenneth "Rosie" Rosencrance—Kadafi's favorite killer. His distinctive solid blood-red Messerschmitt Bf-109. Over fifty Japanese and Israeli flags were said to be painted on his machine. And his sadistic, homosexual wingman, Rudolph "Tiger Shark" Stoltz. He, too, had a distinctive Messerschmitt; black splotched, big yellow marks and shark's teeth painted on his oil cooler and the underside of the cowling. The *Vierter Jagerstaffel.* Based in the Marianas, at the last report. But they could be carrier borne. In any event, he knew he would meet them before this campaign was over. And he would kill Rosencrance if he had to ram him. Why not? He was old. On the verge of being grounded and deep down he knew he was still *shinigurai.*

He rubbed his neck. Horikoshi had warned him about the arthritis a man his age should expect. He never told anyone of the sharp aching pain he felt, especially on long flights. Before taking off, he always doused himself with aspirin and a medication Steve Elkins had given him after he heard Yoshi complain about some of his aches. "Motrin is what they call it, Commander," the American said. And then raising an eyebrow, "Aching joints?"

"Oh, no, no," Yoshi had hastily protested. "A headache now and then. That's all." Elkins had smiled skeptically.

But another discomfort had crept in to exasperate the air group commander. He sniffed, and then cursed as his nose ran into his mask. Pulling the mask aside, he wiped with the back of his glove. Either he had been up and down too many times in the last few weeks, or age was affecting his sinuses, too. They had become very sensitive to changes in pressure. Sometimes there was blood on his handkerchief. Now they felt as if they had been blown up by a bicycle pump, and every other breath sent little flashing lights across his eyeballs. They had never been this bad before. He steadied himself and with sheer force of will looked beyond the sparks.

Ignoring the sinuses and his itching nose, Yoshi looked up. It was a brilliantly clear, cloudless day. At 22,000 feet, the sky above was as bright as well-scrubbed pottery. Looking down, the sea lay beneath him like a bowl whose edges were the ends of the earth. It was a rare day for the tropics. Surely, some clouds would appear soon. And where were the ubiquitous line squalls? When could you *not* see one from this altitude? It was almost as if the gods were scrubbing the heavens to present the best possible conditions for killing men. A vast shooting gallery brightened by celestial lighting.

He wiped his nose again, yawned several times so that his ears popped. To his relief, the pain in his sinuses lessened to tolerable levels. "Thank the gods," he muttered. Something as trivial as stubborn sinuses could kill a man.

Nothing challenging was in sight. No enemy ships or planes or friendly ships, for that matter. Only his squadrons strung out behind him, above and below. Above at 32,000 feet he glimpsed the twelve Zero-sens of Fighter Two. Led by *Yonaga*'s and the *Kujaku* Hotel's champion poker player, Lieutenant Atsushi Fukazawa, the squadron's pilots included a Russian, Dimitri Kozlov; a German, Josef Dietl; the Chinese, Chiang Tang; and their lone Druze, Shafeek Ghabra. Some of the men called Fighter Two "The International Brigade." But they were good. Very, very good.

Head tilted back, Yoshi watched Fighter Two fly one leg of a big curving pattern so wide it covered the massive flights of fighters and bombers spread beneath them. Yoshi smiled. Their vapor trails left giant sign curves, as if Fukazawa were using the heavens as a chalkboard to give a trigonometry lesson to the whole world.

Fukazawa, code named *Kamome* (Sea Gull) Leader, had the most important duty. He had to intercept high-flying enemy fighters before they could dive through Yoshi and the other fighters, and feed on the bombers that flew far below. "I'm a poker player, just like Admiral Isoroku Yamamoto," Fukazawa had said to Yoshi. The reference to the venerated, gambling Japanese admiral who had led the Imperial Navy during the Greater East Asia War, made Yoshi laugh. "Let me have top cover." And then Atsushi smiled, "I promise I won't draw to any inside straights."

"Don't bluff yourself into losing the whole pot," Yoshi had answered. "I'm part of the ante."

"Don't worry, Commander. I only play the cards I have," the young man had assured him.

Yoshi glanced at his wingmen. As usual, Hooperman and York were maintaining station perfectly off his elevators. Behind him and slightly lower, flew the twelve Grumman F6F Hellcats of Steve Elkins' Fighter Three. In their usual "twos," the big squared-off fighters held their formation with precision. Suddenly, Yoshi realized his neck, back, shoulders did not ache as much as usual. "That Motrin helps," he said into his oxygen mask.

A look below found Dempster's and Terada's bombers. Painted swirling blue-gray in a futile effort to make them less visible against the sea, 47 Aichi D3As and 51 Nakajima B5Ns plodded along close to the surface. Only a blind man could miss them. With no protection for their bellies, Dempster and Terada led their bombers at a very low altitude. If attacked, they would skim the surface. Their new fifty-caliber Browning machine guns protruded from their rear cockpits, giving them a formidable look. Still, Yoshi knew their greatest protection lay with the fighter squadrons.

But he did not have enough fighters. He wanted another squadron of Zero-sens. But Fujita insisted on holding eighteen Zeros and all six Seafires for CAP. This left Yoshi with only 27 fighters to escort almost a hundred bombers. "Not enough, Admiral," he had complained.

"I can spare no more," the old admiral had retorted adamantly.

Yoshi reached to the left, found the aluminum quadrant and, by touch, checked the black knobs of his throttle and mixture control which were side by side. With the propeller pitch on coarse, he had thinned the mixture to give him minimum fuel consumption. He eased the mixture control hack slightly until the *Taifu* backfired its objections. It would tolerate no more.

He glanced at his clipboard strapped to his knee. The enemy force was shown 285 miles northwest of *Yonaga*'s last position. Von Hanfstaengle should be about 550 miles southeast of Guam. But with his SOA held down to a mere 140 knots by the lumbering bombers, it would take two hours or more to reach von Hanfstaengl's last reported position. In two hours the enemy force could steam over sixty miles. No doubt, he would close the range on the Marianas and hope for the support of the aircraft based there. Still, Yoshi knew he would find them—kill them.

With radio silence in force, he banked slowly to the right in anticipation of von Hanfstaengl's course. He would close on the Marianas, too. Looking around at his groups he grunted with satisfaction. All squadrons had made the small correction in course. His group and squadron leaders Terada, Dempster, Elkins, and Fukazawa were very alert. Good men all. Would any of them survive the day?

Again he was struck by the clarity of the air. It was like a polished window pane. A fighter pilot's dream. He itched for combat. He had been born to do it. For a moment he hated the bombers. It was like dragging an anchor.

Glancing at his fifteen instruments and the gunsight

mounted just behind the ninety millimeter armorglass windshield, he felt the engine's vibrations coming up through his bucket seat. The *Taifu* was firing sweetly on all eighteen, turbos ticking over with a bare hum. Perfect. He knew his mount better than any mistress he had ever had. He was one with the Zero-sen, an extension of the control column, the throttle. He knew how to fly her on a fine, feathered edge, pushing her to her limits, but never over.

In the dim past, back in China, he had learned the victor was the pilot who had the better feel for his fighter and the touch to get the maximum out of it. He had always flown his fighter to the limit of its design, where even firing his guns could cause a stall. Attuned to his plane's every whim, every tremor, he felt the engine in his bones—could feel it when it edged toward a stall, pushing to the limit of wing loading and maneuverability. He knew how tight he could turn before the controls mushed out on him, a fatal mistake in a dogfight.

Maximum power, lift and maneuverability were controlled mostly by instinctive flying. "The seat of the pants," the Americans called it. And concentration had to be total. He always remained focused in spite of fear, fatigue, aching joints, brimming bladder—never allowing static into his mind. Aerial combat brought a connectedness with one's self, and he knew that small, cramped cockpit was exactly where he belonged. It was more than his home, it was his destiny and, perhaps, his casket.

"The best survival tactic is to always check your ass and stay alert," an old instructor had pounded into him at Tsuchiura when he was a teenage cadet. "If you can hear machine guns but can't see the plane, some *yakuza* is on your tail. Roll out of it or prepare to send your ashes home."

Yoshi had learned to demand hard weight-training of his pilots. Typical of World War Two aircraft, none of his fighters had hydraulically-operated controls. Consequently, dogfighting was very hard work, demanding strong arms, shoulders and legs. At high speeds, controls became extremely heavy. Also, without cabin pressurization, flying at high altitudes drained a man's energy. And so did pulling Gs in sharp turns. A two hundred-pound muscular man turned into 1,000-pounds of lead in a 5-g turn. After a few minutes of combat, a pilot became covered with perspiration and began to pant like a tired runner. The man in poor shape lost his quickness and it showed in slower turns and maneuvers. This flyer quickly became a flag on someone's fuselage.

Yoshi had drummed these and more lessons into his pilots in endless meetings and simulated dogfights. Again and again he pounded his axioms for survival into their heads: "If the enemy is above you, never climb to meet him because you will lose too much speed. You'll be a sitting duck." "Never run, even in the worst kind of trouble. That's what the enemy expects." "Always check your tail when you pop out of a cloud—you could have flown directly in front of an enemy fighter." "Avoid cumulus clouds, they are great hiding places." "Look out for thin cirrus. The enemy can look down through them and see you, while the glare blinds you." "In a head-on attack, be careful with your turns or you will give the enemy your belly as you bank to the side. He couldn't ask for a better target." "Never overshoot an enemy or you will fly right into his gun-sights and give him the easiest kill of his life."

Fukazawa's voice jolted him. "*Yubi* Leader, this is *Kamome* Leader. Enemy fighters at two o'clock high—upsun. Am engaging."

"Very well, *Kamome* Leader." Yoshi stared upsun at a bleary white patch of backlit cloud. The glare was dazzling, but on the far horizon he saw a swarm of specks racing out of the sun toward his groups. A gaggle of fighters. Maybe in squadron strength. Could Fukazawa and his

"International Brigade" stop them all? Probably not, but he would buy them time.

Then Elkins' voice with more trouble: "*Yubi* Leader, this is Rambo Leader. Fighters low at three o'clock. Closing fast on our bombers."

Then frantic calls from Terada and Dempster. "Fighters! Fighters! Low! Closing. I'm going down to the deck!"

Yoshi shouted out commands, armed his guns, turned on his electric sight, went to fine pitch—full rich—and goosed the engine. Then York's voice: "Ships! Ships! Carriers, cruisers, the whole bloody lot at one o'clock."

That was it. Just as he expected. Sixty miles closer to the Marianas. The enemy main force with a massive CAP covering. It was going to be a very tough engagement, especially if the enemy could draw them within range of his Marianas bases. He cursed himself. They were fighting on Otto von Hanfstaengl's terms. He had chosen the arena and dictated the tactics.

He called Elkins. "Rambo Leader. Intercept enemy fighters at three o'clock."

"Roger, *Yubi* Leader. Going downstairs."

Instantly, the big Hellcats dropped off into screaming dives, curving in a wide sweeping turn that would intercept the enemy squadrons before they could hit the bombers. But, again, there were more fighters than Yoshi had expected—at least two squadrons. The enemy carriers must have a greater capacity than he had foreseen, or their land-based fighters' range had been under-reported by Intelligence. However, with *Bennington*'s air groups, and the fighters and bombers from Iwo Jima attacking, the enemy must be hard pressed to defend his land bases, let alone mount an attack over 500 miles to the southeast. *Everyone* was over-extended.

Had they been fed misinformation by the Arabs? He suspected there were more aircraft based on Saipan and Tinian than they had expected. The rumors of the Focke-

Wulf 190 disturbed him. And *Bennington* had an enemy carrier to contend with, too. It made no difference. The mission was the compelling mandate. Their reason for existence. Nothing else mattered. Never had his groups turned back from an attack, and they would not set the precedent today. Damn the fighters. Damn the casualties. The two enemy carriers were now only a few miles to the northwest. They would kill those carrier, or be killed in the attempt.

For the moment he would hold his position. He could be needed by Fukazawa or Elkins. Maybe both. He had to wait to see where the enemy's maximum effort was made. It should be the bombers. Still, it could rain enemy fighters. He punched his combing in frustration.

With his Pratt and Whitney throttle open to full military power, Commander Steve Elkins led his squadron in a long curving dive that would take him to the rear of the attacking enemy squadrons. He threw a hasty glance at his instruments: air speed 480 knots, cylinder head temperature 240 degrees, oil temperature 220 degrees, oil pressure 85 pounds, manifold pressure 57 inches of mercury. None of the numbers really registered, but his subconscious told him they were all "green." "Good," he said to himself. "The old bird is holding together."

Without looking, he knew his wingman, Lieutenant Phil Lunoy, was below and to his right rear. A wingman's job was to stick like glue to his leader's tail while his leader did the shooting. He was the leader's life insurance. Lunoy was one of the best. A superb pilot, he could follow his "top gun's" most violent maneuvers. He was sure if he ever flew through the gates of hell, Lunoy would be there clinging to his tail. Although he was only 23 years old, Lunoy was already a veteran of four battles, with three kills of his own to add to Elkins' nine.

Outnumbered two to one, Elkins knew he would need the massed fire power of his seventy-two fifty-caliber machine guns. He disliked releasing the wingmen, but he had no choice. He spoke into his microphone. "Rambo Flight, this is Rambo Leader. Rambo Yellow, Green and Blue individual combat. Form a line abreast. Let's clobber the bastards." Quickly, the Hellcats juggled and bounced in each other's slipstream as they broke into a saw-toothed line.

Now Fighter Three was swooping down on the enemy's trailing aircraft. Twenty-four Messerschmitt Bf-109s flying in their usual *schwarms* of twos. He cursed. The leading elements of fighters had opened fire on the bombers. But this time the Aichis and Nakajimas fired back with their heavy fifty-caliber guns. Hot flames bubbled out of the bombers and tracers strung across the sky like webs spun by mad spiders. The Messerschmitts curved upward to attack the Aichis, which were climbing to reach dive-bombing altitude. Shells and bullets chewed into their exposed bellies.

One Aichi, its bomb hit, found its moment of glory like a great incandescent nova. A thousands pounds of high explosives lit the sky, rivaling the sun with its luminosity. Another, with a dead pilot, did a graceful half-roll, levelled off and slid across the sea, flinging up sheets of blue water and white spray before it finally stopped and settled into its grave. A third bomber belched flame and shovelled out black smoke. Dropping its bomb, it tried to dive away. The nose went down but the plane did not, skidding out of control directly into raging bursts of cannon fire. Bullet and cannon streams flickered and slashed through it from cowling to tail hook. It flipped on its back and tumbled into the sea.

Elkins heard Blue Leader, Brian Lanigan, curse in frustration. "Come on. Come on. Let's kill the bastards!"

With the advantage of diving speed, Elkins and Fighter

Three quickly closed on the attacking enemy. Trying for a shot at a bomber, a 109 slid into view ahead, perfectly silhouetted in Elkins' sight. It appeared cleanly, so beautifully his lungs expanded for sheer joy. After a short burst, the Arab tried to pull up and Elkins countered by hauling back on the stick. He tasted jubilation as the black fighter swam back into his sights. Every muscle was tensed to hold the Hellcat steady when he pressed the button. Even so, the blaze of fire racing from his wings made him flinch. His six guns shaped a glowing cone of destruction that shot off his enemy's hood and almost amputated his right wing. With big bullets ripping the wing roots and glycol pipes, the Me-109 began gushing white smoke. Rolling onto his back, the enemy pilot dropped out of his cockpit. The parachute blossomed into a big yellow canopy like a great daisy. Then the body plummeted. The pilot had forgotten to lock his harness.

"Ha! Have a refreshing swim all the way to Mecca!" Elkins shouted.

Despite the close pursuit of Fighter Three, the 109s were raging through the bombers, shooting down another four or five within seconds. Hot on their tails, Fighter Three dared their own friendly fire from the terrified bomber gunners to hound the Messerschmitts. Reefing out of his dive, Lunoy fired a long burst into the cockpit of one climbing enemy. The canopy shattered, right wheel—minus tire—dropped, and the port wing cracked, bent and ripped off. Then the whole aircraft disintegrated like a house of cards kicked by a child. The pieces scattered. No parachute.

"Score one for the good guys," Lunoy shouted.

The fighter circuit was full of shouts of triumph, of fear, warnings. Fukazawa's men came through and the bomber pilots, too. Some were unintelligible, a few of the foreign pilots reverting to their native tongue in their feverish excitement and moments of sheer terror. *"Banzai!" "Itbakh alaykum!" "Merde!" "Sterben arschloch!" "Dio mio!"* squawked through, mixed with the usual American expletives, commands and cries of warning. But Elkins could pick out and distinguish one voice louder than the others. It was Lanigan. "Henderson, Jesus. Two on your ass."

"See 'em."

"Break right! Break right—no! No! Right!"

Then a bright white flash, like a soaring rocket, as Henderson's Hellcat pulled up sharply and arced into a long curving parabola; a smoking rainbow that ended in the sea.

"Oh, no. No!"

Then Elkins saw them. Small fighters like scaled down P-47s. The feared Focke-Wulf 190. Eight or ten of them ripping into Terada's torpedo bombers. With each fighter striking with four twenty-millimeter cannons and two 13-millimeter machine guns, it was like watching sharks on a feeding frenzy. Every fighter seemed to score with its first burst. On the first pass, ten Nakajimas were shot out of the sky.

Elkins shouted into his microphone. "*Yubi* Leader, this is Rambo Leader.

"We need help down here. I've got two squadrons of 109s and a squadron of 190s." He looked around in anguish as more bombers crashed. "We'll lose 'em all, *Yubi* Leader."

"Rambo Leader, this is *Yubi* Leader. Coming down."

Fukazawa had driven off the high-flying enemy, which had probably been a diversion, anyway. Yoshi shouted into his microphone, "*Kamome* Leader, we're needed downstairs. Are your weapons free?"

"Enemy has withdrawn. Lost two of my boys. Weapons free."

"The bombers are in trouble. Follow my lead and look for the One-Nineties. They're our first priority! Kill them!"

"Roger. Coming down in your backwash."

Yoshi pulled his nose back and watched the horizon tilt and fall away like a table cloth sliding off a polished table. Then, with Hooperman and York tucked in tight to his elevators and Fukazawa not far behind, he split-essed down, half rolling into a power dive. The world was upside down, the table cloth a gray ceiling where the bombers and fighters were crawling, burning, crashing, killing each other. They grew bigger and bigger every second.

Things were out of control. Bombers were being swatted out of the sky like flies squirted by insecticide. A Messerschmitt and a Focke-Wulf were hit by Elkins' guns. Another Hellcat spun into the sea.

Yoshi increased his dive, but dared not push the throttle into overboost. Pulling out at near 600 knots would knock out a man half his age. Indicated speed four-hundred-eighty knots. Fast enough. Maybe too fast. He had no choice. He would dive vertically through the dogfight and pick off the enemy fighters before they had a chance to react. These were not the kind of tactics he had taught his men in gunnery school, but he and his wingmen had the marksmanship to make it work. He spoke into his microphone. "*Yubi* Two and Three engage the Focke-Wulfs. *Kamome* Flight, targets of opportunity, individual combat."

Within seconds, Matsuhara's flight followed by Fukazawa's ten Zeros plunged into the melee below. It was a barroom brawl devoid of organization. The only aircraft that showed discipline and order were the bombers. Yoshi saw only about thirty Aichis and the same number of Nakajimas in the air. They bunched, trying to concentrate their fire power.

Pulling back on his stick, Yoshi curved toward a 190 hounding a Nakajima. The Zero bounced, vibrated. The fog came. He shook his head, gulped oxygen and concentrated on the three black rings on the hundred-millimeter pink reticle. The Focke-Wulf bounded in, out, and around. "Sacred Buddha, calm down!" he screamed at his fighter. Flattening out and throttling back, the hybrid aircraft finally collected itself in a level, composed attack.

The pilot of the 190 was so intent on killing the bomber, he made the novice's mistake of not looking back. He never knew he was under fire until Yoshi's shells and bullets ripped holes in his wings and fuselage. Then be made his second mistake. He pulled back on the stick, giving Yoshi a target he couldn't miss. Yoshi's shells and bullets shattered his canopy, smashed his instrument panel and blew off his left shoulder. Blood and hydraulic fluid washed and sprayed through the cockpit. As the fighter twisted and flipped wildly, he screamed for the blessing of death. It came quickly, when the fighter bored into the sea at over 400 knots.

Two more Focke-Wulfs were hit. Burning like a comet, the first gradually dissolved into smoking fragments as it arched into the sea. The second, hounded by a Hellcat, gyrated wildly with a dying man at the controls and finally fell into a terminal spin.

Lanigan's voice: "Have a nice day, you prick!"

Fukazawa's ten fighters drove down onto the fight with more destruction. Within seconds, three Messerschmitts had been shot down. Parachutes speckled the view below. Yellow for the Arabs and white for the Japanese. And men were in dinghies. Most were bomber crews.

Despite the heavy losses to the onslaught from above, the enemy pilots whirled and fought back ferociously. Phil Lunoy had just poured a burst into a Messerschmitt that was hanging like a trapeze artist as it fired into the belly of an Aichi, when he heard a frightening sound. Machine guns. Behind him. He threw everything into the left corner, but too late. The four twenty-millimeter cannons and two 13-millimeter machine guns of a Focke-Wulf 190 poured shells and slugs into the Hellcat. One shell ripped a fuel tank.

Fuel and hydraulic fluid gushed over his legs. Lunoy never saw it, never even heard the thumping impact. The stench of fuel had just reached his nostrils and he had just screamed, "No!" when the 13-millimeter bullet struck his oxygen bottle. It exploded. The Grumman flared like a match. Pure oxygen mixed with high-octane fuel made a furnace heat that turned his flight suit to ash in a second; boiled his body in its own fluids and peeled off his skin as if he were molting thin black sheets of tissue. He tried to scream but only sucked flames into his lungs. The cockpit was melting around him and he had just grabbed the Canopy Jettison Lever when the Hellcat blew up like a bomb. Turned into a swirling cloud of debris, the fighter blew away like a handful of dust. From above, Steve Elkins saw only a flash of white as stark as lightning. Then after images blinked across his retinas.

Screaming, Elkins stormed after the 190. But a burst into his port wing sent him rolling into a frantic dive before he, too, was immolated. Beneath him was a Nakajima dribbling smoke with a Messerschmitt hounding it. The enemy fighter was only about a hundred yards ahead. A glance into his rearview mirror told him his tail was clear. He only needed a few seconds. The Messerschmitt loafed into his gunsight. He jabbed the button, pouring all his hate, pain and misery into the vile object. Miraculously, nothing seemed to happen to the enemy despite the smoking tracers that it seemed to be absorbing like a sponge sopping up water. Then its tail flew off. It nosed over but did not dive. Instead, it flopped, flipped and tumbled about in maneuvers never conceived by its designers. The pilot was flung out of the cockpit and was promptly swatted by his starboard wing and hurled like a ball hit by a bat.

"You just got clobbered for four bases!" Elkins screamed, laughing and wiping tears from his cheeks at the same time.

Yoshi Matsuhara had just pulled a mind-jarring five-g

turn when he heard Hooperman's yelp of triumph. "Sent one of the buggers west or east, or wherever those bloody bastards go."

Yoshi didn't have time to respond. Instead, his concentration was on his reflector sight that slowly pulled up and framed a 190 intent on splashing a Nakajima with a dead gunner. With a perfect killing angle, the Focke-Wulf closed in like a predator for the throat. Yoshi could envision the cruel smile twisting the Arab's face. He would wipe it off.

Holding tight to the stick grip, Yoshi gave him the prescribed three rings of gunsight, a quarter length deflective lead, and gently pushed the button. After the first gun-camera pressure, the guns' recoil hit the airframe with the kick of a bull. With elation he saw his shells and bullets chew through the 190's thin metal airframe like a chain saw through dry twigs. The wings flashed on and off with shiny splotches as if he were knocking gold coins out of the paintwork. Then the top half of the cowling was shot loose, bent up and flew back, bouncing off the canopy. Shells struck the big BMW engine, blowing off a cluster of exhaust outlets and the tops of four or five cylinders. Immediately, oil sprayed.

Yoshi's world went black as the 190's engine dumped oil all over him. One loud voice boomed through his earphones. It was Hooperman. "Break, Commander. In Christ's name break!" Then his Zero shuddered under hammer blows of bullet strikes.

Blindly he kicked rudder and rolled into a turn. He knew his attacker was right behind him, no doubt trying to bring him back into his gunsight. But, now, the pelting airstream had begun to clear his windshield. Breathing big gusts of relief, Yoshi got his first glimpses of the outside world. He might have become someone's million-dollar fortune if not, at that moment, he had not climbed into the base of the only cloud in the sky. He was sure that it had been sent by the gods because he hadn't even noticed it before. Blinded again by the swirling vapor, he checked his gyro horizon and eased his climb, until the rate of climb indicator steadied up. He continued straight and level for a moment, his hands trembling and his heart pounding so hard he could feel the pulsations in his throat. This had never happened to him before. Smothered in his enemy's oil. Blind. A new way to die. How devious were the gods?

York's voice: "Jesus, Commander. You ain't bought the whole packet, 'ave you? Where you at, guv'nur? C'mon, c'mon!"

Suddenly, Yoshi burst out of the cloud into the brilliant pristine sky. Enough oil had blown off his windshield and canopy so that he could see ahead, but not very well to the port side. The canopy was very foul. He cranked it open and was immediately struck by a gale. Hooperman and York crowded in protectively. "I say, *Yubi* Leader," Hooperman said. "Can you see, old sport? You've been dipped in oil."

"You look like a rat dipped in cat shit, guv'nur."

"I'm fine. Fine. My windshield is clear enough. I can use my gunsight." He looked around. "Where did everyone go?"

York's voice, expletory but accurate: "Most of them bloody fuckers's bugger-all. But some's still on the block. Got one One-Ninety at eleven o'clock high an' a bunch o' One-Oh-Nines fuckin' with Fukazawa's and Elkins' lads at two o'clock low."

Yoshi saw them. Maybe twenty Messerschmitts, mixing it with about seven Zero-sens and the same number of Hellcats. Before he could turn his head, a 109's Daimler-Benz shot flames over most of its fuselage, lost its rudder and flipped over and over until it ripped itself to pieces on the hard surface of the sea. It sprayed burning gasoline over an area the size of a baseball diamond.

A Zero dipped down low over the grave. The exultant,

heavily accented voice of the Druze, Shafeek Ghabra, broke over his radio. "*Alla akbar,* camel dung!"

The guttural voice of the German, Josef Dietl, "Fukazawa, turn! *Bruch!* The One-Ninety! On your tail!"

Fukazawa's voice: "See him!" Then a scream and Fukazawa's radio went dead.

High and to the west, Yoshi saw his squadron leader's burning Zero-sen curving toward the sea. It left black bobs of smoke behind like ink flicked from a pen. The 190 pulled up behind it triumphantly like a hawk that had just struck a pigeon.

"*Gott in himmel!* Bail out! Bail out!"

But Fukazawa never answered, riding the Zero into its pulverizing impact with the sea.

"Sacred Buddha!" Yoshi agonized. "No! No!" Fukazawa had played his last hand. There was nothing more to lose.

Hooperman's voice jerked his mind from his dead squadron leader. "Our bombers are going in."

Yoshi leaned over the combing and looked around. "Where? Where?"

"Three o'clock."

Then Yoshi saw them. Only about twenty of Dempster's dive bombers were left, but they were at about 3,000 feet, flaps down almost ready for their dive. And below maybe twenty-five Nakajima B5N torpedo bombers were swinging in from both sides of the carriers. The enemy fleet faced a devastating three-dimensional attack. Desperately, the enemy fighters, with Fukazawa's survivors and Elkins' Hellcats hounding them, roared in for their final effort.

Big caliber AA was splattering the sky like thrown sludge. The escorting *Gearings* and two cruisers were firing their DP cannons so fast the ships seemed to be burning. Forty-millimeter, thirty-millimeter and smaller machine guns began to add their own smoking projectiles to the maelstrom. Ugly brown smears pock-marked the unsullied sky like a revolting rash on an infant's skin. The barrage was aimed at aircraft identity be damned. Both friend and foe took their chances.

Commander Oliver Y.K. Dempster put the enemy fighters out of his mind, but not the flak. The nearer he got to the enemy, the more there was. Each burst seemed to spawn two more, doubling and redoubling like a breeding virus until the sky was blanketed with blackness, flecked with small white puffs, streaked with red, green, and yellow. But he led his bombers straight on like blind men walking down the middle of a busy road, never deviating from his run to the bomb point. One bomber just touched the edge of a big black blot and there was a flicker of incandescence that pulverized two men in the time it took to inhale. Almost immediately, another Aichi was hit and angled down as if it were seeking out its executioner. A third D3A was on fire. It dropped its bomb but blew up anyway, before it could even turn.

"*Sacre merde*—Holy shit!" he heard his lone French pilot, the highly capable Lieutenant Charles de Guingand mutter into his open microphone.

"Radio discipline!" Dempster shouted. His whole world was the enemy fleet below. Two carriers. He wanted them both. He would ignore the cruisers and destroyers. The casualties. He would split his forces. He spoke into his microphone. "This is *Kani* (Crab) Leader. *Kani* Blue and Green take the leading carrier. *Kani* White and Yellow take the second."

There were acknowledgments that registered on his subconscious. He was edging toward the lead carrier. It was one of the Russians. *Buzaymah* of the *Kiev* Class. And so was the second, the *Magid*. Unmistakable. Big ships. Fast. Armed with a forest of anti-aircraft. The AA bursting around him was five-inch, 38-caliber from the *Gearings* and 76-millimeter automatic fire from the carriers and cruisers. There would be forty-millimeter, twenty-millimeter and six-barreled, thirty-millimeter Gatlings waiting for him to come into range. And probably more. It made no difference. He would kill the carrier despite whatever it and its escorts could throw at him.

All of his concentration was on the target. He watched as the carrier appeared to pass along his left wing-root. When it was invisible, he closed his cooling fins, set the propeller on full coarse, opened the slat-type airbrakes hinged below the outer wings, and turned on his autopilot.

Glancing at the red rods projecting above the wings to confirm the brakes were open, he shouted into his intercom, "Tomatsu, here we go!"

"Yes, Sir," his gunner replied. "Let's put one down her stack!"

Then he winged over to the left and plunged into his dive. Quickly, he glanced at the red line on his side window and found he had to pull back slightly on his stick to attain the correct 85-degree dive angle. *Buzaymah* was directly under his Windshield and growing. Perfect. Now it was pilot judgement and experience. He had both. He instinctively worked his controls to keep the growing carrier in his windshield. *Buzaymah* was curving to port. Dempster laughed. "No chance, comrade!" He stared through his sight, crosshairs on the center of the flight deck.

The intensity of the AA was unbelievable. It seemed the whole Russian arsenal lined the flight deck in galleries and crammed the superstructure. It was all very clear. Seventy-six-millimeter cannons firing sixty-rounds a minute were mounted in pairs in gun houses, and thirty-millimeter machine guns fired from multiple mounts. There could be 20s, 40s, 37s and 57s firing at him, too. He couldn't tell and it didn't matter. The cannon fire exploded far too high, but the smaller shells came at him in smoking torrents like typhoons of burning embers. He bit his lip and tightened his grip on the control column. He felt like a duck in a shooting gallery patronized by machine gunners.

He wanted to release at 600 feet. But he would probably be dead by then. At 900 feet, he pulled the manual bomb release and felt the huge jar, the tug downward and then upward as the 1,200-pound bomb was swung free of the fuselage and propeller by its crutch like a sling-shot. Pulling back on the stick, he felt the big bomber flatten, the autopilot kicking in to help a pilot who might be fogged out by g-forces. But his senses were clear.

Flattening out at less than a hundred feet, he heard Tomatsu shout with joy. Turning his head, he saw his bomb explode squarely in the middle of *Buzaymah*'s flight deck. Curving away, he passed directly over the big cruiser *Beth-shan* which ignored him, occupied with dive bombers and torpedo bombers. Now that he had dropped his bomb, he was a low priority target. He laughed to himself.

Weaving through the flak and flying over enemy destroyers, he managed to look back. He recoiled with horror. His next three bombers were hit by thirty-millimeter fire, shredded, burned, demolished like toys. He heard de Guingard shout his last words, "*Je suis mort*—I am dead! *Je suis mort!*" as his burning bomber plummeted into the sea.

But the enemy gunners couldn't take all the targets. Dive bombers were attacking and the torpedo bombers were maneuvering to attack from all points of the compass. But the Nakajimas were late. Terada should have had his attack coordinated with the dive bombers. Two more bombs bit the carrier, greatly reducing its AA fire. Its own ordnance began to burn and explode. Then a huge volcano erupted, blowing the flight deck forward of amidships over the side like a table thrown in a barroom brawl.

But carrier *Magid* still had not been hit. White and Yellow Sections only had nine dive bombers. And just as the lead plane reached its dive point, three 109s broke away from the dogfight and struck the bombers. Two were shot down immediately, while the remaining seven plunged into their dive. But cruiser *Babur*, a light cruiser with six new 125-millimeter guns and top-heavy with new AA, had crowded close to *Magid* with four *Gearings*. The seven surviving Aichis dove into a solid wall of flak.

The bomb of one exploded, taking another with it. A Messerschmitt, apparently out of ammunition, raced in from the rear and side and rammed another. Locked together, the two aircraft whirled in a macabre embrace like a pair of mating insects. The engine of the bomber bounced off the bridge of a destroyer.

Another Aichi lost its landing gear and one wing. Flopping over and over, it flung its bomb high into the sky and lunged into the sea. The remaining three, bounced and buffeted by AA and plagued by the two remaining fighters, dropped their bombs frantically before they, too, could be destroyed. A 76-millimeter shell destroyed one and a second was shot down by a 109. The third dropped down so low the AA gunners on the escorts had to depress below the horizontal to fire at it. The Aichi managed to zigzag its way to safety. All the bombs missed.

"*Yubi* Leader, this is *Kani* Leader. No hits on second carrier." Dempster pushed the stick to the left and kicked rudder, trying to avoid the full armament of a *Gearing* directly ahead.

Yoshi heard static and other voices shouting through the circuit. "Repeat! Repeat, *Kani* Leader."

But Dempster would never repeat. A twenty-millimeter gunner on the *Gearing*'s fantail tracked the Aichi as it swung away from the stern, gave it a good lead and depressed the trigger. He held it down until his sixty-round magazine was empty. His first tracers flew past the prop and then he let the big plane march through his tracer stream. He could see flashes like flares being set of all along the belly of the plane. One spatted wheel exploded, bits and chunks of aluminum were ripped from the length of the aircraft. "*Allah akbar!* Die Japanese dog!" his loader shouted, jamming a fresh magazine into the open breech.

Dempster felt the first shell hit the Sakae with sledgehammer force. The bottom half of the cowling flew off and immediately flames shot from broken exhaust stubs. Then his instrument panel exploded in his face and blinded his right eye. His left rudder pedal flew up and hit him in the face. Strange. His booted foot was still in the pedal. More explosions.

Tomatsu screamed, a short blood-spraying cry. A shell had penetrated his seat, punched through his buttocks, shattering the big bones of his pelvis and driving up into the lower intestines before it exploded. The blast nearly blew the young gunner in half. With his lungs splattered all over the front of the cockpit, his scream was cut off before it could form.

Dempster had no time for Tomatsu. He was beyond help, anyway. Parts of the gunner had splattered against the back of his head and neck. He looked down in horror. He had been hit in both legs; disabling, bone-smashing wounds. Blood was spraying from his right leg that had turned to gelatin just above the knee. Fuel was gushing in from the forward tank and mixing with the blood. Flames began to work their way quite slowly up his legs. The pain was beyond comprehension. He screamed and screamed again.

The last piece of equipment to fail was the radio. He had left his channel open to command his other sections, which no longer existed. Now everyone heard his shrieks. Although the control cables had been shot out, the Aichi flew itself more or less level for a surprisingly long time and the flames worked their way up his legs and burned at his crotch. Howling like a maddened animal, he reached for the canopy release and he cried in agony and frustration as he futilely tried to move his shattered legs away from the fire that was eating them. Eventually, the Aichi performed a slow roll and then mercifully drove itself into the sea. The screaming stopped.

The cheering men on the fantail of the *Gearing* pounded each other on the back.

Yoshi pounded his combing. Mumbled bitter curses. One of the finest had just died horribly. There was still one more carrier down there to destroy. The sacrifice of Dempster and his men would be avenged. But it was up to the torpedo bombers. There were ten of them left. Converging on the carrier from the bow, stern, both beams.

Yoshi looked around. Only about five Zeros, six Hellcats, and the two Sea Furies were left to engage about the same number of Messerschmitts. All the 190s had been destroyed. The dogfight had deteriorated into a few low-level scraps that ringed the perimeter of the tightly grouped battle force. At the moment, he had more than half his ammunition left and no target. Then he saw them. Three 109s. Charging after the torpedo bombers. One had York on its tail, another Elkins. The third was in the clear. Yoshi kicked rudder and pushed his stick forward. The Arab had a good angle on a Nakajima. Yoshi cursed. His own attack angle was almost a full deflection shot.

Pushing the throttle through the last stop, the great *Taifu* roared out its throaty power as its turbos jammed oxygen into the cylinders. Overboost. It was dangerous. Could burn up his engine in less than five minutes. He had no choice. He dared a glance at his cylinder-head temperature. Two-sixty-nine and climbing. And the airspeed indicator chased around the clock, pursuing the red danger line. He must be doing over 500 knots. He felt vibrations building in his seat, the pedals, the stick. He dare not let his eyes linger on the instruments. Rarely did he ever look in combat. It was an easy way to die. His attention was riveted on his target which had just wobbled into his gunsight.

The Me-109 was closing fast on the Nakajima. The torpedo bomber pilot's total attention was on the carrier, which was only about a mile ahead. Flak was streaming by. Flashing. Exploding. Filling the sky with its brown and black puffs. Kicking up water in the bomber's path. Yoshi recognized the numbers on the tail and the big "T" on the fuselage. Terada. His bomber leader. Leading his few surviving boys into the mouth of hell. It was a superb, courageous, suicidal attack. The B5Ns were racing in on their target as if it were the hub and they the spokes of a wheel. The enemy was forced to split his fire. Concentration on a single target was impossible.

But the fire was murderous. A Nakajima lost its torpedo then its left wing and cartwheeled into the sea. Another pulled up with a dead pilot and did a full loop before crashing. A third spouted fire and black smoke, dropping slowly until it skimmed the surface and then flipped over on its back as the sea reached up, caught it and pulled it down into its grave. But the eight survivors drove on.

He heard Elkins shout, "Got the bastard!" Then York's shout of incoherent triumph. "His pisser's in the twist. Fry, bugger, fry!"

Now, only Yoshi's Messerschmitt remained in pursuit of the Nakajimas. And the pilot was relentless, either very brave or very foolish. He had to dare his own fire to make his run. He was almost in range of Terada's bomber when Yoshi pulled back on his stick. Momentum and centrifugal force fought him. It took all the strength in his powerful arms, and he had to brace his feet to get added leverage to pull the stick back. The airframe vibrated, bounced about as invisible forces pounded and dragged at his airfoils. His wings actually seemed to flap. Blood drained from his brain and his vision clouded and darkened. His stomach tried to sink through his bowels like a slug of lead, and his legs were petrified wood. Insupportable pressure pushed his head down until he thought his spine would bend and his seat collapse.

But he had closed on the enemy. He was almost in range. But the Arab had turned and given Yoshi a nearly full deflection shot. Seesawing his rudder pedals, he turned first to the right and then quickly to the left, cutting the deflective lead in half. The 109 meandered into his gunsight and then out of it. Yoshi cursed, fought the fog, reduced throttle and brought the black fighter back into the reticle. The Messerschmitt's wingtips touched the inner ring.

The 109 fired a burst. Terada ignored him. He was close to his drop point. Yoshi increased throttle and quickly the enemy's wingtips grew out to the third ring. A touch of rudder to ease deflection a bit more and the fighter filled the pink circle. Gently with a surgeon's touch, he pushed the button. Long smoky trails of gunfire reached out for the 109 and erupted into bright yellow strikes along his fuselage. "Die, you dog!" Yoshi screamed.

Slices of aluminum flaked off the fuselage, flashed in the bright sunlight and then folded back into the slipstream. The Arab refused to die. Miraculously, he was still firing on the Nakajima. Yoshi stared with disbelief. He had never seen such determination this side of Bushido. But it cost the Arab his life. A stream of shells hit the cockpit, turning it into a blizzard of shattered Plexiglas, broken plastic mixed with gore. The 109 swerved, did a half roll and buried itself in the ocean at over 400 knots.

Yoshi had no time to rejoice. An explosion to starboard flipped him almost on his port wingtip. It took all of his adrenalin-driven strength to throw everything to the right and pull the fighter up before he followed the Arab into the sea. Again, in overboost, he clawed for altitude, circling away from the carrier.

He was looking at *Magid* when the first torpedo hit. Then three more in quick succession. With three holes in her starboard side and one in her port, she lost speed and began to settle. Almost immediately, she took a starboard list. There were cheers in the his earphones. But very, very few.

He looked for enemy fighters. But the sky was clear of the 109s. Either the last one had been shot down or the few survivors were trying for the American fields on Guam. None would have enough fuel to reach their fields on Saipan or Tinian.

Now, circling at reduced throttle he stared down. *Buzaymah* was burning from stem to stern. Her crew was abandoning ship. Some were jumping over the side, others were sliding down lines to a destroyer that had come alongside. *Magid* had rolled heavily to starboard. She was nearly on her beams ends. Crewmen slid off or jumped into the sea. They looked like ants floating in a flood. Yoshi nodded with satisfaction. Both carriers were finished.

He spoke into his microphone, "*Yubi* Groups, this is *Yubi* Leader. Form on me. It's time to go home." He glanced at the point option data scribbled on his clipboard. "Vector on Point Delta."

There were acknowledgments, and the aircraft all turned on a easterly heading. Soon, York and Hooperman snugged up close to his elevators. Looking at his depleted forces, Yoshi felt he would vomit. High above, only three Zero-sens of Fighter Two remained to give top cover. Josef Dietl led the "Vic." Except for the German, the "International Brigade" had ceased to exist. Elkins with four Hellcats trailed. Below only five Nakajimas formed up with three Aichis. Yoshi was shocked. He thought all the Aichis had been destroyed.

They had scored well, destroying two carriers. But the price had been high, so terribly high. Once when a young cadet he had heard an officer say, "The price of glory is never too high."

"You're wrong! Wrong!" Yoshi shouted, pounding his instrument panel until the needles jumped. "Too many have died. Too many!" He forgot his circuit was open. Everyone heard him. No one said a word.

They had settled on their course and droned on toward *Yonaga* for a few minutes when Elkins' called York, "*Yubi* Three, you're leaving a marker."

Yoshi turned his head. His heart bulged into his throat. The Sea Fury was leaving a brownish-white trail.

Hooperman's voice: "I say, old boy, you copped it bad."

"Rat shit, your nibs. Just pissin' a smidgin o' glycol," York answered.

Yoshi said: "More than that. You have a fire. Can you smell petrol? Engine temp?"

York: "Engine temps up a bit, petrol stink. She always stinks like a Soho 'ore."

"Bail out!" Hooperman shouted with undisguised alarm. "Hit the silk! Straight away!"

"Ain't nothin', an' I ain't goin' in no drink for nothin', guv'nur. I ain't 'ad a bath since me mudder . . ."

Yoshi was staring over his shoulder when the Sea Fury blew up. It exploded with incredible violence, as if every cavity had been packed with high explosives. A powerful machine of the air, perfectly controlled, was instantly replaced by a brilliant orange ball with a white hot core. Instantaneous combustion consumed its aluminum airframe, the one-ton Bristol Centaurus engine hurled ahead and below Yoshi's port wing like a boulder thrown by a catapult. Bits and pieces of the fighter no larger than a playing card rained in a burning shower.

"No! No!" Yoshi screamed, fighting his controls as the fighter bounced, swerved and tilted upward in the shock waves. Tail down, he nearly stalled. Increasing throttle, he dropped his nose and starboard wing to regain control. His eyes burned and streamed as if he had looked at a welder's torch.

Hooperman's broken voice. "He's gone—gone. My God! Elwyn! My God!"

Yoshi choked back a half-sob, half shout of rage. Wiped his nose, his cheeks. The keen, crusty Cockney was no more. The fearless fighter, tenacious, courageous wingman who had saved his life a half-dozen times. The wit, the humor, the close, great friend. Gone in the time it took to blink.

Again the instruments jerked and jumped under the blows of the gloved fists. "It isn't fair! Amaterasu, it isn't fair. You took too many—the best," he shouted into the slipstream.

There was no answer, only the sound of the wind howling through the cockpit.

Twenty-one
The Killer Bees

"Radar reports unidentified aircraft bearing three-five-zero true, range ninety miles."

"Very well," Fujita said. Pushing by Captain Mitake Arai, he bent over the chart table and plotted the sighting himself.

Standing a good distance from the chart table and out of earshot of the admiral, Gary Mardoff spoke to Brent Ross. "Why doesn't he launch his fighters?" Anxiously, he waved overhead, "We only have six Zeros up there."

Brent answered patiently, while Loren Hobel and Alistair Cunningham huddled close. "Too soon. He's got to wait—conserve his fighters' fuel." He stabbed a finger at the chart table where Fujita and Arai were conferring. Fujita waved at the sky, pounded the chart and the executive officer nodded in agreement. "He'll launch any time, now."

Rear Admiral Byron Whitehead spoke up. "And keep in mind, there may be other aircraft around."

"What do you mean?"

Mardoff followed the rear admiral's hand as he gestured on the bearing. "They like to draw you off on an all-out interception of their main raid and then," he swept his hand low, embracing most of the horizon, "try to sneak a few torpedo bombers in low under your radar—hit from any point of the compass."

Hobel said, "I hear they have a 'Jihad Corps'. A special attack corps."

Whitehead nodded grimly. "Yes. Most are Shi'ites. They'll make it to paradise if they can crash into our ships."

"Like the Shi'ite who blew up the marine barracks in Lebanon," Mardoff offered.

"Exactly. He's wallowing in milk and honey."

"But not the marines," Hobel mumbled.

Mardoff swallowed hard, his eyes popping as if pressure was building inside his skull. He tried to speak but his throat appeared so constricted he couldn't articulate. While Mardoff struggled, Cunningham offered his own observation. "By Jove, isn't that bloody irony, if I've ever seen it."

"What do you mean?" Hobel asked.

The Englishman glanced at the chart table, where Arai and Fujita were now involved in an animated discussion. He spoke in hushed tones. "Just this, Loren. The Japanese invented the Kamikaze attack, and now it's been bloody well turned against them."

Looking at Mardoff, Brent drove in his needle. Using Cunningham's British idiom, he said crisply, "You must face up to it, gentlemen, this show is no cricket match. It's more like a bloody fox hunt."

"You think that's funny?" Mardoff spat.

"Uproarious," Brent said, driving the needle in a little deeper.

Eyeing each other silently, the reporters fingered their video recorders. Hobel brought his up, aimed it in the direction of the still-invisible raid and shot a few feet of sky. The sound of Fujita's dividers thumping the chart caught their attention. The men moved closer to the admiral. The old man spoke to himself more than to Arai.

"First sighted at one-hundred-eighty miles. Their SOA is about one-fifty."

Arai checked a hand calculator. "Right, Sir."

"Check with CIC."

"Aye, aye, Sir." In a moment, the talker reported verification by CIC.

Fujita shouted at the talker. "Sound the general alarm. Stand by to launch all fighters! Battle group to assume AA formation!"

Within minutes, the ship was at general quarters and the reserve fighters launched. Every man on the bridge donned a helmet and life jacket. Quartermaster Rokokura Hio checked the reporters' life jackets to be certain they were properly fastened.

"Fasten your helmet straps tight or not at all," Brent said to the reporters. "Concussion can dig a loose strap right into your chin and than snap the bucket back down hard."

"Or don't fasten them at all, old man?"

"Right, Alistair, so that a blast can blow it clear off."

"But then I'd be exposed," Mardoff said.

"No problem."

"No problem?"

"Yeah, Mardoff, you'll probably be dead anyway."

The reporters fumbled with their straps. Again, Hio checked each man.

"You're in rare form today, Commander," Mardoff said scornfully.

"A naval battle is a rare thing," Brent said casually.

Another command and *Yonaga* returned to base course—a course that drew the ship closer to its returning air groups but, at the same time, made the run of the approaching enemy aircraft shorter. Battleship *New Jersey* and four of the destroyers drew close to the carrier. A grim silence settled over the ship.

Forty minutes before there had been jubilation, when

the radio room first picked up Commander Matsuhara's weak transmission reporting the destruction of *Buzaymah* and *Magid*. Then *Bennington* reported her air groups were heavily engaged in the northeast Philippine Sea, just west of the Farallon de Pajaros. Apparently, General Ibrahim Mohammed Awad had thrown most of his Marianas air force into the battle to support the carrier, which everyone now knew had to be the big, American built *Al Marj*. To support *Bennington* and counter the enemy's land-based reinforcements, the Japanese squadrons on Iwo Jima had been fully committed. The battle worked in Lieutenant General Ichiro Sago's favor. In the time gained in what appeared to be a standoff, his amphibious force was making its escape good. In fact, Sago reported he was under a CAP of fighters based on southern Kyushu.

While eighteen Zeros and six Seafires circled overhead, the force steamed northwestward in near silence. All of *Yonaga*'s 32 dual purpose 127-millimeter cannons and 186, triple-mount 25-millimeter machine guns were manned by helmeted crews. The blowers had been secured, and all water-tight doors and hatches dogged down. The tension on the bridge was as palpable as a steel spring drawn to the breaking point.

"Now we wait," Hobel sighed.

"That's ninety percent of war," Whitehead said.

Then the rumble was heard. Every head turned toward the sound. Raising his glasses, Brent could see the enemy groups on the far horizon. They looked like a swarm of bees. Bombers accompanied by fighters. "Killer bees," he said to himself. The expected Junkers Ju-87 was there in squadron strength. Then he looked for the outdated North American AT-6 Texan and the clumsy Fairey Barracuda torpedo bombers. Both were easy targets. He was shocked. He saw none. Instead, he sighted at least a dozen big, clean mid-wing monoplanes with high tail planes, ventrally mounted radomes, huge spinners on their radial engines and what appeared to be radiators or oil coolers bulging from the leading edge of their port wings. All had big, pregnant-looking bellies. "What the hell?" he said to himself.

"By Jove, that's the bloody Fairey Spearfish," Cunningham exclaimed. "Cracking good bomber. The best the Royal Navy ever built, but a bit late for World War Two."

"Torpedo or dive?"

"Both! They carry their ordnance internally." The three reporters raised their recorders.

Even Fujita and Arai were shocked. "Not a word—not a hint from intelligence," Fujita groused.

Rear Admiral Whitehead, who had been silent, winced and stared through his glasses. He was obviously discomforted. NIC, Mossad and the CIA had all been taken this time.

Fujita shouted at the talker, Seaman Naoyuki. "Radar, any other unidentified aircraft on the scopes in addition to the enemy raid at three-five-zero?"

Naoyuki spoke into his headset. "Nothing, Sir."

"Very well." After a quick check with CIC, Fujita shouted at the talker. "CAP intercept raid, vector three-five-zero. Main battery stand by to commence firing. All ahead flank!"

With oil jetting into the boilers, the four great engines pounded out their power and 84,000 tons of steel stormed through the sea, accelerating quickly. "Thirty-three knots, one-hundred-seventy-five revolutions," came up from the pilot house.

"Very well."

Naoyuki spoke. "Admiral, the chief engineer says he can't hold this speed for more than twenty minutes. Boiler pressure is nearly eight-hundred pounds. He's getting some release on Four and Seven."

"Tell Lieutenant Yoshida to keep the pressure up on all sixteen boilers. They should take eight-hundred pounds. Let the relief valves blow! I need every knot he can give me."

"Isn't that dangerous?" Hobel asked.

Brent waved at the raid. "So are they."

There were puffs of brown smoke as the outlying escorts began to fire their five-inch guns. *Haida* added her four-inch fire. Speaking while staring through his glasses, Arai said, "Maybe four squadrons. Not a big raid—by Arab standards. And from two carriers."

Brent said, "Must've carried a big complement of fighters."

"That's how Hanfstaengl plays it," Whitehead said. And then he added dourly, "There's enough of 'em to sink us."

"Their carriers are sunk?" Hobel hazarded, voice climbing an octave.

"Right," Arai said, still studying the raid with his binoculars. "They're orphans."

Mardoff said in a tremulous voice, "Then they have nothing to lose."

Despite a familiar frozen tremor that skittered the length of his spine, Brent stood erect with squared shoulders, playing the "Yankee Samurai" to the hilt. These reporters would never know his fears, his horror at what was about to happen. This had happened many times before. Dozens of battles had hardened him. He knew how to control himself despite the atavistic terror that could turn a man's blood to ice. In his most casual voice, he responded. "They're already dead men." He managed to chuckle sardonically. "You are about to see one helluva story explode all around you. Have your cameras ready for the scoop of the century."

Whitehead, showing his own brave military face, added his own dig to the reporters' discomfort. "And your epitaphs." Brent and Quartermaster Hio chuckled at the clever quip.

Mardoff exploded. "Get off my back!" His hand swept the sky. "Those goddamned planes can kill all of us. You, too. Or don't you give a shit?"

"Of course we do," Whitehead said.

Mardoff encompassed everyone with his wide, jerky stare, "Then you're scared shitless, too—aren't you. Bushido? Bullshit!"

Overhearing the last remark, Fujita entered the exchange. "Watch your mouth or I will have you removed." Mardoff twitched and stared at his feet like a scolded schoolboy. Fujita continued. "You are here by the grace of the Emperor. Never forget that." Staring from reporter to reporter, he asked in a flat, emotionless timbre, "Do any of you wish to report to the conning tower? There you would be protected by sixteen-inches of armor plate. It is much safer than this exposed bridge." Embarrassed, the trio looked at each other and politely refused, Mardoff with trembling lips. Fujita continued. "Very well. And now, I must insist on bridge silence. We have a war to fight."

Brent gestured at the horizon where engines were snarling like a pack of wild beasts. "It's begun!"

Diving through their own AA, *Yonaga's* fighters pounced on the incoming raid. They were met by at least an equal number of Messerschmitt Bf-109s. There were no Focke-Wulf 190s or the rumored Heinkel He-100s visible. With their four Hispano cannons belching floods of twenty-millimeter shells, the Seafires scored first. Two 109s were shot apart immediately, and another veered off, flames pouring back from its engine. But the enemy fighters blunted and spread the javelin-like thrust of *Yonaga's* fighters. Within seconds, the fighters were tumbling across the sky, locked in personal duels. The bombers droned on. All of them seemed headed for *Yonaga*.

"This is bloody great stuff," Cunningham said, tracking the fight with his camcorder.

"Never shot anything like this," Hobel said.

"Please, God, stop them," Mardoff muttered. But his eyepiece was pressed to his eye and the camcorder was whirring.

A Seafire and two Zeros broke through the fighter screen, zipping into the bombers. A Stuka lost a gull wing and flip-flopped into the sea. Then two more Junkers were hit, one gliding to a sloppy water landing, the other plunging vertically into the sea. It hit so close to *Haida,* the water kicked up by its impact drenched the destroyer's bridge. Parachutes began to speckle the sky.

"My God! It's real. Men are being killed," Hobel said, shooting his pictures. And then in disbelief, "They're trying to kill me."

Brent nodded with a hard set to his jaw as a truth flashed. That's how it was the first time he tasted combat. It happens to all men.

The first Spearfish fell, spewing two white parachutes before it crashed. Another pulled up with a Zero on its tail. Gunfire blew off its radome and shattered the power turret, silencing its rear-firing pair of 12.7-millimeter machine guns. A short burst into the cockpit put a dead man at the controls.

Now enemy fighters were battling *Yonaga's* aircraft amongst the bombers. More fighters were shot down. The enemy pilots were desperate, and very good. A Seafire with a dead pilot flew off to the west in a long curving path like an old ballistic missile, until it finally buried itself in 1,000 fathoms. A burning Me took dead aim on one of the *Fletchers,* but missed the bridge, smashing into the sea only a few yards off the ship's port side.

"He tried to ram him!" Hobel yelled.

"Shi'ites! Shi'ites!" Mardoff screamed.

A Zero exploded, another with its engine shot out glided to a landing. A wounded Stuka tried the same landing. But its landing gear caught a swell and the bomber flipped over on its back and sank immediately. One head bobbed to the surface.

"Horrible. Horrible," Hobel said in a squeaky voice. His face was as white as a bleached bed sheet. But he continued filming.

"Main battery, commence firing!" Fujita shouted.

With a stinging blast like a thousand whips, the sixteen cannons of *Yonaga's* port battery fired as one. Brent had pushed his helmet up and covered his ears. But the reporters were taken by surprise. They all shouted out in pain and clamped their hands to their ears, camcorders hanging at their waists.

"Ow! Christ! That hurt!" they cried out.

Working like madmen, the gunners slammed the semifixed ammunition into the breeches, setting off a steady barking rumble like a hundred bass drums pounded by lunatics. But the bombers bored on, driving through solid brown and black boxes of exploding shells. Twenty-millimeter and forty-millimeter shells from the destroyers reached upward for the bombers. A Stuka exploded. A Spearfish lost its fuselage just abaft the cockpit. Spinning on its horizontal axis, it pinwheeled into the sea. But at least four Stukas and six Spearfish plowed on toward the carrier.

"Some of them are getting through!" Hobel shouted.

"Those bloody fools have guts!" Cunningham yelled.

"They're going to kill us!" Mardoff cried out.

"That's what they get paid for," Brent yelled back.

"How can you be so goddamned shit-assed?"

"Maybe because I'm not scared shitless like you are, asshole."

"Up yours, mighty warrior." He raised his camcorder.

There was a buzz-saw sound that weaved through the bedlam. *New Jersey* had opened fire with her four Phalanxes. With each system's close-looped radar not only tracking its target, but its own projectiles as well, the fire was devastating. Each six-gun Gatlings fired 3,000 twenty-millimeter rounds a minute. Hordes of shells ripped a Stuka apart and shot the propeller and cowling off a Spearfish. Engine howling with an excess of energy and with boiling black oil washing back over the canopy, the Spearfish dropped into a sudden plunge. Pilot blinded by oil, the plunge became a vertical dive. The bomber crashed into the battleship's superstructure, taking the Phalanx that had been its executioner with it. A great effulgent red ball of flame trailing a black tail of smoke ballooned into the air. Burning gasoline washed over Turret Three and a half dozen AA gun mounts. A second Phalanx on the opposite side was enveloped in flames.

"Shit!" Mardoff said.

"Poor blokes," Cunningham said.

"Lousy, stinking break," Whitehead said.

"Maybe he did it on purpose," Mardoff said.

But *New Jersey* never faltered. With fire-control teams attacking the blaze, she crowded even closer to *Yonaga*. But her firepower had been reduced.

Only two Stukas were left. Both had their dive brakes down. The four surviving Spearfish had circled ahead of *Yonaga*; two to port, two to starboard. Their bays were open. Each carried a torpedo.

"They'll coordinate their attacks on us," Brent shouted at the reporters who looked away from their camcorders. "Put us on the 'anvil'."

" 'Anvil'?"

"Attack from both sides."

"They'll get us," Mardoff said.

"Good chance."

"They're ready to die."

"Yes. But we're not."

There was a shriek overhead. Both Junkers had pushed over into their dives. Mardoff made his own dive under the chart table. *Yonaga*'s 186 25-millimeter machine guns all seemed to be firing. A blanket of tracers rose to meet the dive bombers. And *New Jersey's* two remaining Phalanxes and machine guns were adding thousands of tracers to the deluge.

It was like hitting a burning wall. The first Stuka lost its landing gear, then its rudder. Its left wing tip and then its propeller flew off into infinity. Out of control, it twisted in big corkscrew turns until it smashed into the sea. The second Stuka seemed to dissolve like a cheap toy, a dozen shells bursting in big motes of fire all along its nose, wings and canopy. Its bomb broke away and streaked down directly for Brent Ross' head.

"No! No! Not that kind of goddamned fluke," Brent said to himself. Hobel and Cunningham ducked behind the windscreen. Brent felt the cold hand of horror clutch his guts. He fought the urge to join the reporters. Standing next to Admiral Fujita, he watched over a ton of high explosives hit not more than thirty feet from the carrier's port side. A tower of solid blue water shot at least a hundred feet into the air. A deluge drenched AA crews in their galleries. Shrapnel bowled over several of the green-clad gunners. At least two 25-millimeter mounts were put out of action.

"The Spearfish!" Whitehead shouted. "Coming in from both sides!"

Crawling out from under the table, Mardoff climbed to his feet. He clutched the windscreen with white knuckles and cried out. "My God. More of 'em. Won't it ever stop?"

New Jersey shot down one of the bombers to port. The other, wave high and far behind, skimmed low toward her damaged stern. None of *New Jersey's* armament could be brought to bear on the pair to starboard. "Right full rudder!" Fujita shouted. The carrier heeled over into its turn.

Captain Fite's DD-1 shot one of the Spearfishes down as it skirted the bow of the *Fletcher*. However, the second bomber bored in on the carrier. Brent saw chunks of aluminum blown from its wings and fuselage. But, miraculously, it never faltered. Its torpedo dropped and streaked toward the carrier. But Fujita had defeated the enemy's attack with his turn. The torpedo would pass harmlessly to port.

The pilot of the Spearfish did not pull up. Perhaps he was dead. Perhaps he was an insane Shi'ite. Instead of taking evasive action, he headed directly for *Yonaga's* bridge. "Kill him! Kill him!" Fujita shouted.

All three reporter stood rigid, frozen. Dropping their camcorders, they stared opened-mouthed at the doom reaching for them.

Brent could see the pilot's face through the thick armored glass windscreen. His goggles were up and his head was like a big brown melon. The melon burst, turning the inside of the canopy red. The bomber veered sharply to the right. It plowed into a gallery of AA guns on the starboard bow and exploded. Pieces of burning aircraft rained all over the forward part of the flight deck. Blazing gasoline washed through the gun tubs incinerating screaming gunners. More gasoline flamed down the side of the ship. Two howling human torches jumped over the side and were immediately sucked into the blades of the ship's huge thrashing screws. Blood and human flotsam boiled up in the ship's white wake.

"Damage control! Fire and rescue parties to the starboard bow. Stand by to flood magazine number three!" Fujita screamed at Naoyuki.

A lookout shouted. "Bomber off the port side!"

Like an avenging apparition, the lone Spearfish to port burst through the smoke of *New Jersey's* fire and streaked for *Yonaga.* It was so low, tracers from the battleship and carrier struck both ships. Precisely what the enemy wanted. He countered the carrier's desperate turn by sweeping to the right and then turning in toward her beam.

A twenty-millimeter shell slammed against the windscreen. Two or three more hit the foretop. Colorful chunks of recognition lights rained down and clattered off helmets and bounced on the deck. "We can be killed by our own guys!" Hobel cried out.

"That's right! Keep your head down or you won't have one."

To add to Fujita's problems, smoke from the fire swept back, choking the men and obscuring vision. The bomber took hits. The radiator and radome were shot off and a big chunk of rudder ripped away. There were hits all along the fuselage, but the sturdy plane never deviated. Again, Brent could see the pilot. His face was bloody and he was slumped to the side. "My God. He's dead! Dead!" Brent shouted.

Mardoff, who was peeking over the windscreen, shrieked shrilly. "Then what in fuck's flying it?"

"Nothing. It's out of control!"

When the Seafire was only a hundred yards from the carrier, a 25-millimeter shell struck the torpedo bay. The one-ton torpedo dropped part way out, held in place by only the rear crutch.

Cunningham and Hobel showed new courage. Standing erect, they shot it all with their camcorders. Mardoff remained crouched. Every man on the bridge seemed mesmerized by the oncoming doom. Another hit, and the Seafire pulled up slightly and the torpedo broke loose. Just as the bomber reached *Yonaga's* port side, the torpedo struck the flight deck flat and skidded toward the island like a great white glistening cigar.

"We're dead!" Mardoff screamed.

The plane pulled up, caught its port wing on the main director, lost the wing, spun flat like a boomerang, and curved into the sea. The torpedo struck the steel plate of the island and shattered. Eight-hundred pounds of the high-explosives sprayed and shot in every direction. Two handlers were caught in the deluge and knocked from their feet.

"Where's the explosion? Why aren't we dead?" Mardoff cried incredulously.

"Right-oh. We should be corpses," Cunningham agreed.

"It didn't arm," Brent said. "It's got to make a run in the water before it arms. We we're hit by a ton of junk."

"No shit?"

"Jolly good run of luck, I'd say."

"I won't argue with that," Hobel added.

Quickly, Fujita brought the carrier back to its base course. The fire was controlled without flooding Magazine Number Three. But twelve gunners were dead, and twice that number wounded. The two handlers doused with the torpedo's explosives were uninjured. Not one enemy plane was in the sky. All had been destroyed or fled.

"All ahead two-thirds. Left standard rudder. Steady up on three-five-zero," Fujita shouted down to the pilot house. The great carrier slowed into her turn. "Casualty reports. Chief Engineer, I want a report on Boilers Four and Seven." He looked up at the twelve Zeros and four Seafires that had survived. "CAP maintain patrol. We will refuel and rearm one fighter at a time."

"Steady on three-five-zero, speed twenty-four, one-hundred-twenty-eight revolutions," came up a voice tube.

"Very well."

Naoyuki said, "Chief Engineer Yoshida, recommends Boiler Seven be secured, Sir."

"Very well. But I want twenty-four knots."

"Twenty-four knots, Sir."

"Radar reports friendly aircraft bearing zero-one-zero, range one-one-zero, SOA one-one-five knots."

"Very well. Right to zero-one-zero."

Coffee and tea were served to a silent, exhausted group of men on the bridge. The reporters remained. Brent sensed not only a relief at having survived, but a new bravado that can come to men after they find themselves alive after their first battle. The reporters began to laugh and joke amongst themselves, until the casualty reports sobered everyone.

Naoyuki's said: "Admiral, all fires out. Twenty-five-millimeter mounts One and Three destroyed, seven gunners dead, four wounded. Five gunners at twenty-five-millimeter mounts Twenty-four and Twenty-six dead, six wounded. Number Twenty, one-hundred-twenty-seven-millimeter gun out of action."

"Jesus. All those guys dead—burned to death," Mardoff said.

"Two chopped up in the screws," Hobel added funereally.

There was a bleak silence on the bridge as the ship and its returning air groups drew closer together. Then Brent sighted them, dead ahead over the bow. "I see some of them, Admiral."

"Yeah," Whitehead said. "Only a few."

"That can't be the whole lot," Cunningham said.

Fujita said to the talker. "Radar, I want a check on all approaching aircraft."

"There must be more," Whitehead said.

"Eighteen verified, Sir," came back almost immediately.

"Eighteen!" Arai and Whitehead shouted, aghast.

Whitehead said, "We sent out over a hundred."

"One-hundred-twenty-nine," Arai said.

Brent stared through his glasses, turned his focusing knob gently. He brought Yoshi Matsuhara's Zero into focus. "Thank God," he muttered. But one of the Sea Furies was missing. "York! No! My God."

"My God, what?" Mardoff said.

"None of your business, and shut your mouth!"

The reporter turned sullenly away. He remained silent.

This was no time to challenge the officers. All were suffering their own personal hells.

A red flare arced from one of the Aichis. Then two more flares, one from another Aichi and one from a Nakajima.

Within minutes, the force had turned into the wind, Pennant Two two-blocked and the first bomber landed. It had so many holes in it Brent wondered how it could fly. The gunner was dead and the pilot wounded. Still, he made a fair landing. Medical orderlies pulled him from the cockpit and the plane was towed forward.

One after another the bombers landed. All showed hits. Finally, the fighters dropped down and were jerked to a halt. The last plane to land was the red, green, and white Zero of Yoshi Matsuhara. It, too, was perforated as if it had been hit by giant shotguns. Yoshi was so weary, Ota had to nearly pull him from the cockpit. At first, Brent thought his friend was wounded. But then the pilot walked unassisted to the island.

He had to see Yoshi, talk to him, somehow help him at a time when he needed the companionship of his closest friend the most. But it would be an hour or two before he could see the air group commander. First there would be debriefing and meetings with his pilots. He was distracted by a messenger who rushed through the doorway clutching a dispatch.

The seaman saluted, handed Fujita a dispatch and said, "Lieutenant Castagnini's orders—hand deliver this message to you, Sir. A Purple Alpha transmission, just logged in." Fujita took the message and dismissed the messenger.

Everyone watched the old man read. The inscrutable face was as expressive as a stone. Finally, he looked up and spoke to the expectant faces. "Captain Treynor reports *Bennington* has taken two bombs. Extensive damage to her flight deck and hangar deck." Groans. "However, she did damage *Al Marj*. The enemy carrier is burning." Grins.

Nods. "*Bennington's* air groups took casualties, but a number of her aircraft are landing on our fields on Iwo Jima. Our bombers inflicted tremendous damage on the enemy fields in the Marianas. They took heavy casualties. Thirty-six enemy bombers and twenty-seven fighters definitely destroyed. Seven more bombers and ten fighters damaged. We definitely lost thirty-one bombers and twenty-four fighters. The count is incomplete." He looked up.

Alistair Cunningham asked, "Is this privileged information, Sir?"

"Losses of our aircraft is secret. However, when we stand in Tokyo Bay, the whole world will know about the damage to our ships. This you may report." Then, hardening the timbre of his voice, he spoke. "Before we return, I will brief you, inspect your film, and define precisely what is off the record and what films you may take ashore."

Mardoff said, "But, Sir, after all we . . ."

Fujita cut him off. "That is my decision. There is no discussion."

While the reporters shook their heads in frustration, Fujita barked out orders to Naoyuki. Radio silence was reimposed, and the battle group turned northeast on a return course that would keep it out of the range of enemy bombers. The port watch was set with a Condition Two of Readiness. The reporters requested and received permission to leave the bridge.

Brent had just moved to the windscreen and raised his glasses when he noticed Fujita clinging to the bank of voice tubes. He rushed to the old man's side. Fujita's head was down and he was breathing hard. "I am all right, Brent-san," the old man wheezed.

"Respectfully, Sir, I beg to disagree." What Brent left unsaid was that Fujita was over a hundred years old, weighed less than a hundred pounds, and had just fought a battle that exhausted men a fraction of his age. Instead, he tactfully suggested, "Let me assist you to your cabin, Sir."

"This battle may not be over."

A concerned Naoyuki said, "Radar reports the scopes are clear. No blips except friendlies, Sir."

Looking up from his charts, Arai noticed the disturbing scene forward. He came to Fujita's side. "I'll take the deck, Sir, until Lieutenant Shoten relieves me."

A few of the deep wrinkles on Fujita's face curled into a weak version of a grin. "All of you want to rid the bridge of me."

"We want you to rest, Sir," Brent said. "There are still more battles to fight." He waved to the west. "This one is over."

The old man straightened and the haggard face took on a new hard, enigmatic look. "And we won." There was no attempt to hide the irony in the words, the hideous losses that had sickened everyone.

Brent took the old man's elbow. "Please, Admiral, let me help you to your cabin?"

The proud samurai returned, and Fujita shook him off. "Thank you, Commander, I am quite capable of managing that task myself." He turned to Arai. "Captain, you will take the deck." Fujita repeated course, speed, condition of readiness, engineering status, casualties, formation, CAP orders, and concluded with an age old formality. "You have read my orders of the day?"

"Yes, Sir. You are relieved."

Head high and erect, the old man left the bridge.

Brent stared after him. How long could "The Iron Admiral" last? Even iron rusted, deteriorated. A legend. Notwithstanding, even legends die. Could willpower alone keep him alive? Could he will himself to life until the Arab wars were over and the free world and the Son of Heaven secure? It seemed impossible, but Fujita was never daunted by odds or turned away by obstacles that appeared insurmountable. Yet, time and it's companion, death, allow no man to turn his back.

Brent took a deep breath and sighed it out. He had to find Yoshi. He left the bridge and by the time he had entered the main passageway, Fujita had already disappeared into his cabin.

Nearly two hours later, Yoshi Matsuhara and Claude Hooperman were both sipping drinks when Brent entered the air group commander's large cabin. Slouching in their chairs, fatigue lined their dark-stained faces. There was the odor of burned oil, gasoline, and gunpowder in the room. Yoshi waved the American to a chair, and poured him a Chivas Regal without even asking. Mumbling his thanks, Brent sipped the marvelously mild scotch.

The Japanese said with the same bitterness he had just heard in Fujita's voice. "We won a great victory, today, Brent-San."

"You sank two carriers."

"The price was high."

"I know."

"We lost a lot of good men, Brent-san."

Brent nodded silently and drank. There were no words that could console these men. It was best to let them talk it out.

Yoshi wiped a hand across his face as if he could pull off and cast away his tension, his grief. "Hanfstaengl put up a lot of fighters. The Focke-Wulf 190 is a real killer."

Hooperman said, "Bloody tough—tremendous fire power."

"Y.K. Dempster's dead, Atsushi Fukazawa, Shafeek Ghabra, Chiang Tang, Dimitri Kozlov, Philip Lunoy and most of the best gone." He tapped his glass on the table until a few drops of *saké* spilled over, and then drained it with one quick toss of his head. "Never have I suffered such casualties. My bomb groups have ceased to exist. Dempster was right. We need better bombers. He was incinerated in his." He pressed his palms to his temples as if he were countering growing pressure, and then poured *saké* until his glass was filled to the brim. "Our Aichis and Nakajimas are hopeless." He pounded the table with a big fist. "We couldn't protect them all."

"You sank *Buzaymah* and *Magid.*"

The pilots nodded. Exchanged a glance as if the destruction of the carriers had slipped their minds. The loss of their comrades possessed them, was eating at them as if they were drinking acid instead of liquor. So many. The cream of the air groups. All three men realized the actual count of dead pilots and aircrew would be well over two hundred.

Hooperman said, "Sheer guts. Never saw men drive home an attack like Dempster and Terada. AA in sheets, fighters . . ." He shook his head and drank.

"York's gone."

"I know, Yoshi-san."

Hooperman turned his hands up in a gesture of futility. "He just blew up—like a bomb."

"I told him to bail out." Yoshi clenched his fists and pounded his knuckles together. "Bull-headed Cockney. One of our DDs could have picked him up."

"Had guts. Always gave them what's for. One of the greatest natural flyers I ever saw, and a tough little bugger." Hooperman smiled to himself. "But I could always beat him at whist."

"I'll write his family."

"He had none. We were his family—the whole lot."

Yoshi nodded. "I forgot." He held up his glass. "To Pilot Officer Elwyn York. If there is a heaven, I'm sure he can talk his way in."

"Or fight his way in."

"Hear! Hear!" The men drank.

Hooperman tabled his drink, blew his nose and said to Brent, "*Yonaga* got knocked about a bit."

Brent welcomed the change in subject, even if it was unpleasant. At least the pilots would be distracted. "Right. Some casualties to gun crews, and one boiler had to be secured. But the old girl's still in fighting trim." He took a large gulp. "They threw a new plane at us. The Fairey Spearfish."

"I heard," Hooperman said. "Best RAF bomber to come out of the recent unpleasantness." He shook his head. "Bloody arms dealers. If you've got the quid, you can buy anything."

Yoshi's fist slammed down on the table. "Money's killing my men!"

"It always has, Yoshi-san. It's the fuel of war." Brent took a drink, swirled the liquor through his teeth, savoring the mild charcoal flavor. He looked at a leather-bound copy of the *Hagakure* that was on the table near Yoshi's right hand. Bushido, the code of the samurai. The code Yoshi Matsuhara lived by. The greatest single force that drove *Yonaga.* Brent nodded at the book. "Our book, Yoshi-san."

Yoshi knew what was on Brent's mind, but played along with his friend. "The wisdom of Yamamoto Tsunetomo. We have lived by his words for almost three-hundred years."

Brent glanced at Hooperman. "In a way, all fighting men live by these words."

Hooperman smiled. "We all have our codes, Commander Ross."

"And the codes are often analogous."

"True, Commander. In many ways they are universal."

Brent reached across the table and placed his hand on the leather cover. "The book tells us that the true warrior must be constantly prepared to make the ultimate sacrifice of his life in the service of his cause—his lord."

"Without a moment's reflection or conscious consideration," Yoshi added, brightening slightly.

"This is what York, Dempster, Fukazawa, Lunoy, our gunners and the others rushed to fulfill," Brent said. "Japanese or not, they were all samurai. Isn't that true?"

Yoshi nodded and smiled for the first time. Glancing at Hooperman, he said, "He's a wise one, this young man. He knows the great thinkers, the philosophers."

"Right, you are, Commander." The Englishman smiled at Brent. "And he's quite the psychologist."

The speaker hummed and the men all turned toward it expectantly. "Commander Yoshi Matsuhara, report immediately to Admiral Fujita's cabin," squawked through. "Flying Officer Hooperman to Debriefing."

"To Debriefing? I just talked my bloody head off." The Englishman ran a hand over his chest. "Got to get this filthy shroud off."

"They're never satisfied," Yoshi said.

The two pilots tossed off their drinks and struggled to their feet. Brent followed Yoshi into the passageway and then walked to his own cabin.

Throwing himself on his bunk, the young commander felt every joint and muscle ache. That's how it always was after a battle. He was drained, felt like he needed a transfusion. He was worried about Yoshi. He had never seen him so depressed.

"Maybe I helped him. I was corny, but maybe he felt a little better," he said to himself. He glanced at the big brass ship's clock on the bulkhead. He would relieve Tokuma Shoten of the OD watch in three hours. He needed rest. Closed his eyes.

The scotch helped him unwind, but true, restful sleep was impossible. The spring had been wound too tight. Throwing his head back, fatigue intruded on his mind like a dark cloud. He fell into a weird world of half-sleep, half-wakefulness where his subconscious took over, conjuring up strange images that flashed on and off kaleidoscopically. Bombers, fighters, exploding bombs, and burning gunners seemed permanently fixed on his retinas. It was all too real. They were in his cabin. He could hear the screams, smell the gunpowder, the burning flesh. He pounded his head with his fists. "Go away! Go away!" he shouted at the overhead. "I've had enough. Let me sleep!" Then Sally Neverland heard him.

She was there, smiling down from the overhead. Sweet, vulnerable, appealing. Her big blue-green eyes were warm with affection. "Sally Neverland, what in the hell are you doing here?" He wanted to hold her again. Follow that one kiss of so long ago with more, many, many more. Then he heard her voice, the words she had used in his apartment, the words he would always remember. "I could fall in love with you, Brent Ross."

"I'm bad luck," he cried back at the overhead. She began to fade into the gathering darkness. "Don't leave! I need you!" He reached up. Tried to touch her. Stop her. Found nothing but air. "Don't leave, Sally. Please don't leave."

She smiled again and was gone.

Twenty-two
In the Eyes of the Lord

"Don't leave Sally, please don't leave," Reverend Ezra "The Word" Freestone said. He moved closer to her on the couch and took her hand.

"But I'm very tired, Reverend. I need sleep." She did not pull away.

"Just a few minutes. I want to talk of our mission."

"Of course."

"We've done good work for the Lord, Sally."

"Yes, Reverend. Saved nearly five thousand heathen souls from the fires of damnation."

"You have turned into a fine servant of the Lord, Sally."

"Thank you, Reverend." She waved at the appointments of one of the *Kujaku* Hotel's finest rooms. "This is a fine room. And mine is very nice, too."

Freestone smiled. "Why not? This is my last night—ah, with you. Then back to Hollywood."

"Those streets are foul with the devil's work."

"Yes, Sally. Our work will never end. We must battle him at every turn."

She bit her lower lip and looked down at her feet. "The great sea battle is over. The news reports say many lives were lost."

"More of the devil's work."

"Yes. Horrible."

"You are worried about your young friend—this Commander Brent . . ."

"Commander Brent Ross."

"Yes. You mentioned him before." He tugged on the beard that hung to his chest. "Do you love him?"

"I love all of mankind."

"That isn't what I meant."

"I know."

"Well?"

She sighed out air through clenched teeth in a sign of her confusion. "I could."

"But do you?"

"I don't know."

"Someday you will mingle flesh with man again. It is your right, your destiny. But it must be the right man, a man chosen by God." He tightened his grip on her hand and stared down at her.

She searched his face. His eyes gleamed with a strange light she had never seen before. She could almost feel the presence of the holy spirit. "Perhaps," was all she could say.

"Did you save him?"

"No. If he was killed, his soul is lost in the fires of hell."

"You tried."

"Of course. I invoked the gospel—prayed for him and still do."

"Good. Good." He looked at her drawn, pale face closely. "You've lost weight. Look a little pale, Sally. Have you been eating?"

She shook her head. "It's nothing, Reverend. I've lost a few pounds, that's all. I still have the energy from God to do his work." She did not tell him of the persistent diarrhea, the two sores that had broken out in her mouth just the week before and refused to heal. Sometimes, they made eating painful. And the night sweats that had awakened her for two nights in a row. She knew what was wrong. Despite her prayers, she had picked up one of those mysterious oriental viruses. She had even run a low-grade fever for two days. But she had prayed and the fever vanished. Soon she would pray away all of the other symptoms. She was doing God's work and she knew the Lord watched over his own. There was no reason to trouble Reverend Freestone. The poor man was burdened enough with his own work, his own problems.

Freestone lifted her hand in his and dropped them back in her lap between her legs. She could feel him pressing down but knew it was entirely innocent. He said, "I talked to God this morning."

Sally was not surprised. The reverend carried on lengthy conversations with God almost every day. "And what did he say?"

Freestone ran a hand down over his beard. "He commandeth that man should be with woman." The hand slipped up. "As man and wife."

"Adulterers burn in hell. 'Thou shalt not commit . . . ' "

"Yes, true. But He commanded that you and I should be such—as man and wife. The Seventh Commandment would not be violated."

She was stunned. "To marry. To know each others flesh?"

He turned his face up to the ceiling as if he were addressing God himself. "I am an ordained minister of the church of 'The Voice of God in Jesus'—the one true church." He looked down on the girl with benevolence in his eyes. "In the name of the Lord, I proclaim us man and wife." The hand broke away from hers and stole up even further. "Our union is sanctified."

Bewildered, she caught her breath. "I don't know if I could do that."

An arm circled her shoulders, and a hand began to toy

with her breast. "It has been commandeth. Have I ever lied to you?"

She shook her head. "No, you have never lied."

"Do you love God?"

"You need not ask that. You know I do with all my heart and soul."

"Then you accept his charge that we be as man and wife, that we attain divine grace by joining together?"

She sighed, a deep sound that hissed in her throat. She looked at his hand that had found its way all the way up her leg and was pressing down on her mound. She could feel his other hand toying with her nipple. It wasn't right. This was what other men had done to her. But it was a command from the Almighty. This could not be refused.

He quoted the scriptures. " 'Wives submit yourselves unto your own husbands, as unto the Lord'."

She let her shoulders sag, and watched as his hand curled under her skirt and traced a line up her thigh. In a moment, her panties had been pulled away and she could feel a trembling finger begin to explore. A cold wave swept up her spine on the feet of tiny insects. She stiffened.

Feeling her reaction, he resorted to the gospel again. " 'A man shall be joined unto his wife, and they two shall be one flesh'."

The hand caressed, parted her, probed deeper. She heard him murmur in her ear, " 'Let the wives be to their own husbands in everything'." He pressed his lips to her ear. "Do you believe."

"It is the word of God. I believe. We are man and wife."

His eyes were mesmerizing. "Will you serve me—serve the Lord?"

She hesitated. Finally, she almost whispered, "Yes."

Rising, he took her hand and led her to the bed. Slowly and solemnly, he undressed her. Finally she lay on the bed and stared up at him as he disrobed. His body was flabby and very white. His erection large, glans red with a round purple head. His entire visage was repulsive. Suddenly, she thought of Brent Ross. Strange, he could come to mind now.

Then murmuring another verse, " 'For the husband is the head of the wife, even as Christ is the head of the church; and he is the savior of the body'," he lowered himself between her legs. She felt the big turgid thing slide into her.

She circled her arms around his big body as he worked, thrusting and grunting. But God wasn't there. It wasn't divine. It was like being with any other man. There was the usual discomfort that bordered on pain. The patina of sweat that bound their bodies together. Then, he began his buildup. Grunting, grasping her buttocks and lifting her completely off the bed until the explosion finally came. He cried out, slobbered on her neck, and dug his fingernails into her buttocks. Then he sagged as if his life's blood had spurted from him.

She thanked God. It was finally over. But she was wrong. There was a brief respite and he was on her again. More shouts, digging fingernails, and he sagged between her legs like a great sack of gelatin. Then she hoped sleep would come and she could leave. But, again, she was wrong. He kept her trapped in his arms and bore down on her with his weight. There was no escape. She remained all night. Finally, just before dawn, he took her again. Thankfully, he had a plane to catch. It was the last time.

When she finally went to her room, she felt filthy. And she was filled with his seed. Some of it ran down her leg, slimy, disgusting. Yet, she did not have the energy to bathe. Incredibly, somehow, she did not feel she had the right. She must remain in filth because that's what she was.

Bitterness filled her. Now she knew the reverend was just another man. Nothing more. He had used the gospel to betray her. She had been defiled in the name of the Lord. "Piano Legs" Nell had been right when she said, "You wouldn't have a friend in the world if you didn't have that pussy." Freestone was nothing but another Howard Cook, Nicholas Vance, and a hundred other vulgar johns.

The only man who had never come on to her had been Brent Ross. And he had had his opportunities. This big, handsome man with his own code, own set of values, was the most moral man she had ever met. And he was a sailor and was supposed to be horny. He had treated her with respect and a curious kind of affection that he could not hide behind that tough warrior exterior. She remembered their one kiss—sweet, tender. Oh, how she had wanted more. Had clung to him, wishing he would love her. If she could ever love a man, love him in every way, it would be Brent Ross. But that was past. Could never be. It was all over.

She would write Brent Ross first. She sat down at a small desk and turned on a floor lamp. She wrote steadily for a few minutes, placed the letter in an envelope and wrote, "Commander Brent Ross, Carrier *Yonaga*," across the front and sealed it. Then she thought, he *might* be dead. She shrugged. It made no difference.

Rising from her chair, she unplugged the lamp. Then a pair of scissors snipped and hacked until the cord broke loose from the lamp base. She tested it. Long enough and very strong. She smiled. There wouldn't be much strain on it and she could double it, anyway.

Walking into the bathroom, she looped the doubled cord around her neck and tightened it. Then, she pulled a stool into the shower and tied the cord to the shower head. She tested the shower head with a hard tug. It was sturdy enough. Then she stood on the stool and snugged the cord up close to the head. That should do it.

She looked upward and called on God for the last time. "Yea though I walk through the valley of the shadow of death. I fear no evil; for thou art with me . . ."

She kicked the stool out.

Twenty-three
The Greatest is Love

At eighteen knots, and following a wide sweeping course to the northeast to remain out of bomber range of the Marianas, it took a week for the battle group to return to Yokosuka. Yoshi Matsuhara and Lieutenant Akira Terada led the few surviving aircraft into the air when the force was a hundred miles at sea. They would fly to Tokyo International Airport and Tsuchiura. It was a sad moment when the crewmen watched so few leave the deck.

"Just a week ago I darkened the sky with my eagles," Brent heard Fujita muttered bitterly. "Now most have fallen like dry leaves." Brent remained mum. There was nothing to say.

When the ships stood in the Uraga Suido, vast crowds lined the Boso Peninsula to starboard and the mainland to port. There were cheers and shouts of *"Banzai!"* But as the damage to *Yonaga* and *New Jersey* became evident, the throngs quieted.

Four *Rengo Sekigun* boats raced around the carrier. Filled with the usual foul-mouthed, filthy demonstrators, they flashed signs: "Capitalist Butchers;" "Imperialist Pigs;" "American Lackeys;" "Free the Arabs From the Zionists;" were the most prominent. Turning his focusing knobs with a feather touch, Brent brought a big man standing on the bow of one of the boats into focus. He had a flat nose, filthy matted hair that hardly stirred in the stiff breeze, no front teeth, and a massive scar up his left cheek that terminated in a hole where his ear used to be.

"Well, I'll be goddamned," Brent said to himself. "My old friend from the *Kujaku.*" Then the man held up a sign, pumping it up and down. "Yankee Samurai Eats Shit," was the message.

"I get the impression that chap is not very fond of you, Brent," Whitehead quipped.

"We should run the bastards down," Brent muttered, staring through his glasses. Gary Mardoff, the only reporter on the bridge, turned and stared at him. A strange grin twisted his face.

"That's just what they want," Whitehead said. "They'd have their martyrs."

Brent nodded silently. "Of course. Just an impulse. I hate the sons-of-bitches." He stabbed a finger at "No Ear." "Especially that one."

"Who doesn't?"

When *Yonaga* finally moored at Dock B-2, Brent could see *Bennington*, which was high and dry on her blocks in the great graving dock. Only her upper works were visible and fire damage was evident all the way up to the navigation bridge. "It will take months—months," Fujita said. "She will not be ready for our next operation."

"Next operation?" Mardoff said to Brent. "He's thinking of the next battle already?"

"Of course," Brent said. "We have to earn our pay."

Four hours later, Brent and eighteen other officers were given permission to rent rooms at the *Kujaku* Hotel. It was a "port" and "starboard" R-and-R, with each man reporting back aboard every other day. The weight of duty was heavy, and preparations for the invasion would begin immediately. Delay worked against the Japanese forces. The enemy air groups on the islands had been decimated. Time would permit the enemy to bring in new squadrons and repair his damaged installations.

When Brent arrived at the *Kujaku*, the picket lines had already been established. Immediately, when he was spotted, a great cry went up: "Traitor;" "Pig;" "Jewish Lackey;" "Killer." And his friend with no ear was there, spraying spittle through the gap in his teeth as he waved his sign, challenging Brent. "Go home, fascist pig," he screamed, trying to block Brent's path.

"Out of my way, 'Toothless', before you lose that other ear and the rest of your ivories!"

The mob crowded closer. Then Chief Boatswain's Mate Shin Kanemura and a squad of his seaman guards arrived. Quickly the mob was herded across the street and Brent was able to enter the hotel.

He had just entered his room and did not even have time to unpack when the knock came. When he opened the door, he found a squat, husky policeman standing in the hall. The officer looked familiar, but Brent could not place him immediately.

"Lieutenant Yohei Kono of the Yokosuka Police," the officer announced.

Then Brent remembered. The officious boor of an officer who had been so abrasive the day of the fight with "No Ear" in front of the hotel. "What do you want?" Brent asked curtly. And then sarcastically, "I didn't hit a single person—not one man, woman or child."

"Please, Commander," Kona said in an unexpected conciliatory voice, "may I come in?"

Brent waved him in. The men sat facing each other over a Formica finished coffee table. Kono said, "Ah, you knew Sally Neverland."

The use of the past tense and the man's attitude set off an alarm. "Why do you ask?"

He avoided Brent's eyes, "She committed suicide—in this hotel a week ago."

For a moment Brent was unable to speak. Grief and shock locked his jaws, his brain numbed. It took him a while to collect a coherent thought. Then his thoughts congealed and flooded.

More death. Hadn't there been enough off the Marianas? All the young men they had left fathoms deep, or fried in their gun tubs. And now Sally was gone. An ethereal little bird of a girl, beautiful and guileless. Only now did he realize how much she had meant to him—how much he had anticipated seeing her again. To hear her, to hold her. But now she was dead, the ultimate finality. Death dogged his footsteps. Ruth, Devora, and now Sally. He was cursed.

He breathed hard, in short gulps, until he thought he would hyperventilate. Then, he took several slow deep breaths and was finally able to collect himself. Looking at the concerned Kono, he said in a choked, husky voice, "I can't believe it."

"She meant a lot to you." There was genuine concern in the voice

"Yes."

"I'm sorry."

Brent shook his head negatively. He didn't need sympathy and he felt slightly embarrassed at his show of emotion. "How—how did she do it?"

"She hanged herself in the shower."

Brent rubbed his temple with big knuckles. "Oh, Lord. Poor, sweet little Sally." The lieutenant watched silently. Finally, a new thought intruded and Brent looked up. "Why do you want to see me?"

"You knew her well?"

"I saw her a few times and I liked her."

The professional police officer returned. "Nothing more?"

"What do you mean by that?"

"Precisely what I said."

"I told you I knew her. I was very fond of her. We were friends. That was it."

"And she was more than fond of you. She left you this note." The lieutenant pulled a long envelope from his inside pocket.

Brent opened it and pulled out a single sheet. "Why, this is a photocopy."

"Right. The original is evidence."

Brent read:

Dearest Brent,

I am not worthy of this life. I am filth. An eternal shower could not cleanse me, although when they find me, they will know that I tried. That is why I chose the shower.

You are the only decent man I have ever met. You respected me and treated me like a lady. The man I trusted, sought guidance from, and who introduced me to our savior, is no better than the rest. And I let him. I share the guilt of the Seventh Commandment.

Once I told you I could love a man like you. That was not true. Now, I know, I do truly love you. You kissed me once, but only once. In this I was cheated. I needed so much more of you. I will carry you and that moment in my heart for all eternity.

To remember me, look to your Bible. First Corinthians tells us, "There remains then, faith, hope, love, these three, but the greatest of these is love."

Love for all eternity,
Sally Neverland

Brent stared silently at the letter. He could not trust himself to speak. He wiped his nose, then stared at Kono with eyes heightened by moisture to the intensity of blue steel. "That son-of-a-bitch preacher Freestone did this."

"Apparently, they had sex, yes."

"Where is he? I'm going to kill him."

"No you're not."

"You can't stop me."

"Geography can."

"What do you mean?"

"He's gone back to Hollywood. Left a week ago."

Brent slammed a big fist down on the table so hard a vase filled with artificial flowers almost toppled. The police officer grabbed it. Brent's deep voice seemed to rumble from his chest. "Godamnit! I'll get to him some day. He'll be easy to find. This has to be squared. Don't you understand?"

"I understand she had sex with him and then she killed herself. There was no criminal act on his part." Kono tugged on his nose as if he were trying to lengthen it. "And, Commander, she was not that angel you've idealized."

"Don't give me any lectures. I'm quite aware of her past. I just want to get my hands on that preacher. You may not understand, but he's responsible."

The lieutenant's face was twisted by a strange smile, an amalgam of humor and irony. "You won't have to find your revenge."

"What do you mean?"

"Remember, I asked you about how well you knew Sally Neverland?"

"Yes. It's none of your business."

"But it is." His pudgy fingers drummed on the table. "We did an autopsy—required after a suicide." The fingers stopped their skirmish with the table and his black eyes drilled into Brent's. "She had AIDS."

"Oh, God."

"A virulent new strain of Kaposi. So you'd better be thankful you weren't more than 'good friends'."

"We weren't." Brent hunched forward. "Then there's a chance Freestone got it?"

The policeman shook his head. "Not just a chance, it's almost certain. It's the most contagious strain ever isolated."

"But, could he get it from one exposure?"

"Of course. But according to our M.E. he had been exposed more than once. Sally Neverland had been penetrated repeatedly. He could tell by the amount of . . ."

"I know. You don't have to tell me." Elbows on knees, Brent leaned toward Kono. "Then you think he's HIV positive?"

"Freestone is a dead man, Commander."

"You're sure?"

"Yes. And it won't be pleasant."

The next day, the entire staff was assembled in Flag Plot. Brent was still terribly depressed by the death of Sally Neverland, and his inability to lay his hands on Freestone. Notwithstanding, when he took his seat next to Yoshi Matsuhara and surveyed the room jammed with the most important men in his life, his spirits lifted. Sally Neverland would never be forgotten, but for the moment he must put her out of his mind. Glancing at Yoshi, he realized his friend, in a very real way, had suffered even greater losses—was tortured in his own special hell.

No time to feel sorry for yourself, Brent said to himself. He put on his best military face despite the lingering anguish and rage that seethed in his guts.

Fujita began the meeting by gesturing to Colonel Irving Bernstein of Mossad, and the young CIA man, Elliot "Ellie" Amberg. "Intelligence reports the enemy carrier, *Al Marj,* has returned to Surabaya along with three cruisers and numerous escorts." There were groans. "She is not severely damaged and should be ready for operations within a few weeks." He tugged on the single white hair dangling from his chin. "She may come out, challenge our invasion."

"Then, what?" Amberg said.

"We will destroy her."

Cheers, shouts of *"Banzai!"*

"My boys hit her with at least two bombs, and she was burning," Captain Paul Treynor of the *Bennington* protested, silencing the shouts.

"Apparently her damage was not as severe as your pilots reported. Our reports indicate she will be back in action very soon." Bernstein and Amberg nodded.

"We inflicted heavy casualties on her air groups," Treynor insisted. "Almost wiped them out."

"Replacements are already being brought to Indonesia. She can rebuild her air groups nearly as fast as we can," Fujita said.

Yoshi asked Treynor, "Did you encounter the Heinkel He-100?"

"Yes. Six or seven. They and the Focke-Wulf 190 accounted for a lot of our casualties."

"Were they carrier borne?"

Treynor pursed his lips and made a small popping sound. "It was hard to tell, but it appeared they were not equipped with hooks."

Yoshi nodded. "Then they were land based."

"Yes, that is what my pilots concluded."

"Did you destroy any, Captain?"

"Yes. My pilots claim three He-100s definitely destroyed, two more probables. We shot down six 190s. I'm sure fighters from Iwo accounted for some of them, but that has not been confirmed."

Yoshi licked his lips, eyes narrowed, and his visage took on a hawk-like aspect. "*Oberst* Rosencrance and his *Vierter Jagerstaffel* did you . . ."

Treynor was ahead of him. "Yes, the Fourth Fighter

Squadron. They were there flying a new souped-up Me-109." Bitterness entered his voice. "They inflicted heavy casualties on us. We got two or three of them."

"Souped up?"

"Yes, Commander. My pilots claim they were as fast as the 190s."

"Rosencrance? Stoltz?"

The captain shook his head. "No one claimed either of them. They're still out there."

Yoshi's big fists pressed against the table. "A solid red machine with a wingman painted black and yellow with shark's teeth up front?"

"Those are the two."

"Amaterasu," Yoshi muttered so that only Brent could hear. "I will kill the swine, yet."

Fujita interrupted impatiently. "All of you know our losses in aircraft were heavy."

Yoshi winced, clenched his fists, and looked down at the table. Fujita continued, describing casualties to the Japanese forces. The heaviest losses were sustained by *Yonaga's* air groups. There were groans as he gave the count. But other losses were not nearly as crippling. The Iwo Jima command had lost nine Zeros and four AD-4 Skyraiders. *Bennington* had lost twenty-seven bombers and fifteen fighters. Thirty-four of her aircraft had landed safely on Iwo. However, *Bennington* would be out of commission for at least six months. She was out of the operation. Fujita called on Admiral Whitehead.

Standing, the American rear admiral glanced at some documents. "Gentlemen, the Pentagon is deeply concerned about the Arab presence in the Western Pacific. Rightfully, they see a threat to their base on Guam if we do not prevail." He looked around at the expectant faces jamming the room. "Consequently, new squadrons of TBM torpedo bombers, SB-2C dive bombers, Bearcats, Tigercats and A-4 Skyraiders are enroute to Japan as I speak." There were shouts, cries of *"Banzai,"* and Brent slapped Yoshi Matsuhara on the back. The glum air group commander looked up and brightened slightly.

"*Yonaga* can't handle those heavy aircraft," Paul Treynor said.

Fujita countered. "We are installing new arrester gear sent by the American Navy."

"Most of my pilots have never flown these aircraft," Yoshi Matsuhara said. "They need forty to fifty hours in a new aircraft—minimum."

"They are manned by highly trained volunteer crews," Whitehead said. "Most are American and British, and are carrier capable."

More cheers. The ancient scribe, Commander Hakuseki Katsube, sprayed *"Banzai,"* waved a hand, and dropped his head down on the table with a sound like a thumped melon. As usual, he was ignored.

Yoshi said, "Then you're saying they can fly from *Yonaga*, Admiral Whitehead?"

"Correct, Commander—from any carrier."

"No problem with our nine-meter elevators?"

"No problem, Commander."

More shouts, excited babble. Katsube remained inert.

Fujita gestured to Lieutenant General Ichiro Sago, who sat next to his aide, Captain Gorsuko Uchimura. "General Sago will describe our plans for the invasion of Tinian."

Sago stood, walked to a large chart of Tinian attached to the bulkhead, picked up a pointer and spoke. "The Arabs do not learn from history. They expect us to repeat it—attack Saipan first. Then when we move against Tinian," he stabbed the chart at the northwest corner of Tinian. "Mohammed Awad will expect us to hit him here," he circled the tip, "at White Beach One and Two, where the Americans landed in 1944."

"How do you know?" Whitehead asked, his old dislike tainting his voice. His animosity for Sago was well known to everyone. The huge blowup they had when they first met had not been forgotten by any man who saw it. Brent feared another head-on collision.

"I know because I have operatives on both islands," Sago answered brusquely. "They have noted the enemy's preparations and have even taken pictures."

A startled babble seeped through the room. Amberg and Bernstein exchanged a surprised look. Whitehead shook his head, a look of incredulity on his face. Sago had done better than Mossad and the CIA.

Whitehead pointed at the chart. "You said you don't intend to land on the White beaches?" The voice was military, not hostile.

"Correct, Admiral," Sago responded cordially. The rubber tip dropped down to the southwest coast of the island. "In the American invasion a big demonstration was made here, in Sunharon Bay off Tinian Town. Here there are good beaches. Landing craft even started toward the beach in a feint that drew Japanese forces to the south." He thumbed the chart. "I know. As I told you, I was there and our commanding officer, Colonel Kiyochi Ogata, was as stupid as a carp."

"You'll reverse it?" Whitehead asked.

"Yes. We will make a false attack on the White beaches and," he struck the chart with a sharp sound. "We will land in Sunharon Bay."

He turned to Admiral Fujita. "I need *New Jersey* and as many *Fletchers* as you can spare to shell the beaches south of Tinian Town. Also, White Beach One and Two must be bombarded to complete the deception."

Fujita nodded. "Of course. As we agreed." Brent saw a new glint dancing in the rheumy black eyes. The old man smelled gunpowder. He was revitalized. Already he was forgetting the terrible ordeal of a week earlier.

Fujita continued. "In fact, with *Bennington* out of the operation, we will have her fourteen escorts for other duties and I can give you additional fire support ships. I should be able to assign ten of them to you for shore bombardment."

"Fine, Sir, more than I expected. Air support, Sir?"

"We will bomb both landing sites with our bombers from Iwo and *Yonaga's* bombers will join them. The enemy should be completely confused." He smiled, and then showed his vast knowledge of World War Two. "We will not make the same mistake the Allies made at Normandy when their heavy bombers dropped their loads far inland. We will bomb the beaches, not waste our bombs inland where they serve the landing troops very little. Those bombs that miss can blast holes in the sand where our troops can take cover." He thumped his little fist on the table. "Demolish their bunkers, pill boxes, emplacements, blast the senses from the defenders."

"Banzai!" "Hear! Hear!"

Amberg's shrewd mind broke through the noise. "Admiral, what are your contingency plans if *Al Marj* sorties?"

"That's precisely what I want. *Yonaga* will engage her. *New Jersey*, destroyers, and bombers from Iwo Jima will provide the fire support for General Sago's amphibious forces."

Treynor said to Sago, "This is a massive, complex plan. Do you have the men, the equipment and the bottoms to execute it?"

Sago dropped the tip of the pointer to the deck. "While you were at sea, we received some very good news, indeed. The Americans have been sending us more ships. At this moment, I have forty attack troop transports, twelve attack cargo ships, four LSDs and sixteen LSTs. I can hit Tinian with two infantry divisions and an armored brigade."

Nobomitsu Atsumi entered the discussion. "A hundred-thirty tanks?"

"One-hundred-fifty tanks, all Abrams," Sago said.

Atsumi had more questions. "Merchantmen? You'll need them to meet the logistics of a prolonged campaign."

"The Maritime Self Defense Force has leased twenty-seven merchant ships manned by merchant seamen to supply our forces once Tinian is secured."

"How many tanks can you land in a single wave?" Whitehead asked.

"I have the landing craft to put twenty-four tanks ashore with the first three waves."

Whitehead thumbed his chin. "You know the enemy forces on Tinian have been reinforced. It is garrisoned by a reinforced brigade of infantry—maybe eleven thousand men, three companies of combat engineers, four batteries of 122-millimeter guns, and a company of T-62s."

"I'm well aware of his strength," Sago said in an even but cordial voice. "And G-2 has learned that Awad's chief of staff, Brigadier General Habib Shihaded, has taken command."

Whitehead nodded. "He's a tough, tenacious fighter. If anyone can discipline Arab troops, he can."

Bernstein chuckled. "Then, he can create miracles—walk on water."

"Right across the Indian Ocean and back home," Brent added. There were laughs.

Captain McManus of *New Jersey* said through the noise, "We'll need to land a lot of artillery if we're to neutralize General Awad's guns on Saipan, General."

The men fell silent.

"True. I have twenty batteries of 105-millimeter guns, and ten batteries of 155-millimeter guns. Also, we will put ashore several batteries of howitzers of big caliber."

"How big?"

"My largest are 240-millimeter."

Fujita intervened. "Gentlemen, now you can see how our plan is developing. After we capture Tinian, we will have control of the air and sea and can put in place nearly two hundred pieces of artillery. Then we will keep Mohammed Awad's forces on Saipan under continuous sea, land, and air bombardment. He will have no alternative except to surrender or see his command obliterated by our bombs, shells, or by starvation. An invasion of Saipan will be unnecessary." He nodded at Captain McManus and Captain Fite who sat side-by-side. "Captain McManus' sixteen-inch guns and Captain Fite's five-inch guns should prove to be very persuasive." There were chuckles and Katsube managed a *"Banzai,"* into the table top.

Elliot Amberg asked, "You expect Awad to surrender, Admiral?"

The admiral tapped the table to accentuate each word. "He will be in an untenable position. Only a fool would continue to fight."

Amberg said, "Respectfully, Sir, millions of fools follow Kadafi."

Colonel Irving Bernstein said to Amberg, "You have to understand the Arab psychology of battle. When they're winning, they become wild men, charge like lunatics."

Brent Ross interrupted. "But, Colonel, when they're losing, they become wild men again and run like lunatics all the way back to their goat herds."

Snickers and a few guffaws.

"Right, Brent," Bernstein said, "and they are quite capable of surrendering in droves—by regiments, by divisions."

Amberg said, "You've fought them for a long time, Colonel."

"All of my life."

Captain Treynor said, "The natives. Our ordnance doesn't know the difference between Arabs and civilians."

Whitehead responded, "We will offer them transport to Palau or Yap. Guam is a possibility, but I have not contacted the Pentagon because of security reasons."

Fujita took over. "All of you understand the plan?"

There was a nodding of heads, looks exchanged. "Any questions?"

Treynor looked troubled. "Admiral, there are a lot of contingencies in our plan."

"There always are."

"No plan ever survives contact with the enemy, Sir."

"Of course, that is the nature of war."

"I'm concerned about *Al Marj*," Treynor said. "If she breaks past *Yonaga*, our entire invasion force will be in jeopardy."

Fujita's brittle jaw took a hard set. "She will not defeat *Yonaga*. Let me remind you, *Yonaga* is actually a carrier built on a battleship hull. If necessary, I will close with her and sink her with artillery."

"Her cruisers?"

"I will sink them, too."

"Banzai!" "Hear! Hear!"

Treynor sank back. There was a look of apprehension on his face that matched that which Brent felt in his heart. Fujita dismissed the meeting.

As Brent stepped into the passageway, he stopped Yoshi Matsuhara. "Come over to the *Kujaku*. I'll buy you all the sushi and *saké* you can hold."

The pilot smiled. "Why not. I have a room there."

When Brent and Yoshi walked into the waiting alcove of the *Kujaku* Hotel, they were stopped by a boisterous, friendly voice calling from a small room adjacent to the bar. It was Gary Mardoff, standing and waving. "Come over—buy you a drink, shipmates."

Looking at the reporter, Brent realized his attitude toward the man had changed. Men who risk their lives together establish an arcane bond that grows despite mutual antipathy, even hostility. Mardoff had risked his neck on the bridge of *Yonaga* along with the rest of them.

This had earned him entree to a very select fraternity. There was no denying it. And Brent and Yoshi both felt it. And the reporter felt it, too. It glowed in his eyes, could be heard in the timbre of his voice.

Brent glanced at Yoshi. The pilot shrugged and said, "Why not?"

As Brent entered the room, he saw her, Helen Whitaker. She was seated with Mardoff and sipping a drink. He broke stride and Yoshi stopped with him, staring curiously. Then to Brent's astonishment, Helen stood, waved and said with a smile, "Come sit with us—Please."

Staring at the reporter, Brent realized the prissy, reserved Helen was back: shapeless gray suit, white blouse buttoned at the high lace collar, hair swept severely into a bun, thick glasses. This was a different person from the pernicious, foul-mouthed harpy he had slapped at the *Shibu*. She actually appeared to be happy to see him. Muttering, "Ah, what the hell," he nudged Yoshi forward and walked to the table.

Greetings were exchanged, and the officers seated themselves. Brent stared at Helen and felt an old hostility rise. She spiked his guns immediately. "I heard about Sally Neverland. I'm very sorry. Terrible tragedy."

Waves of confusion clashed in his brain. What kind of woman was this? She seemed to have two distinct personas, not just an alter ego. She had called Sally a slut, and, now, she showed genuine sorrow.

"Yes," Brent agreed simply. "A terrible tragedy."

Mardoff interrupted by waving at someone behind Brent and calling out *"Jochu."* Brent could hear a waitress approaching.

Immediately Brent felt a presence behind him and recognized the voice of Fumi. "Welcome back, Commander Ross," the waitress said into Brent's ear. "I heard you had checked in."

Brent turned and stared up. He had forgotten how beautiful the young girl was. "Thank you, Fumi-san."

"What would you like?" she asked. Then leaning close to his ear, she whispered, "I can give you anything you need."

Helen smiled slyly and Brent felt his face warm. He ordered scotch straight up, Yoshi ordered *saké,* warm and spiced. Before the girl could leave, Helen said, *"Shimaki,* please."

Yoshi looked at the reporter. "That's a sweet cake," he noted.

"Brent introduced me to it the first time we met," Helen said.

"That isn't all he introduced you to," Mardoff said, looking over his glass and snickering.

Brent felt a deep hot stirring. "What do you mean by that?"

Mardoff laughed, a friendly sound. "Nothing, old buddy—I mean *war* buddy. Only that you introduced her to the world's toughest interview."

"You're sure?"

"Of course."

Helen said to Brent, "There isn't anything more and Gary knows it. He's trying to have fun with you."

"That's right, shipmate."

"You filed your stories?" Yoshi asked.

Mardoff nodded, but the smile evaporated. "Yes. What Admiral Fujita allowed us."

"Wasn't that enough?"

Mardoff shook his head. "In our business, *never* enough."

Brent took a deep swallow. "Did you enjoy your cruise?"

Mardoff's good humor returned. "Better than the 'Love Boat'."

Helen laughed. Brent and Yoshi stared. Then Mardoff

surprised the officers. "I'm going to show you how to win the next one."

"Win the next one?"

"Yes," the reporter said. "At the Emperor's request, Fujita has given permission for Cunningham, Hobel and me to accompany you on your invasion of Saipan."

"Saipan?"

"Yes." The reporter grinned craftily. "Everyone knows it. It's common talk. Didn't you know that?"

Brent almost laughed and Yoshi had a hard time keeping a straight face. On several occasions Brent had heard the old admiral mention the impending invasion of Saipan within earshot of the reporters. The clever old man had planted the seed where he knew the tight-lipped mouths could not remain zipped. There would be leaks and he was right.

The officers played the game. "I guess the whole world must know."

Yoshi carried it further. "They can't stop us."

Mardoff emptied his glass and signaled Fumi. He was feeling expansive, exhilarated. He chided Brent. "Do I get a medal? After all, I did take as many chances as you."

Yoshi said, "Our fleet does not award medals to live personnel. It's tradition that goes all the way back to the old Imperial Navy."

"You mean I've got to get killed first before I can show off my medals?" He took a sip from a fresh drink Fumi had unobtrusively placed onto the table. She glanced at the other drinks, Mardoff nodded, and they were quickly replaced.

Brent did his own chiding. "That's right, and you'll have to stay away from the chart table. The admiral said he tripped over you."

Mardoff laughed uproariously. "I found out the damned thing's made of wood. Right?"

"Right."

"How's about a steel chart table?"

"No chance. Try the conning tower."

The reporter became serious. "No way. I'll stay on the bridge. I want to be there when you take on *Al Marj*."

The officers looked at each other. In some ways, these reporters knew almost as much as they did. And Mardoff was showing a trace of courage.

"What makes you think she'll come out?" Yoshi asked.

Helen broke her silence with more information that surprised the officers. "She isn't badly damaged, and they have no choice, do they?"

Brent shrugged and stared at Helen. "The winds of war can be as whimsical and unpredictable as the moods of a woman," he said.

Helen picked up on the double entendre immediately and caught Brent with those strange blue-gray eyes. "Sometimes, those moods can be poorly controlled and offend, when that is the worst possible thing."

"You called Sally a . . ."

"No, please, Brent. I'm sorry. I didn't think."

Mardoff broke the mood, "I hear that Admiral Suleiman Franjieh has taken command of *Al Marj*."

Yoshi beetled his brows and looked at Brent. This was news—to both of them. If true, the reporters knew more than they did. "Ah, he's a Shi'ite fanatic," Yoshi said.

"Right," Mardoff said, "a real first-class Shi'ite crazy. Hell, they call him 'The Mad Mullah'. He'd have Mother Teresa drawn and quartered if he thought it would help the jihad. He's the kind of cat that would rush into paradise by ramming *Al Marj* right up *Yonaga*'s butt."

Brent said, "How can you know this. This must be a rumor."

"It is. CNN reported it just an hour ago."

"So that's it."

"Yeah, Brent, that's it. Take it for what it's worth." The reporter gulped down half his highball and opened another matter. "We'll be shoving off in about a month. Right?"

"Who knows?" Brent said, skirting the delicate subject. "That's another gust from the winds of war."

Pushing himself to his feet, Yoshi announced, "Sorry. I must prepare some reports for the admiral, or he will have me keel-hauled."

Mardoff held up his glass and his voice was serious. "But first, Commander, to a successful campaign."

Everyone drank, and Yoshi left.

As the pilot disappeared in the crowd waiting at the bank of elevators, Mardoff proposed another toast. "And here's to no medals."

Brent smiled. They all emptied their glasses.

Glancing at her watch, Helen said, "Sorry to break up the party, but I've got to be leaving, too. My plane leaves at five." She glanced at Brent, "Ah, I mean seventeen-hundred hours."

"Plane?"

Mardoff answered for Helen, "Helen's been transferred to the Washington bureau."

"I thought I'd have a farewell drink here with Gary and hope that I could find you," Helen said. She smiled broadly. "You're hard to catch."

She stood and turned toward the door. Gary began to rise but she halted him with, "Brent, walk me to my cab. I want to talk to you."

He looked at Gary. The reporter shrugged, grinned and nodded toward the door. Brent followed Helen out to the sidewalk. For once, the entrance was deserted. No demonstrators, no pedestrians. The only other people there were two seamen guards who saluted Brent and then slouched back against the building with bored looks on their faces.

Brent waved at a cab that was passing by. The driver

nodded, and drove to the end of the block to make his U-turn.

Helen said in a hardening voice, "This hair is so damned tight I can't blink." She loosened it, shook her head and it tumbled to her shoulders. Then she brushed out the tangles with long strokes. The seamen guards watched with amused looks on their faces. Brent wondered at this strange behavior. Professional women just didn't do this in public.

The shock came. "Glad I didn't fuck you, big man," she said.

Brent was speechless for a moment. The other Helen was back. He turned. She grabbed him by the arm. "That little whore had AIDS, you know. A delightful way to go."

He pulled his arm free, but seemed rooted by the animal-like stare of the blue-gray eyes. He had never experienced anything like this. It was almost as if two separate women inhabited the same body. She continued, "You fucked the little slut, didn't you? AIDS and all. You sailors are so goddamned horny you'd screw anything that'll hold still for thirty seconds."

He felt rage boiling up from his stomach that churned like a mixer, filling his mouth with a sour taste. His muscles tensed, fists clenching and unclenching spasmodically. The anxiety and tension of battle was still there. His fuse was very short. "Shut up!" he shouted.

His voice caught the guards' attention. They straightened.

"Why don't you slap me?" she sneered.

"Good idea."

The big palm caught her squarely, spinning her half around with its force.

The guards started toward them.

Grabbing her cheek, Helen screeched. "You son of a bitch!" and rushed toward him, fingernails extended before her like the claws of a beast. Not wishing to hit her again, Brent retreated. He already felt like a fool and a coward. And enlisted men had seen it all.

Rushing hard and nearly stepping on his toes, she managed to take a swipe at his face that barely nicked his chin. He felt warm blood begin to ooze. Then she kicked at his crotch and missed. At that moment the two seamen guards grabbed her arms and held her motionless, completely off the ground.

"That whore-mongering bastard attacked me," she screamed, twisting and kicking out at Brent.

Brent heard the calm voice of Chief Shin Kanemura behind him. "You attacked Commander Ross, madam. There are three witnesses who saw it all." The two seamen guards muttered concurrence. "Either you get into that cab," he pointed at the cab which was waiting at the curb, "or I'll have you thrown into jail." He turned to Brent, "With your permission, Sir."

"Granted."

"You bastards all stick together, don't you!"

"We see and speak the truth, madam." The two guards nodded and grinned. "Put her in the cab!" the chief snapped.

"That's not necessary. Let go of me." Kanemura barked an order and the guards relaxed their grip. She pulled herself free and walked to the curb. Entering the cab, she turned to Brent. "I'm not finished with you, oh mighty 'Yankee Samurai'," she said, voice acid with sarcasm. "The next time I see you I'm going to kick your balls off. If you have any."

As the cab pulled away Chief Kanemura and the guards all snapped a rigid, mocking salute.

"Fuck you, motherfuckers!" she screamed, half-leaning out of the window and waving a fist as the cab roared into traffic.

The chief and his men laughed. Brent remained silent. Turning to enter the hotel, he found Gary Mardoff standing a few feet behind him. Mardoff wore a rare look of anguish. He took Brent's arm and said, "I need a drink, Brent."

"So do I."

The men returned to their table and Fumi brought fresh drinks. Both drank deeply and silently, Brent dabbing the blood off his chin with a clean napkin. Finally, Brent said, "She has a problem."

"Both of her," Mardoff answered.

"MPD, Gary?"

"Yes, Multiple Personality Disorder. It's not uncommon and she's a classic case."

"She's a female Jekyll and Hyde."

"You hit it right on the head, Brent."

"She needs psychiatric help—maybe she should be committed."

"She was committed once, for three months."

"Can't you do something about it?"

"It's hard."

"Hard?"

Mardoff gulped down more liquor and turned his head away as if he were searching for an invisible presence. He revealed a side of himself men rarely show other men. "I'm not family, and I—I love her."

Brent stared at the tortured reporter. He had always suspected there was more than a professional relationship between the two. "And she loves you?"

"The pro journalist thinks she does—sometimes."

"And the other one?"

"The bitch?"

"You said it, Gary."

"The bitch hates me. She wants you."

Brent's laugh was flat and humorless. "She has one helluva way of showing it."

"She's crazy."

"Both of her?"

"Right. Both of her, Brent."

"Let's have another drink."

Fumi replaced their empty glasses. They drank until dark, Gary downing two to Brent's one. Then Brent helped the reporter weave his way unsteadily to his room.

Twenty-four
For These Brave Men

Driven by a newly-revitalized Fujita, preparations for the invasion moved swiftly. Lieutenant General Ichiro Sago met frequently with Admiral Fujita, Captain Mitake Arai, Rear Admiral Whitehead, and other members of the staff. On occasion, Whitehead and Sago exchanged malevolent glances, but there was no repetition of the hostile outbursts of their first meeting.

It was confirmed that "The Mad Mullah," Admiral Suleiman Franjieh, had taken command of *Al Marj*. The officers were astonished by CNN. "Sometimes they scoop our own intelligence services," Whitehead said on hearing the news.

"Maybe we should hire them," Brent jested.

Brent's days at the *Kujaku* were few, most of his time taken by the furious pace of the preparations for the invasion. New aircraft was arriving daily, and little was to be seen of Yoshi Matsuhara. He spent most of his time at Tokyo International and Tsuchiura. When Brent did see the air group commander, his despondency seemed to be wearing off with the arrival of each new squadron of American aircraft. To everyone's delight, the support was lavish.

Mardoff, Cunningham and Hobel had been cleared for the operation. But Fujita would not allow them aboard while preparing for the invasion. The world expected Saipan to be attacked, and that was how Fujita wanted it to remain.

Finally, after five weeks of frantic preparations, Fujita called a staff meeting.

General Sago reported he was ready. He had trained his forces to the point of exhaustion. To Brent's surprise, the captain of subchaser *Edo*, Lieutenant Dov Poraz, sat at the far end.

Fujita introduced Poraz and explained. "Lieutenant Poraz has requested to participate in this operation. I have given my permission for *Edo* to serve on lifeguard duty. With her speed and versatility, she will be valuable in rescuing downed aviators."

"Arabs, too?" Lieutenant Akira Terada asked. The bitterness of the terrible losses his torpedo bombers had suffered was imprinted on his face in deep, new lines, shifting unblinking eyes, and a tick that jerked the right corner of his mouth down.

"They'll get the Geneva Convention," Poraz said.

"That's more than they give us."

Poraz said to Terada, "That's the Israeli way. We're not savages."

Terada came half out of his chair, anger and belligerence clear in the pitch and timbre of his voice. "You can't talk like that . . ."

Fujita voice rang like steel from the scabbard, "Enough, Lieutenant. Back in your chair!"

Glaring at the Israeli, the pilot sank back down slowly. Fujita gestured to the chief engineer, Lieutenant Tatsuya Yoshida, asking about the condition of his department.

"All boilers capable of giving you seven-hundred-fifty pounds of pressure. We're ready, Sir. Bunkers topped off," Yoshida said.

Then, quickly, all other departments reported. All were ready for sea. Fujita beamed and turned to Captain John

Fite. The escort commander reported three completely reconditioned *Fletchers* had been bought from Taiwan, giving the force a total of thirty escorts.

"Good. We cannot have too many escorts." He gestured to Yoshi Matsuhara. "*Yonaga's* air groups?"

Yoshi stood and reported one squadron of Zero-sens, a squadron of Grumman F6F Hellcats, two squadrons of F8F Bearcats, and a squadron of F4U Corsairs ready to operate from *Yonaga's* flight deck.

"Bombers?"

Yoshi shocked and delighted the men. He nodded at Terada. "We have one squadron of Nakajima B-5Ns, twenty-four Douglas AD-4 Skyraiders, twenty-four Grumman TBF Avenger torpedo bombers, twenty-four Curtiss SB-2C Helldiver dive bombers, and three Aichi D3As."

"Iwo?" McManus asked.

Yoshi explained that *Bennington's* thirty-six surviving aircraft would operate from the island. The total force was twenty-four Tigercats, thirty-six AD-4s, twelve Vought Corsairs, and ten A-1s. Commander Emmitt Hopp, *Bennington's* air group commander, was put in command of the Iwo groups.

There were shouts of enthusiasm. Fists were waved. Backs pounded.

Fujita silenced the men with raised palms. "This is truly an international force," he said. "Fighting men of stout heart have joined us from all over the world, especially America and England." His fingers found the white strand hanging from his chin. "For the first time since she was commissioned, *Yonaga* will operate more pilots and crews of foreign nationality than Japanese." Everyone stared at him oddly. He raised his tiny fists as if he were saluting the gods. "For these brave men I give thanks."

"Hurrah!" "Hear. Hear!" *"Banzai!" "Tenno heiko Banzai!"*

Fujita quieted the shouts. "Gentlemen, all is ready. We get underway at zero-three-hundred tomorrow."

A sudden soberness filled the room. Then the usual prayers were given. Fujita lead in Shinto and Buddhist, Whitehead in Christian, and Bernstein a few verses in Hebrew.

"Our ships are ready, our machines are ready, and we have enlisted the aid of our gods." Fujita's small black eyes burned into every face. He shouted, "Destroy the enemy! Kill him, send him back to his desert!"

More shouts of approval. The men were in high spirits when the meeting was dismissed.

Because she was small, with poor sea-keeping, *Edo* put to sea at midnight. She would trail the big ships at her best cruising speed of fifteen knots until the battle began. Then it was up to Dov Poraz to position himself for his lifeguard duties. It would be risky. Very, very risky.

The rest of the force was at sea by 0900. Again, the fleet set a southerly course for a point off the Bungo Suido, where a rendezvous would be made with General Sago's forces. The rendezvous was made perfectly, and the great armada headed for the Marianas.

Just as the *Yonaga* cleared Shikoku's Murato Zaki, word was received of heavy air raids on the enemy fields on Saipan and Tinian. The aggressive Emmitt Hopp was sending his bombers and fighters against the enemy. Fujita had planned on these attacks to "soften up" the enemy. Actually, they were battles of attrition, and both sides would suffer.

Then came the shocking news. *Al Marj*, three cruisers and perhaps ten escorts had sortied. When last seen, they were steaming at high speed into the Coral Sea.

"Let them come," Fujita said. "I want them."

Then he dispatched orders to the fleet and to Hopp's forces on Iwo Jima. "Continue with plans. *Yonaga* will engage enemy fleet."

"Aren't you taking unnecessary risks, Admiral?" Whitehead said. "I suggest you have Sago's forces go into retirement. Take *New Jersey* with us. We need her firepower."

"*New Jersey* remains with Sago. He needs her firepower, too."

Whitehead brought up a sensitive bit of history.

"When the Imperial Navy came out in June of 1944 to challenge our attack on Saipan, we sent our amphibious forces into retirement until Task Force Fifty-eight turned back the threat. Only *then* did the transports return."

"I will take your suggestions into consideration, Admiral Whitehead." Fujita fingered his wasted chin. "There is much merit in it, and tactical considerations may make a retirement mandatory. But, for now, I intend to proceed with our attack as planned."

"Yes, Sir. Of course, Sir."

After four-days sailing, the Japanese ships stood 500 miles off the Marianas. Hopp reported his Skyraiders had inflicted severe damage on the enemy installations. His own losses had not been severe, and he was continuing his attacks. Apparently, the enemy had many more aircraft than anyone had suspected. This unexpected strength forced a change in plan. *Yonaga*'s air groups were needed, but *Al Marj* was closing. Fujita faced a maddening dilemma. He took Whitehead's suggestion and sent Sago into retirement.

"Sago will steam zero-six-five and its reciprocal until we clear the skies of the enemy," he said.

Whitehead nodded, smiled and said nothing.

But where was *Al Marj*? She hadn't been sighted in days. "We need reconnaissance," Fujita said.

"We have our scouts out, covering all sectors," Whitehead said.

"Not enough range."

"We need a submarine picket," Whitehead insisted.

"Yes, Admiral," Fujita agreed. "We need just one submarine picket—one picket in the Coral Sea would do it."

"We lost *Blackfin* down there."

Fujita nodded silently. The loss of the doughty old diesel boat and her fine crew was too painful to articulate.

"Captain Seitz, we're approximately eighty miles southwest of Palau, latitude seven degrees, ten minutes, longitude one-thirty-three."

"Angaur Island, Lieutenant Levinthal."

"Correct, Captain," he nodded. "The southernmost island in the group."

Seitz turned to the diving officer. "Ensign Verlander, depth?"

"As before, Sir, sixty feet."

Seitz patted his Type 18 all-purpose periscope. The solid feel of the instrument was reassuring. Submarine *San Jose* had taken a terrible pounding from the Arab fleet. The perfect circle of Number One Section had been hammered into an ellipse, and some welds had ruptured. The forward crews' quarters and the missile room had flooded. But the yards in Guam had done an outstanding job of repairing her. Number One Section had been reconfigured, ruptures hand-welded, a turbine rebuilt, and a thrust block turned and realigned. She was cleared for 500 feet and 40 knots.

Now he was supposedly on a shakedown cruise—trials and drills that must be completed before he was cleared to return to "Pearl." This gave him options of number of days running and area of operation. He had more than tests on his mind. He had lost seven men, including his executive officer and best friend, Randall Turner. He had sunk a destroyer, true. But that was not enough for his dead men, for the treachery and cowardly attack on the neutral *San Jose.* For the first time in his life he felt hate, pure and irrepressible.

A big thing was brewing in the Western Pacific. The old "Iron Admiral," Hiroshi Fujita, was mounting a major effort and "Mad Mullah" Franjieh had barrelled out of Surabaya to stop him. According to his calculations, Franjieh would pass somewhere to the west. Somehow, he would get a piece of him; track him, shadow him, announce to the world his position. And there was something else—he wanted to be nearby when the "Iron Admiral" and the "Mad Mullah" collided. It would be the show of the century.

He turned to the OOD. "Lieutenant Lee, call me if sonar picks up a sea gull crapping on the ocean."

"Aye, aye, Sir." Seitz walked forward to his cabin. He was tired. He needed rest.

An hour later he was called to the sonar room. He stood behind Jim "Big Tooth" Smiley. Smiley gestured at his console, " 'Sierras', Sir. Lot's of 'em. Helluva racket. Sounds like the 'Come and Go Motel' after a high school prom." He threw a switch so that the speaker hissed and popped. But through the distortion, Seitz could her the faint "chunk, chunk" of dozens of screws, and the pinging sounds of searching sonar.

"How many?"

Smiley pointed at a series of white lines at the far left of the display. "Cavitations of a whole fleet, Sir."

Seitz ordered all sensors brought on line, and the other three screens in the room lit up. More white lines, some wider and more intense than others. Smiley threw some switches, tapped a flurry of keys, clamped a hand over his earphone and said, "We've got these babies in our threat library, Captain." He looked up, "That big mother's *Al Marj*."

"Cruisers?"

"Got 'em. Two heavies, *Beth-san* and *Arad*, the light cruiser, *Babur*. And maybe ten escorts. It's the Arab Fleet, Sir. No doubt about it." A broad smile flashed the big white teeth.

"Ten escorts? Are you sure?"

"That's all I get, Captain."

Seitz rubbed his temple. "Should be more, maybe seventeen."

Smiley shrugged. "That's all I identify."

"Must've taken casualties."

"They've been whittled down, Sir."

"Range?"

"Not close."

"Course? Speed?"

Sonarman Jim Eberhard at the next console said, "Northeasterly, Captain. High speed."

Seitz pulled down the corners of his mouth and grunted, "That must be 'Mad Mullah' Franjieh. Always in a hurry."

Eberhard said, "He ain't trolling for sardines, Captain."

Seitz slapped both sonarmen on the back. "Great work." He pulled a microphone down from the overhead. It was time to bring his computers on line. "Lieutenant Lee, lock Target Motion Analysis on the contact. It should be on your BSY monitor."

"I have it, Sir."

"Good. It's the Arab fleet. We'll trail them—no closer than ten miles. Course zero-five-zero, SOA twenty-eight. Report course or speed changes of 'Sierras' to me immediately." He looked at the expectant faces of the sonarmen, "The 'Mad Mullah' just grew a shadow."

He spoke into the microphone, "TMA, I want verification of *Al Marj's* position, speed and course." Quickly, a voice in the speaker gave him latitude, longitude, speed, and course.

Seitz's mind was working, as if it were interfaced with one of his computers. "Communications Shack!"

The voice of cryptographer Kip Jones answered. "Communications Shack, aye."

"Send a message, HF, addressee COMWESPAC: Arab fleet, carrier *Al Marj*, three cruisers, ten escorts contacted at latitude seven degrees, twelve-minutes north, longitude one-three-two-degrees, forty-minutes east. Speed twenty-eight, course approximately zero-five-zero."

"Crypto, Sir?"

"Plain language."

"Plain language?"

"You heard me, Jones, plain language."

There was the hum of a small electric motor as the antenna whipped upward to the surface.

Seitz studied the waterfall displays on all four consoles for a moment, turned and returned to his cabin. He tried to doze off, but was too excited to relax. Again, before Seitz had been in his bunk an hour, Smiley called him to the sonar room. Staring at his display, the sonarman said, "Captain, I have a strange 'Sierra' trailing the Arab fleet. Not close, doing maybe sixteen knots."

Seitz studied the faint white line, flickering and refracting. Smiley said, "Well I'll be damned."

"Speak up, man."

Turning in his chair, the sonarman spoke over his shoulder, "It's one of those old Russian AGIs—intelligence gathering ships of the *Primorye* class." Returning to his keyboard, he punched several keys and watched line after line of green characters race across the screen. He read. "Five-thousand-tons, two-hundred-seventy-four-foot length, forty-five-foot beam, speed twenty."

Seitz tugged on his jaw and ground his teeth. A scrap

of news copied months ago tried to break through. Then he had it. An Israeli subchaser had tangled with a trawler in the East China Sea. He spoke into the microphone. "ESM, I want a reading."

"Many powerful radars over a hundred miles north. The Arab flotilla, Sir."

"There's a small ship trailing."

"Have her, Sir. Sea and air search radar. Big stuff. S-band, nine gigahertz, about fifteen kilowatts. Military stuff, Captain."

"Check your threat library."

A short silence. Then, "Got something, Captain. Could be 'Trawler X-ray'. A new addition to our threat library, just programmed into our computers by the fleet internet. It could be the Arab trawler that tangled with that Israeli sub-chaser back in July."

"*Edo*?"

"Right, Captain. The subchaser stored all her emissions in her computers. It can't be certain, but it appears to be 'Trawler X-ray'. Or a twin."

Seitz palmed his hair back from his forehead. "Well, there's only one of them in *these* waters, and she definitely isn't on a pleasure cruise. That's for sure. Must be 'Trawler X-ray.' We'll track her, too."

Lee's voice: "Want a look, Captain. We can be in visual range in less than an hour."

"Negative, Mister Lee. The 'Mad Mullah' is our first priority."

Seitz gave his orders, and then walked back to his cabin. This time he had no trouble dozing off.

Twenty-five
The Show of the Century

The surprised voice of Talker Naoyuki commanded the attention of every man on the bridge. "Admiral Fujita, *San Jose* reports carrier *Al Marj* with three cruisers and ten destroyers at latitude seven degrees, twelve-minutes north, longitude one-three-two-degrees, forty-minutes east. Speed twenty-eight, course approximately zero-five-zero."

"*San Jose*? The gods are with us," Fujita said.

"The reconnaissance we needed, Admiral," Whitehead said.

"*San Jose* has something to settle with those Arabs," Arai said.

Quickly, Fujita and Arai leaned over the chart table, plotting, talking in quick bursts. Brent Ross, Rear Admiral Whitehead, and the reporters watched silently. "About a thousand miles," the navigator said.

"West and south," Fujita said.

"When he clears the passage between Yap and Ulithi, Suleiman Franjieh should steam almost directly east. However, Admiral, he could head north instead," Arai ran a finger up the chart in a northerly direction. "Into the Philippine Sea to support General Awad's forces from here." He thumped the chart just west of Saipan and Tinian.

"True, but that is not how the 'Mad Mullah' thinks. His Shi'ite mind tells him to smash us, bulling his way into paradise by destroying us or dying in the attempt." His finger followed Arai's tracing north. "And if he does steam into the Philippine Sea, we can counter by heading north at flank speed, follow him into the Philippine Sea and block his retreat."

"Yes, Admiral. We'd have him then."

Fujita struck the chart with the pointed end of a pair of dividers. "If, as I suspect, he continues on his present course, we will engage him here between Guam and the Western Carolines."

"Then he could be in range in about a thirty-six hours."

"I want AD-4s to search that area. Give the order."

"Aye, aye, Sir."

The next morning two AD-4s found the enemy fleet, steaming precisely where Fujita expected it. One of the Skyraiders was lost to enemy fighters. And there was another plain language transmission from *San Jose*, confirming *Yonaga*'s reconnaissance.

Fujita was exuberant. "We have an ally, a shadow following the 'Mad Mullah'."

"That's a big advantage, Admiral," Whitehead said.

Fujita studied the chart. "We will change course. Head north. This way we will close on our bases and draw him away from his. And," he thumped the chart with his finger, "I wish to engage him at dawn."

He turned to the other men on the bridge and smiled. "He still does not know our precise position. Let him guess, and burn up his fuel at twenty-eight knots."

Mumbles of agreement, nods.

The next morning the fleets were less than 500 miles apart. *Yonaga*'s position was no longer secret. A Fairey Spearfish had roared in, skimming the wave tops. It transmitted the battle group's position and was promptly shot down by the CAP.

"It's all even, now, Admiral," Whitehead said.

Another transmission from an Aichi gave Franjieh's position. Fujita pounded the chart with his gnarled knuckles. "That is where he should be! Here, between Guam and the Western Carolines. It is time."

He turned to the talker and ordered the air groups launched. Slowly, the big carrier turned into the wind.

Yoshi led an eclectic assortment of fighters. Hooperman was to his right, flying his Sea Fury. To his left his new wingman, another young Englishman, Pilot Officer Humphrey Cummings, handled his Sea Fury with the delicate touch of a maestro conducting Debussy. Yoshi had had little chance to acquaint himself with the young Liverpool man, but he did know he was a rabid Beatle fan. This seemed strange to Yoshi, because his new pilot had not even been born when the group was at its height. But, Cummings loved them. "Them blokes all came from me home digs," he had heard him say on two occasions. And he had CDs of every song the Beatles had recorded.

High above Josef Dietl led the twelve Zero-sens of the newly rebuilt International Brigade. Trailing Yoshi was Steve Elkins and his twelve Hellcats. But echeloned out to both sides of Elkins were two squadrons of the vicious little F8F Bearcat. Both were American led and American manned. The squadron of F4U Corsairs and six Seafires had remained with *Yonaga* as CAP.

Far astern were the bombers. Two squadrons of AD-4s with newly installed power turrets, two squadrons of TBMs and two squadrons of Curtiss SB2Cs. Never had Yoshi led such power. Not only did each bomber carry awesome loads of ordnance, they were all heavily armed and extremely durable. In fact, *Yonaga's* three Aichis and twelve B5Ns were being used exclusively for reconnaissance.

Lieutenant Akira Terada had screamed his objections, but Fujita had adamantly refused to allow the old aircraft to join the attack. Finally, arguing to the point of insubordination, Fujita grounded Terada. It was a wise decision. Yoshi was convinced Terada was on the brink of madness.

Raising his goggles and straining his eyes over his starboard wing, Yoshi saw the ships and the fighters simultaneously. Carrier *Al Marj* surrounded by three cruisers and ten destroyers of the *Gearing* class broke over the horizon at high speed. The fighter circuit came alive. Josef Dietl: "*Yubi* Leader, this is *Kamome* Leader. Many fighters at twelve o'clock low."

"Roger. I see them." Yoshi studied the enemy squadrons. They were climbing. Apparently, the warning had come late. Sloppy radar search. But there were no bombers.

The usual Messerschmitt Me-109s were there. More than two squadrons of them. But what he thought at first were a dozen Focke-Wulf 190s, were not 190s at all. Needle nosed, high Galland-style canopy, sawed-off tail, ventral radiator, and a small wing-span of not more than thirty feet. The feared Heinkel He-100. No doubt about it. Yoshi gripped his control column until his knuckles hurt. The samurai was never daunted by the length of his enemy's sword, or the thickness of his armor. He would kill this new enemy, too.

He spoke into his microphone. "This is *Yubi* Leader. *Kamome* Leader remain in top cover, all other *Yubi* squadrons, engage!"

Thirty-nine fighters plunged out of the sky and swept through at least forty Messerschmitt 109s and He-100s. The enormous firepower of the Hellcats and Bearcats told immediately. At least eight of the enemy fighters shredded on the first pass.

But the Heinkel was a superb acrobat. One of them, darting like a bumble bee, caught a diving Hellcat with a three-second burst. Streaming oil and black smoke, the Grumman began to turn for home. The little Heinkel bored in like a ferret for the kill. With his concentration on the Hellcat, the enemy pilot never saw Yoshi. He caught the He-100 in a one-quarter deflection shot from behind. With precisely the right deflective lead, Yoshi fired a short burst. The Galland canopy disintegrated and most of the pilot's head was blown into the instruments.

"Ha, super-fighter. You can die, too."

Order vanished, the dogfight sprawling across the sky in dozens of individual duels. The enemy pilots were good, and built their score. Yoshi saw two more Hellcats and a Bearcat crash into the sea. Now, AA from the ships began to blot the sky. Big ugly puffs that killed friend and foe alike.

Yoshi's fighters kept the pressure on. With more firepower and just as fast and maneuverable, the Bearcat was more than a match for the He-100. More 109s and 100s burned, spun and disintegrated. Yoshi was euphoric. He commanded the greatest pilots on earth, and the Bearcat was the most lethal fighter in the sky. The enemy pilots seemed to lose spirit, began to flee north. "Go ahead. Run to Saipan, cowards. We'll kill you there, too."

He put a burst into a 109 and watched it blossom into a big red ball of red and orange. The pilot had no chance.

Suddenly, like a miracle, the sky was empty of enemy fighters. Now it was the turn of the bombers. His six bomber commanders had all taken Greek code names, "Plato Leader," "Archimedes Leader," "Socrates Leader," "Pythagoras Leader," "Pericles Leader," and

"Hero Leader." Collectively they were the "Greeks." He would send them all in. Overwhelm the enemy AA defenses.

"All Greek squadrons, this is *Yubi* Leader, attack. Attack! Attack!"

There was a series of "Rogers" and "Wilcos." Most the voices American, and the Skyraiders, Helldivers and Avengers raced into the battle like hawks on doves. But these doves had claws. AA rose in smoking columns, splattering the sky with acres of black splotches.

Yoshi had seen *Buzaymah* and *Magid* destroyed just a few weeks before by old Aichis and Nakajimas. Both carriers had been Russian-built, not nearly as fast or armored and compartmented like the American built *Al Marj*. And *Al Marj* bristled with AA: rapid-fire cannons, thirty-millimeter Gatlings, and machine guns.

The first bombers to attack the carrier were a twelve-plane wave of AD-4s. Flying into a solid wall of AA, six were shot down immediately. Five of the survivors, taking evasive action, missed in low-level runs, bombs exploding harmlessly to port and starboard. However, the last Skyraider brazenly swooped low over the stern, as if the pilot were approaching for a landing. Like a giant bird laying eggs, the bomber dropped a stick of six five-hundred-pound bombs. Thirty-millimeter fire ripped the bomber and killed the two-man crew. Disintegrating, the AD-4 roared over the bow and plowed into the sea.

But she left hell behind her. Four bombs exploded in a precise row down the center line of the flight deck. With five-inch armor plate, the bombs failed to penetrate the flight deck. However, AA crews were killed or stunned, her entire defense scheme disrupted.

Then it was the Helldivers' turn. Bomber after bomber streaked down, releasing uranium-tipped 1000-pound bombs that slashed through the armor like Excalibur through reeds.

A carrier is a floating ammunition and fuel dump. The ignition of one or the other can cause catastrophe. The explosions on *Al Marj's* hangar deck set off both; ready bombs, torpedoes and gasoline.The result was calamitous, a spectacular display of pyrotechnics seldom seen on this earth.

Aft, the deck heaved up and the sides of the ship blew out, hurling chunks of plate and men hundreds of feet to both sides. Then, forward a hundred-foot section of flight deck was flung skyward on a giant yellow-white pillar of flame. Most of the wreckage landed on a *Gearing* close to her port side. Immediately, the destroyer began to burn and list.

Yoshi could feel the concussions buffet his fighter about as if he were in the heart of a storm. He watched ammunition explode in mammoth, white-hot bursts, fizzling, flashing like giant electrical fires. Balloon-like luminescent balls of flame whorled skyward, flaring yellow and white with heat. Armor plate, decking and twisted girders were flung into the sky with each blast, raining down and pockmarking the sea in a radius of a half-mile. Dense black smoke rose above her, roiling and swirling thousands of feet into the sky and casting an enormous shadow on the sea. The day actually darkened.

But *Al Marj* did not die easily. She did not slow, did not change course. The tough hull was still undamaged. "Let water into her!" Yoshi screamed.

Avengers and torpedo-carrying Skyraiders swarmed in from both sides. The escorts shot some down, but most of the sturdy bombers released their torpedoes. *Al Marj* fairly leaped from the sea as four torpedoes hit her almost simultaneously. Slowing, she skewed off course, began to settle. Now, she was a burning, sinking wreck. More bombs, more torpedoes hit her.

"Banzai!" Yoshi shouted.

"Good show!" Hooperman cried out.

"Allah Akbar, and have a nice day," Elkins jeered.

"Die Arab *schweine,"* Dietl spat.

"Wallow in your bloody milk and honey, 'Mad Mullah'," Cummings revelled.

Yoshi spoke into his microphone. "Greeks! The cruisers. The escorts!"

Within minutes, three *Gearings* were sinking and cruiser *Babur* was dead in the water. But Yoshi had lost at least six more bombers to the murderous AA. They still had an island to invade. "The Mad Mullah" was finished. He had to conserve his power. Yoshi glanced at his point option data and spoke into his microphone. "This is *Yubi* Leader to all squadrons. Well done. Return to 'Point Foxtrot'."

With the fighters hovering protectively over the bombers, the squadrons turned and began their return flight to *Yonaga.* Yoshi was puzzled and concerned. Where were the enemy bombers? He had seen none. Maybe they had never been launched—went down with *Al Marj.* He shook his head. Something was amiss.

Gripping the handles and staring into his search scope, Commander Richard Seitz whooped. "Jesus! What a show! That big baby just blew!"

There were excited cheers throughout the boat, as the crew stared at monitors that showed precisely what the Type 18 periscope saw. Elation raced like wildfire through the submarine. The hated Arabs, who had nearly sent them to a hideous death—the killers of seven of their shipmates—were being massacred.

Quartermaster Roy Whitlow at the helm grumbled. "I can't see the monitor and steer this boat, too, Captain." Other duty personnel in the control room muttered agreement.

"I'm taping it. You can rerun it, just like 'Deep Throat'."

The diving officer, Ensign Rick Verlander, asked, "What's happening, Captain?"

Seitz pressed his eyes against the soft rubber lining of the eyepiece. "*Al Marj* has had it. Blowing up. Spouting more smoke than Mount Saint Helens. A real first class case of pollution."

A magazine exploded with Vesuvian force, blowing cannons, men and flaming wreckage high into the sky. There were cheers, cries of awe.

"This is better than Disneyland," one of the men in ESM shouted.

"In glorious living color," another technician said.

"And American pilots did it! They're flying the bombers," Verlander said.

"That's the scuttlebutt," August Lee said.

"It's more than scuttlebutt," Verlander countered, "that's the word."

"Right," Seitz said. "Yanks." And then staring into the periscope, he described the action to the control room watch. "The carrier's down by the head and listing. The crew is abandoning ship. A light cruiser, must be *Babur*, is on her beams end. Three destroyers are burning and listing. They're out of it."

Smiley's voice came through the speaker. "A lot of pinging, Captain."

"But they haven't acquired us. The cans are busy picking up survivors."

"Yes, Sir. But they're searching, and there's one bearing three-zero-zero relative that's snooping this way."

Seitz swung the scope a hundred degrees to port. "Got her. She's picking up some aviators." He looked around at the expectant faces. "It's time to put more water over us, but I want a reading first."

Technician Carl Anselmo, manning the ESM console,

said, "Captain, got the cans and the cruisers, but there's something else coming through the clutter. Can't believe it."

"What's that?"

"I've got 'Trawler X-ray' bearing two-six-zero true, range sixty."

Seitz scratched his head. "Are you sure? She doesn't have that kind of speed."

"She's faster'n we thought. It's her, Captain. No doubt about it. She's been taggin' right along."

"I'll be damned."

Smiley's voice: "Captain, that can's drifting down on us."

Seitz turned to the Verlander. "Take her down to two-hundred feet. Down scope." He snapped the handles up. There was a hum, and the instrument began its drop down into the well.

"Aye, aye Sir. Two-hundred feet. Course, Sir?"

Seitz rubbed his chin and looked at his navigator, Joel Levinthal. "For now, zero-six-zero. Speed six for an hour, and then we'll run the reciprocal. I want to stay in this area and see the second act."

"The show may be over, Captain," planesman Neil Marz said.

"Maybe. But you must admit the first act was a show-stopper."

"Right, Captain, better than 'Tom and Jerry'."

"Not as violent," someone said.

Everyone laughed.

But something nettled Seitz. Through the smoke, he thought he had glimpsed blue at the foretop of cruiser *Arad*. White stars on a blue field. He had assumed Admiral "Mad Mullah" Suleiman Franjieh had had his flag on *Al Marj* and probably died with her. But an admiral's pennant could have been flying from *Arad's* masthead.

He shrugged. What difference did it make? *Al Marj* and

Babur were sunk, and three destroyers sunk or disabled. The battle group was finished. There was no doubt about that. And the trawler piqued him. He wanted a look. With his speed, he could lay to for a day and still catch *Yonaga* and the "big show" up north.

Seitz smiled. This was going to be very, very interesting.

Twenty-six
Great Footage

The familiar chilling cry rang out, "Unidentified aircraft bearing one-four-zero-true, range eighty."

Fujita and Arai checked the chart. "They've covered fifty-five miles in fifteen minutes, Admiral."

Fujita nodded. "That is a SOA of two-hundred-twenty knots. If they are bombers, must be the Spearfish. The Ju-87s and Texans cannot make that kind of speed." He turned to Talker Naoyuki, "CAP to intercept raid, vector one-four-zero true. AA crews stand by. Escorts AA formation."

Gary Mardoff, Alistair Cunningham, and Loren Hobel all stood tall near the aft end of the bridge. Brent smiled to himself. The new bravado of men who had survived their first taste of combat was obvious. "Let's see what they do when the shooting begins," he said to himself. And then, turning to the reporters, "There's room under the chart table for three, you know."

"We won't need it," Mardoff shot back. Cunningham and Hobel laughed.

Watching the destroyers close in to both sides, Cunningham said, "That raid's closing in from the southeast, Commander Ross."

"Correct."

"But the enemy battle force is to the southwest."

"Right. The bombers must've swung far to the east to avoid our fighters."

"You mean Commander Matsuhara's squadrons."

"Right."

"We could use them," Mardoff said, betraying a note of anxiety.

"They're on their way."

"They got *Al Marj*, a cruiser, and some destroyers."

"That's the report," Brent said.

Hobel said, "This time the Arabs planes can land in the Marianas."

Mardoff asked, "Well, why don't they?"

"They have a job to do," Brent answered.

Mardoff's tightened his jaw, "And we're the job."

The reporters fell silent. They faced a well-equipped enemy, desperate and determined. It would be a tough battle. Brent could see the expressions change as some of the new confidence leaked away.

"Aircraft!" a lookout on the foretop shouted.

Raising his glasses, Brent focused on over thirty big mid-wing aircraft. "Spearfish!" he shouted. One-four-zero true, elevation angle twenty-five, range eighteen."

"Fighters?" Fujita asked staring through his glasses.

Brent searched for a moment. "None, Sir."

"None? Are you sure?" Fujita dropped his glasses. His eyes were not good enough for this work and everyone knew it.

"Yes, Admiral. The only aircraft visible are Spearfish."

"Very well, Commander Ross."

Hobel said to Brent, "I don't get it. Shouldn't they have an escort?"

"Could be a mistake in coordination. The fighters could be far behind or they could have missed us completely," Brent said.

"Like Torpedo Eight at Midway," Whitehead offered calmly. "They attacked unescorted, with those awful Vought 'Vibrators' and lousy torpedoes, and were all shot down without inflicting a scratch."

Mardoff showed his knowledge, "Ensign Gay was the only survivor."

"Right."

"And don't forget," Brent said to the staring reporters, "we're dealing with the Shi'ite mind. The tactics of the 'Mad Mullah'. Don't expect rational tactics."

At that moment everyone fell silent, watching the twelve Curtiss F4U Corsairs and six Seafires of the CAP strike the enemy formation. Then hundreds of voices were raised in cheers as the fighters raged through the Spearfish, cannons and machine guns reaping a bloody, flaming harvest. Within four minutes nearly twenty of the bombers were destroyed. Some of the survivors turned north, others dived. Wherever they fled, the fighters hounded them like a pack of wolves savaging sheep. More bombers dove, spun, disintegrated. One, carrying a one-ton bomb, exploded in a blinding flash that left only swirling smoke and raining debris.

The reporters, eyes to camcorders, filmed it all, crying out excitedly as they panned through the carnage. "Great stuff!" Hobel cried out.

"Men are dying," Mardoff said.

"Who cares," Hobel retorted. "You're getting good footage, aren't you?"

"Great footage!"

A burst of AA low on the water caught their attention. Not one AA gun had been fired up to this moment.

"What the bloody hell?" Cunningham said.

Then Brent saw it. One of the Spearfish that had fallen

into what had appeared to be a terminal spin had pulled up just a few feet above the sea. He had fooled everyone.

Already, the bomber had hopped over the outer ring of escorts and was drawing fire from the inner *Fletchers.* However, it was so low friendly fire was hitting the ships and bouncing off or bursting in little motes of fire. The pilot was desperate and very clever. And he was, also, probably suicidal. His nose was pointed at *Yonaga's* port side.

"Commence firing! Commence! Commence!" Fujita screamed.

The port battery burst to life, hundreds of tracers racing to meet the bomber. Cannons shot into the water ahead of the Spearfish, shells sending columns of water spouting in its path. It seemed nothing could survive the barrage. But the Spearfish plowed on, shedding aluminum, backfiring puffs of black smoke.

"My God," Cunningham said. But he continued to film with Hobel and Mardoff.

There were some winking lights along the wing of the bomber. "Jesus," Mardoff said. "He's strafing us."

Staring at the approaching bomber and the winking lights, Brent felt those old familiar icy pests using his spine for a race track. The war drum was in his chest and his mouth went as dry as ashes. Choking it back, he squared his shoulders and gripped the windscreen.

There were snapping sounds, as if someone were cracking a whip over his head. Then clangs and bangs as 12.7-millimeter bullets ricocheted off the bridge. Not all ricocheted.

There was a scream, and Hobel was hurled backwards against the bulkhead as if he had been struck by a sledgehammer. Brent felt someone spraying his neck with a warm stream. A quick glance backward. Hobel, mouth open in a frozen scream, eyes like billiard balls, was sliding to the deck. Blood was bubbling out of his mouth and a stream of blood at least five feet long shot out from his chest, spraying Brent and painting the windscreen in mad designs.

Mardoff shouted, "No!"

"Shut up!"

Only a few feet from the carrier, the Spearfish's four guns fell silent. But the plane came on, engine barking and missing, now unfurling a solid banner of smoke. It pulled up slightly and Brent could see the huge bomb in its bay. Just before the bomber crossed over the deck, the bomb dropped.

"We're dead!" Mardoff screamed. Everyone on the bridge became rigid, fixed in place like actors in freeze frame.

The bomb hit the deck flat and skipped into the ocean. It was followed by the Spearfish that plunged into the sea off the starboard side.

"It didn't explode," Mardoff choked out incredulously.

"Too close. It didn't arm," Brent said.

Mardoff jerked a finger over his shoulder at Hobel. "He won't know."

"Or bloody well care," Cunningham added.

"He got great footage," Brent said.

"And he's dead."

"C'est la guerre, Gary," Brent said.

"It's as simple as that?"

"As simple as that."

"Sixty feet, Captain," Ensign Rick Verlander said.

"Very well, up scope."

Seitz grasped the handles and swept the horizon. He said to the OOD, Lieutenant j. g. Barry Wolstan, "The

Arab battle group's over the horizon, on a northerly heading."

"Northerly, Sir? Strange," Wolstan said.

"Yes it is. Must be looking for survivors. Their aviators parachuted over a big chunk of the Pacific."

Jim Smiley's voice from sonar: "Captain, got 'Trawler X-ray'. Bearing one-nine-zero true, range six-thousand-five-hundred. Should be in visual range."

Seitz swung the periscope around to the south. Immediately, he focused on the big trawler, which was steaming to the south and east of *San Jose.* She was flying Arab colors. "What in hell is she up to?" he asked himself.

Then he saw the pair of yellow rafts, barely visible to the low-riding periscope head. They were tied together with a short line. The Arabs used orange rafts, the Japanese yellow.

These were some of *Yonaga's* airmen. Two men in each raft. Bomber crews. No doubt about it, they must be American. The trawler was headed directly for the rafts.

"She's spotted some of *Yonaga's* aircrews," the captain said. "Going to pick them up."

Then he saw the men in both rafts, waving at the approaching ship. "Good," Seitz said. "They would've died out here. There is some humanity in . . ."

Flashes from amidships and from the bridge stopped him in mid-sentence. "They're killing them!" he screamed.

As he watched, bullets from two machine guns ripped through the bodies of the four men in the pair of rafts. The bodies tumbled into the sea and the riddled rafts sank.

"No! No!" Seitz pounded the periscope. He jerked the microphone down. "They just murdered four aviators—Americans!"

There were shouts of anger. Curses. Fists were waved. "Get even, Captain!" "Square it!" "Don't let them get away with it!" "An eye for an eye," resounded in the steel cylinder.

Using all of the self-discipline at his command, Seitz collected his thoughts through the turmoil churning his mind. His Rules of Engagement specifically stated, "Fire only if fired upon." But Americans had been slaughtered—murdered while helpless in their rafts. "Fire on my countrymen and you've fired on me," he muttered under his breath.

"We've been fired upon," he yelled at the control room crew.

"We've been fired upon!" they roared back.

Calming suddenly, he became the cold, calculating commander. He put the sub in combat mode and began TMA tracking of the trawler which was turning onto a northerly heading. "Torpedo Room, make Tubes One and Two ready in all respects."

Chief Torpedoman Weldon Shallenberger acknowledged. "With pleasure, Sir."

Seitz turned to the Attack Officer, August Lee, "Range and bearing?"

Lee glanced at his consoles. "Range six-thousand, bearing three-zero-zero, relative."

Voice trembling with controlled fury, Seitz fired off his orders. "Torpedo mode active, keep the wire. Short Range Attack Mode, search depth fifteen, high speed setting—and I want them twelve degrees off the intercept line, left and right, Ensign."

"Cover our whole one-hundred-eighty degree front, Captain."

"Right, Mister Lee. At least one of the fish should acquire the bastard." Then, glancing at the consoles. "Are the dots stacked?"

"Not yet, Sir."

Seitz stared into his eyepiece. The trawler was turning away and heading north at high speed. "Godamnit, what's holding up the show? We've got our nose up her ass."

"Dots stacked. We have a firing solution, Sir," a technician cried out.

"Match bearings and shoot!" Seitz shouted.

San Jose shuddered as if struck by a Force Eight earthquake, and two Mark 48 torpedoes streaked at 65 knots toward the target. With their seeker heads pinging almost 180 degrees all around, and technician monitoring the runs at his console, "Trawler X-ray" had no chance.

The first blast shook the sub. Then another. "Two out of two," Lee shouted.

Eyes glued to the eyepiece, Seitz switched on the monitors. The submarine was filled with cheers, whoops, cries of elation. The trawler had broken in half. Bow and stern pointed at the sky, the shattered ship formed a "V" as she died. Burning fuel spread across the water. Men jumped into the flames, others swam away frantically. In less than two minutes, "Trawler X-ray" had vanished.

"Sir," Barry Wolstan said, "will we pick up survivors?"

"Negative. There are starving sharks around. They'll welcome the snack."

Wolstan smiled. "Good idea, Sir. Help preserve the ecology."

Seitz turned to Lee, "Secure the attack team." And then to Wolstan, "Steam zero-four-zero, depth one-hundred, speed thirty-five. Now, it's the third act I want to see."

"Aye, aye, Sir. The third act."

"The final act," Lee said.

"Yes," Seitz agreed, "the final act."

Twenty-seven
The Final Act

While *Yonaga* closed on the Marianas, General Sago's transports remained in retirement. Despite mounting casualties, Emmitt Hopp's bombers and fighters from Iwo Jima continued their relentless pounding of Saipan and Tinian. All of the enemy bombers were either destroyed or hidden. However, fighters were still encountered. Rosencrance's *Vierter Jagerstaffel* was the most formidable. Hopp's pilots verified that the *Jagerstaffel* was equipped with a new, far more powerful version of the Messerschmitt Bf-109. It was believed the squadron was flying from a concealed field near Saipan's Marpi Point; the infamous suicide cliffs of World War II.

A squadron of Heinkel He-100s and a few bombers appeared after *Yonaga* sank *Al Marj*. Identified by their markings, they were definitely fugitives from the sunken carrier. Most of the bombers were shot down by Hopp's Tigercat snoopers, but some of the fighters landed, and it was believed they were hidden in revetments dug into the foothills of Saipan's 1550-foot Mount Topatchau.

With a CAP of Hopp's fighters, *New Jersey* had brought the old invasion beaches on Saipan under fire. These were the beaches of Charon Kanoa—the beaches soaked by the blood of hundreds of American Marines during World War Two. This is where the Arabs expected Sago's assault troops to land. At first the battleship fired from long range, but moved closer with each salvo. *Fletchers* and *Haida* joined in on the deception, steaming close to the island, sometimes firing over open sights.

Yonaga had paid a cruel price for her victory over *Al Marj*. Lost were nine AD-4 Skyraiders, six TBM Avengers and four SB2C Helldivers. Yoshi Matsuhara had seen his fighter strength reduced by four F8F Bearcats, three F6F Hellcats and two F4U Corsairs. However, *Yonaga*'s air groups were still very formidable. She could still hurl 66 bombers and 60 fighters against the enemy.

Steaming at eighteen knots, it took *Yonaga* only two days to move to her launch point for the assault on Saipan and Tinian. All units were informed by a new code, Purple Alpha Two, which had been created specifically for the invasion. *Yonaga, New Jersey*, and Sago's armada all moved on Tinian in perfect coordination.

In the early morning of the third day, *Yonaga* arrived at a point 250 miles northeast of the target. This was "Victor One," the launch point. As dawn broke, Yoshi Matsuhara led his eagles into a sky that was clear and nearly empty of clouds except to the south. Here, a seething wall of black clouds boiled over the horizon. Even from a distance, the fury of the thunderhead's enormous electrical charges was evident, lightning brightening the glowering black mass as if huge arc lamps were popping continuously. However, the sea was still relatively calm and the wind only Force Three. But this one would bear watching.

Staring ahead at the still empty horizon, Yoshi felt a new determination. This would be the ultimate assault. This was a battle to drive the enemy from bases that threatened the sacred homeland. And although it was never mentioned in the presence of Americans, this would be the battle to rid this island of evil *kamis*.

From this ten by four-mile spit of land, Enola Gay had

taken off to drop the world's second atomic bomb on Hiroshima—to vaporize, to burn; to disfigure; to conceive monster babies; and to slowly kill survivors over decades of agony. A bizarre, inverted vengeance, true, but vengeance of a sort was there and all samurai sought to savor this cup. Yoshi Matsuhara was especially parched.

As Yoshi approached the islands at low altitude, not an enemy aircraft was in sight. Above, at 22,000 feet, Dietl and his International Brigade kept their usual top cover. Dietl was anxious for action. In the battle against *Al Marj*, his squadron had not fired a shot. The red-faced German had been distressed, complaining in his usual mixture of German and English, *"Gott! Ich* need *aktiviti."*

"You'll get action," Yoshi had assured him.

"Wann? Wann?"

"When? Over the islands. That's when."

The German had grunted more displeasure and downed a beer.

With the islands clearly in view, a vast panorama of battle began to unfolded beneath his wings. Scores of transports were laying-to off Tinian. Some were anchored. Dozens of landing craft were already plowing through the sea in huge circles off White Beach One and Two. *New Jersey* was blasting the same beaches with full broadsides from only a mile. Her special bombardment ammunition, with super-quick contact fuses, blasted bunkers, guns and men. Destroyers, too, were bombarding the White beaches and the beaches in Sunharon Bay. Others were exchanging fire with Arab batteries on southern Saipan, which had brought some of the transports of Sago's diversionary force under enflading fire.

Tigercats, Skyraiders, Zeros, Helldivers, Bearcats, Hellcats, and Corsairs from Hopp's Iwo Jima squadrons bombed and strafed the enemy installations on Saipan. *Yonaga's* air groups had the responsibility to attack Tinian's defenses. Until observers were in place on ground stations, the air group commanders were ordered to "seek out and destroy targets of opportunity."

AA from both islands was ferocious. The gunners were laying down carpets of black bursts at precise altitude. Radar control. No doubt about it. Only radar could lay the shells in with such precision. Yoshi saw an A-1 with its engine blown off slide off ludicrously on its tail, flip over on its back and fling out two bodies that quickly blossomed parachutes. A diving F4U ran head-on into a stream of thirty-millimeter shells and was shredded into swirling eddies of burning fragments. No parachute.

A concussion just to the left jolted Yoshi. The first shell was on altitude. Then more bursts all around. Immediately, Yoshi led his squadrons in evasive maneuvers, trying to confuse the gunners. But the bursts continued to hound them. A Skyraider was lost, and then a Helldiver. Casualties. Always inevitable. Always hard to endure.

Gritting his teeth, Yoshi scanned the sky all around. Still, not one enemy plane was to be seen. Where was Rosencrance and his *Vierter Jagerstaffel*? Perhaps they were all dead. Or, maybe, what air strength Awad had was being saved to attack landing craft once the landings began. Could it be? Assault craft presented the greatest danger. They were the first priority. Once tanks and infantry stormed ashore, half the battle was lost. You didn't need to be a Von Clausewitz to know this. A half-century earlier, Imperial forces learned this lesson on dozens of islands in the Pacific; the Germans at Normandy.

And Yoshi could see heavy counter-battery fire from Tinian. Apparently, Brigadier General Habib Shihaded had prepared exactly as Fujita had anticipated, concentrating his power in the north. "Those who imitate history are risking destruction by it," the old man had declared. The way the scenario was unraveling, Fujita had been very accurate, indeed.

Suddenly, large splashes rose among the Japanese vessels off White Beach One and Two. Artillery, and it was very accurate. No doubt registered months in advance. Yoshi knew there must be concealed observation posts on Mount Lasso. A *Fletcher* was hit and was forced to turn away from the beach. A transport took two heavy caliber shells and began to burn. Without artillery spotters on the beach, it was up to the sharp eyes of the aviators to pick out targets of opportunity—to find those guns.

Without even using his binoculars, Yoshi spotted flashes at the base of a small hill, just north of Mount Lasso. Big stuff. At least four batteries of 122-millimeter guns. It was time to send in the Greeks. He checked his grid map and spoke into his microphone. "Aristotle Leader, this is *Yubi* Leader. Enemy artillery at coordinates Charlie, Bravo, one-seven." He paused, tracing a finger over the Cartesian overlay, "Mike, Delta, four-three. Take them out!"

The nasal New York twang of Lieutenant Michael Craig came back. "*Yubi* Leader, this is Aristotle Leader. I see the flashes. Going in!"

Twelve Skydivers streaked down on the target like a column of hawks all hungry for the same mouse. Not only were the coordinates hit, but most of the west-facing side of the hill was blown apart and set ablaze by napalm. And *New Jersey*, too, fired three broadsides into the fiery maelstrom. The island was becoming the true hell that festered and burned in every Japanese heart. Two of the Skydivers were shot down. Turning to the southeast, Michael Craig set a course for *Yonaga*. They would refuel, rearm, and return.

It was time for the landings. Sago's transports, *New Jersey* and twelve destroyers moved south to the Sunharon Bay. Steaming in close to Tinian Town, the ships turned the high ground behind the beaches into an exploding, heaving mass of leaping flame, smoke, debris, and dust.

Now Brigadier General Habib Shihaded knew he had

been tricked. Desperately, he tried to reinforce his defenses at Sunharon Bay. At an altitude of only 3,000 feet, Yoshi could clearly see troops in trucks and on foot rushing south from the White Beach defenses. He called Elkins, who was orbiting 5,000 feet above. "Rambo Leader, this is *Yubi* Leader. Troops on the main road headed south." He glanced at his grid map to give precise coordinates. It wasn't necessary.

"I see them, *Yubi* Leader," Elkins answered. "Let's give them a warm welcome."

"Don't forget the ditches, Rambo Leader. Follow my lead."

Rolling into a dive, Yoshi streaked down on the enemy column. AA of every kind rose to meet him. Thirty-millimeter Gatlings. Machine guns. Rifles. He was certain he saw an officer firing a pistol at him. Tracers, like bright beads, flicked past his wings, under his propeller, over his canopy. There were bangs, thumps. The Zero jerked, bounced, vibrated from the hits. He ignored them. The long, dense line reminded him of ants. Racing closer, the ants became men and vehicles. The brown column swam into his sights. Shihaded had been very foolish. It was too easy. Like exterminating insects.

Flattening his dive, Yoshi pressed the red button and sprayed the length of the column. Skimming the road, his shells and bullets cut down men like corn and set two trucks afire. Panicky soldiers leaped into the ditches lining the sides of the road. But Hooperman and Cummings raked them with cannon fire. Bodies fell in heaps, some were blown to pieces. Wounded roasted in burning trucks. Yoshi was glad he couldn't hear the screams.

In over a half-century of fighting, Yoshi Matsuhara had killed hundreds of men. But never like this. Never had he strafed men, cut them down in windrows like slaughtered animals. There was no joy of victory here, no elation. He felt a little nauseous.

Glancing back, he saw Elkins' Hellcats racing in for their share of the slaughter. The big fifty-caliber bullets knocked men about like mannequins. Dismembered and eviscerated. There would be very few survivors. But Elkins paid a price. Yoshi saw a Hellcat pull up and twist high into the sky, pause as if held by an invisible wire, and then tumble back to bore itself into the southern slope of Mount Lasso.

Then, Yoshi spotted the big brown beetles. Ten tanks crawling south toward the invasion beaches. Before he could open his microphone, one of the Greeks, Lieutenant Louis Goodman, called him. "*Yubi* Leader, this is Plato Leader. I have ten tanks moving south. Request permission to attack."

Yoshi gave his permission, and the Helldivers dropped off into their dives. Within a minute, the tanks were concealed by heaving earth, flashes, smoke, and dust. Two emerged from the bombed area, continuing south at high speed. Yoshi sent in Pericles. The last two tanks were blown into burning junk by 500-pound bombs. But now, three of his bomber squadrons were on their return run to *Yonaga* to rearm.

He flew over the landing beaches where the first two waves were already ashore. And he could see tanks with big Japanese ensigns painted on the tops of their turrets moving off the beach. One exploded. Another lost a tread. Then he saw flashes and spotted a row of bunkers dug into the slope of a small rise. He sent in the rest of the Greeks—Archimedes, Pythagoras, and Socrates. The big bombers raced the length of the enemy works, dropping high explosives and napalm. The enemy batteries were silenced, and more Japanese tanks moved inland. He lost three bombers. The survivors turned northeast for their return flight to *Yonaga.*

It was going well. According to plan. Landing craft were already beginning to shuttle back and forth from the anchored transports to the beach. In less than an hour, tanks and infantry had already pushed at least a half-mile inland. The Arabs had been completely surprised. And now, with spotters on the beach, *New Jersey* and the destroyers were finding targets with greater accuracy.

Suddenly, Yoshi was galvanized by a message from *Yonaga* that burned in his earphones. "*Yubi* Leader, *Yubi* groups, this is *Saihyosen.* Am engaging enemy surface force of two cruiser and seven destroyers at point Victor Two. All Greeks with ordnance remaining return to Victor Two. All other aircraft return to *Bara* (Iwo), rearm, and engage enemy at Victor Two. Expedite! Expedite!"

Yoshi pounded the padded combing. "Impossible! Impossible!" he screamed. "We smashed the *Al Marj* force. They should be headed for Surabaya!" And then, collecting himself, his mind clicked over with the precision of a well-oiled machine. The run to Iwo Jima was 550 miles. Then the return to *Yonaga* would be at least another 500 miles. Over a thousand miles, rearm, refuel. He howled in anguish. Five to six hours minimum. Frustration choked in his throat like rotten food. Then, grimly, he called *Yonaga* and informed Fujita that all bombers had dropped their ordnance. He was ordered to Iwo Jima.

Then in a voice of pain, futility, and barely contained rage, he ordered his groups to turn north.

Yonaga was on her own.

"We are on our own," Fujita said grimly, glassing the horizon over the stern.

Brent was stunned. Just twenty minutes earlier, *Yonaga* had been cruising on a northwesterly heading, closing on Saipan and Tinian to reduce the range for her returning air groups. Then, out of the vortex of the massive storm to the south—whose fierce electrical disturbance had cluttered their radar with ghosts and false images that made the scopes an unreadable jungle—*Beth-san, Arad* and seven *Gearings* had charged at over thirty knots. Radar and ESM had picked them up at twenty-two miles, when they were still far out of visual range. Every man had realized then that the enemy had a few tricks of his own.

Immediately, Fujita had launched the remaining aircraft of the CAP, so that all twelve Corsairs and six Seafires circled over the battle group.

"I should have expected it from these Arabs," Fujita had screamed. "It is the Shi'ite mentality." He pounded a tiny fist against the steel windscreen. "It is I who did not learn from the past."

"We're out of range. We can outrun them. Stay on this heading, Admiral," Whitehead advised. "Call *New Jersey.* Lead those cruisers right into her guns. *Beth-san* and *Arad* would have no chance against her sixteen-inchers."

"*New Jersey* will remain with the invasion forces. They are already nearly a mile inland. I cannot jeopardize the landings." Fujita stabbed a finger at the horizon. "*We* will engage them."

"A surface battle?" Whitehead said incredulously. Brent Ross, Arai, Mardoff, Cunningham, and even Quartermaster Hio and Seaman Naoyuki stared at Fujita with the same incredulity. "A carrier against two cruisers—with armored turrets, centralized fire control?"

"Yes. Remember, Admiral Whitehead, *Yonaga* is built on the most powerful battleship hull ever constructed. We will engage. Those cruisers must be stopped. They could sink our transports, kill thousands of men, before *New Jersey* could engage them. Those fanatics would find nothing more desirable than to die in the midst of our flaming transports."

"They'll cut us to pieces, Admiral."

Fujita's withered jaw took an unyielding set. "Let them try."

Then he ordered the whole force to come about and

speed increased to thirty knots. Fite's eleven destroyers were directed to prepare for torpedo runs. At least, in escorts, Fujita had an eleven to seven advantage.

Within minutes, a lookout shouted. "Ships bearing zero-five-zero, hulled down!"

Brent brought the sighting into focus with his superb Zeiss lenses. "Two fighting tops, Admiral. Big directors—lots of radar. The cruisers, Sir. About three miles apart."

While the two forces closed, the silence of smoking death filled the bridge. In a short while, most of the enemy fleet was visible. Then Brent saw the blue bunting. "Sir, an admiral's pennant at *Arad*'s masthead."

Whitehead said, "Admiral Suleiman Franjieh. He's the only flag officer with the fleet. It's got to be him."

"Of course. The 'Mad Mullah'," Arai said.

"Good. We will help him find that paradise he seeks so frantically, put him at Allah's right hand." Fujita pointed at the enemy fleet. "We will split them," he announced. "Steam between *Beth-shan* and *Arad*." He waved a tiny fist. "We will fight our final, decisive battle. The battle all samurai seek."

Brent heard Mardoff gasp. Then both reporters began to pray.

Whitehead said, "That's what he wants, too, Admiral. That final decisive battle. He'll have us in a cross-fire."

"And they can hit each other while we engage him with thirty-two five-inch guns." He called the crew to General Quarters. "Main battery, load AP! All hands stand by for surface action!"

Cunningham, face bleached white by an amalgam of anxiety and apprehension, spoke softly to Brent. "I say, split the enemy line. Those were the tactics used by Lord Nelson at Trafalgar."

"He won, didn't he?"

"Yes. But he bloody well bought it."

"We fought a *Brooklyn* class cruiser in the 'Med' in eighty-four and sank her."

Cunningham nodded. "Yes. I remember."

Mardoff commented, "*Yonaga* got the shit kicked out of her."

"We took some casualties," Brent understated. "But we sank her."

The reporters traded a distressed look, turned toward the bow and raised their camcorders. With a hard tug, Brent pulled his jaw to the side and then clenched his teeth. He felt little of the confidence he tried to show the reporters. They were in for a bloody battle. Was he playing his last hand? All men who fight are gamblers. Maybe, this time, his chips would be swept from the table. His old dark companion was clutching at his guts with a cold hand.

Fujita looked overhead at the twelve Corsairs and six Seafires of the CAP. He said to Talker Naoyuki, "Order the CAP to strafe enemy cruisers when I engage."

Now Brent was staring through his glasses at the enemy fleet. It was closing fast. The cruisers were in range but had not opened fire.

"I say," Cunningham said, "he has bigger guns. Aren't we bloody-well in range?"

"Yes," Brent answered.

"Then why doesn't he shoot?"

"Franjieh is a madman. I can't read his mind."

Cunningham said, "Maybe he thinks he can toy with us."

"He's lost his advantage in range and *Yonaga*'s one lethal toy," Brent said.

Naoyuki's voice: "Admiral, radar reports enemy cruisers in range."

"Very well. Main battery local control." And then a command as old as naval warfare, "Engage as your guns bear. Commence firing. Commence! Commence!"

* * *

"They've opened fire," Seitz said. He gripped the periscope handles so tight, his knuckles shone nearly white in the red glow of the control room. "*Yonaga's* opened up with about eight or ten five-inch bow guns."

"Nothing else bears, Captain?"

"Right."

"The cruisers, Sir?"

"Only their forward turrets are unmasked. Six guns each. And both ships just fired salvos."

There were excited shouts from crew members watching monitors in other compartments.

"Jesus," Seitz said, "it's an old-fashioned shoot-out. The cans are laying down smoke and going after each other."

"After each other?"

"With five-inch, thirty-eights, and fish—that's what I mean. The old-fashioned, unguided fish with a half-ton warhead!"

"Tear your guts out."

"One just did."

When Fite's pair of torpedoes struck the *Gearing,* the double punch fairly lifted the 2,200 ton ship out of the water. Then, keel broken, she sank back and almost immediately took a hard port list. Cheers rang through *Yonaga.*

"Missed some of it—that goddamned smoke!" Mardoff complained, staring through his eyepiece.

Fite's destroyers were attacking in two columns, laying black smoke that seemed to roll on the water like slimy black tubes. The consummate destroyers skipper, he hoped to break through the enemy *Gearings* and make runs on the cruisers. But the enemy destroyers blocked him, firing and launching their own torpedoes. A *Fletcher* staggered, dropped out of line, and began to list. Then a *Gearing,* hit by at least fifteen five-inch shells, began to burn. Slowing, she turned away. Fite's attack was succeeding against the destroyers, but he had not distracted the cruisers.

The fighters were strafing. One after another, like wasps stinging an elephant, they raced the length of the cruisers. Their bullets and shells killed AA crews, but could do no damage to the armored turrets. And the elephants struck back at their tormentors. A Seafire was hit and plunged into the sea. Then a Corsair exploded. But the survivors never hesitated, pressed home their attacks. Another Seafire spun into the sea, followed by a burning Corsair.

The attention of every man on the bridge was on the cruisers. They were firing, now, as fast as the big guns could be loaded. The smoke screen helped confuse the cruisers' gunners, but their first three salvos roared in very close—bursting just over *Yonaga's* stern. To Brent, the ripping whoosh of the passing shells reminded him of the sound of passing trucks on a freeway. Then, the fourth salvo from *Arad* burst so close, torrents of blue water rained down on *Yonaga's* starboard side. A few men were bowled over by shrapnel.

"They have the range!" Whitehead screamed.

"And so do we," Brent answered, watching shells explode on both cruisers' forecastle and bridge.

And now more of *Yonaga's* guns were brought to bear, at least ten guns on each side firing. More hits. The gunlayers cheered. Worked their weapons with desperation. Ramming the semi-fixed ammunition home, standing to the side as the big guns recoiled. Before the recoil was complete, the gun captains opened the breech, which vomited hot brass casings. The gunners kicked them aside.

Then, a full salvo from *Arad* hit *Yonaga* at the waterline. The shock of the explosions shook her down to her triple bottom. Curtains of water rose and collapsed, soaking gunners in their tubs.

"Ha," Fujita laughed. "You have hit my sixteen-inch armor belt. We can fix that with paint."

But *Beth-shan's* next salvo could not be repaired with paint. Brent actually saw the salvo as it descended and slowed like six big blue bowling pins. Two hit off the port quarter, the other four came aboard and punched through the flight deck into the 33-inch armored box beneath. Teakwood and steel plate were flung into the air, mixed with latex, box beams, cement, sawdust and girders that filled the armored box. Not one shell penetrated into the hangar deck. There was smoke, the stench of cordite, the screams of wounded. Quickly, the smoke blew away. The flight deck was wrecked.

More salvos roared out on long orange tongues of flame. Spires of water spouted skyward on every hand. Two shells hit *Yonaga's* foretop. Pieces of director, radar antennas and men rained down. A man's chest, bloody with ribs protruding like a roast, hit Mardoff on the head. Screaming, the reporter recoiled into the far corner of the bridge. Quartermaster Hio threw the chest over the side.

The cruisers turned slightly away, unmasking their Number Three turrets. Instead of firing on *Yonaga*, the big guns blasted Fite's destroyers. Three shells hit a *Fletcher* just forward of her bridge. Ammunition detonated in Number One and Number Two gunhouses. Then her forward magazines exploded in a brilliant, incandescent flash, taking the forward third of the ship with it and hurling the entire bridge into the sea. What remained of the ship rolled over and sank.

In quick succession, three more *Fletchers* were hit and smashed like cans under a man's boot, while shells continued to rain on *Yonaga*. Fite's torpedo run had been completely disrupted. Now his remaining ships were fighting for their lives.

Hits obliterated a four-gun battery on *Yonaga's* starboard quarter. Flipping over and over like a flicked cigarette, a five-inch gun splashed into the sea, its dismembered crew raining around it. Ready ammunition exploded, killing more gunners.

Then a fire began aft. Horror after horror came on so fast a man's senses were overwhelmed. More destroyers were burning, sinking. A few fighters strafed. *Yonaga's* cannon fire was an uninterrupted, thundering barrage. Smoke enveloped the bridge in a choking cloud. To be heard, Fujita had to lean close to Naoyuki and scream into his ear.

Mardoff staggered back to the windscreen. "We're being slaughtered!" he screamed.

But the carrier's high-velocity, armor-piercing shells punched into the enemy ships. A half-dozen hits forward on *Beth-shan* opened her forward magazine. Then a shell smoked in like a match to a fuse. The explosion blasted both forward turrets into the sea and the entire bow vanished. Engines driving her at flank speed, she scooped up water that crushed her forward bulkheads and drove her to her grave.

Cheers, shouts of "*Banzai!*" Both reporters focused their camcorders. For a moment, they were both brave.

Their courage vanished with the next salvo. At least three shells hit *Yonaga's* flight deck on her port side amidships. A piece of shrapnel the size of the end of a water heater hit Quartermaster Hio in the chest, nearly separating him into two parts. The force of the impact threw him across the bridge, crashing into the chart table. Blood splattered in every direction. It looked as if a maniac had thrown a bucket a blood across the table and against the bulkhead. Mardoff cried out in terror.

Captain Arai pushed the carrion away and then another hit to the foretop sent a thin sliver of steel driving down through Arai's left shoulder blade and into his chest, puncturing his lung and heart. Vomiting blood, he fell on top of the dead quartermaster.

The ship rolled and Brent slipped, barely able to support himself in the heel-thick layer of blood which covered the deck like fresh paint. Grabbing the windscreen, he saw both of the reporters cowering in the corner of the bridge. He had no trouble understanding them. Only his will of tempered steel kept him from joining them.

Yonaga's firepower was being reduced, and only four or five of Fite's *Fletchers* were engaging what appeared to be an equal number of *Gearings.* So much smoke obscured the southern horizon, it was impossible to tell how the destroyer battle was going. But one *Fletcher* charged out of the smoke and turned broadside to *Arad.* D-1 was painted in big white letters on the destroyer's bow.

"It's 'Slugger Fite'!" Whitehead shouted. "He's making a torpedo run."

The cruiser fired, and the forward part of the destroyer was hidden by columns of water and spray. "They missed!" Mardoff screamed. There were flashes amidships and long tubes leaped from the destroyer.

"Fite's launched his fish!"

"Six, seven miles. Too long," Whitehead said. "And Franjieh is making over thirty knots. World's toughest target. It'll take a miracle."

There was no miracle for Captain John "Slugger" Fite and his D-1. *Arad's* next salvo plowed into the destroyer's stern, set off the depth charges and blew off the aft part of the ship, all the way forward to the secondary director. At once, the bow lifted high and the destroyer began to slide, stern first, into the depths.

"Shit!" Mardoff cried.

"Goddamnit! Poor, brave bastards," Whitehead lamented.

Brent pounded the windscreen and sputtered curses. His stomach churned and his morning coffee surged up to sear his throat. He had lost a dear old friend, and one of the bravest men he had ever known.

Yonaga punished *Arad* with renewed fury. She was burning amidships, and Number Two turret was out of commission. But only seven of *Yonaga's* starboard cannons were still firing.

Fury wasn't enough to bring victory. Hits high on the damaged flight deck finally penetrated into the hangar deck and blew a fuel tank to pieces. Immediately, a tidal wave of fire rolled through the hangar deck.

"Damage control! Fire and Rescue Party!" Fujita screamed.

More shells came aboard, holing the funnel and destroying the aft director. Now only two guns of *Yonaga's* starboard battery could fire and there was no chance Fujita could unmask his port guns. The "Mad Mullah" saw to that by circling to starboard at high speed. As Fujita turned, Suleiman Franjieh turned with him.

"We're finished," Cunningham said.

"We're dead. Dead," Mardoff choked.

Smiley's voice through the open circuit: "There's a ten fish spread in the water, Captain. Headed toward the cruiser."

"How close."

"They'll pass across our bow at a thousand yards in about a minute-and-a-half."

"Guidance?"

"Not active, Captain."

"Speed?"

"Slow. It'll take 'em another six or seven minutes to reach the target area, and it looks like they'll all pass astern—but really can't tell for sure."

"Very well." Seitz peered into his eyepiece. He grimaced. "Shit, the 'Mad Mullah's' got him."

"*Yonaga's* finished," August Lee said, glancing at a monitor.

There were angry shouts from the crew. "That fuckin' Arab's killing the carrier," one of the men in ESM agonized.

There were underwater explosions nearby that shook *San Jose.*

"Depth charges?" Rick Verlander asked.

"Negative, Ensign," Joel Levinthal said. "Ship breaking up sounds, or a magazine going up."

"Sonar, those explosions?"

Smiley's voice: "Probably the can that fired those fish, Captain. She's sinking fast."

"The fish?"

"That cruiser's doing thirty-two knots. It looks like they'll all miss, Captain."

Seitz turned away from the periscope. "We can't allow this."

"Our rules of engagement," Levinthal reminded him.

Seitz said to Levinthal, "Didn't those explosions sound like depth charges?" The navigator looked at the captain curiously. "Well, didn't they?"

Levinthal nodded thoughtfully. "Well, they *were* underwater, and Smiley wasn't sure . . ."

Seitz command cut him off. "Torpedo room, make all tubes ready in all respects! High speed!"

Barry Wolstan suddenly spoke out, "Captain, you could be court-martialed."

Seitz turned to Wolstan. Every eye was on the captain. A silence as cold as crypt filled the control room.

"That's my decision," Seitz finally said.

Although *Yonaga's* hull was intact and her machinery was functioning perfectly, she was quickly becoming nothing but a burning target for *Arad.* Fires were raging on the hangar deck, and burning fuel had seeped down into the second deck. There was danger of Number One magazine and Number Three Torpedo Locker exploding. Fire would destroy *Yonaga,* not water. Fujita ordered the magazine flooded, but the threat to the torpedo locker had to be met by men wielding hoses and spraying foam. And only two five-inch guns on her starboard side still fired.

There would be no more help from the escorts. They were out of it. Only a few destroyers were visible on the horizon. Still exchanging fire.

A yellow flash, an ear-numbing report, and the last two guns were knocked out. The mad circling continued, but Fujita could never win this race. The nearly intact port battery would never be brought to bear.

The old admiral raised a fist to the heavens. "Oh, Amaterasu, have you forsaken the Son of Heaven?"

At that moment, two water spouts soared majestically along the cruiser's starboard side. The big ship, rocked, slowed and skewed about out of control. Flames were boiling and arcing amidships. Wreckage rose high above the smoke. Then either a magazine or her boilers exploded, nearly breaking her in half.

Yonaga's crew went wild. Screaming. Crying out to the gods and lavishing thanks. Whitehead pounded Brent on the back. The young American nodded, smiled, waved a finger at the dying cruiser. "Torpedoes! 'Slugger' Fite hit her? He did it. From that range? A miracle shot."

"A miracle, miracle," Whitehead concurred, still not able to believe what he had seen.

The reporters ignored the conjecture. They were busy with their camcorders. "Great footage! Great footage!" they both shouted.

Suddenly, Brent heard Naoyuki's alarmed cry. "Admiral! Admiral!"

Turning quickly, Brent stared at the piled corpses. The

heap had grown. Fujita was sprawled across Arai, with the talker bending over him.

"No! No!" Brent shouted. He rushed to the admiral.

Twenty-eight
The Duel

"Captain Poraz, we're right on the twentieth parallel, one hundred miles west of Farallon de Pajaro."

Clutching the windscreen of the rolling, rocking submarine chaser, Lieutenant Dov Poraz studied his new executive officer and navigator, young Ensign Gershon Manis. "Very well, Mister Manis. We will continue on a southerly heading."

Manis raised his cap and brushed an unruly lank of red hair back under it. Then he clamped the cap back down. "Ah, Sir. We're only two-hundred-seventy miles from Saipan, now. Easy aircraft range."

"True, Ensign. But a lifeguard can't do his job unless he's on the beach."

"Sir, we've picked up four aviators here. We're right on the route from the Marianas to Iwo Jima."

Dov Poraz nodded. *Edo* had been running a hundred-mile line off Farallon de Pajaro for over three weeks. Aircraft flying to and from Iwo Jima had flown hundreds of sorties over the tiny ship. Then, at 0900 hours, his radio room had picked up *Yonaga's* shocking message stating she was engaging two cruisers in a surface battle. Within thirty minutes, her air groups had begun to stream overhead.

Two badly damaged aircraft—a Hellcat and a Helldiver—had made water landings close aboard *Edo.* The pilot of a third, a Zero, had bailed out and had been kept afloat by his life belt until pulled from the water. In all, four men had been rescued. One, the Helldiver's gunner, had died. The three pilots were being tended by the ship's doctor in the mess hall, which had been converted into a sick bay. The doctor, a Japanese named Yonezawa Kawano, had been assigned for the ship's lifeguard duty only. He had brought three of his own medical orderlies aboard with him.

Now, with the subchaser ready for duty in the Middle East, the entire crew was Israeli. In fact the new name *Maccabees* had already been chosen to replace *Edo.* The subchaser would take her new name when her lifeguard duty was completed and she departed for the war in the Middle East. But now, her job was to save lives, not take them.

A voice ringing up the voice tube from the electronics shack attracted the officers. It was Cryptographer Menachem Zucker, who sat in the same chair where Technician Tochi Nakahara had bled to death. "Captain, I have a Purple Alpha Two transmission from *Yonaga.* 'Have engaged two enemy cruisers and seven escorts. Both cruisers and five escorts sunk. I have sustained heavy casualties. Unable to operate aircraft. Underway for Yokosuka with five escorts. All vessels damaged'."

Poraz piped the good part of the news over the P.A. system. There were cheers and happy exclamations from the crew. Then Zuker decoded another message that dampened it all. General Sago reported enemy air raids. Three transports had been hit and *New Jersey* had taken a bomb. He closed with, "Fighters! I need fighters! Where are you?"

An hour later, Japanese fighters streaked overhead, headed south for the battle. But not as many as Poraz expected. He counted eight Hellcats, four Corsairs, ten Bearcats and twelve Zeros. The whole fighter stream was led by a wedge of three aircraft. The tip was easy to identify. It was the red, green, and white, over-engined Zero of Commander Yoshi Matsuhara, flanked by the two Sea Furies of his wingmen.

Poraz leaned over the voice tube. "Pilot house!"

"Pilot house, aye."

"All ahead full."

Looking down, Yoshi Matsuhara saw a tiny sliver of a ship leaving a thin white scar on the sea. Probably *Edo.* That was close to her station. All noncombatant vessels had long cleared the area.

He was in a foul mood. The Arabs had cheated, played another dishonorable card. Violating a basic rule of war, three Spearfish with Japanese markings had slipped into Iwo's landing pattern and destroyed most of Emmitt Hopp's fuel supplies, trucks, and refueling equipment. All of the bombers had been shot down and two surviving crewmen executed. But that was little consolation. It was impossible for the base to refuel all of the aircraft that had swarmed to it. Worse, for a few hours there would be no fighter protection for Sago's invasion forces. The window was open, and the Arab aircraft were taking advantage of it.

Even without the air raid, Iwo Jima's facilities had been taxed by *Yonaga's* aircraft. With fuel tanks burning and the base in an uproar, it seemed Yoshi's air groups faced an almost impossible problem. Hopp was determined to put as many of his fighters in the sky as possible, Commander Matsuhara be damned.

Yoshi fought him. He was in a vile mood. *Yonaga* had been badly mauled. Was returning to Tokyo Bay with only five escorts. Many of his closest, oldest friends were dead. No doubt about that.

In a shouting match with Hopp, in which Yoshi threatened the base commander with a court-martial and even violence, Hopp finally agreed to provide 37 of *Yonaga's* fighters with enough fuel and ammunition for another run to the Marianas. Yoshi wanted more, but Hopp was adamant. He would service his own squadrons. He had to protect his own base and send fighters south. The rest of *Yonaga's* fighter groups would remain on the tarmac until Iwo's squadrons were ready.

It had been close to 1400 hours before Yoshi led his fighters into the sky. It was late. They could return after sunset. But that was of little concern. Their amphibious forces were under air attack. The rumors about hidden aircraft were true. Something, it must have been a friendly *kami,* told him Rosencrance was there. Yoshi licked his lips. It was coming. He was sure of that. He would meet the killer.

He had pushed his throttle far beyond the most favorable cruising speed. Now, passing over *Edo,* he was burning fuel lavishly. But he had no choice. If he were caught in a long dogfight, he would never make it back to Iwo Jima.

A quick look around told him his squadrons were perfectly ordered. Behind and slightly below, Elkins led a squadron of eight Hellcats and four Corsairs. To Elkins right and slightly higher, one of *Bennington's* best pilots, Lieutenant Gene Oshry, flew at the head of ten Bearcats. And above, Josef Dietl gave top cover with the twelve Zeros of the International Brigade. He had 36 of the best pilots in the world at his back. They could handle anything the enemy threw at them. But the enemy was still over two hundred miles away. He twisted in anger, clenched and unclenched his teeth until his jaw hurt.

After the longest hour of his life, he sighted Saipan. Then Tinian came into view. Junkers Ju-87s and Spearfish were attacking the transports. AA fire was very heavy. Three transports and a LST were burning. Another transport was rolling over. *New Jersey* was smoking amidships, but was firing both her main battery and secondaries. She appeared to be in fighting trim. Sago was continuing with the attack. Landing craft were still shuttling to and from the beach in Sunharon Bay.

He said into his microphone, "Rambo Leader, this is *Yubi* Leader. Destroy the bombers. *Kamome* and I will give you top cover."

"My pleasure, *Yubi* Leader. Keep my ass covered." With that, Elkins led eight Hellcats and four Corsairs into their dives.

There about twenty enemy bombers. The fighters swept through them like a typhoon through *papier mâché.* Six were shot down on the first pass. The remainder fled to every point of the compass with Elkins' fighters pursuing.

Dietl's voice: "*Yubi* Leader, this is *Kamome* Leader, fighters closing from nine o'clock on my altitude. Intercepting."

Yoshi looked at the sighting. Heinkel He-100s. Ten or twelve of them streaking in for the attack. Dietl would get the action he craved at last.

Hooperman's voice: "*Yubi* Leader, I have four Messerschmitts at three o'clock on our altitude, and twelve more at five o'clock high."

"See them." Yoshi called Lieutenant Gene Oshray. "Asphalt Leader, this is *Yubi* Leader. Engage One-Oh-Nines high and to the northwest."

"This is Asphalt Leader. Got 'em, *Yubi* Leader."

In their usual pairs, the fierce little fighters banked sharply to the right and streaked into the enemy formation, cannons stammering out yellow flames.

Staring down at the remaining four enemy fighters, Yoshi came erect as if his spine had been instantly petrified. A solid blood-red Me-109 with a black and yellow splotched wingman led. There were shark's teeth painted on the wingman's lower cowling and oil cooler. Rosencrance and Stoltz. No doubt about it.

"Rosencrance, you murdering ronin." He choked for a

moment remembering how the renegade American had murdered Willard-Smith in his parachute. Huskily, he spoke into his microphone. "*Yubi* Flight, it's Rosencrance."

"Bully," Hooperman said. "We owe that bugger something."

"Let's cuff the pommy bastard," Cummings said.

"Follow my lead on the first pass! Then individual combat."

Yoshi rolled into a steep right bank and brought the Zero around through a sharp ninety-degree turn. With surgical precision, he rolled her out, the wings snapping level to the horizon with a slight tremor.

Rosencrance, too, turned to meet the threat. The 109 could not outrun or out-dive the monstrous Zero. He had no choice. He must meet the attack head on.

The four Messerschmitts were in a line abreast, and Hooperman and Cummings edged up on Yoshi's wingtips. All seven aircraft opened fire simultaneously. Cannon shells from Hooperman blew off one of the black Me's propeller. The damaged fighter dove for the ground. The odds were even.

Immediately, Stoltz and the surviving black 109 banked off to the right. Hooperman and Cummings turned with them. But Rosencrance bored on, never deviating, growing in Yoshi's sights. Both men were firing. Lacy strings of tracers tied them together like spider's webs. At a combined closing speed of nearly a thousand-miles-an-hour, both planes expanded with explosive speed to the pilots. At the last second, spinner to spinner, Rosencrance pulled up and wracked the fighter into a tight turn.

At the same time Yoshi punched the stick brutally over with his right hand, matching the move with his right foot for rudder control. Wings almost vertical, the belly of the 109 nearly touched Yoshi's left wing tip. Buffeted by the slipstream of the passing Messerschmitt, Yoshi pulled back sharply on the stick, drawing it to him, sucking the fighter around in a punishing, tight turn. The wings trembled with the tremendous load. For a moment, Yoshi felt light-headed from the g-forces. He managed to shake it away, but it took too long—much too long.

Options raced through Rosencrance's mind while his enemy came about. He could run. He could dive. Both those choices would probably kill him. His simplest and most practical maneuver was to continue his turn, wracking it around so that he could bring his guns to bear in the shortest possible time. But he couldn't turn with the Zero. Nothing could. But he was a master pilot with 74 kills. There *was* a way. He cracked the flap handle that dropped the flaps back to maneuvering position, increasing his lift and giving him better turning ability. He shuddered and bounced close to stalling speed, but his turn matched Yoshi's.

Yoshi was startled by a sight he had never expected to see. Rosencrance had turned with him. The Japanese had time for a short burst only, as glowing coals flashed by him. That was all. The fighters passed each other with only inches to spare.

Both pilots pulled back on their sticks and kicked rudder. The Zero won this contest. Just as Rosencrance pulled out of his turn, the 109 shuddered as bullets slammed into his starboard wing. Holes appeared along the leading edge, and a cannon shell exploded under the fuselage. He was in his enemy's sights. Instinctively, the American battled the controls even as he judged the situation. Pushing the stick to the left, he hit hard right rudder, kicking the Me into a flat, sloppy skid. Enough. Barely enough to throw off the glowing hornets hounding him. It had been incredibly close. Another foot or two to the side and twenty-millimeter shells would have poured into his cockpit.

Now both fighters were out of firing position, and they

flashed past each other. Yoshi caught a glimpse of Rosencrance—goggles up, white face, a broad grin on his face. And the sky was strangely deserted. Dietl, Elkins, and Oshry were fighting on the southern horizon. It was then Yoshi realized his fight with Rosencrance had taken him far to the north of the islands. It was almost as if these two blood enemies had been left to settle their hatred in a private arena.

The fighter circuit was filled with commands, warnings, shouts of triumph. But Yoshi had no time to respond. One, however, shocked him. It was Hooperman: "Cummings, my bloody firing circuits are shot out. Can't get off a round."

"Get under me. I'll cover your arse."

"Look out! Stoltz behind you!"

"See him. Tally ho!"

Yoshi was fighting for his own life. There was nothing he could do to help his wingmen. He pulled back on his stick. The fighter with altitude always had the advantage. Rosencrance pulled up, too, but nothing could climb with Yoshi's hybrid Zero.

High above the American, Yoshi kicked rudder and horsed the stick back. He came at Rosencrance in a turning dive.

Rosencrance studied his enemy's move. It looked like a straight-forward attack out of the Zero's constant curving dive. The Japanese would have a difficult gunnery problem, but he was an excellent marksman. Rosencrance was in trouble. To escape, he would have to time everything perfectly. Be a target for only a split-second and answer with his own weapons.

He stomped on his rudder pedal and pulled back hard, turning into the diving Zero. Now there was no way for the Japanese to fire at him without steepening into a near vertical dive. The 109 bounded upward, curving higher and higher into a loop. Rosencrance held her in tight rein, bringing her around in the tightest possible circle.

But Yoshi had anticipated, corrected, fired a short burst. A few holes appeared in the 109's fuselage and tail. To an extent, Rosencrance had foiled Yoshi's attack. The Zero screamed down past the Messerschmitt.

Shouting with triumph, Rosencrance rolled after the plunging Zero.

But Yoshi's big engine pulled him ahead. He steepened his dive even more—glimpsed his air speed indicator passing 500. The controls stiffened in his hands, the fighter vibrated from the tremendous air pressure building against it. Now the whole cockpit shook—the stick, rudder pedals, seat, canopy, instruments. The lid of his binocular case chattered like the teeth of a freezing man. Dust rose from the floor and drifted down from the canopy. A glance into his rearview mirror—the gap had widened and the sea was rushing up. Time to pull out and give Rosencrance a squirt.

Gritting his teeth and holding his breath, he pulled back on the stick. G-forces tried to suck his guts out, pulled the blood from his brain. His nose ran, jaws sagged, head so heavy it sagged to the side like a leaden weight, and his bladder was no longer under control. His bowels threatened. There was a hissing in his ears. The fog came, filling the cockpit. The shaking control column began to slip from his hands. Never had g-forces hit him like this. He felt the fighter mush and slew off just as he began to climb to meet his enemy. There was time, *if* he could control the Zero. But he couldn't. His age. It was killing him. Fujita and Horikoshi had warned him he was too old. Now, the ultimate test had proved them right. He would never get the last shot. He was cold meat and he would die helplessly like an amateur.

Rosencrance couldn't believe his good fortune. The Zero had slewed off, out of its climb, and was banking gently to the right. An easy shot. His million-dollar bounty was in reach. All of his concentration was on his target. He brought his reflector sight to bear, gave a one-quarter deflective lead, and pushed the red button. The airframe shook from the concussion.

He never saw the blue blur racing in high from the side and rear. He only had time for a short scream before the five-bladed Rotol propeller of the Sea Fury crashed through the canopy and drove his dismembered body all the way through the fuselage and out the bottom.

There was no explosion. The 109 wrapped itself around the Sea Fury and the two fighters whirled and tumbled into the sea like two insects in a mating frenzy.

Yoshi screamed out in agony. His hated enemy was dead, but he had lost Hooperman. He had sacrificed his life. He pounded the instrument panel. Cursed. Cried. Never would he have bargained for such a trade. And then his engine barked out in its own agony. Cannon shells had blown part of the hood and cowling off. His oil pressure was dropping and engine temperature soaring. He reduced throttle almost to the stalling point. But the engine was dying. There was no doubt about that. And his controls were mushy. The aircraft was not responding the way it should.

Collecting himself, he leaned over the edge of the cockpit and looked down. Nothing but ocean. Empty and very blue. A nice cool place to die. Then he saw the tiny ship, ahead and very close. Either it was a reckless fishing boat or *Edo.* Bail out or ride her down? A water landing was dangerous at best. He could be injured, trapped in the cockpit.

Then Cummings helped him come to a decision. "Hit the silk, Commander. That's *Edo* down there. You're bloody well shot up. You could buy the farm if you tried to ditch."

Yoshi looked around. The Sea Fury was behind and above. "Roger. Bailing out."

He disconnected his radio and oxygen leads and unfastened his safety harness. He checked his parachute lock, straps and D-ring. Then he fingered the toggle to his life belt's cartridge. Everything was correct, ready. Finally, he reached up and pulled the red ball. Immediately, the canopy flew off and a gale whipped through the cockpit.

He took a deep breath, set his jaw, and rolled the fighter over.

Twenty-nine
At the Head of Heroes

Destroyer *Yamagiri* relieved *Edo* the day after the submarine chaser picked up Commander Yoshi Matsuhara. Although the pilot had landed close to the subchaser, he had been fouled by his parachute and had nearly drowned before a rescue team of two swimmers from *Edo* freed him.

Doctor Kawano worked furiously over the pilot, forcing out the water. Yoshi gagged, vomited and finally was able to breath freely. However, he was very weak and, at first, unable to eat or even drink coffee.

Part of it was remorse, he knew it. He had lost his incomparable wingman and cherished friend, Flying Officer Claude Hooperman and many, many more. He felt a terrible guilt, a hollow void as if his spirit had been gutted. Rosencrance's death brought little consolation.

Lieutenant Dov Poraz had visited him minutes after he was lifted over the gunwale. Yoshi thanked him. "I wouldn't be alive if your rescue team hadn't dragged me out."

The Israeli smiled broadly. "It was a pleasure, Commander. And, anyway, it was a hot day and the boys needed a swim. Now get some rest."

It would take *Edo* nearly five days to reach Tokyo Bay. Yoshi suffered the tortures of the damned worrying about his squadrons and his friends on *Yonaga*. No more information was forthcoming regarding casualties from the sea battle. However, *Edo* monitored the fighter frequency. He did find comfort in learning that Steve Elkins and Josef Dietl had survived. However, Gene Oshry was missing and the squadrons had lost twelve fighters. But every enemy aircraft had been shot down, including Stoltz, who Cummings had killed.

One day out of Tokyo Bay the glorious news arrived. Sago had overrun Tinian. His Abrams tanks had smashed Brigadier General Habib Shihaded's T-62s. Japanese infantry, in furious attacks, had routed the Arab infantry. Most surrendered, but a few hundred fanatical Shi'ites, screaming *"Allah akbar!"*, had died in a final suicide charge. Brigadier General Habib Shihaded shot himself when his bunker was overrun.

Almost two hundred pieces of heavy artillery had already begun to bombard the enemy defenses on Saipan, and more guns were being unloaded and brought up. *New Jersey* and a dozen destroyers had been replenished by an ammunition ship and a tanker. They were adding their firepower to the bombardment.

Emmitt Hopp's fighters and bombers had complete control of the sky. Bombing and strafing runs were incessant. It was a siege—a bloody, brutal siege just as Admiral Fujita had envisioned. Outclassed in artillery and manpower, the Arabs were isolated. The Japanese had absolute control of the sea and sky. The pounding was merciless. Already, Japanese radio was calling on Major General Ibrahim Mohammed Awad to surrender. Britain, France, Germany, Italy, India, and China all called on Awad to surrender and stop the useless sacrifice of lives.

One day out of Tokyo Bay, Yoshi climbed up to the bridge. He enjoyed the view from the platform and liked Dov Poraz's company. He found Poraz staring over the bow and Ensign Gershon Manis bending over the chart table.

After greeting the pilot and inquiring about his condition, the captain said, "Awad's a tough old fighter. I know, I fought him in the Middle East."

Yoshi's lips twisted mirthlessly. "True, but he has a lot to learn from the Japanese."

Ensign Gershon Manis said, "He's taking a terrible pounding."

"Yes," Yoshi said, "outmanned, out-gunned, out-thought."

Manis said to Yoshi, "Will Sago invade?"

"Never. Admiral Fujita has taken a page from General Douglas MacArthur's book of tactics."

"MacArthur?"

"Yes. Let them 'wither on the vine'."

The next day *Edo* entered Tokyo Bay. The battle group was already tied up at their moorings at Yokosuka. As usual, *Yonaga* was at Dock B-2. When Yoshi saw the burned, blasted hulk, he almost wept. "Sacred Buddha," he muttered, "she must have lost hundreds."

Just as the small ship was being warped into her berth, the joyous news broke. Major General Ibrahim Mohammed Awad had surrendered unconditionally. Sago's troops were occupying Saipan.

It was over.

Cheers roared out from the docks, the warehouses, the ships. Ship's whistles were blown, bells rang, cars and trucks honked their horns. Men hugged each other, shook hands. Long hidden stores of liquor were broken out.

But Yoshi felt little joy. He was the first man to disembark when the submarine chaser tied up. He ran to Dock B-2.

Yoshi Matsuhara saluted the duty officer, Lieutenant j. g. Tokuma Shoten, on *Yonaga's* charred quarter deck. His first words were, "Admiral Fujita?"

The young man bit his lip. "Ah, Commander Matsuhara, he's in his cabin."

"Is he well?"

"No, Sir. Not well."

"Wounded?"

"No, Sir."

"Then what?"

"He seems to have collapsed."

"Commander Ross?"

"Commander Ross is in Admiral Fujita's cabin."

"Rear Admiral Whitehead?"

"Ashore, Sir. Reporting to the American ambassador."

"Already?"

"The President of the United States demanded it, Sir."

"Commander Atsumi?"

"The gunnery officer is well, Sir."

Yoshi wanted to ask about the casualties, but his first thought was of the admiral and Brent Ross. The elevator had been destroyed, so he was forced to race up endless ladders to Flag Country.

When the exhausted pilot entered Admiral Fujita's cabin, he found Brent Ross and Chief Hospital Orderly Eiichi Horikoshi bending over the admiral's bed. The admiral's appearance was frightening. His sun-shaded skin had taken on the cast of ashes. The thin lips were a purple slash, and the eyes were closed. His breathing was barely perceptible. He was obviously unconscious.

"Yoshi! Yoshi!" Brent cried out, clasping his friend's hands. "Thank God you're alright. I heard *Edo*'s report."

"Amatersasu has been watching over you, too, Brent-san." Yoshi gestured to the bed.

Before Brent could speak, Horikoshi said, "If you two wish to reminisce, please do so elsewhere. We have a sick man here."

Yoshi ignored the insult from the irascible, rank-hating physician. "How sick is he?"

"Ha! He's over one hundred years old, has just fought the battle of his life, lost two-hundred-twenty dead, three-hundred-fifty-four wounded, twenty-seven missing and his executive officer and chief engineer are dead." He thumped the bulkhead with a little fist. "And you ask me how he is?"

"Yes!" Yoshi came back sharply. "How is he?"

"Dying. That's how he is."

All three men were shocked by a weak faltering voice from the bed. "I'm not dead—yet."

For the first time since Brent had known him, Horikoshi was at a loss for words. Fujita said, "I have something to say. Bring me my scribe."

Brent opened the door to the passageway and found a throng of officers and men crowding close. At first he didn't see frail old Hakuseki Katsube. Then he found the commander, standing at the back of the crowd next to a lone Buddhist priest. He called the scribe in, and Fujita nodded to a chair. Katsube sat almost erect, pad and brush in hand. There was no slobber on his chin and he actually looked alert. Every man in the room suspected they were about to hear a dying declaration.

Fujita said, "I, Admiral Hiroshi Fujita, declare Commander Yoshi Matsuhara promoted to the rank of captain per this date. Upon my death, he is to take command of carrier *Yonaga.* Commander Brent Ross will be his second-in-command." The old man paused, breathing in short hard gasps, as if the words had exhausted him.

"Anything else, Sir?" Katsube asked, eyes unusually wide and moist.

"No. You are dismissed, Hakuseki-san." Brent helped the old man to the door. The bent scribe was crying into his sleeve when he left.

Yoshi spoke, "Sir, I deeply appreciate the honor you have given me. But isn't Gunnery Officer Atsumi alive?"

"Yes."

"He is a line officer. Doesn't he better fit the command?"

The old man took several short breaths. "No, Yoshi-san. A carrier is best commanded by an officer with flying experience. Do not forget, I started in naval aviation." He closed his eyes and opened his mouth, as if he were trying to gulp in more oxygen. His voice dropped off. "We captured Tinian?"

"And Saipan."

A dark silence crept through the room while the old man struggled for air. "Tinian was the one. We had to take it. It is a place of great evil." Again a long pause, and the old man seemed to be fading away, back into unconsciousness. Looking at Brent, he spoke in a dry rustling sound and he repeated himself. "We have captured Tinian?"

"Yes, Sir."

"Then that bomber can never take off."

The two officers looked at each other in confusion. Fujita continued, still speaking to Brent. "The one that can carry that bomb—the bomb that can give birth to a new sun and take a city with it."

Now they knew. The admiral was slipping into delirium. Yoshi remained silent while Brent picked up the thread. "Yes, Sir. It will never take off."

Now, Fujita was drifting back over half a century. Reality was gone. "And you, Kazuo, my eldest. You are at my side when I need you."

Brent felt Yoshi nudge his arm. He played it. "Yes, Sir, I am here."

"The rays of the new sun will never sear our home," he assured himself again. "It can never happen now and we will all be together again—your mother, your brother Makoto."

Brent felt a swelling in his throat, and he drew a deep breath before he could speak. "It can never happen, Sir. You must have had a nightmare."

"Yes, Kazuo, just a nightmare." The old man stared straight up with unblinking eyes. "Hiroshima is still beautiful."

"Yes, Sir. Beautiful, green, filled with the sounds of laughing children."

"Good, good, it is truly a beautiful city."

"Yes, Sir. A wonderful place to live."

"We will build that new shrine in the garden. At the end of the bridge next to the pair of lanterns. You know the spot, Kazuo."

"Yes, of course, Sir. The perfect place."

"I have already ordered fine, white Italian marble for it. It is just what we need for our garden." Again, a long pause. In time Fujita said, "I will leave you soon, my son. I fear for my spirit."

"Your karma shines bright like new armor, Sir."

"Bright enough for the Yasakuni Shrine?"

"At the head of the heroes, Sir."

"You are a good son, Kazuo."

"I try to be worthy of you, Sir."

The old withered face cracked as a smile tried to work its way in. "You are more than worthy, my son."

Then, without warning, the old man sagged back, and the breathing stopped.

Brent waved to Horikoshi. Quickly the orderly examined the admiral. Then, slowly, he turned to the officers. "Admiral Hiroshi Fujita has entered the Yasakuni Shrine."

Yoshi tucked the bedding down neatly. Unashamed, Brent pulled out a handkerchief, wiped his eyes and blew his nose. Then, he took the admiral's sword from a closet and laid it at his feet.

"It's over," Horikoshi said, straightening and staring down at the corpse.

Yoshi said, "For the admiral, yes."

"What do you mean, Commander—ah, I mean captain?"

"It's never over."

"More killing, Captain?"

"As long as there is evil in this world, there will be *Yonagas* to fight it."

"*Yonaga* is a wreck."

"*Yonaga* will come back."

"And why?"

"Because it must."

Horikoshi snorted with disgust and turned to leave. Yoshi stopped him with a hand to the sleeve. He nodded to Fujita, "Make the arrangements."

"I already have. The chief priest from the temple at Daisen-in is in the passageway." The physician pulled away and walked to the door.

As the door closed, Yoshi placed a hand on Brent's back. "Come, Brent-san. We have much work to do."

They both took a last lingering look at the admiral, bowed, saluted, and left the room.

MORE FROM BEST-SELLING AUTHOR NOEL HYND!

A ROOM FOR THE DEAD

(Hardcover, 0-8217-4583-2, $18.95)
(Paperback, 0-7860-0089-9, $5.99)

Detective Sgt. Frank O'Hara should have seen it all in his twenty years as a state cop. But then he must deal with a grisly murder spree marked with the personal signature of a killer he sent to the electric chair years ago. If it isn't Gary Ledbetter commiting these murders, then who can it be? Is it someone beyond the grave—a demon from Hell come to exact a chilling retribution against his executioners? Or is Frank losing his mind, his sanity slipping beneath grueling pressure and the burden of guilt and rage carried by every good cop . . .

GHOSTS (0-8217-4359-7, $4.99)

For Academy Award-winning actress Annette Carlson, Nantucket Island is the perfect refuge from a demanding career. For brilliant, burnt-out cop Tim Brooks, it's a chance to get away from the crime-ridden streets of the big city. And for Reverend George Osaro, ghost hunter, it is about to become a place of unspeakable terror . . .